International acclaim for Michelle de Kretser's

THE HAMILTON CASE

"Simply put, *The Hamilton Case* is one of the most extraordinary novels I have ever read. . . . It makes the English language sing."

— Kenneth Champeon, *Bookpage*

"A splendid, intelligent, and at times mesmerizing work of fiction. . . . As Sam Obeysekere lingers over the events of his life, his cool Edwardian narrative voice is as deceptive as that of the butler Stevens in Kazuo Ishiguro's *Remains of the Day*. . . . By novel's end, it is Ms. de Kretser's great skill that has allowed us to become so thoroughly involved in a sordid family drama that we almost neglect to notice the great events passing by in the background."

— Sudip Bose, *Washington Times*

"Multilayered and beguiling. . . . *The Hamilton Case* — which beautifully renders the sensuality of Ceylon — is a very artful and evocative plea for interpretation over explanation. . . . Through a rich family history replete with joys and tragedies, Michelle de Kretser has adroitly demonstrated just what a baffling, intractable, multifaceted thing one person's life can be." — William Boyd, *New York Times Book Review*

"De Kretser's prose is powerfully evocative. She deserves comparison with J. M. Coetzee and her countryman Michael Ondaatje."

— Fiona Stager, *Courier-Mail* (Australia)

"Absorbing, elegantly written. . . . A many-layered, fascinating novel, finely attuned to both history and humanity. . . . *The Hamilton Case* displays a formidable talent."

— Charles Matthews, *San Jose Mercury News*

"Opulently atmospheric. . . . It is de Kretser's style that seduces, a somersaulting bird of paradise. . . . At the close, a chain of revelations sews together chance and innuendo in surgically tight stitches. . . . Sam's Victorianisms transmute to poignant irony, Maud's losses bloom into poetic exactitude."
— Kai Maristed, *Los Angeles Times*

"There is a mystery at the heart of *The Hamilton Case*. . . . De Kretser takes her subject — which is how the English language, and with it a way of looking at the world and at people, has penetrated the psyche of Ceylon — and twines it into the fabric of her story. In other words, this is no protest novel, but an elegant, seductive, and manipulative work of art. . . . Sam Obeysekere's life, as an old friend of his describes it, is 'a devastating lesson in how a man might see every detail with perfect clarity and yet misread the shape of the whole.' De Kretser has pulled off something remarkable, writing a novel that charms and beguiles without soothing us into making a similar and unjust mistake."
— Laura Miller, *Salon*

"I devoured this book. De Kretser misses nothing."
— Christopher Ondaatje, *Literary Review*

"De Kretser has given us the classic whodunit wrapped up in a beautiful and tragic literary novel."
— Ella Walsh, *Vogue*

"A miniature masterpiece of a mystery. . . . Sherlock Holmes haunts *The Hamilton Case*. . . . Sam Obeysekere's story takes some time to reveal itself as a mystery, but it does so when Obeysekere takes on the case of a respectable English planter — Hamilton — who gets shot in the chest. 'Murder, a moonless night, the jungle crowding close.' . . . De Kretser's prose is stunning and subtle in depicting Sam's downfall, evoking the glittering excesses of colonial life — after a party 'you could have strolled across the lagoon on the champagne corks' — and the tropical fecundity of Ceylon with equally irresistible power."
— Lev Grossman, *Time*

"A bewitching novel. . . . An utterly captivating blend of intellectual muscle and storytelling magic."
— Boyd Tonkin, *Independent*

"A dazzling performance. . . . *The Hamilton Case* ratifies every dream one might have of a tropical landscape with its account of a rich and eccentric family and its complex and serpentine history. De Kretser is, however, as smart and up-to-date as she can be. . . . It is impossible to describe her prose as anything but rich, luxuriant, intense, and gorgeous."
— Anita Desai, *New York Review of Books*

"Prose as lush as a tropical jungle. . . . A poignant mediation on colonialism, family ties, race, and national identity."
— Adam Woog, *Seattle Times*

"*The Hamilton Case* is one of the most remarkable books I've read in a long while — subtle and mysterious, both comic and eerie, and brilliantly evocative of time and place. I've never been to Sri Lanka but I feel it's become part of my interior landscape, and I so much admire Michelle de Kretser's formidable technique — her characters feel alive, and she can create a sweeping narrative which encompasses years, and yet still retain the sharp, almost hallucinatory detail. It's brilliant."
— Hilary Mantel

"A razor-sharp evocation of a place and time. . . . *The Hamilton Case* has a way of insinuating itself into the reader's mind. . . . De Kretser, like Ishiguro in *The Remains of the Day*, finds a heartbreaking dignity in her hero's pathos."
— Bill Ott, *Booklist*

"Beautifully written. . . . There are mysteries, but de Kretser is more concerned to explore most movingly the characters of the dangerous, pompous, and ultimately tragic Obey and his family. . . . *The Hamilton Case* is haunting, lush, and delicately nuanced."
— Peter Guttridge, *Observer*

"Absorbing, elegantly written. . . . A many-layered, fascinating novel, finely attuned to both history and humanity. . . . *The Hamilton Case* displays a formidable talent."
— Charles Matthews, *San Jose Mercury News*

"The novel's beautiful, delicate, and scathing prose . . . provides the ruminative gratification of serious literature."
— Brenn Jones, *San Francisco Chronicle*

"Part colonial whodunit, part Faulknerian gothic, the beauty of this book is its ability to constantly surprise. . . . *The Hamilton Case* is an important novel that gives up more of its secrets with each reading."

— Liam Davison, *Weekend Australia*

"Stunning. . . . Rich with evocative writing that brings to life its lush locale, made all the more exotic by its teetering place on the precipice of history." — Laura DeMarco, *Cleveland Plain Dealer*

"De Kretser has given us the classic whodunit wrapped up in a beautiful and tragic literary novel." —Ella Walsh, *Vogue*

"A bewitching novel. . . . An utterly captivating blend of intellectual muscle and storytelling magic." —Boyd Tonkin, *Independent*

"Rewarding, thought-provoking, witty, and often disconcerting, *The Hamilton Case* takes the reader into a world of transformations."

— Clare Griffiths, *Times Literary Supplement*

"Every so often there comes a novel for adults that combines a fastidious literary sensibility with that intense, urgent childhood readability, and then the result is as magical as the old childish enchantments. *The Hamilton Case* is like this. . . . De Kretser is a virtuoso in language. Whatever the linguistic equivalent of perfect pitch may be, she has it."

— Jane Shilling, *Telegraph*

"I read *The Hamilton Case* in a single day, greedily, absorbed in its narrative drive, its poised voice, its rich texture, its dense sense of life."

— Delia Falconer, *Sydney Morning Herald*

"Ambitious, gracefully composed. . . . *The Hamilton Case* is really about something far more absorbing than the tidy and classic plot twists of a British murder mystery. . . . 'Who isn't drawn to what he pities?' The signal accomplishment of de Kretser's hypnotic, lush, and calmly observant novel is that we feel this same sentiment on Sam's own behalf, even after we learn in the story of his life how deeply suspect it must be. That is the final, remarkable mystery that endlessly enlivens *The Hamilton Case*."

— Chris Lehmann, *Washington Post Book World*

THE HAMILTON CASE

Michelle de Kretser

BACK BAY BOOKS
Little, Brown and Company
New York Boston

ALSO BY MICHELLE DE KRETSER

The Rose Grower

Back Bay Books / Little, Brown and Company
Time Warner Book Group
1271 Avenue of the Americas, New York, NY 10020
Visit our Web site at www.twbookmark.com

Originally published in Australia by Knopf and in Great Britain by Chatto & Windus
Originally published in the U.S. in hardcover by Little, Brown and Company, May 2004
First Back Bay paperback edition, April 2005

Library of Congress Cataloging-in-Publication Data
De Kretser, Michelle.
The Hamilton case / Michelle de Kretser. — 1st American ed.
p. cm.
ISBN 0-316-73548-5 (hc) / 0-316-01081-2 (pb)
1. Colombo (Sri Lanka)—Fiction. 2. Failure (Psychology)—Fiction. 3. Loss (Psychology)—Fiction. 4. Mothers and sons—Fiction. 5. Problem families—Fiction. 6. Trials (Murder)—Fiction. 7. Scandals—Fiction. I. Title.

PR9619.4.D4H36 2004
823'.914—dc22 2003060759

10 9 8 7 6 5 4 3 2 1

Q-FF
Book design by Jonathan D. Lippincott
Printed in the United States of America

For Chris, with love

PART I

I always made it my business, at least,
to know the part thoroughly.

G. K. Chesterton

A WISE CHILD

A name is the first story that attaches itself to a life. Consider mine: Stanley Alban Marriott Obeysekere. It tells of geography, history, love and uncertainty. I was born on an island suspended midway on the golden trade route between East and West—a useful bauble, fingered and pocketed by the Portuguese, Dutch and British in turn. In 1902, when I was born, Sir Alban Marriott was Governor and he agreed to be my godfather. How could he refuse? He had been in thrall to my mother ever since she sent him the skin of a leopard she had shot, along with a note. *I shall call on you between five and six this evening. The skin is for the small blue reception room, which is ideally suited to fornication and whatnot*. Her name was Maud and she was a great beauty. Also a first-rate shot. In Scotland she had stalked deer with the Prince of Wales; his performance, she reported, was mediocre. He presented her with a brooch fashioned from an eagle's talon mounted on silver and onyx. Mater dismissed it as *monumentally obvious* and palmed it off on her stewardess in lieu of a tip on her voyage home.

My father insisted on calling me Stanley, although my mother hated the name. I have often pondered the significance of Pater's uncharacteristic resolve. His father, too, was a Stanley, so he might simply have been affirming family tradition. On the other hand, might his assertion of my paternal provenance betray some anxiety about it? My mother had a certain reputation. It was alleged that she once swam in a jungle pool wearing only her bloomers, even though there were gentlemen and snakes present. Half of Colombo society followed the lead of Lady Marriott, who was stout and afflicted with shingles, in cutting her dead. Mater said Stanley was fit only for a peon, so it was just as well my initials spelled Sam. These days there is no one left to remember that I was ever called anything else.

Stanley Alban Marriott Obeysekere: between the names that define me as my father's child falls the shadow of an Englishman who didn't serve a second term as Governor. Shortly after his death eight years ago a package from a firm of London solicitors found its way to my desk. It contained a small murky oil painting of a large and largely unclad female gathering flowers and berries against a backdrop of broken marble columns in a woodland glade. The artist—quite unknown to the works of reference I have consulted—signed himself Tom Baltran. The executor's letter accompanying the painting explained that the Baltrans and the Marriotts were cousins. Moreover, it continued, the Hon. Thomas was descended on the distaff side from the first Duke of St. Albans, Charles II's illegitimate son by Nell Gwynne. The artist's hefty nymph was held, *in family lore*, to represent the orange seller, but this was purely speculative. *Sir Alban*, wrote his solicitor, *was most anxious for this painting, the gem of his small collection, to pass to you. He retained the warmest memories of his years in Ceylon, and often referred to happy times spent in the company of your mother*.

An ambiguous legacy, wouldn't you say? I keep the painting in a cabinet, along with Sir Alban's other gift, a silver eggcup presented on the occasion of my christening. Now and then I set these objects before me and study them. An egg, a mistress, a bastard son: their message seems unequivocal. But the testimony of signs is unreliable. Within minutes I have reasoned that an eggcup is a wholly conventional gift on the part of a godparent, and that the Hon. Thomas's daub points only to the ill-judged sentimentality of a nonagenarian. The argument prevails for a brief interval; then doubt creeps in again. These sessions always end the same way: I cross to my mirror where reassurance waits in the solid evidence of my flesh.

If you wish to ascertain a man's lineage, read his face not his birth certificate. My skin is as dark as my father's, our branch of the Obeysekeres being famously black. Like Pater, I am of average height and inclined to portliness in age. We share a high forehead, thick, springing hair, a curved nose and assertive ears. We are not handsome men. But we have *presence*. Whereas Sir Alban, as he appears in my parents' photograph album, is tall and hollow-chested, with pointed features and an entirely unconvincing mustache. He clasps his left wrist in his right hand, holding himself together.

By now it will be apparent that my pen is not constrained by decorum. I have always set great store by the truth, a virtue not usually prized in my profession. But it was my ability to see accurately and to speak the truth, without concern for convention or fear of reprisal, that made my name in a different sense. The very notoriety of the Hamilton case has seen it shrouded in the fog of rumor, conjecture and misinformation that passes for analysis in the drawing rooms of this country. In these pages I intend to set down the facts of the matter at last.

A REMEMBRANCE OF THINGS PAST

My grandfather, Sir Stanley Obeysekere, was a *mudaliyar*, an office that placed a man at the pinnacle of our island's social system. A *mudaliyar* was a leader of men, with considerable influence in his ancestral district. By tradition he was a gifted soldier and a skilled diplomat, abilities he placed at the service of his sovereign. With the advent of the Europeans, however, the role of the *mudaliyar* evolved. The Kandyan kingdom remained unconquered in the hills until 1815, but as the Portuguese, Dutch and finally the British occupied larger and larger areas of the maritime provinces, it was for their administrative talents, above all, that my ancestors came to be valued by the colonial powers. Their education, the respect they commanded among their countrymen and their knowledge of the island's customs meant they were ideally suited to assist in the colonial administration: as record keepers, as intermediaries and interpreters, as presidents of the courts that dealt with native disputes concerning land, contracts and debts.

The Europeans rewarded loyalty with land: whole villages were given in gift to the *mudaliyars*, vast tracts of jungle, tax-free estates. Pater's inheritance included landholdings throughout the southern provinces, four properties in Colombo, six or seven outstation bungalows, a cottage in the hills, a tea plantation and a plumbago mine; as well as Lokugama, our country seat, where my childhood unraveled in splendid isolation.

I have no doubt that my ancestors were vigorous men. One of my lasting regrets is that I never knew my grandfather, who was by all accounts a wise and able administrator. I have by me a copy of the confidential memorandum from Government House recommending his knighthood. It notes that my grandfather possessed *a most complete and accurate knowledge of the practice and procedure of the Island* and describes him as *a man of the highest character, honourable, high principled and unswervingly loyal*.

Alas, Sir Stanley met with disaster at the age of thirty-four. He was boating on the lake in Kandy one afternoon when he noticed that a party of English girls, who had ventured out without a boatman in the spirited way of the young, had gotten into difficulty. Before his horrified eyes, one of the girls, who had unwisely risen to her feet, was pitched overboard. Ten years earlier my grandfather had swum the Hellespont, *cheered on by a smelly band of very villainous Greeks*, as he recorded in his diary. Now he dived at once into the lake and reached the young lady's side in a few swift strokes.

All would have been well had it not been for the hysterical reaction of Miss Daisy Dawson, one of the ladies left shrieking in the boat. Afterward her father, the Government Agent for the Jaffna Province, offered in extenuation the terror and confusion his daughter felt at the prospect of capsizing (none of the ladies could swim) and her extreme distress at seeing her friend, a sweet girl on the threshold of womanhood, being manhandled by a native. In her understandable terror, confusion and distress, Miss Dawson brought her oar crashing down on my grandfather's skull. He drowned, of course.

Miss Dawson's party, including the sweet girl in the water, was rescued by two Scottish engineers, whose presence on the lake was taken as proof that my grandfather had acted courageously but precipitately. Two white men would not have sat by and watched an English girl drown. Sir Stanley would have done better to attract the engineers' attention with manly shouts. The sentiment in billiard rooms and newspaper editorials was that the Ceylonese, even the ablest among them, were prone to exaggeration.

Pater was a boy of nine when his father drowned. Some said Sir Stanley had been murdered; it came down to one's point of view. His death served as a pretext for a halfhearted attempt to stir up anti-British sentiment, which floundered at once since the Obeysekere clan failed to support it. In fact my Great-Uncle Willy wrote a strongly worded letter to the *Times of Ceylon* regretting his brother's impetuousness, and absolving Miss Dawson, *a mere inexperienced girl*, of all blame.

It so happened that Willy was involved in litigation at the time. He was the subject of a lawsuit brought by a man called Perera, who was contesting Willy's title to some twenty acres of forested land near Chilaw. This fellow Perera claimed that the land had belonged to his family for generations, although he could produce no certifiable title of ownership. He alleged that Willy had acquired a spurious title to the property and then sent a band of thugs to seize it by force.

Such allegations—indeed such practices—were common enough in those days, when everyone who could afford to do so was mad to get his hands on land that could be used for cash crops. One might argue that the land grab had been set off by the government, whose Waste Land Ordinance had declared that all lands not permanently cultivated or in certifiable ownership were the property of the Crown. In this way the British acquired acres of primeval forest that were sold for plantations. The local elite followed suit, clearing land for coffee and tea and rubber and coconut with so much zeal that the government was eventually forced to consider measures for preserving the jungle and slowing down sales of uncultivated land.

Willy and Perera had hired teams of lawyers who had been fighting it out in our tortoiselike courts for years. In fact the case had dragged on for so long that Willy had grown quite fond of his adversary, whom he referred to affectionately as The Blasted P. He regaled his relatives with details about this character: his hair oil, the sturdy umbrella that accompanied him everywhere, his habit of picking his teeth with a long fingernail, his numerous offspring ("I counted at least fifteen. Huge, hairy hulks. And as for his sons . . . !"). When he learned that The Blasted P's eldest daughter was to be married, Willy sent her a handsome canteen of cutlery. It was returned the next day. Willy slapped his forehead. "Of course! The Blasted P scorns cutlery. Should have sent the girl a set of fingerbowls."

Whenever the clan gathered at Lokugama, Pater and his cousins would entertain the adults by acting out imaginary episodes from the life of The Blasted P, who had quickly passed into family myth. The Blasted P at Buck House: much hilarity from the spectators as our hero presses betel on the Crown Prince, slurps his tea from a saucer, ogles the behind of a lady-in-waiting, asks a footman when the arrack will be served, all under the unamused eye of Victoria (my Aunt Sybil, much padded with cushions, who at the age of twelve bore an unnerving resemblance to that redoutable monarch).

Willy once took The Blasted P aside and made him a sporting offer: settle the matter once and for all like gentlemen, weapon of his choice, circumvent the bally lawyers. But The Blasted P was a devout Buddhist. "Lectured me on the taking of life and whatnot. Blighter's bleeding me to death in the courts but that's different, it seems."

With the shift in government policy on the sale of forested land, the matter was no longer farcical. Willy's lawyers expressed pessimism about the final ruling, expected in a few weeks. Then my grandfather died and Willy wrote his letter. The court found in his favor. His jungle acres were cleared for coconuts and in time returned considerable profits. The Blasted P faded from view, although Willy always sent him a card at Christmas. Yet he died a disappointed man, poor Willy, because the OBE he yearned for never materialized. The English have long memories, you see. Their great talent lies in the reconciliation of justice and compromise. A formidable race. I miss them to this day.

RITZY

Would Pater have turned out differently if Sir Stanley's accident hadn't deprived him, at a tender age, of a father's loving sternness? Speculation of that kind is irresistible and pointless. For myself, I believe that sons are born to disappoint their fathers. In that respect, every man fulfills his destiny.

My father was an indulgent, insouciant man. There was something spongy about him, like a fish that has lain too long out of water. This was perhaps the consequence of his moment in history. With the development of the colonial Civil Service, the *mudaliyars'* power had eroded, and a preoccupation with status had taken its place. Senior chaps like Pater had little to do but advise the British on the doings and the opinions of the Ceylonese. In this way, they came to wield enormous influence in the twice-yearly distribution of imperial honors among their countrymen. Pater traveled at the center of a retinue eager to laugh at his witticisms and compliment him on his judgment. In private, lists of the coveted honors were drawn up on the backs of dance cards. Resentment at being passed over would be elaborated into an extravagant narrative of insult and vengeance as obsessively detailed as the petit point over which generations of ladies wore out their eyes in drawing rooms.

Pater loved parties, champagne, horses. His generosity was legendary. If he had particularly enjoyed himself at a house party, his hostess might receive three bottles of priceless Tokay Essence or a comb that had last belonged to a Chinese empress. Sentimental songs made him weep. Once, learning of a critically ailing child on the estate at Lokugama, he despatched a carriage to Colombo for his own specialist. The round trip of two hundred miles took the best part of a day, and the child died hours before Sir Humphrey arrived; but that was not the point.

At Lokugama, petitioners thronged at the gate whenever Pater was in residence. In his hearing true friends desisted from admiring this painting, that bibelot, because, "Take it! I bought it for you! Take it!" he would urge, and if they remained adamant in their refusal, he had it sent around to them the next day, anyway.

Like all admirable qualities, this liberality was hard on those in its vicinity. I learned to keep prized possessions hidden away after Pater spotted my beloved lead soldiers on the verandah, scooped up the Duke of Wellington and pressed him into the grubby hands of our cookwoman's grandson. I flew at the brat and kicked his ringwormed shins, for which I earned myself a thrashing. That night I cried myself to sleep. Not for the sake of my backside—my father's strokes were so light and glancing that in his hands a cane was an instrument of love—but for the injustice I had suffered.

It was Pater's iconic largesse that had first brought him to my mother's attention. Mater, her cousin Iris, and Iris's parents were taking tea at the Savoy on the girls' first visit to London, when Great-Uncle Bertie adjusted his monocle: "Isn't that young Obeysekere over there by the window? But who on earth is that frightful fellow with him?"

The frightful fellow turned out to be an out-of-work coachman who had stopped my father in the Strand and asked for money, saying he was hungry. Pater invited him to tea. Dumbstruck waiters fetched apricot jam, lemon curd, cheese tartlets, asparagus rolls, shortbread fingers, coffee éclairs, tongue sandwiches, ginger biscuits, coconut meringues, shrimp paste, a raspberry sponge, a chocolate blancmange, plum cake, seed cake and a trembling mandarin orange jelly. After all, Pater was known to tip royally. The coachman rose splendidly to the occasion, filling his stomach and his pockets at the same time. Mater swore she saw him snaffle the sugar tongs, wedged between two currant buns.

Dowager ladies began sniffing and asking in ringing tones for the manager. All oblivious, Pater smoked his pipe and chatted away. When Maud's party approached, he was saying, "You must promise me, as a man of honor, never again to soil your lips with China. Ceylon tea! The flavor, you know, is incomparable. If you could see those hillsides on an April morning!" There and then, Mater decided to marry him.

Beware of what you fall in love with. I have often observed that we are attracted to those characteristics that we ourselves do not possess; so it is not surprising that they quickly lose their fascination. My mother, a shrewd, pragmatic woman, was charmed by this informal, open-handed stranger. Within days she was calling him Ritzy: a nickname that revealed her disdain for detail (she had met him, as you will recall, at the Savoy) as well as her craving for glamour. But as love's feast was succeeded by familiarity's reckoning, she would realize she had married a man who liked nothing better than giving things away.

Society is intolerant of this impulse—only think where it might lead—and so it was fortunate, from my father's point of view, that a ready-made, socially sanctioned outlet was at hand for his weakness. The horses came from Ireland and Arabia, from Cape Town and Calcutta, beautiful, smooth-muscled beasts, nervous as harpstrings. In the hills during the Season, in Colombo all year round, with a gardenia in his buttonhole and his lucky moonstone set in embossed silver on his little finger, Pater proceeded to unburden himself of my inheritance. From time to time he couldn't help winning. On such occasions he was visibly downcast.

My parents quarreled frightfully. Or rather Pater dodged about the room, while my mother hurled abuse and whatever she could reach at his maddening smile: cushions, fruit, fruitstands, first editions of Tennyson, eighteenth-century candlesticks, a set of ivory figurines, a silver salver, a game of dominoes, a maidenhair fern. She plucked a canary from its cage and launched it on a stream of curses. It flew into a mirror and died. Mater seized the yellow corpse and dropped it into her teacup, then flung the lot at my father's head.

She was a great smasher, my mother. Crystal was her speciality. My father took pains to ensure that she always had a supply of costly glassware at hand. Did she never realize he was making her his accomplice in his grand scheme of beggaring us? Vases, decanters, a wine-red Venetian swan and five little cygnets: they shivered apart and Mater's yellow eyes glistened. Her lizard tongue slid over her lips. Once, peeping awestruck from behind an armchair while she raged and smashed a Baccarat jug and a dozen ruinously expensive water glasses, I saw her grow still. She strode over to Pater, thrust him back onto the ottoman and straddled him. I thought she was going to murder him, slit his throat with an icy splinter. Squeezing my knees together, I rocked for joy. She would be mine, all mine! Imagine my disappointment when she moaned and he laughed, and next thing they were sitting side by side, the best of friends.

But what I remember most about my parents is that they weren't there.

LOKUGAMA

I remember the coming of the monsoons, that intoxicating sensation of rules disobeyed as the earth darkened and the wind grew huge and swung around to a different quadrant. I remember the grassy inner courtyard, where I lay on my back through slow afternoons and waited for a disheveled cloud to move across the sky.

Beyond the servants' quarters, on the far side of the wall that marked the rear boundary of the compound, loomed the jungle. Green birds flew in and out of it. One day I stacked bricks at the foot of the wall and heaved myself level with the parapet overhead. There I gazed into the face of a cobra, who was coiled in a patch of sunlight. I did not repeat the experiment.

My earliest companion was my smooth gray pony, Moonshine. Every morning and evening I would ride him to the trunk road and back, bracketing each day with his comforting presence. There were dogs, too, five or six Great Danes reeking of Lifebuoy soap sprawled about the place like trophies. Pater was fond of the breed; perhaps they reminded him of horses. He used to feed them toast spread with Gentleman's Relish. They never lived very long: those the snakes didn't get, the ticks finished off.

Forty years earlier, when a fire had destroyed part of the house, my grandfather himself had drawn up the plans for its reconstruction. The resulting admixture of styles and periods bore eloquent testimony to the triumph of zeal over talent. The courtyards typical of our ancient homesteads were now imprisoned between verandahs tiled in the tiny mustard and rust hexagons of any Civil Service bungalow. Satinwood doors, three inches thick, that had withstood Dutch bullets, opened onto lavatories. A corridor turned an angle and collided with a bricked-up doorway. An ancient fresco on the gateposts, restored by an artist who had toiled on these scenes from the life of the Buddha for three years, jarred with the marble nymphs and shepherd boys Sir Stanley had shipped out from Genoa to lurk about the compound. Fortunately Miss Dawson and her oar intervened at this juncture and my grandfather's vision of battlements was never translated into stone.

I had been bored in every cranny of the vast, ill-assorted house he had created. The table in the dining room could seat thirty-two; morose with boredom, I once lay under its ebony expanse throughout a nine-course luncheon, rousing myself now and then to inspect the ankles of a cabinet minister's daughter. Boredom inspired me to gouge our family tree into a calamander sideboard and take a single huge bite from every biscuit and cake in the pantry. Spiteful with tedium, I tortured frogs and birds in oleander thickets, only to weary of their suffering no sooner than it had begun.

At last, desperate for distraction, I would make a tour of all the cabinets in the house, studying the fabulous flotsam of Empire: scarlet-lacquered boxes, ivory-stemmed opium pipes, pewter card trays, an ostrich egg mounted on a filigree stand, even a jade-green tika from New Zealand. Scattered through this priceless collection was a democratic assortment of leather camels from Aden and seashell ashtrays from Brighton. No distinction was made between the relative worth of these articles. A Georgian tankard might hold a gaudy paper fan emblazoned with cherry-blossom in Birmingham, or a seventeenth-century Persian wall tile painted with ruby pomegranates. All served equally to link our old house, dozing in the jungle, with the great electric world of merchants and machinery. I was the center that drew and held them all—or so I imagined, and would grow lightheaded with pride. Years later in London, as I strolled through the perfumed abundance of Mr Selfridge's emporium, I was visited by the same delightful sensation. Such profusion, such variety! A cornucopia of disparate items, lace-trimmed handkerchiefs and rattan parrot cages, collected *en bloc* from every outpost of the globe. My gaze alone lent meaning to its surreal topography, rescuing it from chaos.

If I close my eyes I can still conjure the liniment smell of the medicine chest that stood in Mater's bedroom at Lokugama. It was painted white and locked with a small brass key. My mental taxonomy pairs this faintly sinister cupboard with an angled cabinet that occupied a corner of Pater's study. Objects that had been in our family for generations were heaped on its shelves in disarray. Ornamental daggers dulled by time, palm-leaf scrolls bearing royal signatures, statuettes of the Buddha, tooled betel boxes, gold-inlaid areca nut cutters, perforated chank shells, a jumble of tortoiseshell and silver hair combs: they all gave off a disagreeable odor of dust and neglect.

We had at least a dozen indoor servants and a regiment of gardeners and grooms. I remember the commotion when a servant-girl threw herself down the kitchen well; for a week, all the household water had to be drawn from the estate wells and brought to the big house in a cart, a welcome bump in the monotonous graph of our routine.

From time to time, out of nowhere, the kitchen courtyard would be full of squawking and feathers. An orchestra from the nearest town would show up in a bullock cart. At least, their instruments arrived in the cart; the musicians trudged along beside it. Tuning up was invariably accompanied by complaints about bunions. Later my parents would arrive from Colombo, sweeping in with presents and anywhere from three to thirty friends. I would rush to Mater and grasp her about the knees. Sometimes, not knowing how else to express my longing, I sank my teeth into the folds of her skirt and worried the material. She patted my head. Her tea-brown hands were diamond-shaped and scented with Russian tobacco. A cat's-eye bracelet winked at her wrist.

Pater always bought champagne by the twelve dozen. The parties lasted until dawn. After everyone had gone away again, I used to line up the empty bottles along the verandah and shoot them with my air rifle. That's what comes to mind when I think of my childhood: a boy in short trousers and long socks, the listless, bright, empty afternoon, birds flying up from leaves at the first explosion.

LESSONS

Once a week, with a servant in attendance, our buggy cart carried me into the nearest town, several miles distant, for my elocution class. The cart was drawn by a black ox with silver bells around its neck. A few years ago, as a pert little BOAC stewardess strapped me into my seat on a flight to England, I thought of that ox, with its lustrous eyes and hay breath. From buggies to airplanes in the span of a man's life. Is there a phenomenon more emblematic of our century's accelerating trajectory?

My teacher, Miss Vanderstraaten, seemed wholly ancient to me, so she was probably about forty. She lived with her mother in a dark house devoid of oxygen set within the blackened walls of the Dutch fort. Her academy was run from an antimacassared back parlor, where the starched children of local notables were delivered to her to be drilled in enunciation. Its furnishings included an occasional table crowded with photographs in heavy frames, and a row of monogrammed Delft plates on a shelf.

Miss Vanderstraaten was the first Dutch Burgher I knew. The European purity of her race was her great pride, and she guarded it with the zeal that brands all lost causes. One day I arrived a little early for my lesson, and so encountered a Mrs. de Jong and her beefy daughter, Phyllis, in the hall. Phyllis and I eyed each other with mutual distaste, while her mother, one of those women who sticks, exchanged a protracted farewell with Miss Vanderstraaten.

As soon as the door closed behind the de Jongs, my teacher's sugared tones altered. "The cheek of that woman," she hissed. "Black as the ace of spades and always passing herself off as one of us. As if everyone doesn't know she was one of the railway Rosarios before she married." My mystification must have been apparent, because she added impatiently, "A Portuguese Burgher. A lot of *very common* Sinhalese took Portuguese names when they converted."

"Pater says there's not a Ceylonese without mongrel blood in his veins," I replied, gratified that I could keep up my end of the conversation. "He says we've all got at least one skeleton in the family closet—a Tamil, a Moor, a Swiss mercenary, someone we'd rather keep quiet about."

"That might well be true of *your* people," said Miss Vanderstraaten, enunciating with great clarity. Her eyes flicked over me from head to toe. "Although you look *extremely Sinhalese* to me."

Whenever I tripped up in my recitations, Miss Vanderstraaten's wooden ferule thudded down on my knuckles. Mosquitoes congregated in the dim space under the table where I swung my legs. "How now brown cow," I intoned until the itching grew wild and I had to break off to tear at my shins, while the ruler crashed about my shoulders for fidgeting.

Miss Vanderstraaten often left the room in the middle of a lesson. I assumed this was for reasons to do with her bed-ridden mother, whose voice quavered down the stairs from time to time. Now I am not so sure. My teacher's habitual odor of lavender water and camphor was subtly different when she returned. In Oxford I was once at a party where a bottle of gin slipped from a girl's fingers. The sweetish whiff of those fumes transported me instantly across the years. I found myself once again in that cramped parlor, I could see the swing of Miss Vanderstraaten's coral beads, feel the nubbly texture of her plum-colored tablecloth beneath my elbows as I leaned over my book of exercises.

One day when my teacher had gone to the solace of her flask, I crossed the room to study her photographs. I picked up a studio portrait of a raven-haired goddess on the arm of a stout European gentleman at least twenty years her senior, posed against a painted backdrop of snowy mountain peaks. Peering at the photograph, I had just realized with a jolt that the beauty was my teacher—the mole fastened like a tick under her left eye was unmistakable—when the ruler caught me hard across my arm. Miss Vanderstraaten snatched the photograph from me and clasped it to her pintucked bosom. She brought her face down so close that I could see the grains of powder caught in the downy hair at the corners of her upper lip: "Don't you ever, *ever* touch my belongings with your *black hands*."

Behind Miss Vanderstraaten's house lay a harbor that had seen the fleets of Phoenician merchants; beyond it, the Indian Ocean rolled without interruption to the southern ice. But that spacious blue view was invisible from the parlor, where the blind was always pulled down behind elaborate lace curtains.

My formal education in those years was dispensed by a series of tutors, Englishmen whom the years have blurred into a single pinkish young man with an archetypal chin. The product of a minor public school, he instructs me in Ancient Civilizations (which is to say Egyptian, Greek and Roman) and is tormented by prickly heat. We study Geography with the aid of a globe supported by ormolu caryatids. In Arithmetic he allows that fractions are dashed confusing. He hears out my Latin declensions slapping at mosquitoes; he scratches his bites, which grow red and inflamed. He takes tea on the verandah, staring out at the vegetation that crawls about the house looking for a way in; the milk has turned, again. If he's a good sort, he plays the piano and teaches me a bawdy song; we belt out the chorus together. Once a month he goes into town, where he tries to work up an interest in the magistrate's sister, a lady with buck teeth who conducts séances. After a while he packs up the blank notebooks he intended to fill with piquant detail for his *Travels in the East*. A card at Christmas informs us that he has settled into his post of assistant housemaster at his old school. A wistful postscript adds that in England tea simply doesn't taste the same.

But the most enduring lesson of my childhood was provided, against all expectation, by my father. It happened when I was eight years old. Discipline on the estate at Lokugama was strict, although by no means harsh. As was usual in those days, village cattle that strayed onto the estate were shot. Our overseer, who prided himself on his loyalty to our family—and who no doubt relished the power and prestige that came with his post—always flogged any villager caught stealing coconuts. Yet conditions on our estate were far more lenient than on many others, where it was not unknown for landowners to keep laborers in stocks overnight to prevent them deserting during the coconut-picking season.

One morning, not long after daybreak, we heard a commotion in the compound. It happened that Pater was down from Colombo, seeing to the sale of a few acres to pay off a creditor who was proving a bore. He went out onto the verandah, still in his lounging slippers and foulard dressing gown. There he found our overseer, two watchmen propelling a sniveling youth and, at a respectful distance, a small group of laborers.

The overseer, who was in some distress, told his story haltingly. For some weeks now, coconut thieves had been operating on the estate. Traps had been set, extra watchmen hired. The overseer questioned villagers for miles around and had one or two known troublemakers thrashed for good measure. Still the thefts had continued. Thereupon the overseer announced that he was docking every laborer a tenth of each day's pay until the thieves were caught. This was grossly unfair; but it produced a startling result.

A few of the men, goaded by the loss of income, decided to institute their own watch, an initiative they discussed with no one. On the third night, two dark hours before dawn, they managed to lay hands on one of the thieves. To their amazement he turned out to be the overseer's youngest son, a fifteen-year-old boy who confessed to working in cahoots with some ne'er-do-wells from the town. Being privy to his father's security measures he had passed the information to his accomplices, and thus they had evaded detection. But that night the thieves had been startled by the unexpected presence of the laborers; the thugs from the town had gotten away, but the boy had panicked and been taken captive.

Seeing Pater, the boy flung himself to the ground and kissed his slippers, pleading for clemency. But it was no use. During the telling of the story, the number of onlookers had swelled until the entire working population of the estate had gathered in our driveway. Needless to say, the overseer and his family were not greatly loved. All the house servants came out onto the verandah. The gardeners and other outdoor workers clustered on the lawn. The watchmen removed the boy's shirt. His hands were tied, and the ends of the rope fastened around the trunk of a convenient flamboyante tree. The overseer himself, tears streaming down his face, handed the lash to my father.

I am certain Pater was as gentle as he could be, under the circumstances. Nevertheless, by the sixth and final stroke, the boy's back was streaked with blood. He was a screamer: he had been at it since the rope first rose in the air. I had an excellent view from the top of the steps. I remember standing very straight and still, and being careful to keep my face from betraying my emotion. For truth to tell, I was in the grip of a queer exaltation. What I was witnessing was the grand and terrible spectacle of justice.

At breakfast, Pater said as much. He had heaped his plate from the dishes on the sideboard. Now he sat staring at his rashers, tomatoes and green chili omelette. "Without fear or favor," he said, at last. Then he left the room, neglecting to close the door. The sound of vomiting reached me from the hall lavatory.

The whole episode left me much to ponder. Like all children I had believed fairness to be synonymous with justice. *It's not fair!*—so runs the eternal cry of childhood. Was it fair that the overseer's son was thrashed while the men who had led him astray went unpunished? I now realized that it was a childish question. It was essential to the harmonious functioning of our little community that the boy paid publicly for his crime in spite of his privileged standing on the estate. Pater had taught me, by his example, that while we might dread what justice requires of us, our fear cannot be allowed to interfere with the benefit to society.

You see, don't you, why I have made prosecution my life's work. In the popular imagination, defense is the noble choice—what my old pupil-master liked to call *le beau rôle*. But I have invariably found that it appeals to childish men; a flabby brotherhood that calls it justice when a blackguard who should be ornamenting the gallows strolls away from the dock. Give me prosecution every time! It is a stern and thankless calling. But it has a grandeur that the sentimentality of defense can never hope to rival.

I see I have neglected to mention that I had a baby sister, then aged three. Claudia was standing beside me on the verandah that morning, but as soon as the overseer's son began his racket, she burst into tears and ran sobbing into the house. Thus from a tender age she displayed the hysterical turn of mind that was to overwhelm her later in life. I had a brother as well, Leonard, born a few weeks before the incident of the coconut thieves. The sight of Mater crooning over that puny stranger had filled me with loathing when Claudia and I were taken to Colombo to admire him. Claudia, being a girl, had never posed a threat to my standing. But in Leo I intuited an adversary, a pretender to my throne.

I need not have feared; my resentment did not have long to simmer. Leo's life was a short one: he died in his cot when he was only six months old and plays no further part in this testimony.

SONS OF EMPIRE

At the age of thirteen I was enrolled in St. Edward's School in Colombo as a boarder. Neddy's had been founded in 1862 by an Anglican bishop on the pattern of Eton and Rugby. There, some five hundred boys were educated in English, Classics, Mathematics, Divinity and the Sciences. Many of us went on to Oxford and Cambridge, and returned home to forge illustrious careers. Government, the judiciary, medicine, education: to this day Old Edwardians are disproportionately represented in all the leading professions. Even in its present degraded state, Neddy's has no rival in the land. Preposterous claims have been made for Queen's College; but as we Edwardians like to say, Queen's is all balls and no brains. Which has never prevented us from routing them at cricket.

Neddy's occupied a prime site in Colpetty, a former coconut plantation that stretched between Galle Road and the sea. After the close green canopy of Lokugama, I thrilled to the wide skies and salty, invigorating air. When the wake-up bell sounded at ten to six, we boarders had to assemble in the quad for twenty minutes of drill. How I relished those mornings: the cool breeze, the drum roll of breakers beyond the boundary wall, a dozen boys moving as one under the ghost moon that still haunted the pearly sky. Decades later, it was the memory of those mornings that prompted me to buy Allenby House. I did not realize—

how could I have?—that the sea is a cruel companion to the old. To a young man it sings of change, boundlessness, the beckoning future. Later it changes its tune. Every day now I wake to the same complaint, a relentless whisper of frustrated endeavor.

I was a boarder rather than a day boy because Pater was still wending his merry way toward financial ruin and it had been necessary to sell all the property we had once owned in Colombo. Shortly after I entered Neddy's, my parents moved in with my Aunt Iris, who lived in the newly fashionable suburb of Cinnamon Gardens. Although my aunt and her husband were childless, their palatial house could have accommodated half a dozen boys; but I suppose my parents didn't wish to presume further on their hosts' kindness and include me in the household, and so I remained a boarder throughout my time at Neddy's.

Uncle Kumar, Iris's husband, had once been briefly engaged to my mother. When she threw him over for Pater, Kumar promptly married her cousin to show he didn't care a fig; but for years he couldn't stand to be in the same room as Pater and was famous for having walked out of a ball at Government House when my father was announced. Unfortunately he was halfway through a waltz with Lady Marriott, a singular honor. I believe it was the last time she danced with a Ceylonese.

Over the years, things had been patched up between Pater and Kumar. Still, I was surprised to hear that my parents were putting up at Cinnamon Gardens. Today, the only conclusion I can draw is that Mater had embarked on an *affaire* with Uncle Kumar. The three of them—Kumar, Iris and my mother—called at Neddy's one Saturday during my second term and treated me to a feed at the Dragon Restaurant. All the boarders came out to admire Kumar's shiny blue motor car and I was much envied when I climbed aboard. Kumar, I recall, was in rattling good spirits and tipped me ten chips. Pierced with sudden loneliness when I was returned to Neddy's, I pressed my lips to Mater's cigarette-scented cheek and wound my arms about her neck. "Goodness, Sam," she said, disentangling herself. "Anyone would think you had a claim on my affections and whatnot." Then she tapped me lightly on the head with her folded fan and was gone. Three months and eighteen days passed before I next saw her.

Most of us Edwardians came from Sinhalese or Burgher families, but there were several Tamils among our number, a sprinkling of Moors and Chinks, an Indian from Bangalore and even two woolly-haired brothers from East Africa. But racial divisions were played down at Neddy's, as a matter of school policy. We were Edwardians first and Ceylonese a long way second. Of course a fellow's name proclaimed him a Sinhalese or a Tamil, a Burgher or a Moor; but these distinctions passed almost unnoticed.

It's true that we routinely referred to the Chinese boys as Ching-Chongs. And yes, we never bothered with the Kaffirs' jawbreaking name but dubbed them the Kalus for their glossy black skin: at sixteen, Kalu Dwarf already stood over six feet tall; while cheerful Kalu Dhodhol enlivened any gathering, like the sticky black sweetmeat that inspired his name. But these appellations were no more sinister than calling a chap Four Eyes because he wears spectacles or Fatty because he runs to lard; all schoolboys everywhere seize on physical attributes that deviate from the norm.

As any Old Edwardian will attest, the prevalent tone of the school was one of comradeship unmarred by racial or religious strife. We spoke English, our only common tongue, to each other as well as to our masters. Most of us were Christians, and attended the daily service held in the school chapel, while the dozen or so non-Christian boys did extra prep or listened to an uplifting talk by Warden Metcalfe's wife. Friendly rivalry, encouraged in the classroom and on the playing field, served only to strengthen our common bonds and provided healthy lessons in character and confidence. I myself had the highest regard for Kalu Dhodhol, a formidable opponent on the tennis court. He died last year, poor devil, hanged in one of those coups the Kaffirs are so keen on. I have such a vivid memory of him leaping the net, all graceful limbs and a wide white grin. "Pukka show, Obey," he would say and mean it, despite having beaten me in straight sets. He put it about that he and his brother were of royal blood, a claim I received with skepticism; I believe the savage races do not distinguish between fact and fable as rigorously as we do. But he was certainly one of nature's gentlemen. Hard to believe he's gone now, forever.

PLAYING THE FOOL

I emphasize the harmony that prevailed at Neddy's because one of my classmates was none other than Donald Jayasinghe. That's right: the architect of racial hatred, our erstwhile Minister of Culture. The champion of Sinhalese who couldn't read or write the language and delivered his Cambridge-inflected speeches from transliterated scripts with nervous aides standing by to prompt him when he tripped over his tongue. The famous Jungle Jaya, with his talk of Aryan supermen that pandered to the vanity of villagers and won his party its landslide election victories. The British made a fatal error when they brought in universal suffrage. It might be plausible in Europe, but here, with our ignorant masses, what can it lead to but the disasters we've seen since independence? Would you ask a child to operate on your appendix or a lunatic to advise you on your investments? Yet we entrust our choice of government to villagers with no discernment or finesse, no training in sustained analytical thought. Inevitably, their crude emotions carry the day. We all suffer the consequences.

Jaya was a day boy, so we were never close. But as academic rivals we kept an eye on each other. I trounced him at Greek and Latin but he had the edge on me when it came to French and Geometry. In English we were neck and neck. And to this day you may see our names bracketed in gold on the Honors Board. (I had half a mark more, I believe, but the examiners, with questionable wisdom, decided to award us equal first place.)

Even as a boy, Jaya was extraordinarily hairy: at fifteen, with his blue-and-silver school tie knotted around his neck, his collar was edged with thick dark fur. If you ask me, all that parading about later in a sarong had nothing to do with rejecting the dress of our imperial masters and everything to do with showing off his breastplate of matted curls.

Women are notoriously attracted to that kind of thing; it appeals to the primitive mind. "What a perfectly delicious young man," I remember Mater saying at one prize-giving. It was 1918 and I had just collected the Bishop's Medal for Poetry, the school's most coveted award, for my sonnet "On the Fallen." It was the first time in Neddy's history that the prize hadn't been carried off by a Sixth Former and I think I may say without exaggeration that my victory caused a small sensation. After the speeches and ceremonies had ended and we boys were free to mingle with our guests, I went straight over to my parents, carrying my usual haul of books, supplemented with the Bishop's gold medal. Mater ruffled my hair. "What a perfectly delicious young man." For a dizzy moment, I thought she meant me. Then I followed her gaze—and there was Jaya, encircled as usual by a pack of doting juniors, looking my mother over with his sticky brown eyes.

Several Old Edwardians swear that no one who knew Jaya as a boy could have predicted what he would become as a man. They are wrong. Oh yes, yes, the outward show, the aristocrat turned demagogue, handmade shoes from Bond Street exchanged for thick-soled sandals of local manufacture, single malt replaced by that vile fruit cup at official functions, all that I grant you. But these things were mere props; in essence, Jaya's politics were wholly consistent with his antics at Neddy's. His old friends feel betrayed by the social revolution he engineered when he allowed priests and villagers to impose their prejudices on the entire country, and their sense of grievance blinds them to the truth. It is also soothing to subscribe to the notion of a clean break between the two halves of Jaya's life; in accentuating that discontinuity, we seek to underplay the fact that the man who let us down so shamefully grew from the boy we idolized.

I use the pronoun rhetorically, you understand: I am proud to say that I, for one, always thought Jaya shone with a very dim wattage. But far too many of our comrades were dazzled. It is unusual for a clever boy to be popular, too. I myself, while of course looked up to by the others, was treated with a certain deferential reserve, which could on occasion turn malicious. (I well remember the incident of the dead bandicoot placed under my coverlet. And even if nothing was proved, I know who was responsible.) But Jaya had the common touch. Consider our choice of games: I got my colors in tennis, where outcomes hinge on individual talent and strategic intelligence, and a certain discernment is asked of the spectator. Jaya, on the other hand, was a cricketer. There is no surer route to popularity in a country where any urchin can parade his expertise in an alley with a plank for a bat and a kerosene tin for a wicket. When Jaya made 133 not out against Queen's in March 1920, a tide of boys rolled onto the field and chaired him around the ground, paying no heed at all to my prefect's whistle. Decades later, more than one Old Edwardian would confess to me that it was the memory of that golden afternoon that had prompted him to vote for Jaya. This despite the incontrovertible evidence that as a batsman the blighter possessed little innate talent and the style of an ebullient bear. Viewed analytically it is obvious that his famous victory was only the compound of his indefensible risks at the crease and some spectacularly inept fielding by Queen's.

But it was not just cricket that won Jaya his following. He was also a joker, you see, always playing to an audience. His pranks were legendary, chuckled over by everyone from Olympian prefects to the greenest juniors, regularly finding their way into the Glee Club's end-of-term skits.

There was the time our form had a new Latin master: Neville Willoughby, pink-eared, black-robed, as fresh off the boat as the morning's catch. When he entered our classroom we rose to our feet and greeted him with our chorused *Salve, Magister*. Baring his narrow brown teeth in a grimace intended to convey camaraderie, Willoughby asked us to tell him our names, as we were all going to be *great chums*. Jaya had planned accordingly. When the new master pointed at him and his cronies in turn, each boy called out a Sinhalese obscenity. The spruce young Englishman strolled up and down between the rows of desks carefully repeating *Son of a whore! Frog's arse!* in his Oxford drawl, while behind his back boy after boy collapsed in silent mirth.

It is quite true—I am not the least ashamed to admit it—that I followed Willoughby out of the room at the end of the lesson and informed him of the deception. My conscience dictated it. Was it gentlemanly to mock a newcomer to our land? Was it honorable to take advantage of his ignorance? Of course I was justified in acting as I did. Yet I confess that I quailed when I emerged from the boarding house the next morning to find Jaya, a suspiciously early arrival, lounging in my path. Half a dozen boys had followed me out after breakfast and now crowded close; I felt their breath on my neck and thought of noble Actaeon, torn to pieces by his hounds. It is possible that I whimpered.

But Jaya only looked at me. "It's in your blood, isn't it, Obey?" Even in those days he had a large furry voice like an actor reciting poetry. "Your people were Buddhist under our kings, Catholics under the Portuguese, Reformists under the Dutch, Anglicans under the English. You can't help yourself, can you? Obey by name, Obey by nature."

Before recess the taunt was all over Neddy's: Obey by name, Obey by nature. Fellows grinned all over their faces when they saw me coming. I could have pointed out that what Jaya had said of the Obeysekeres was equally true of the Jayasinghes—indeed of all our leading families. I could have argued that there is no shame in adaptability and keeping an open mind. But Jaya didn't operate within the parameters of rational argument. His popularity was founded on the base instincts that schoolboys share, the cheap laugh, the dagger in the spine.

His most notorious stunt took place in the science laboratory. Chemistry was taught throughout Neddy's by a hunched and ancient Tamil by the name of Sudaramani. Suds, as we called him, had a temper as explosive as the chemicals with which he surrounded himself.

The slightest misdemeanor, even the suspicion of inattention, and Suds would have the culprit by the ear and his cane at the ready. We lived in terror of him. Once, when we were lined up outside his lab, I was seized with a fit of hiccoughs. Suds arrived, shoulders around his ears, hauled me out of line and ordered me to bend over in the doorway. He then invited my classmates to plant a muddy boot in my backside as each boy entered the room, which I regret to say they did with alacrity. Suds himself delivered the final kick, sending me sprawling to the floor, where I remained for the rest of the lesson. I must say it cured my hiccoughs.

Chemistry lessons with Jaya meant stink bombs, and test tubes that mysteriously slid from benches to smash on the floor whenever Suds was preoccupied with a particularly tricky experiment. Jaya had more thrashings in Chemistry than I had in all my years at Neddy's; eventually he took to slipping an atlas down the seat of his trousers before entering the lab.

One morning he was uncommonly provocative, hurling inky litmus pellets around the room and breaking wind loudly. But when Suds came roaring down from his dais, cane twitching, Jaya leapt off his stool and scuttled to a corner, shouting, "Sir, I can't stand it any longer, sir! Sir, you have destroyed me, sir!"

He reached up to the shelf above his head, grabbed a jar clearly labeled Hydrochloric Acid, pulled out the stopper and took an almighty swig. Old Suds howled like an injured dog. Clutching his chest, he tottered toward Jaya, who had fallen writhing to the floor. Seconds later, as we boys watched petrified, Suds's cane swished through the air. Jaya was rolling to safety under a bench, gurgling with laughter. It transpired that he had climbed in through a window the previous day and replaced the contents of the jar with water. Warden Metcalfe himself administered the caning at a special school assembly, after which Jaya was suspended for a fortnight.

You see the relevance, don't you? What has Jaya's entire political career been but a hideous practical joke perpetrated on our country? Calling us the Lion People, telling every Sinhalese lout with a chip on his shoulder that he was the rightful master of the land: what arrant nonsense the man came up with to wangle his victories at the polls.

Jaya used to boast that he taught his countrymen to be proud; the truth is, he taught us to hate. We're no longer Ceylonese: we're Sinhalese, Tamils, Malays, Burghers, Chinks, Moors, Colombo Chettys, and ready to cut each other's throats at the slightest provocation. How providential that the blackguard drove his car into an embankment before he could send the whole country slamming into a brick wall. Not that he didn't set us well and truly on our course; and he'll be splitting his sides among the hellfires when the grand collision comes.

But I see that Jaya has quite usurped this account of my schooldays, which is not what I intended at all. He was a minor player on the periphery of the happiest times I've known. These days, Neddy's has come down in the world. It might still be the finest school in the country, but it has little in common with the institution that nurtured me. Do you know that they no longer teach Latin? And they've begun phasing out English-medium instruction. Are we to become a nation capable of talking only to itself, a lunatic on the world stage? The Tamils will learn their Tamil, the Sinhalese their Sinhala; if they end up unable to understand each other, so much the better for mutual hatred. *Divide et impera*: wasn't that one of their charges against the British?

I am proud to have attended Neddy's in the days when it turned out gentlemen and scholars. As a boy I often thought what a great pity it was that Ceylon had no empire of her own: we Edwardians would have made such a splendid job of sallying forth and ruling it.

THE DREAMING SPIRES

This morning the sight of a grizzled face in the mirror so startled me that for a moment I feared an intruder had slipped into my room. Yet I am all too conscious that I have grown old. I, who once prided myself on coming to the point, on the succinct phraseology of my addresses to the jury, have become a man who rambles. In my youth I had no patience with the conversational detours of the elderly: how long it took them to reach their destination, I would think, searching for shortcuts to bypass their meandering. I couldn't understand why, when so little time remained to them, they would squander it in this way. Now I see that it was not a matter of being wasteful, but of hefting each moment, acknowledging its due weight. *Tempus fugit*; so old men cling to it as it passes, and its wings beat a fraction slower overhead.

Nevertheless I must press on if I am to arrive at the events that spurred my pen. The first lesson the Bar taught me was that narrative is chiefly a matter of selection. What one leaves out is quite as important as what one chooses to disclose—indeed more so. I must endeavor to keep the precept in mind as I compose this account.

And so I shall not allow Oxford to detain me long. I spent four years there, reading Greats. Warden Metcalfe had advised against this course of study, warning that students who didn't have an English public school preparation usually fared badly. But when he saw that my mind was made up he offered me every encouragement, tutoring me himself in Ancient Greek and extra Latin. His words came back to me on my first night in Hall, as the scholars stalked disdainfully past my table. The long dark rustle of their gowns left me pincered between envy and resolution. I knew very well that to be their equal I should have to prove myself their superior. Thus I applied myself with diligence to my books, and eventually took a very decent Second in Honor Mods.

Mater and Claudia were visiting England that year and came up to see me. They were pleased that I had done well, but their congratulations were perfunctory. Women are rarely impressed by intellectual achievement. My father would have appreciated my success more keenly but he had remained behind in Colombo. Mater had refused to cover his passage—she had sold Granny's star sapphires to raise the money—and he had no means of paying for himself.

Over tea in my set my mother recited a litany of complaints. The arrangement with Kumar and Iris had come unstuck, and now my parents were renting a poky little house with only three bedrooms in Havelock Town. The few parcels of land that hadn't been sold were mortgaged to the hilt. Our dwindling revenues were being sunk into my education. Pater had sneaked off to Lokugama one weekend, packed up the contents of the cabinets in both drawing rooms and sold the lot to a flat-faced Malay. Mater had been obliged to pawn a gold chain to pay for Claudia's piano lessons. They could no longer afford a motorcar. Even the Great Danes hadn't been replaced when the latest litter succumbed to tick fever.

Meanwhile Claudia picked at her sleeve and her teacup rattled in her saucer. She had grown into an attractive young woman with a slim yet rounded figure and our mother's long golden eyes. Yet she avoided one's gaze and her fingernails were hideous: raw, bitten down to the quick. It was plain that the dear girl was quite overcome with emotion at being reunited with me at last.

After tea I proposed a stroll around the colleges. It was a flawless afternoon, all restless leaves and the river slow and green, stonework like sculpted honey. We had paused in Tom Quad so that I could discourse on its history when I was interrupted by a shout—and to my dismay there was Jaya, shambling toward us in the sunlight. Really, the fellow bore an astonishing resemblance to an ape; one looked around in vain for his keeper.

He stood before us and stroked his mustache, examining my mother with an auctioneer's frank interest. She, wretched woman, narrowed her eyes still further and her nostrils quivered like a deer's. He claimed he was over from Cambridge to visit friends, but that didn't prevent him attaching himself to us for what was left of the day. With my mother on his right arm, he strolled the pavements as if he owned them, laughing in that coarse way with his head thrown back, or bending close to Mater and snuffling in her ear. I followed, rigid with rage. Beside me, Claudia gnawed at her fingers and screamed when a bicycle bell sounded at her shoulder.

Mater informed me, in a brief letter I received a few days later, that Jaya had invited us all to Brackwell Hall, Sir Geoffrey Alderton's place in Norfolk, for a week. Sir Geoffrey, you'll remember, claimed to be a Communist, and liked to collect exotic guests whom he could pin out like so many specimens for the instruction of his neighbors. How utterly typical of Jaya not only to have wangled his way into Brackwell Hall, reputed to be one of the country's finest examples of Georgian domestic architecture, but to extend invitations to all and sundry like the lord of the bally manor. I was determined to put the kibosh on that little show. Two hours before we were due to set out for Norfolk, I turned up at the hotel in Bayswater where Mater and Claudia were staying and announced that I had no intention of leaving it. I ordered Claudia to remain in London with me, as I did not believe our father would approve of her being on intimate terms with Reds. She wept, as she always did when overstimulated. Mater raged like a leopard but I would not be swayed. It was scarcely proper for her to turn up unaccompanied at Brackwell Hall; some things are simply not done, even by Communists. And yet, you know, as the hour of the train's departure drew near, she stabbed a pearl-headed pin through her hat and swept out of the door, swearing like a fishwife in primrose linen.

ORIGINALITY AND ITS DISCONTENTS

Claudia and I spent a soothing week together: early morning strolls in the park, the occasional concert, an outing to Brighton. My sister had had her hair bobbed and looked absurdly young. My company was all the tonic she needed; after a day or two of skittish agitation, she grew used to the excitement of being alone with me in London and was soon jabbering like a mynah.

I had forgotten my sister's trick of twisting commonplace sayings into unexpected configurations. The whole family picked up her coinages. *It's a long worm that has no turning* became an Obeysekere standard. *No point spoiling the soup for a pennyworth of tar. Give a dog enough rope and hang him*. Now, speaking of a lackluster acquaintance, "He's no oil lamp," she remarked. I grinned. It was amusing; even astute. At the same time, I was faintly irritated. As a child I had memorized the proverbs that headed the pages of my copybook, committing each one to heart as my pencil traced its lines and loops. I was word perfect. No one noticed. That was the point, in a way: to have the fluency to pass unremarked. Nevertheless it was galling when Claudia's mistakes drew admiring laughter from our parents. I have always favored the classical world, in which perfection is synonymous with flawless imitation. The ancients understood that there is no art to being original. It's only a matter of getting everything wrong.

If I indulged now and then in these uncharitable thoughts, it was only because Claudia could be a trying companion. For a start, she badgered me with questions about Jaya. Where did his people live? Would he call on us when he returned home? Had a marriage already been arranged for him? I refused to answer. It was obvious that she was troubled by the nature of Mater's relations with Jaya, and I judged silence to be the best way of calming the unhealthy frenzy of her suspicions.

One evening, when we had returned from a late stroll around the West End, Claudia grew excited. It was unwise of me to have allowed her a glass of hock with dinner. Prowling around her room, she hurled a foam of garments from drawers and upended hat boxes. The cause of the hullabaloo was the disappearance of a short length of corded blue silk. The thing was fraying, worthless. But it was her *special rope*. She slept with it under her pillow. If she thought I wasn't looking, she would take it from her pocket and finger it. It was a habit she had retained from her earliest years, when her imagination would pounce on an unsuitable object of one sort or another and dig in its claws. The cord was the same shade of bruise-blue as a cushion she had dragged everywhere as a small girl; it took Pater to pry it from her when it finally grew too filthy to be tolerated.

I hated seeing my sister handle that grubby little cord. A few hours earlier, I had taken advantage of a diversion to abstract the thing from her evening bag and drop it under a chair. Now, when it became obvious to Claudia that she had lost it, she wanted to scour the pavements we had walked that night. The idea was absurd. I was tired and had no intention of trawling the streets pretending to search for that dingy fragment. But she became rebellious, raising her voice and even trying to push past me as I barred the door. I envisioned being summoned to an interview with the hotel manager, who always wore a brown suit and looked at me as if I were something that had turned up in his toothpaste. He would announce himself *entitled to an explanation*. Embarrassment ran its cold feathers down my spine, curled itself between my shoulder blades.

In the end I was obliged to remind Claudia of certain unfortunate facts. There are instabilities that appear in old families like flaws in the finest china. Take our Aunt Sybil, who never married and displayed a keen interest in missionaries. One afternoon she lured a Methodist into a bathroom and locked the door behind her. Then she hurled the key out of the window. They remained there for several hours, until the minister's hoarse cries succeeded in rousing the servants. Afterward, Sybil was confined to the care of a brother-in-law who thrashed his eleven children every Sunday morning to strengthen their characters. It was not that I threatened Claudia exactly. But at length she grew limp. I stayed with her all night, fearing she might yet blunder downstairs and into the streets, whimpering for her lost treasure. I need not have been anxious. At breakfast she was a model of propriety. The rest of our time together was entirely harmonious.

As for what went on in Norfolk, I hate to think. At a Law Asia dinner some forty years later, I found myself sitting next to a desiccated chief justice from Lahore. He told me he had once met my mother at Brackwell Hall. "A remarkable lady. Tremendously kind to me, yes tremendously." He fussed a moment with his spectacles. There had been some awkwardness, he recalled, over a crystal rose bowl. "Been in the family since Queen Anne. The maids were picking shards out of the rugs for days." He smiled at me, the old toad, and I glimpsed the ghost of a boy in his ruined face, and summers that had grown to fullness, leaf by leaf, Mater in a bronze straw hat and Claudia walking down a grassy path that fell away toward water, all vanished now, everything over.

MURDER CONSIDERED AS A FINE ART

Oxford remains with me as a quintessential day: liver and bacon and toast and marmalade, a couple of lectures, a cold collation in my set at noon. Into flannels for tennis, which we played on a meadow reached by taking a ferry across the river. A meadow: I had never understood the word, so familiar from books since childhood, until I encountered that soft, yielding grass, with its embroidery of buttercups and daisies, utterly unlike the coarse blades and knotted weeds that passed for lawn at home. I would lie down between sets, intoxicated by the sweet scent of earth and grass. All around me boys sprawled under a high, blue sky, young gods in an antique glade.

There would be a huge tea in a pavilion, more tennis, then back to college for a bath and dinner. This was followed by an hour or so of talk and pipes in the JCR or billiards at the Union. With Moderations behind me, I felt able to relax the rigorous program of study that I fear had turned me into something of a swot in my first two years. Fisher, my tutor, encouraged a leisurely approach, advising me to do no more than read generally as initial preparation for Schools. This left plenty of leisure for idling in a punt or penning a short story for the college magazine.

The news from home left me in no doubt that I would be obliged to earn my living on my return. Not for me the debonair cultivation of eccentricities while pretending to manage the family estates; for the very good reason that there would be no estates left to manage. The prospect of a career struck me as no bad thing. There were plenty like my father, natural leaders of our countrymen, who dissipated their talents in frivolities because their wealth freed them from the necessity of earning a living. I determined then and there to seek my fortune at the Bar. A noble profession, and ideally suited to one so amply endowed with reason and eloquence. I borrowed a couple of books on criminal law and lost no time in mastering their contents.

My reading soon led me to the famous murder trials of the day. Thereafter, when I went down to London it was not to visit the Tower or the Houses of Parliament but to stroll down Hilldrop Crescent, where little more than a decade earlier Dr. Crippen had made away with Belle Elmore and buried her remains in the coal cellar of number 39. In the seedy little secondhand bookshop that stood at the crossroads, I bought a twopenny pamphlet and gave myself up to its sensationalist account of the initial police bungling of the case, the subsequent pursuit of Crippen across the Atlantic and the cable received over the ship's wireless that sealed his fate.

From Hilldrop Crescent it was a short walk to 63 Tollington Park, where Frederick Seddon had murdered Eliza Barrow for her money. My research took me also to the chemist's shop in Crouch Hill where Seddon's daughter purchased the threepenny packet of arsenic-laced flypapers that had figured so prominently in the prosecution. I bought a packet myself as a memento, while picturing the revolting sickroom described by witnesses: the sluttish bed linen, the chamberpot that required emptying, the sickening clouds of flies whose squalid buzzing filled the room. Because whatever purpose those flypapers had served, it was plainly not the murder of flies.

Although I could not know it at the time, I was living in the heyday of the English murder. What novelist, even one possessing imaginative powers of the highest order, could have invented a scene such as the one that took place in Bismarck Road, Highgate, where Joseph Smith played "Nearer, My God, to Thee" on his landlady's harmonium while his latest bride drowned in the upstairs bath? Only think, if you dare, of that parlor. I see a determinedly respectable room: a brass-potted aspidistra in the bay window, china dogs on the mantelpiece, looped curtains made of a heavy brown material that doesn't show the dirt. And Smith descending the stairs, flexing his fingers.

Wonderful stuff, don't you agree? I was most impressed by the cold brilliance with which the great English murderers planned their crimes, the slow maturation of the project in logic and cunning over weeks and months. It was quite the converse of the way things were done at home. There, lack of premeditation was the rule. Murder was frequent—far more frequent than in England—with at least half the number of recorded murderers giving their occupation as *cultivator*. Such men carried knives for agricultural purposes, and fought with them, rather than with their fists, over the most trivial causes: a fence line that was out by an inch, the disputed yield from a single branch of an overhanging breadfruit tree. There was no art to such crimes. The psychology of the murderers was as simple and dull as the alphabet. In many cases the killer made no effort whatsoever to avoid detection and was apprehended at once by the authorities. It struck me as a thoroughly brutish state of affairs.

From the art of murder it was a short step to murder as art. It was at this time that I discovered the complex pleasures of the detective novel. I was soon immersed in Conan Doyle and E. C. Bentley, and the early works of the sublime Mrs. Christie. I shuddered over "The Murders in the Rue Morgue." I thrilled to the adventures of Father Brown. Holmes and Poirot, my favorite fictional detectives, became quite as real to me as anyone I knew. I loved to sharpen my wits on the ingenious puzzles devised by their authors, and may say without vanity that once or twice I succeeded in cracking them before the solution was revealed in the final pages. Modesty compels me to add that my unraveling of the Hamilton case (variously described as *masterly* and *a dazzling piece of detection*) probably owed more to a mind steeped in the stratagems of detective fiction than to the genius with which I was credited by so many commentators.

Here I must ask you to grant me the indulgence of a parenthesis. Only last week I attended a lecture at the British Council on the subject of classic detective fiction. The lecturer, a Dr. Sims, dressed like a poacher and sounded like a barrow boy, but claimed to be a don at the University of Liverpool. When my ear had adjusted to the peculiarities of the fellow's accent, he was arguing that the popularity of the detective novel springs from its shoring up of conservative values. "By its strict adherence to formal conventions, the whodunnit seeks to bring the socially disruptive act of murder under control," he brayed. "The murderer is unmasked by a representative of authority, who provides a rational, logical explanation of the crimes. Thus we see that the detective novel raises the specter of a threat to society only to exorcise it. The murderer is removed from our midst, and the reader is reassured by the restoration of order and the perpetuation of the status quo."

Have you ever heard such rot? I almost rose from my seat to set the silly ass right there and then. Dr. Sims had missed the point entirely. The true drama of the whodunnit lies not in the clash between murderer and detective, but in the skirmish between author and reader. The fictional murderer is brought to justice, yes. But when an author succeeds in outwitting his reader, *there* is the "destabilizing of convention" so prized by that nitwit from Liverpool.

Consider for a moment a classic work like *Hercule Poirot's Christmas*. Doesn't the success of Mrs. Christie's inspired plot hinge on the rules that govern the conduct of policemen? The reader who accepts that convention is outwitted by the author, who dares to flout it. Contrary to Dr. Sims's argument, the whodunnit is an invitation to social disobedience. It is enthralling precisely to the extent that the principles it sabotages are considered beyond question. Who but a fool would describe this process as *shoring up conservative values*? The detective novel is nothing short of a literary insurgent.

Over coffee and biscuits I attempted to put my argument to Dr. Sims, but he paid no more heed to me than to the dandruff lying in dunes on the shoulders of his corduroy jacket. His tiny eyes leapt about the room like flies. As soon as I paused, he muttered an excuse and headed for the urn, where busty Miss Amita de Silva, the assistant librarian, was arrayed in a fetching scarlet sari and tight black blouse. That is at once the strength and the weakness of the English mind: always more interested in practical outcomes than abstract speculation. Not that Dr. Sims got very far with Miss de Silva. She is a Marxist-Leninist, I believe, with a stern outlook and a fine disdain for Europeans. Other than Marx or Lenin, of course. At any rate, she contrived within minutes to spill a cup of steaming coffee into our lecturer's lap. He yelled blue murder.

THE QUALITY OF MERCY

In time I exchanged Oxford for London, where I would be eating my dinners at Gray's Inn. Thanks to Fisher, I was reading for the Bar with Douglas Dartington-Clay, the most sought-after pupil-master in England; the two men were related by marriage. Dartington-Clay recommended lodgings off High Holborn; the rooms were cheap and clean, he said, and conveniently situated. All of which was true, but my master was either ignorant of or chose not to mention the overwhelming attraction of 6B Feathers Lane. I became aware of it one icy November afternoon, when my landlady entered my room unannounced and crossed to the table where I sat huddled over my papers. Somewhat taken aback, I was rising to greet her when she placed her hand on my shoulder, indicating with downward pressure that I should remain seated. Then she bent over, unbuttoned my fly and knelt in front of me.

Mrs. Arthur Timms must have been in her thirties when I made her acquaintance. Part Maori, part Irish, part Scottish, she was a large-boned woman with smooth olive skin and eyes of the clearest grey. She had met and married Timms, an able seaman in the merchant navy, when he was on three days' shore leave in Dunedin. My bedstead of dainty, if chipped, white iron, like the wreaths of bluebells and pink rosebuds on my wallpaper, hinted that the original occupant of my room had been a young girl. However, the Timmses marriage did not appear to have produced any children; at any rate, I saw no photographs or mementos to suggest the contrary. Mrs. Timms—I never knew her first name—rarely volunteered information about herself and, despite the nature of our relations, I was always too shy to ask questions. There was something dignified and regal about her, a compound of her slow gait, the heavy black hair she always wore pinned up, the dark rings around those pale irises that gave her an air of intense remoteness, even when she was engaged in the most intimate acts.

She, on the other hand, encouraged confidences. Soon I found myself whispering to her what I hardly dared acknowledge to myself. Thereafter she often brought a springy length of rattan to our encounters. As for Timms, he was away on his ship for months at a time. I saw him only once, in the dim hallway, a blue-jowled chap with a shiny raincoat and lips as red as geraniums. When he went away again, his wife had a black eye and violet bruises along her thighs. What I remember most vividly about her is that, unlike the English, she always smelled clean.

There were five other boarders, all of us students from Asia. At first I flattered myself that Mrs. Timms had singled me out for her attention. I was soon disabused of that notion. A month after our first encounter, alerted one evening by a familiar creaking, I crept upstairs to the third-floor landing. After a brief hesitation, I approached a door and applied my eye to the keyhole. A diminutive Burmese was busy with Mrs. Timms, whose dress was rucked up around her hips; he had fastened himself to its dove-grey billows like a small golden ornament. It was fortunate that my moans coincided with his or surely I would not have escaped detection.

After that I listened attentively whenever I heard my landlady's step; and thus ascertained that she came and went from all our rooms, never staying longer than half an hour or so. She fitted us in: between putting a pie in the oven and serving up supper, between stepping out of her bath and stepping out to the corner-house on a Saturday evening, resplendent in a mauve satin hat.

The service Mrs. Timms did us lonely young men, strangers in a strange land, cannot be overestimated. Oddly enough, we never discussed her among ourselves. For my part, I had the sense of living under an enchantment; to speak of it would have broken the spell. There was also the fact that I felt an instinctive antipathy for the Parsi from Bombay with whom I shared a landing. Sodawallah was always pushing smudged tracts about vegetarianism and Gandhi under my door. I finally put a stop to it by informing him that I would far rather live under what his literature persisted in calling *the imperialist yolk* than put my trust in a fellow who went about in sandals. From then on Sodawallah affected not to see me when we met in the hallway or passed on the stairs. When Mrs. Timms enquired into the cause of our strained relations, I confessed at once. She spanked me soundly with my clothes brush. The roses on my wallpaper blossomed in crimson splendor.

You will think, perhaps, that I relate these details from a vulgar desire to titillate. Not at all. I wish, belatedly, to pay tribute to Mrs. Timms. Until I met her, I had believed that no woman would willingly have congress with me. Ugliness is a terrible affliction. I was painfully conscious of the discrepancy between my unprepossessing appearance and the subtlety of my mind. Oh, those large English girls with their small English smiles! How I yearned for one of them, more discerning than her sisters, to see beyond my appearance to the delicate play of intellect and wit in a mind nurtured on all that was finest in literature and philosophy. *I am not what I seem*, I wanted to cry. *I am no different from your brothers. We have read the same poems*. But those bloodless lips twisted, and the girls looked away. I do not believe this was due to racism. Jaya's skin was almost as dark as mine, yet mutual friends were always barraging me with reports of his success with the wives and daughters of peers and publicans alike. The difference was that he was tall and broad-shouldered and that women deemed him handsome.

I was not a virgin when Mrs. Timms made herself available to me. In Oxford I had frequented ladies of easy virtue. Although "frequented" is hardly accurate: a timid visit now and then when need drove and my allowance permitted. But I had thought that the real price

I would always pay for a woman's caresses would be the revulsion I saw in her eyes—until that autumn day when Mrs. Timms proved otherwise.

I wrote to her after I returned home but received no reply. Once, she had asked me to read out a circular—a trivial matter concerning missionary work in the Far East—saying, by way of explanation, that she had mislaid her reading glasses. It occurred to me at the time that I had never seen her wearing spectacles, but I attributed this to the natural vanity of a woman with beautiful eyes. Now, thinking the matter over, I wonder if she might have been illiterate. Or perhaps it was simply that like most of her sex she preferred to live in the present, and saw no point in lingering over an episode that had reached its conclusion.

Five or six years later, Dartington-Clay's Christmas card brought the news that Mrs. Timms had tripped on the steps to the coal cellar and broken her neck. He added that one of his pupils, a Tamil from Penang who had been lodging at 6B, had made *rather an ass* of himself at the funeral.

POSH

On the day I was called to the Bar, I returned to Feathers Lane to find an orange envelope waiting for me on the hall table. The telegram informed me that my father was dead. Typically, Mater gave no details. A last-minute cancellation provided me with a berth on a ship sailing in four days. A starboard cabin, unfortunately. Port out, starboard home: only in my case home meant traveling east, not west. After Port Said, where the stewards changed into their whites, I simmered slowly on the wrong side of the ship. At night I would linger on deck as long as possible, hoping for a shred of breeze off the water. But a trio of Australians who came aboard in Aden took possession of the piano every evening after dinner and I fled from their music as if from contagion. "Black Mammie, Black Mammie": sung at the top of a woman's voice, it pursued me into my dreams. She had hips as broad as her continent, that fair maid of Perth, and her eyes were the vacant blue of the ocean.

Pater had been dead a month when the *Alberta* entered Colombo harbor. I saw a forest of steamer funnels, and the low white buildings like sun-dried droppings that the English left wherever they paused. But well before they came into view, from the moment I first glimpsed a fuzzy green ribbon unrolling along the horizon, my heart had swollen in its cage. My own, my native land. After London it looked small and shabby, a relative last encountered on a distant afternoon and now discovered standing cap in hand at your door. It announced itself as a scent made up of tar, damp, rot and water that has stood for days in vases. My mouth filled with saliva. I had promised myself a feast of crab claws that night; or stringhoppers and chicken curry; or deviled prawns or biriani or egghoppers, but in any case all the fried *brinjal* I could eat. Settling my hat more firmly on my head, I turned away from the rail; a boy no longer.

A RIVER OF CHAMPAGNE CORKS

There is no man on earth who is not emboldened by the death of his father. Saddened, perhaps. When I looked down at the orchids I had placed on Pater's grave I knew, with piercing certainty, that now there was no one left in the world who would always be glad to see me. At the same time, it was as though a mist lifted and the landscape stood out with the crude confidence of a child's drawing: a broad road lit by a crayoned sun. Sitting behind Pater's desk, fingering the objects that had once signified adulthood (a gold-clipped fountain pen; a Florentine leather blotter), it was not my father's absence I felt but my own presence: a solid form that occupied space in the world, that had weight and quiddity and cast a shadow.

Pater had died as the sun rose a week after his fiftieth birthday. He was riding in Queen Victoria Park when his heart seized up and he slumped forward on his horse—or rather Uncle Kumar's horse, because my parents were back in Cinnamon Gardens. Major, a chestnut gelding, continued to canter around the track. An English engineer who attempted to grasp Pater's reins slipped from his own saddle, caught his foot in a stirrup and broke his leg. His horse came to a halt and began grazing. But round and round the track went Major, a single-minded beast, schooled in routine, impervious to the unfamiliar distribution of weight on his back. Bystanders—there are always bystanders in this country, fellows who appear from nowhere like a rope trick in reverse—bystanders shuddered and stared at the dead man on the tall horse. The phenomenon was surely *moospainthu*, a bad omen. As such, it was best not to intervene.

At last a gardener who recognized my father had the wit to send word to the house. Mater and Kumar arrived, accompanied by a groom. Major slowed, trotted across to the servant, lowered his head, whinnied for sugar. Pater slid sideways into Kumar's arms.

The Englishman, whom no one had liked to touch, continued to lie moaning on the grass. The next day Mater had a basket of fruit sent to him in hospital. Several rude weeks later, she received a stiff little note of condolences. "Really," she said, tossing it to me, "anyone would think I'd sent round a sack of durians."

Pater had made me his executor and sole heir; the tears that had remained unshed beside his grave prickled my lids as I learned of his confidence in my judgment. The weeks that followed my return were spent in consultation with solicitors and accountants and bankers, and I was vain enough, even surrounded by the wreckage of my inheritance, to be gratified by the deference they paid me. An Oxford degree, the London Bar: they invested me with an authority before which men twice my age bowed their heads.

All the same, anger rose in me like bile as I discovered the full extent of my father's profligacy. His desk was jammed with letters of credit, unpaid bills, bounced checks, notices of arrears. Yet the week before he died he had thrown a party for three hundred guests at our place by the sea in Bentota. Kumar assured me you could have strolled across the lagoon on the champagne corks.

There was also the envelope I found at the back of a drawer. Its contents revealed that Pater had put our old overseer's son through a mission school and subsequently paid out a sizable bribe to have the fellow employed as a peon in a government department. A bundle of letters scrawled on lined paper in an ill-formed fist thanked my father for his generosity at Christmas, at Sinhalese New Year, on the letter writer's marriage, the birth of his son, et cetera. Hundreds of rupees squandered on soothing Pater's conscience over a rightful thrashing administered years before: that was the kind of excess I found difficult to forgive.

One of the last things Pater had done was to sign over our estates at Lokugama. I managed to save the house itself. But only by selling everything: teak almirahs, ebony headboards, Malay pewter, Irish linen, Japanese erotica, my lead soldiers, Claudia's dollhouse, our sturdy old rocking horse, Willy's enameled snuffbox with the view of St. Petersburg on the lid, Granny's chamberpot handpainted with French roses; everything of value that had survived my father's depredations. I ransacked steamer trunks, turned out mildewed handbags, rummaged through the pockets of long-discarded suits. I went through my ancestral home like a thief. It was an experience not unmixed with exhilaration.

MIXED DOUBLES

I trust you have understood that I had no choice in these matters. That didn't spare me a blazing row with Mater. It was kindled by the Bentota property, the deeds to which were in her name as she had inherited it from a great-aunt. I explained that the sale of the house would ease the burden of debt on Pater's estate; my mother refused to entertain the idea. "Claudia will have Bentota as her dowry," she said, and directed a jet of smoke at my face. "It's not as if you've left her anything else."

As Pater's heir and executor I was entitled to dispose of his estate as I saw fit. But Mater, with the illogic that women buff to a high polish, had already made it plain that she was piqued by my failure to consult her. "All that money squandered on you at Oxford. Classics and whatnot. How many Ancient Greeks do we know? And then you come home and try to pinch the one thing left to your sister."

I remained calm and forbearing. To my surprise, Pater's death had left my mother badly cut up. I had imagined her to feel nothing but an ill-disguised contempt for the husband she had spoken of with habitual impatience and betrayed so brazenly. Yet by all accounts she had made a spectacle of herself that morning in the park, on her knees beside Pater's body, pulling up fistfuls of grass by the root. When Claudia was a child, I could make her cry by picking up her favorite doll and shaking it until its china eyeballs shifted out of alignment. Almost three months after my father's death, Mater still had the look of that doll: jarred, out of true.

It was my first insight into the nature of marriage: a conundrum only two can solve no matter how transparent it appears. And then, too, over time, I have come to realize that as we grow older we experience any death as diminishment—no matter how shallow the acquaintance, how profound the enmity; another flake of self scraped loose by the knife. I remember opening the newspaper and reading the headline about Jaya: there came upon me the sensation of retreating water, and the curved world falling away under my toes.

My voice was gentle, then, as I endeavored to reason with Mater. I pointed out that without the Bentota sale, the estate could not afford to keep up her allowance. I explained that the expense of running a house in Colombo was out of the question. I intended to move to Lokugama, I said, and practice out of chambers in the nearest town. Claudia could keep house for me. Mater would be welcome under my roof, of course; but with only a barrister's uncertain income to sustain the household, I could offer her no more than board and lodging. If she wanted an independent income and a place of her own in Colombo—and I was certain, knowing my mother, that she would have no desire to bury herself away in Lokugama—the Bentota bungalow would have to be sold. Besides, I added, my sister was still a girl, and a timid little thing at that. It was ludicrous to be thinking of marriage settlements.

Mater had just lit a fresh cigarette. There was a chrome smoker's stand beside the piano; ignoring it, she placed her cigarette on the gleaming instrument. I watched it burn down, knowing it would leave a furrow in the lid of Iris's Pleyel. That was Mater all over, utterly heedless of the damage she caused other people. Beside the fading ash, her crimson nails beat time for long seconds. Then, with no more ceremony than if passing on a trivial piece of gossip, she said, "Claudia has accepted an offer of marriage."

When I could speak, I blurted out the question. "Donald Jayasinghe," said Mater. Even in the midst of my distress, I noted the sly satisfaction with which she purred those syllables.

Jaya had been home for over a year. I had heard of his First of course—he might as well have taken out a notice in the *Times*—but his alleged brilliance notwithstanding, he had been idle since his return, squandering time and money in the usual way on drink and cars and women. He lived two streets away, in his father's house in Green Crescent. I had seen him once, at the tennis club, where he had come up to me and offered his condolences. I had answered politely and turned away. And all the while the blackguard had been engaged to my sister.

Piece by jagged piece, I fitted the story together. They had met over mixed doubles at the club, said Mater. "Jaya spoke to your father on the evening before the accident. Afterward, with Ritzy barely in his grave, we decided to say nothing for a while. It didn't seem right to be announcing a marriage."

That should have tickled me: Mater constrained by social niceties! But I was in no frame of mind to be amused. It was the casualness of that pronoun: *we* decided. "What about me?" I spluttered. "How could you not have said anything to me?"

"Because I knew you would make a scene," she said calmly. "You've always been so absurdly jealous of Jaya. And I didn't want you upsetting Claudia. She's been through quite enough, with the shock of losing her father and whatnot."

From my sister's earliest years, Pater had recognized the delicacy of her nerves and singled her out for special indulgences. Knowing her dread of the dark, he would remain by her bedside for hours on his visits to Lokugama; sometimes I woke at midnight to hear his slippers padding past my door. He had the gift, not uncommon among those who have little to do with children, of being able to enter imaginatively into their world. On Claudia's fifth birthday he had rosy apples hung from every tree in the garden to surprise and delight her. So I had attributed my sister's jangling tears and hammered silences to grief. Now I recalled her watery eyes scuttling away from mine, the cunning with which she had avoided tête-à-têtes, her convenient fit of weeping, face down on the coverlet, when I cornered her one afternoon in her bedroom. She had conspired with Mater and Jaya to deceive me.

From the *suriya* tree outside the window, a saw-edged cry was hacking through the thick air. My ayah used to say that when a rice stealer died, his soul entered the body of a crow. The irrelevant detail floated around my brain; I batted it away, endeavoring to concentrate on Mater's news.

"How do you intend to get by without an income?" I inquired, as unpleasantly as possible. "Carry on sponging off Uncle Kumar?"

"Don insists I make my home at Green Crescent after the wedding. You know what a pile the old boy built—there are corridors and staircases by the mile."

They had arranged everything. I clawed at the back of the nearest chair. Mater, however, had regained her composure. She settled herself on the settee, lit another cigarette. "The suite in the tower will do me very well. As for pocket money . . ." She waved one of those narrow hands that so resembled a snake's head, setting ash falling and bracelets clinking like coins. "I daresay I'll scrape by."

In that instant I saw everything, the sickening pictures garlanded in wavering blue smoke as if conjured from an evil Aladdin's lamp. Mater and Jaya. Claudia, poor child, could have no inkling of what they were about. Perhaps Jaya's widowed father— *the old boy* —was in on it too. Mixed doubles, screamed the crow in the *suriya* tree, mixed doubles!

Mater's voice followed me out of the room. "I'm sure you would be welcome too, Sam."

The next day or the day after, I contrived to get Claudia alone on the croquet lawn, out of earshot of the house. I had it all planned, the sentences arrayed with parade-ground precision, the arguments—veiled but unmistakable—rehearsed like troops. Then I looked into my sister's face, those long eyes, so like Mater's, yet so different in their defenseless transparence, and knew I could no more utter my thoughts than bring my heel down on a nestling and grind till I reduced its softness to a bloody mash of bone and feathers. Instead—and I am ashamed to confess this, but I have set out to tell the truth—I sat on a garden roller and cried like a child.

After a while Claudia came and sat at my feet. She put out a little hand and stroked one of my conker-brown brogues with a tentative finger. "It's all right," she said. "Everything's going to be all right."

When at length I had mastered myself, I clasped her by the wrist and led her to the house. She preceded me into the hall. There was a grass stain on her skirt, its dampness visible even on the dark frock she wore in mourning.

THE VOICE THAT BREATHED O'ER EDEN

Six months later I found myself walking up the aisle at St. Luke's, Claudia quivering on my arm. An Englishman called Canning had recently been appointed vicar. At a christening held the previous week, he had dropped the baby; an alert godmother sprang forward just in time to prevent the eggshell skull from cracking open on the marble basin of the font. Now the silly ass contrived to drop the ring. The slim platinum band rolled a few inches, came up against the bridegroom's monumental foot, fell flat with a tiny clattering. You could see everyone thinking it was an omen.

Less than a year had elapsed since Pater's death so the reception was a muted affair, just two hundred or so guests. My brother-in-law danced first with his wife and then with her mother. Did anyone else notice his paw straying below Mater's waist? Probably not; he leashed it in promptly like a wayward puppy. An occasional whim would lead my mother to abandon European dress, and that night she was decked out in a crimson Manipuri sari, with a royal-blue blouse that left a scandalous quantity of midriff on display. Even the Reverend Canning was unable to keep his eyes from drifting toward that expanse of taut brown flesh, like fish trailing a lure.

I glanced at Claudia, enthroned beside a Jayasinghe crone who was informing the room in an imperious shriek that she had broken her ear trumpet when she threw it at her dhobi. My sister had on the strained expression she habitually wore in company, like someone determined to follow a conversation in a foreign language. As for me, I played my part in exemplary fashion, smiling and chatting away. I even suffered Jaya to mangle me against his chest at the end of the evening. He almost crushed my collar bone.

I rose very early the next day and went out into the dewy garden with Kumar's rifle. I got that crow with my first shot. When I came down to breakfast I looked out of the window and saw the gardener's boy nailing it to the *suriya* tree. Two centuries earlier the Dutch had planted hundreds of those trees, all up and down the coast. As they built their forts and counted their gold they must have gazed at those tulip-shaped, greenish-yellow flowers and wondered if they could bear it any longer: the scent of cinnamon, the approximations.

A DISTURBING EPISODE

Freed from the duty of providing for Mater and Claudia, I decided there was nothing to be gained from moving to Lokugama. As soon as word got around that I intended to remain in Colombo, Pater's old friend Aloysius Drieberg offered me a place in his Hulftsdorp chambers. There I soon acquired a reputation for brilliance. The soundness of my arguments impressed the Bench; the fluency and wit of my delivery delighted juries. I seldom lost a case. My fees rose correspondingly.

Rents in the capital were exorbitant. Colombo landlords treat their tenants in much the same spirit as a cookwoman handles coconuts: split them open, scrape them out, throw away the shells. Fortunately I was spared these trials: Kumar and Iris insisted I stay on and make my home with them, and there was no withstanding their resolve. Iris, who had never enjoyed good health, was diagnosed with Parkinson's disease around this time. I hope that my presence in their house brought a measure of cheer into the lives of those two simple souls, whose relations with my parents were far from uncomplicated, yet who throughout those years showed me nothing but kindness.

For a while I tried to find a tenant for Lokugama, but the isolation of the house proved a disincentive, and so it continued to stand empty and grew more bedraggled with each passing month. The first signs of shabbiness had appeared even before I left for Oxford, and continued apace in the last years of my father's life, when no one in the family was spending more than a few days on the estate and there was no money to spare on repairs deemed nonessential. But in latitudes where rot is the status quo, preservation is a war that must be waged hourly, skirmish by skirmish; inaction is synonymous with defeat. An assault by termites on one of the back-verandah posts proceeded unchecked. In the time it took to replace a row of missing tiles a monsoon had torn three more from the roof; and the rats had grown so bold that they would stroll across a room in daylight.

On my return I had sacked all the servants Pater had quite unnecessarily continued to employ. With so little to occupy them, they had fallen into idleness and insolence—our head servant even having the temerity to protest that my father had promised them all pensions in their old age. Out they all went with no further ado. I brought in a man and his wife to look after the place, and went down now and then to keep them up to the mark and arrange for a little work on the house. On one of these visits, the bungalow keeper told me that Claudia and Jaya had dropped by on a motoring trip and stayed for a cup of tea.

With the ménage in Green Crescent I had as little to do as possible. The newlyweds had spent an extended honeymoon on the Continent. After they returned, I pleaded the demands of my flourishing practice to excuse myself from family gatherings. On those occasions when I could not decently absent myself, I found consolation in quiet talk with Claudia. Jaya seemed attentive enough to her, but then attentiveness to women was a reflex with him. And I had only limited opportunities for observing them together, because in those days the ladies gossiped over soft drinks in one room, while the gentlemen discoursed over their whiskey and tobacco in another. I cannot understand why some of our more forward misses have lately begun to protest this arrangement, when it is so plainly advantageous to both sides: the less contact, the greater the mutual allure.

I was rarely able to see Claudia on her own. So when I ran into Jaya at the club late one afternoon and he told me that Mater was spending the week with friends on their rubber estate at Maharagama, I strove to conceal my delight. Jaya was heading out to Mount Lavinia for a swim, attended by his usual little cluster of toadies. There would be cocktails afterward, leaving the coast clear for hours. I pleaded a sudden headache, abandoned my tennis partner and drove straight over to Green Crescent.

As the car nosed into the gate, a man stepped out of the way. I paid him no heed: one of the many household servants, I supposed. But he must have taken note of me, for as I pulled away he called, "*Mahatheya! Anay, mahatheya*." I braked, and watched him come hurrying up behind me in the awkward half-trot half-shuffle necessitated by his sarong.

"Well?" I barked, when he drew level with my window. "What do you want?"

He bent toward me. I had left the engine running, but a minute later I switched off the ignition and climbed out of the car to stand beside him. It was not a tale I wanted to hear while sitting down.

My informant was Claudia's tailor. Once a month he spent a day at the house, making up garments according to the designs she sketched for him. That afternoon in the course of the fitting, as he circled her with his mouth full of pins, an accidental disarrangement of her petticoats had afforded him a view of her back: it was scored with tiny slits just starting to scab over.

The tailor paused. He kept his eyes fixed on the ground, although now and then he cast a sly glance toward the house, which was screened from view by a bend in the drive. Big *nonamahatheya* and Jayasinghe *mahatheya* were not at home, he said. He hoped he had not done wrong in speaking to me . . . The little *nonamahatheya* would be angry if she knew, and he was a poor man with seven children. Seven daughters! Seven little catastrophes!

The conversation had shifted into a familiar groove. My mind raced with its habitual agility. "You've done no harm in telling me about this," I said airily, as my fingers brushed a few coins in my pocket. I must have been agitated, because I slipped the fellow thirty cents—an absurdly generous tip. He stiffened. Primitive people, like animals, react with unease to any deviation from a pattern. Snatching back two coins from his palm, I went on, "But what you saw is of no importance at all. You should forget it at once if you want to return next month. Above all, not a word to anyone here."

The tailor touched his hands to his forehead. But as I approached the bend in the drive, I glanced back and saw him still standing there, peering after the car. It crossed my mind that he might yet come in useful as a witness.

Jaya's father kept to his own suite in the house, where a small servant-girl, employed for that purpose, rubbed his feet and heard out his reminiscences of hounds he had bred, bearers he had thrashed and illnesses he had outlasted—the good old days, in short. The old boy was, in Claudia's parlance, as deaf as a doormat. There was scant danger of him overhearing or interrupting us, but I took the precaution of locking the music room door, anyway.

Claudia shrank away from me, cowering between the piano stool and the lustrous black instrument. I was having none of that. A few terse sentences conveyed what I knew, as I grasped her by the shoulders and swiveled her about.

In my distress I handled my sister, a slightly built girl, more roughly than I intended. The soft blue housedress she was wearing ripped at the neck. My heart flickered at the sight of a rusty gash showing beneath a shoestring strap: an ugly thing rendered still more repulsive by its proximity to satiny brown skin and ivory lace.

Running my fingertips down Claudia's camisole I located the gruesome herringbone of scabs that framed her narrow back. I wanted to weep. I wanted to commit murder. "*He* did this, didn't he?" I cried. "Is it the first time? Tell me, tell me *at once*."

At that, Claudia's head jerked up. "No, Sam, no."

She struggled in my embrace. I tightened my grasp. She flailed uselessly for a minute. "Tell me," I whispered, my mouth against her hair.

Between sobs, she confessed that the wounds were her own handiwork: she had cut into her flesh with Jaya's razor, she said. "Stop covering up for him," I hissed. "I'll prosecute the blackguard myself. You'll be rid of him forever. We'll live together, just the two of us. I'll look after you."

Her weeping grew frenzied. I shushed her with a hand over her mouth, afraid that the servants would hear. But even when her tears had quieted, she insisted that Jaya had nothing to do with it. She slid down and clasped my knees: "I swear it on Daddy's grave."

Distorted by weeping, smeared with mucus, her angled face was still beautiful. It always had the power to undo me. I squatted beside her and folded her in my arms. By degrees, I managed to comfort her. We rocked back and forth.

As the knot in my chest loosened, it occurred to me that Claudia's self-mutilation was a form of protest. "You can't bear him touching you. That's it, isn't it?" I asked, as I stroked her.

"Oh yes, Sam," she murmured.

At the thought of Jaya's hands crouched like tarantulas on her sweet flesh, I could not repress my own shudder. But what could I do? When I begged her again to leave him, her hysteria revived. She was terrified of what he might do in retaliation, of course. It required all my skill to calm her.

In the end, the best I could do was to extract a promise that she would not harm herself again. I spoke of our childhood. I reminded her that she could always turn to me. And then—and all these years later it still grieves me to write it—then I went away and abandoned her to him.

Iris was playing the piano when I got home. I stood listening on the dark verandah, and recognized an old melody that Pater used to strum on his ukulele: *Believe me, if all those endearing young charms* . . . I thought of childhood holidays in the hills before everything went wrong, my head against Mater's knee and Claudia sleepy-eyed on the rug, the circle of our family as gleaming and unbroken as a wedding band.

The verandah was lined with square red planters holding leafy clusters of dieffenbachia and caladium. A creeper studded with pale stars wound about a pillar, releasing scented cadenzas into the night. My sister's face rose before me, her smile pasted into place as we said goodbye. *For the heart that has truly lov'd never forgets*. I put my fingers in my ears. The moon, flat and white, had on its idiot stare.

Time passed. Word of Jaya's growing interest in politics reached me now and then. He had been to India, where he had an audience with the Mahatma. He had joined the Ceylon National Congress. He had addressed an anti-British rally on Empire Day. He was stirring things up on behalf of whichever cause would tolerate his interference: working conditions on tea plantations, standards in village schools.

But I refused to listen to talk about Jaya. I snatched private moments with Claudia when I could, and assured her that she could rely on my help if she left her husband. I immersed myself in my work. I played tennis four times a week. I blocked my ears.

THE ELEPHANT'S POINT OF VIEW

Kumar was one of those chaps given to enthusiasms. Once he had devoted months to the breeding of tropical fish. Later an entire year had been given over to horology. Malodorous jars of fish food still stood forgotten on windowsills, and not one of the clocks in the house kept reliable time. He had recently emerged from an artistic phase, so that you never knew when a bungled sketch or a tube of cadmium yellow might turn up behind a cushion or at the bottom of a lavatory bowl.

His current ambition was to shoot an elephant. He had a whole repertoire of near misses that he would relate with a disarming blend of despair and drollery. On one memorable expedition, his new gun had jammed not once but three times. On another occasion he had been charged by a cow elephant and fractured both ankles scrambling out of her way.

"I was born too late, Sam," he lamented. "Sixty years ago there were elephants running about all over the bally place. A fellow had only to let off a gun. Like this Major Rogers chap—"tapping the collection of Victorian hunters' tales that was his vade mecum at the time—"fourteen hundred elephants. *Fourteen hundred*. And his friend Skinner is credited with half that number. Two fellows accounting for over two thousand elephants between them. Those were the days, Sam. We poor buggers can only dream."

Good old Kumar! The best of chaps but undoubtedly a duffer. His approach to hunting exactly mirrored his attitude to life: wildly enthusiastic, potshots at everything in sight, but no strategy, no disciplined attack. No wonder Mater had broken off their engagement. "Kumar's like a spaniel," she once observed with disinterested indulgence. "All snuffle, snuffle, snuffle. It's sheer luck if he turns up what he's looking for."

Enthusiasm is a shallow but infectious emotion. After yet another evening of listening to Kumar hold forth about elephants, I found myself scanning the shelf of books he had amassed on the subject. Soon I was enthralled. What had begun as an idle notion, no more than shifting light and shade on the edge of my consciousness, took on definition and bulk, crashed through all other thoughts as the weeks passed.

An elephant presents such a vast target that shooting one would appear to pose no great difficulty. But that is far from the case. The colossal beast is so strong that unless it is killed with the first shot, it will almost certainly get away. Hence the preferred method of a bullet in the brain.

And there the difficulty lies. An elephant has a massive skull in order to afford a surface sufficient for the attachment of the powerful muscles of the trunk and jaws. However, its brain is very small. It is also situated far back in the skull and surrounded by such a huge, irregular mass of bone and flesh that its exact location, in a living animal, is hard to determine. Most other land quadrupeds possess a thin, solid cranium wall, easily shattered by a blow or a bullet. But an elephant's skull, although of considerable thickness, is made up of long, narrow sections perpendicular to its surface, irregularly shaped, pocked like honeycomb. A shot might pass through these airy cells only two inches from the brain with no effect other than to make the animal run farther and faster than it would otherwise do.

Kumar and I would sit up until all hours, poring over diagrams that showed cross sections and angled views. One evening, just short of midnight, a shadow fell across the crimson Turkey rug and I looked up to see Iris. The library was strewn with diagrams, maps, the breathing bodies of dogs. "A Number 8 gun," Kumar was saying. "Nine pounds, twelve ounces."

Iris came closer. Mater's people were typically long-limbed and light-skinned, but in Iris the stock ran anomalous. She was a little round guava of a woman, thick-waisted and blunt-nosed, her coarse complexion disfigured forever by acne. Two years younger than Mater, she looked a decade older. The contrast when they were girls must have been cruel; and Iris's defining trait was that infinite capacity for self-effacement that a woman no one looks at learns when very young.

She stood there now in a shapeless blue housecoat, her hair, which she wore bundled up in a knot during the day, plaited into a gray rope as thick as my wrist. The tremor was not yet very pronounced. Nevertheless the cup she was carrying quivered on its saucer.

"You shouldn't keep Sam up late," she said to Kumar. "He works so hard."

"We'll be through in two ticks, Aunt Iris," I assured her. "We're just deciding which kind of gun is best. Tricky business, you know. Expert opinion is divided."

"Double muzzle-loading," said Kumar firmly. "Smooth- bore."

Iris peered at the litter of catalogs surrounding us. Then she said, "It probably comes down to the same thing, child. From the elephant's point of view."

She padded away to the faint clatter of bone on bone. Kumar and I raised our eyebrows at each other. Women so often leave one with nothing to say.

UNDER THE STARS

We camped in a grove of *palu* trees, near the confluence of two clear brown streams. Kumar, who knew the area of old, had seen to all the arrangements. We had set out at dawn and reached a village of scattered huts early in the afternoon. The bearers and trackers hired by Kumar were waiting there for us. We followed them along jungle paths shrill with the calls of monkeys and birds and the screams of the tree beetle, until we reached our camp site two hours later.

It was an idyllic spot. The *shamas* that had piped us on our way were still calling from the trees as we drank smoky tea and watched our cook busy himself with the hunk of venison that would form the basis of our supper. The other servants settled on their haunches at a respectful distance from our camp stools, chatting quietly over their betel. Soon the irresistible aroma of roasting meat would creep into our nostrils and the *shamas* would fall silent one by one while the nightjar cleared its throat. God was in his heaven. All was wrong with the world.

Kumar had waited until the previous evening. Then, when I went into the library, wound up and ticking with the pleasure of inspecting our equipment for the last time, he wandered over to the window, shuffled his feet and told me that Jaya would be joining us.

"For dinner, you mean?" I asked, horribly jolted. But from the way the old boy avoided my eye and fiddled with a crimson tassel, I knew where the conversation was headed.

He tried to pass it off lightly, as one of those spur-of-the-moment things. He had been shopping for tick gaiters in the Fort when he bumped into my brother-in-law and told him of our plans for the weekend. Jaya had been so enthusiastic that Kumar felt it was *the sporting thing* to invite him along. "No harm done," he concluded with brittle cheer, looking at last into my face. What he saw there led him to turn away in haste, rubbing the bridge of his nose, always a sign that his emotions were perturbed.

With glacial calm I checked over our guns and ammunition, took a last look at the cross sections, read once more through the recommendations of experts I already had by heart. Across the room Kumar pleaded silently for forgiveness. He had damp brown eyes like the sludge at the bottom of a coffee cup. Chaps like that are incurable sentimentalists; absolutely fatal on a jury. I ignored him for the rest of the evening, repulsing his feeble attempts at conversation and declining to join him in a lime blossom, a cocktail made from gin and lime juice shaken with crushed ice that was our standard pre-dinner tipple.

Poor Kumar. It was wrong of me to punish him. Even as I ate my Scotch eggs, tasting only ashes, I could see that he was not really to blame. Given Jaya's unshakeable conviction that he was a boon to any gathering, it would have been almost impossible to prevent him from encumbering us with his presence. But no amount of reasoning could dispel the cold fury in the pit of my brain. The jungle was infested with monkeys. Why saddle ourselves with another?

Jaya was uncharacteristically subdued when we called for him at Green Crescent the next morning. He mumbled something about having had *one too many* at the club the night before and sat slumped in the front seat for the entire journey, stirring himself now and then only to address a remark to the driver. You don't for a moment believe that rot about Jaya renouncing alcohol to comply with Buddhist doctrine, do you? Booze had played such havoc with his liver that his doctors left him no choice in the matter.

On arriving at our camp site, we cooled off with a refreshing dip in the stream. Regrettably this had a restorative effect on Jaya. He had begun the day clad in trousers and a bush shirt, but now draped a checked sarong around his fleshy nether regions and sat bare-chested in the fading light, like any village lout. Drops of water glistened on his matted torso and quivered in the black fur along his arms. One longed to enquire if he had had an accident with a bottle of hair restorer.

When I remarked on the beauty of our surroundings, he snorted. "A grove, a glade—why use words designed for an English forest? They have nothing to do with this jungle of ours."

"And what would you say instead?" I enquired in the silky tones I had perfected in cross-examination.

But Jaya was ever adept at sidestepping inconvenient questions. "The British occupy our imagination as well as our country," he intoned, drawing on his foul-smelling pipe.

I recognized the prelude to a sermon. "English is our inheritance too," I interrupted. "Why shouldn't we mold it to our needs? Grove and *palu* in the same sentence—isn't that distinctively Ceylonese?"

Through rolling smoke, Jaya winked at me like a gargoyle. "Obey by name, Obey by nature," he hooted. "I say, Kumar—I don't suppose you've heard about the time when . . ."

Things got worse. No sooner had I launched into the rather amusing story of a match I had won in straight sets, than Jaya got up and strolled away. His manners had plainly been tailored to match his costume. He thrust himself into the circle of servants sitting by the water, and soon their noisy hilarity was drowning out my voice.

When I could bear it no longer I picked up my rifle, called for one of the trackers and set out before the light deserted us altogether. Within a quarter of an hour I had a brace of the small green pigeon whose bubbling calls had greeted us on arrival. I returned to camp to find that Kumar had joined the raucous group beside the stream. Even the cook had deserted his fire. Not a head turned in my direction. I stood there unnoticed, holding my handful of soft bodies in the dark.

SHOOTING AN ELEPHANT

To bring down an elephant requires a stout heart and steady nerves. One must walk boldly up to the animal and fire from twenty paces or less. Men survive the claws of leopards and bears, but the hunter who comes within range of an elephant's legs or trunk never lives to boast of his exploit.

These things were in my mind the next morning as I shook a scorpion from my boot. I had often seen elephants in the wild, the gray arch of a back looming above the bushes, or a scattered herd feeding on a hillside. I had watched, from a distance, and contented myself with plover and pigeon, deer and monkey. But now that other death, elephant-shaped, was waiting in the shadow of the trees.

We came upon the trail almost at once. When traveling through the jungle a herd of elephants will follow each other in single file. This produces a broad, well-trampled path. Our trackers followed it with ease for over an hour. It led to a marshy area of rank, shoulder-high grasses, where the herd had broken up, leaving the mud stamped into craters eighteen inches deep. It was an empty, stagnant place. I picked my way through with rushing strides, eager to leave it behind. A glance over my shoulder showed Jaya shambling in my wake, as cheerful as a golliwog. A certain refinement of the mind is of course the *sine qua non* of sensibility to atmosphere.

In the scrub on the far side of the marsh we called a halt. The first mouthful of coffee sweetened with condensed milk was just slithering down my gullet when it sounded in the jungle to the east: a single tone followed by three ascending quavers that came to rest on a high, clear note before leaping down an octave for its resonant finale. It was repeated obligingly at intervals over the next hour as we drew closer to the herd.

The air, moist as a bath, was perfectly still. My tracker beckoned me on, signaling caution with a wave of his hand. I slid forward and flattened myself against a teak tree. The jungle ahead was relatively open, with low, scattered undergrowth. Forty paces away, a dozen elephants were feeding on bamboo. They pushed their way through the thorny clumps, snapping stems fifteen feet high as if they were stalks of asparagus.

When awake, a wild elephant is never still. One foot swings and then another, while the animal's tail and trunk are in constant motion. Mesmerized by this lumbering ballet, I barely noticed my tracker reappear at my side. He touched my elbow. I followed his gaze and saw that a female and her calf, in search of the choicest stems, had wandered off from the rest of the herd and were scarcely twenty paces away.

Reaching skyward with her trunk, the old elephant hooked down one juicy shoot after the other for her calf. It stood less than three feet tall, that calf, and its hide was smooth and shiny, a brown so dark it was almost black. As it wandered around its mother, she caressed it with her trunk. At one point it stood directly beneath her, swinging its tail, and I thought what comfort it must draw from that massive, wrinkled belly. For the queerest moment I was conscious of an emotion akin to envy.

The vulnerable point of an elephant's skull may be located anywhere on a horizontal line drawn around the head from the ear opening, three inches above the eye, to the very center of the bump in the middle of the face, which is really the base of the trunk and the nasal cavity. With my finger I traced the diagram on my thigh. Meanwhile, the old cow elephant had begun crushing a fallen stem of bamboo with her forefeet. The calf, now half hidden from me by the bulk of its mother, put out its trunk and stole soft fragments on which it champed.

I took a deep breath and stepped out from behind my tree. Raising the gun to my shoulder I prepared to take aim at the female's head, adjusting the imaginary line I had drawn around it to compensate for the angle of fire.

And then a hulking, shapeless form rose in the scrub ahead. For a long, hideous instant my muscles clenched with fear. This was succeeded by a swift rush of fury. Jaya, whom I had last glimpsed somewhere to my left, had worked his way around me until he was less than a dozen rash paces from the female and her calf. I saw the glint of sun along his barrel. My skull filled with light. The cow elephant was mine, mine! I saw my sister's delicate limbs crushed against that vile pelt. I adjusted my aim downward.

I had forgotten the tracker at my side. Now he made a sound that was not quite a sound, the merest flutter of breath. I turned my head and we gazed at each other. His mouth hung agape. *Darkness visible:* the quotation ballooned in my mind. I stared at half a dozen broken yellow columns in a black cavern ringed with crimson, and knew I had been granted a vision of the portals of hell.

When the blast ripped through the morning, the cow elephant threw her trunk aloft and shrieked. She took off into the jungle, trumpeting as she went. The herd was scattering in every direction. It is the most dangerous moment in the hunt, since you might find yourself in the path of an elephant and be crushed in the animal's startled rush. I fell back behind my cover. Then abruptly it was over, the elephants had regrouped and vanished into the jungle beyond the clearing and all that could be heard was an iron silence.

It was broken by a shout. I stepped around my tree and there was the body, surrounded by prostrate bamboo. The calf had died where it had fallen. Jaya was making a racket beside it, grinning and slapping his tracker on the back. I went closer and saw the red hole at the base of the trunk.

It was an outrageous piece of beginner's luck. His bullet must have passed through the female's skull, leaving the brain untouched but deflected downward in its trajectory as it exited. And so the calf standing beside her had died. In fact I had heard it fall to the ground as I cowered behind my tree, but had mistaken the noise for the crash of bamboo.

I still have the photograph Kumar insisted on taking. The sun is a bleached starburst in the sepia sky. Jaya stands beside the fallen elephant, head thrown back to expose his massive neck, left hand on hip, right hand clasping his gun, one enormous boot planted on the animal's flank. It is an ironic pose. The faint but perceptible exaggeration of the stance parodies all those photographs of self-satisfied Englishmen lording it over the corpses of their Empire's fauna. Here the usual proportions are reversed: the elephant is small, the hunter looms large. Instead of evoking the noble victory of man over nature, the image suggests a shabby little coup.

Oh, Jaya was first and foremost a trickster, a past master of the conceptual sleight of hand. Having shot his elephant, he repudiates all the men who have shot elephants before him. Having claimed what was mine, he judges me for wanting it in the first place. His smile is mocking, intolerably superior. Every time I see it, I relive that moment when I had the blackguard in my sights. I squeeze my knees together. My finger tightens on the trigger.

COFFEE WITH THE KING'S ADVOCATE

One afternoon as I emerged from a courtroom in Hulftsdorp brushing off the defense counsel's reluctant congratulations, a peon in a white sarong and khaki jacket slashed with the black-and-red government sash handed me a message. It was a summons to the office of Sir George North, the King's Advocate, where I was sounded out, over a cup of excellent coffee, about a change of direction. The magistrate of Tangalle was to retire at the end of the year. The KA, with many an allusion to my brilliant grasp of the law, wondered if I had ever considered transferring to the Bench?

I had, of course, as he very well knew; it is a prospect no ambitious young advocate ignores. There was no career more prestigious than the judiciary; and I can say without immodesty that I believed the scrupulous weighing of argument and impartial reasoning that came naturally to me would prove an asset to the Bench.

Sir George, a large red man with incongruous dolls' feet, had crossed one knee over the other and was speaking in circumlocutions of *measured reform* and *propitious times*. His meaning was transparent. Judicial posts below the Supreme Court, which was made up of English judges, had traditionally been filled by civil servants—who were, of course, Englishmen. The police courts at the lowest level of the judicial system were presided over by magistrates, whose ranks included my countrymen. But our island boasted no judicial service per se.

Recently, however, there had been rumors of change afoot; of pressure from Westminster on the Colonial Secretary to appoint more Ceylonese to senior judicial posts, thus setting in train the process of establishing a judiciary independent of the Civil Service. Conjecture overran the legal community at Hulftsdorp faster than morning glory engulfing a fence. Senior advocates in black alpaca jackets and white trousers speculated in circumspect whispers behind the stout Dutch pillars that flanked the corridors of the courthouse. The scriveners who squatted at their writing boxes under the shade trees composing petitions for illiterate clients passed on speculation as certainty. The lowly bun proctors, who spent their days in the crumbling yellow hotel opposite the court where they would take on a case for the price of a cup of tea and a bun, embellished all facts with the baroque flourishes of master craftsmen. Men swore they had *reliable information* that all district judgeships would henceforth be filled from the Bar. Various fellows claimed to have heard from various other fellows who knew a *highly placed chap* that an all-Ceylonese Supreme Court was *in the bag*. Now here was Sir George tacitly confirming the foundations of such talk, if not its airier reaches. An able man embarking on a judicial career could look forward to rapid advancement: that was the gist of it.

I was flattered; who would not have been? Yet I hesitated. There were, in the first instance, financial considerations. I was already pulling in fees well in excess of a magistrate's salary. To give up the Bar would mean a considerable drop in income. My equivocation was fueled also by a sense of injured pride. Magistrate of Tangalle: it was hardly an illustrious beginning, even if Sir George was hinting at more to follow. One would have thought that my education and reputation entitled me to a district judgeship at the least, even if my relative lack of experience ruled out a more senior appointment.

As well as coffee, Sir George's peon had brought in a silver salver laden with sweets and pastries. The KA was known for his sweet tooth. At a cocktail party where the usual trays of deviled eggs and angels on horseback were circulating, he was said to have reached into his pocket and brought out a handful of marzipan-stuffed dates: "Do have one. They're frightfully good."

While talking to me he had helped himself to potato *aluwa*, milk toffee, *thala guli*, coconut rock and two cream horns. Now he produced a large, blinding handkerchief with which he dabbed his lips as I considered how best to reply. At last, while stressing my sensibility to the honor I was being shown, I asked for time in which to reflect on my position. I hinted at financial difficulties, perhaps slightly exaggerating the unenviable state of affairs I had inherited from my father.

Sir George nodded. The English understand money even if they do not always respect it; with us it is the other way around. Could my decision be postponed for a few weeks? "By all means," replied Sir George.

Two years later the KA made a first-class ass of himself over a Mrs. Jansz, whose cardamom-scented love cake was greatly in demand at birthday parties. He was obliged to leave the service in disgrace. That morning, as we shook hands, his fingers were just a little sticky.

A LITIGIOUS PEOPLE

The day after my conversation with Sir George I received a telephone call from Marcus Fernando, an old friend of Pater's who lived up-country. Marcus and his two brothers, Clifford and Ronnie, were embroiled in a testamentary case over their father's will that had dragged on for years and long escalated out of all proportion. But we are a famously litigious people. In 1849 Major Thomas Skinner noted that our love of litigation was probably not exceeded anywhere in the world; and the major, whose relentless application of engineering and ambition over nineteen years produced the Colombo-to-Kandy road, was quite a connoisseur of obsession.

The original suit brought by Marcus had branched into a forest of countersuits and claims and writs and injunctions that outdid each other in improbability. For instance Clifford had sought damages against Marcus for allegedly sending a henchman to urinate on his wife's dahlias, thus destroying her chances at the annual flower show. ("Ever heard such rot?" spluttered Marcus. "Why would I pay some bugger to urinate on her bally flowers? As if I'm a *godeya* who's never heard of weedkiller.")

Recently there had been signs that the Fernando case was drawing to a close. Whereupon, for no reason I could see (other than the prospect of being deprived of ongoing drama), Marcus got the jitters about his advocate and dumped him on the spot. Then he put through a call to my chambers and pleaded with me to take on his brief.

At first I demurred. The Fernando saga was something of a laughing stock among the legal fraternity and I feared my involvement would appear infra dig, at best. On the other hand, the case I should have been prosecuting had come to an early conclusion when the chief witness for the defense came over to the Crown, and it so happened that I had nothing else to do.

Marcus, sensing my hesitation, mentioned an outrageously high fee. I said I couldn't possibly consider less than twice that sum. He agreed at once. His wife was a cinnamon heiress and the old boy was rolling in it. I told him to put his solicitors in touch with me and set about clearing my desk.

UP-COUNTRY

March nights in the hill station of Nuwara Eliya were bracing. In my room at the Windsor, a fire crackled in the grate, and on my morning constitutional around the golf course I sported the tweed overcoat I had last worn in London.

With its rose bushes and frosts and half-timbered cottages, the township offered a very passable simulacrum of an English village. My eyes stung with woodsmoke as I strolled its streets on my first evening, and there came into my mind the memory of young men in long scarves crowding around a bonfire while I looked on from the shadows. I left the European quarter and went down into the bazaar, where a fellow with his head swathed in a gunnysack against the cold was doing a roaring trade in piping hot *mas paans*. But neither the spiced fragrance issuing from his stall nor the fiery beef curry on my tongue could dispel the images conjured by the smoke: shaggy chrysanthemum faces peering out of a foggy college garden, crisp fortunes that gardeners raked up with casual disdain.

As a boy I had loved the hill country. Every April, when society fled the worst of the pre-monsoon heat, Claudia and I joined our parents for a holiday at our place in Nuwara Eliya. The annual exodus broke the tedium of our routine at Lokugama and was the occasion of much excited anticipation. Our ayah hunted out warm vests and woolens in camphored trunks, while I reminded Claudia of treats in store: toasted marshmallows around the fire, rugging up for morning rides beside the lake on our ponies. Best of all, a week on our tea estate, some thirty miles out of Nuwara Eliya, where our bungalow looked out on near green hills and far blue ones, and we went for walks and picked wildflowers like children in a storybook.

In those days, when the motor car was a rarity, we traveled upcountry by train. Like all children, I inhabited a world of potent symbols. The iron span of the bridge over the Kelani River was one of them. As soon as we had steamed across its girdered expanse I would insist on donning my jersey. No matter that our engine had not even begun its assault on the improbable gradients that lay ahead and that it would be hours before the sweetness of cool hill air penetrated our compartment. I sweltered happily in wool, waiting for Claudia, the crybaby, to burst into tears when the first stretch of tunnel cutting into the mountains engulfed us in darkness. Everything happened this way, always. It was very satisfying.

The itch of wool against my skin, the moist green ferns that sprang from rocky crevices as the track wound skyward, Claudia vomiting on the hairpin bends while I leaned out and waved to the third-class passengers in their bulging compartments at the front of the train: each discrete element contributed its part to my happiness. But I believe the deeper source of my pleasure was the certainty that on these holidays we would all be together, as a family. The upcountry season, with its endless rounds of parties and dances, drew Mater as Lokugama never could. Her scented presence flashes like iridescence through my memories of those holidays. Here, she places a vase of sweet peas on a white-painted windowsill. There, she wears a striped ribbon in her hair and whacks a ball clean through three hoops on a velvet lawn.

Our house in Nuwara Eliya was always full of people. But Pater had a rule that our week at Cumberland tea estate was for the four of us alone. Every morning there before breakfast, while shadows were still thickening into mountains and a late rooster crowed from the coolie lines like a faulty alarm, Pater and I would follow dazzling gravel roads between fields where the small hands of Tamil pluckers darted along the surface of the tea. Each woman carried a rod with which she checked that the top of every bush had been plucked level: not easy to determine on the steep hillsides, and a point of pride with the pluckers.

MacKenzie, our manager, had wonderful eyes, blue stones in a blunt red face. He always greeted me with a handshake and answered my questions with proper seriousness. From him I learned that plucking is called fine when a bud at the tip of a shoot and the two young leaves just below it are taken. Fine plucking produces pekoes, while older leaves yield souchongs and congous. Pekoes consisting only of the buds or tips are known as flowery; those containing also the first young leaf are orange pekoes. I tried out the strange words, rolling them like sweets on my tongue.

In the evening, when we settled around the fire, I would parade my erudition before my parents, and my father would applaud while Mater blew me a kiss and a smoke ring. Yet as the week wore on she would grow restless, and remind Pater of the parties they were missing in Nuwara Eliya. After dinner the furniture in the drawing room would be pushed back against the walls and the rug rolled up. My father would pick out a tune on the ukulele he played with talentless verve, while Mater tried out this or that new dance step, breaking off in irritation when Pater wandered further off key than usual.

We spent our last holiday at Cumberland when I was twelve years old. The usual reason saw the tea estate sold a few months later, along with our house in Nuwara Eliya. That last April, almighty rows erupted between my parents. At those elevations, verandahs are glassed in against the evening cold. One morning Claudia and I woke to find every pane smashed and our apu painting flour-and-water paste onto strips of paper with which he taped cardboard over the frames.

That day, our last on the estate, Mater was sleepy and tender, no trace of the flaring temper that had had us children tiptoeing around her all week. Claudia gathered up the crimson seedpods that had fallen from the *madhitchi* tree on the edge of the lawn and I threaded them onto cotton. Mater bent her head and Claudia fastened the necklace around her throat. There it glowed for the rest of the afternoon, its splendor far above rubies.

SUPERINTENDENT NAGEL'S DREAM

Fearing lengthy sessions over the whiskey decanter at night, I had turned down Marcus's offer to put me up. I explained that the quiet privacy of my hotel room was essential in order to weigh up each day's proceedings and plan my strategy for the next. In fact, the case was running itself and I had little to do. Being by nature a sociable chap, I therefore gladly accepted an invitation to dine at the Danville Club. This venerable institution on Danville Road was the Ceylonese response to the Hill Club, which admitted no non-European members. Unfortunately, the Danville had not existed five minutes before some wag whose application for membership had been blackballed dubbed it the Downhill Club—a sobriquet it never managed to shake. Nevertheless, between six and eight of an evening it was a jolly little place: billiards, bridge, pretty Burgher girls sipping long drinks on the verandah, the soothing hum of talk.

My host was a chap called John Shivanathan, a proctor with his own practice in Nuwara Eliya. Shiva and I had been friends at school, where we had shared a study for a term or two. He was a couple of years behind me, and when he became a day boy we drifted apart. In fact, if not for the artificial intimacy enforced by the small boardinghouse at Neddy's, we would have found little to say to each other. We were very different types, you see. He was a duffer at games: the kind of boy who cowers behind the crease instead of stepping out to meet the ball. And like most Tamils he was rather a swot, nose always in a book. I suppose it had paid off, since he seemed to know his way about the law. But he was a nondescript fellow, Shiva: definitely less to him than met the eye. Still, we bagged ourselves a couple of chairs in a corner of the verandah and chatted away over whiskey and sodas, reminiscing about old times, bringing each other up to date on the doings of mutual acquaintances. He enquired after Claudia, and I remembered that our sisters had been friends at school. I could dimly recall Anne Shivanathan, a lumpish girl with a polio limp, who had dropped by at the house shortly before Claudia married. She herself was about to go abroad, she said. The two of them ended up at the piano where they thumped out "The Blue Danube" for old times' sake: Claudia providing the melody, the Shivanathan girl supplying the da-dums.

As the hour for dinner drew near and the crowd at the Downhill started to thin, a tall, fair man came up the clubhouse steps. Pausing in the doorway, he glanced in our direction. Shiva raised his hand, and the stranger came over to greet us, walking with an easy, long-limbed stride.

I warmed at once to Conrad Nagel. I imagine most people did. He had one of those regular, chiseled faces that draws men, while his dark eyes held a hint of that recklessness guaranteed to enthrall women. You pictured him with his chin uplifted, leading men in a doomed cause. It didn't surprise me to learn that he was the superintendent of police for the district, despite his double handicap of race and youth.

Nagel's manners were impeccable: deferential, quietly sincere. As soon as we had been introduced, he told me what an honor it was to make my acquaintance. Turning to Shiva, he recounted my shrewd demolition of the defense in a murder case that had attracted attention the previous year.

"Come, come," I said at last, modesty insisting I put an end to his eulogy. "DSP at your age? That's no mean achievement either."

Nagel laughed. "Oh, I'm just acting the part. And only thanks to a damnfool accident, at that."

He explained that the district superintendent, an Englishman, was on home leave, the first he had taken in fourteen years. He would be gone for months. His assistant, another Englishman, was to have acted for him in his absence. On his fifth day on the job, the new man called for a bacon sandwich at lunch. Sitting at his desk under framed photographs of rugby-playing policemen, he bit into the bread, choked on a piece of gristle and died. After considerable dithering on the part of his superiors, Nagel was promoted from chief inspector to fill in until his DSP returned.

"Hell of a piece of luck for me," said Nagel. "And it wouldn't have happened six months ago. But London's been applying a little heat: more senior posts to go to Ceylonese, whisk the rug out from under the Bolshie buggers who claim we're always being passed over for promotion."

"All the same, you wouldn't have been promoted if the chaps upstairs weren't sure of your abilities," I said, for I could see that Nagel was the sort of unassuming fellow who would always underrate himself. "And now's your chance to prove them right. *Carpe diem*, man! Who knows? You could end up captaining the ship for good."

"Oh, I wouldn't like that," said Nagel.

"Why not?"

He hesitated. Like many Burghers, the DSP had kept the fair complexion of his Dutch East India Company ancestors. Shiva and I watched the blood rise in his cheeks, spread to the roots of his tight brown curls.

"Horses," he managed to say at last. "One day I'm going to breed horses. The Cape. Or Australia. Wonderful animals. Never let you down."

Pink-cheeked, he looked off into the distance. For the blink of an eye that snug verandah with its framed watercolors and coils of tobacco smoke was as insubstantial as a mirage. A stallion thundered over a scorched plain. On a bald hilltop a knock-kneed colt lifted its head and whickered at the moon.

A DUSTY PROVINCIAL MIND

I suggested to Nagel that he join us for dinner. Shiva was obliged to second the invitation, but I had the impression he did so without any great enthusiasm. He had grown quieter since the superintendent joined us, and his subdued mood continued over the meal. It occurred to me that Nagel's frank admiration of my legal prowess might have put Shiva's nose out of joint. Envy is the soul's rust; and the corrosion is nowhere more evident than in small towns, where men clamp on their petty ambitions like armor.

Bearing this in mind, I tactfully steered the conversation away from professional matters. We spoke of tennis—Nagel was a keen player—and I entertained my companions with the latest scandals doing the rounds in Colombo. Over the beef olives I ventured a risqué story or two. The superintendent laughed until his broad shoulders shook. Shiva managed a watery smile.

Nagel told us that he had surprised his twelve-year-old brother poring over a copy of *The Well of Loneliness* in a brown-paper cover. Banned books were circulated among schoolboys at a cost of five cents for two days, the page numbers of juicy passages noted on an accompanying sheet of paper.

"I gave the little bugger two tight slaps and confiscated it on the spot," said Nagel. The book was currently doing the rounds at his station; ten cents per night and constables bicycling in from all over the district to put their names down on the list.

Shiva laughed this time, but still looked uncomfortable. One of those chaps who's incapable of letting himself go. I know that reek of virtue and *pro bono* cases. Perhaps after all it wasn't the difference in our professional status that Shiva found galling, but the contrast between his own arid manner and Nagel's easy style.

We took coffee in a cozy little den that we had to ourselves. As soon as the boy had banked up the fire and retreated, Shiva turned to the DSP. "Any progress on the Hamilton case?"

Nagel shrugged. "Your coolies still swear they found the watch near the path where Hamilton was murdered. But they would, of course." He tugged at his silky mustache, frowning a little. "I must say I was damn wild, that pawnbroker bugger going straight to you."

Shiva helped himself to three lumps of sugar, stirred, tapped his spoon against the rim of his cup. "Well, you know how it is," he said, gazing at his coffee. "He's a Tamil, the suspects are Tamils, I'm a Tamil . . ."

"None of that counts for anything with me," broke in Nagel. "If those men are innocent they have nothing to fear. It's not as if—" He braked abruptly. But we all knew what he had been going to say: *It's not as if I'm a Sinhalese*. Burghers are always trumpeting their immunity from Sinhalese–Tamil tensions; I suppose it's true, in the sense that they consider their European blood renders them superior to both races.

Shiva sipped, then placed his cup on the arm of his chair. Behind his spectacles, his eyes looked slept in. "No one doubts your impartiality, superintendent. But you saw Rajendran. He's a creature of the alleys. And people like that are afraid of the police. It was brave of him to go to you. Afterward he needed a little reassurance, from one of his own people, that he had done the right thing."

He paused, and I was about to ask a question, when he rolled on. "You see, I have a notion that the ordinary man tries to make sense of our legal system by filtering it through his understanding of religion. He knows that deities at the upper end of the scale dispense justice and punish humans only with good cause. They correspond to magistrates and judges. Perhaps also to DSPs." This last with one of his thin smiles. "But demons and minor gods and the lower denizens of the spirit world have no such scruples. They must be influenced through sorcery and ritual if they are to do good rather than evil in the world of men. Hence the bribes paid to witnesses and officials to manipulate evidence in such a way as to produce a favorable result, and the widespread perjury in our courts. The common man recognizes that telling the truth is desirable, but when it comes into conflict with a more important value—justice, say—he is quite prepared to lie."

With admirable self-control, I refrained from letting him know what I thought of this little lecture. That is another consequence of outstation life: the mind, starved of real stimulation, nourishes itself on absurdities. It wouldn't have surprised me to learn that Shivanathan belonged to one of those earnest groups that meet once a month in a mildewed public hall to discuss theosophy or ectoplasm.

It was plain that Nagel shared my opinion. "Are you suggesting," he asked, with a touch of acid, "that your pawnbroker made a false statement?"

"Not at all." Shiva inclined his head. "Merely pointing out that our legal system is literally foreign to our people. And so they strive to make sense of it as best they can. Sorcery provides an effective precedent. Rajendran came to me because as a Tamil proctor I represent a friendly exorcist or a kindly spirit. Whereas the police are minor gods, who might or might not be well disposed to him."

He looked set to take flight again, so I intervened hastily. "The Hamilton case—I say, Nagel, are you in charge of that show?"

The DSP set down his empty cup and turned to me with a troubled look in his eyes. "I am," he said, "and I don't mind saying it's a hell of a business. Dashed grateful for your views and all."

"I'd be delighted," I said at once, moved by the man's gruff appeal. "Tell me about it."

We rang for more coffee, and a bottle of brandy. Then, with the firelight chasing shadows around the walls, they told me about it.

AUTHOR'S NOTE

These manuscript pages were found among Sam Obeysekere's papers after his death.

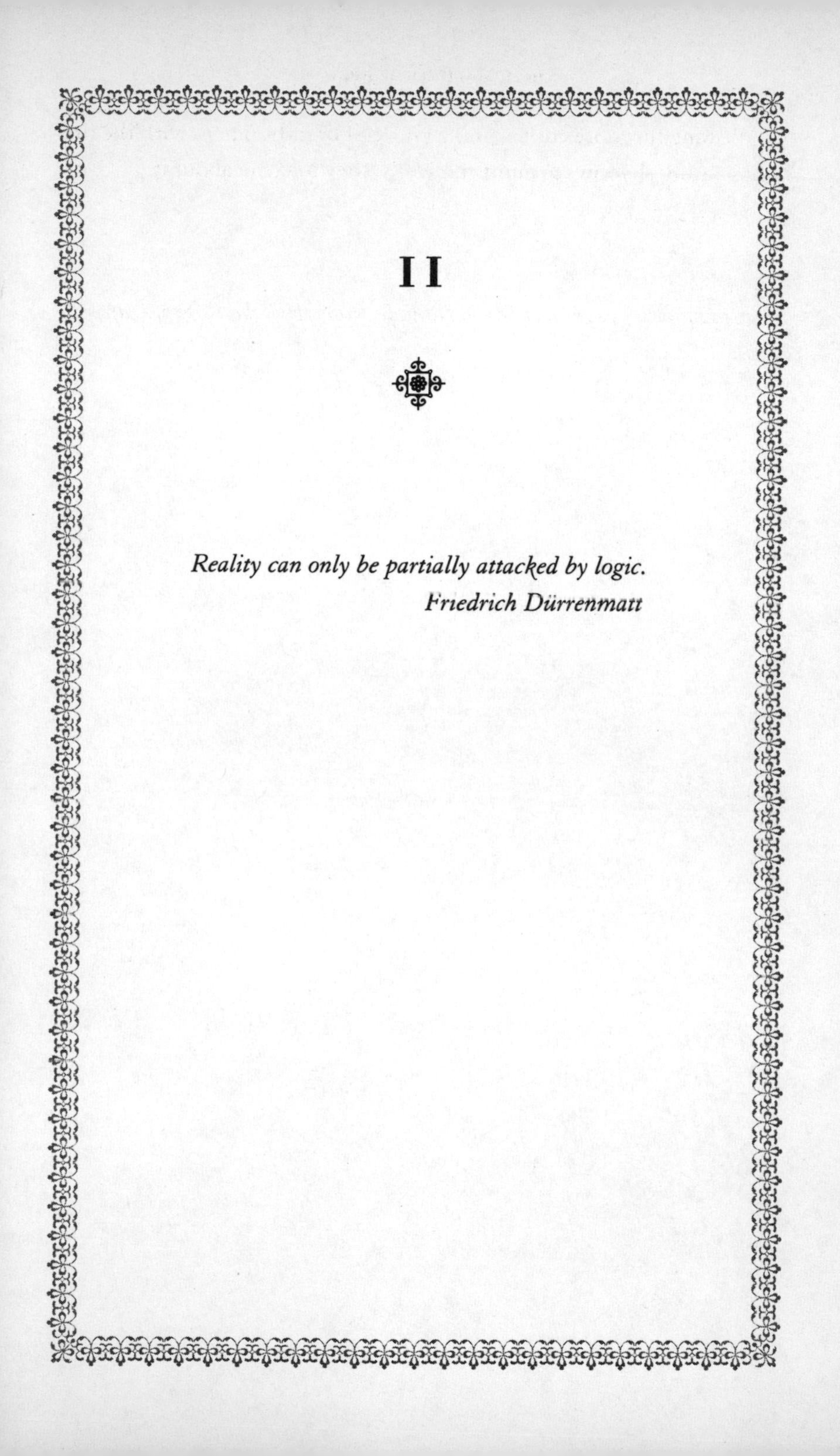

II

Reality can only be partially attacked by logic.
Friedrich Dürrenmatt

Hamilton had gone out as a downy-cheeked boy of seventeen, first to Assam, later to Ooty. He worked hard and wasted no time on suppositions, thereby commending himself to the company's management in London. Nor was he devoid of ability. He understood tea: which is to say weather, soil, pruning. He drank only coffee himself.

Seven years previously they had transferred him to Ceylon and White Falls Estate, in the Nuwara Eliya district. White Falls was performing poorly when Hamilton took over, but he turned all that around. Success is a matter of applying oneself with diligence to one problem after another and he had the knack of that. The result was a respectable yield of high-grade teas, well-maintained roads, an orderly and efficient workforce. The other planters in the district agreed he was a *thoroughly good chap*. He drank in moderation and played a decent game of billiards. Something of a loner—if they hadn't married by a certain age, they usually were—but he turned up to the socials at the club now and then, and you could count on a welcome if you dropped in on him without warning. His assistants found him fair-minded and capable. No one sought the opinion of the pluckers or the factory workers. In any case, their relations with the *dorai* were purely ritual: they flung themselves into the nearest ditch as soon as they heard the clip of his horse's hooves on the gravel.

About a year before he died, Hamilton had announced that he was expecting the arrival of an old friend who had fallen on hard times. Gordon Taylor turned out to be one of those fellows you found as reliably as mileposts across the breadth of the Empire: amiable, aimless, never sticking at anything. Empires exist to provide such men with occupation and background coloring.

Hamilton had run across Taylor in India when they were both young creepers, apprentice planters in the same company. Inevitably Taylor lost interest in tea; he moved to Burma, where he managed a ruby mine for a few years. Later he drifted to Malaya and got into rubber. Somewhere in the Straits he married a girl whose eyebrows were so fair as to be invisible. Opinion at the club had her down as *a nice little thing*. As for Taylor, he was *pleasant enough*; but you felt he would *never amount to much*. Hamilton was sentimental about him, in the way practical men choose one thing to be foolish about and sink their teeth in. Perhaps Taylor reminded him of something he could not articulate, a sentiment—only nothing as definite as that, a suggestion, a hint—dating from India that life could encompass the unexpected. At any rate he now took the Taylors in, borrowing a motor to go down to Colombo and fetch them himself. Their luggage—a tin trunk, two large carpetbags and a springer spaniel—came up later by cart.

Even before the Taylors' ship had docked, Hamilton was going around trying to stir things up on his friend's behalf. He wrote letters; looked up acquaintances on the flimsiest pretext. Later he would go up to chaps at the club and harangue them with recommendations, while Taylor hung about, grinning and sheepish, nursing a long one. Somehow nothing came of it. After a while, Hamilton gave up. The newcomers fitted into life at White Falls, became part of the pattern. Adaptability was their great skill; in that respect they exemplified the species. Taylor lent a hand with the accounts. The two men went shooting pigeon together. Visitors discerned Yvette Taylor's influence in cretonne cushion-covers and two kinds of cake at tea. The spaniel lay wherever you were certain to trip over it, and snored.

One night Hamilton didn't come home.

He had left early for the township, where he had gone to the bank and drawn out the wages for the entire estate as he always did on the first Wednesday of the month. He had called in at the post office and Cargills. He had taken lunch at the Hill Club. There, his dentist's wife, an optimist saddled with a pudding-faced daughter, extracted him from the bar and allowed him to win at bridge. Later, as the evening mists came up, two nuns spotted him on an estate road, approaching the turnoff to a track that ran through a patch of jungle. Hamilton always traveled that way; the jungle path, cutting diagonally across two estates, trimmed an hour off his journey.

Taylor said he saw no reason to be alarmed when the planter failed to return that evening. If Hamilton was held up in town, as occasionally happened, he would put up overnight at the club. But some hours later, after the Taylors had retired for the night, they were roused by the apu; the *dorai*'s horse had returned, riderless. Taylor sent for the tea maker and Hamilton's two assistants. Taking lanterns, the four men set out to search for the planter. A thin drizzle was falling. They found Hamilton near a bend in the jungle track. He had been shot in the chest and lay where he had fallen.

Murder, a moonless night, the jungle crowding close. The men who stood around Hamilton's body were not given to introspection. Yet in the conjunction of those elements each recognized a certain kind of recurring nightmare and was visited by the conviction, momentary but forceful, of something cold and mad at the core of their endeavor.

Suspicion fell on the coolies. That would have happened anyway. And Taylor, stammering in his haste to make his statement to the police, pointed out that Hamilton's watch and chain were missing. Nor was there any trace of the two canvas bags containing the estate wages. That clinched it: Hamilton had been murdered for the money. Taylor, his hands dangling between his knees, choked on his own conclusion. For a dreadful moment it looked as if he might break down. "The best of fellows," he stuttered. "The best . . ."

Nagel had expected it to be over quickly. He was of the opinion, he said to Sam and Shivanathan, that murderers were dull-witted. That was why they were obliged to fall back on murder to achieve their ends. The laborers at White Falls were questioned, then questioned again. The coolie lines were searched. Nothing was found. No one was missing. The police investigation was extended to the neighboring estates, then to the whole district. The usual suspects were hauled in for questioning. Informers were leaned on. Everyone could account for his whereabouts on the evening Hamilton died. No one had seen anything. No one had heard anything. Finally—and this was the most baffling aspect of the case—there was no sign of the money. The bank had recorded the numbers of the notes, and the list was circulated throughout the island. From one minute to the next Nagel expected a telegram, a trunk call. Days clotted into weeks. He swore at his sergeants. Behind his desk, at midnight, he stared at photographs of victorious Englishmen. Those trophies. The way their socks bulged over their calves.

Sam studied the superintendent, as Nagel refilled their glasses. He saw: a father in the railways, a brace of siblings, a fourth-rate school. A bright boy, athletic. Immense pride when he first paraded the uniform: aunties, cousins, tumbling babies, everyone jammed into a cramped room; tots of cheap whiskey and backslapping uncles. Examinations: the household on tiptoe, his mother lighting candles in a side chapel, children slapped for speaking above a whisper. Inspector. Chief Inspector. And then, astonishingly, the last unreachable bauble falling into his hand.

At that moment Sam understood why he warmed to the superintendent. Who isn't drawn to what he pities? In the planters' clubs and the estate bungalows, they would be saying that Nagel had bungled it. An Englishman would have had Hamilton's murderer swinging before the body was cold. It was all the fault of the blasted Civil Service, kowtowing to some damnfool scheme hatched by Westminster. Look what happened when you gave them responsibility! No one safe in their beds! In Nagel's eyes the bewilderment of a child who never meant to climb so high jostled the understanding of a man who has measured the drop below.

Yet two days earlier, the superintendent's luck had turned. A scrawny Tamil presented himself at the police station. Rajendran ran a thriving bicycle-repair business in a filthy alley that was known to all the tea pluckers in the district: he would lend two rupees against their anklets, five cents above the going rate.

For his encounter with authority the pawnbroker wore a tweed jacket above his *verty*, and cracked, exquisitely polished oxblood brogues on his bare feet. Brought before Nagel, he reached into his inside pocket and produced a handsome half-hunter. The superintendent examined the watch in silence: *A. G. H.* His heart flipped like a coin.

Two coolies, a father and son, had brought it in, the pawnbroker said. He thought the younger man was called Velu. They worked on Rowanside, one of the estates Hamilton had traversed on his shortcut. Velu had said that he and his father were taking the same path home when he stepped into the undergrowth to relieve himself. There his toe encountered something smooth and cold. He stooped; retrieved a watch stuck over with black leaves.

Nagel himself went to Rowanside, put his boot through the door of the ten-foot-square room in the coolie lines. They found the father within. The son, spotted running away from the latrine block, was brought to the ground with a flying tackle by an ambitious constable.

At the police station the pawnbroker identified the suspects and was allowed to go. He went straight to Shivanathan, who telephoned Nagel and expressed his willingness to represent the men if charges were laid against them.

Nagel had interpreted this, correctly, as a warning: Shivanathan was letting him know there was nothing to be gained from forcing a statement that wouldn't stand up in court. As if the superintendent was a brute-fisted sergeant extracting confessions on which judges could hone their weary sarcasms. It was the implicit insult to his intelligence—rather than the slur on police methods—that rankled.

The DSP cracked his knuckles and glared at Shivanathan, snug as a walnut on the other side of the fireplace. "They're guilty of theft, at least," he snapped.

"But not of murder?" asked Sam.

Nagel turned to him. He had the policeman's instinctive mistrust of lawyers. Nevertheless he heard himself saying, "I don't think so."

A moment later, relief at having blurted it out collided with the fear of what he had set in train. He excused himself. In the lavatory the cramps came in waves, crinkling his guts. He hung his head between his knees. He wiped the clamminess from his forehead with a handful of Bromo paper.

When the DSP rejoined the other two, Sam asked if he could meet Taylor.

The man had stiff little ruffles of brown hair parted low on the side to show a line of cicatrix-pink scalp. They found him in the White Falls factory, running his fingers through a sample of Broken Pekoe, his pale eyes alight. His tea maker stood by, radiating disapproval.

Nagel introduced Sam casually, implying that he was helping the police prepare their case against the Rowanside coolies. Without actually lying, he conveyed the impression that the men had confessed. It was admirably done.

Taylor rattled on all the way to the bungalow. He had a scheme for determining the exact point at which to check the fermentation of tea leaves. He spoke of scientific accuracy and quoted statistics with the fluency of the demented. The company had appointed him manager in Hamilton's place, at least until the end of the year; he was determined to make a go of things, he said. His dog ignored him, waddling down the steps to Nagel and licking the superintendent's hand with extravagant delight.

"Good-for-nothing brute," said Taylor affably. "Prefers forty winks on my wife's bed to an afternoon's shooting." He offered cigarettes from a yellow tin. His nails were carelessly trimmed and not altogether clean; but beautiful, each with its nacreous half-moon. One of his eyes was smaller and set a fraction higher than the other; the asymmetry rescued his face from blandness by suggesting unreliability.

The apu appeared with a tray. They drank sublime tea from thick Pettah china. All the while, Nagel improvised questions. Had Hamilton had anything to do with coolies on other estates? Had he ever spoken of Rowanside, and if so what had he said? Any shred of evidence that pointed to prior dealings with his murderers would be useful in making the charges stick, he assured Taylor.

Taylor repeated his opinion that robbery was the motive for the murder. On more than one occasion he had voiced his concern about the wisdom of carrying so large a sum back to the estate and offered to accompany his friend; but Hamilton had always laughed him off, saying there was nothing to fear.

Sam, sitting back in a rattan armchair that gave off an odor of spaniel, decided that Taylor talked too much, was probably capable of petty duplicities and doubtless a fool. But he couldn't see audacity in the man.

Then Yvette Taylor came out of the house.

She was young, that was the first thing Sam noticed, much younger than her husband: twenty-two or -three at most. Fairhaired, fine-boned. The men got to their feet. She nodded at the visitors, but didn't hold out her hand. What she thought of Ceylonese on her verandah was plain. Which explained the china. There would be a good set in a lead-paned cabinet, thought Sam, fluted English bone in a shade between rose and apricot. He pictured the apu lifting out a translucent cup; and the expression on Mrs. Taylor's face as she caught him at it.

She was wearing a green cotton housedress sprigged with white flowers. Sam saw himself divesting her of it: her small high breasts, shell-tipped. The vision left him stunned, his chest aching. Nagel, he saw, was studying his boots. He understood that women would unfailingly underestimate Mrs. Taylor; and that their husbands, meeting her, would always picture her undressed.

Her accent was not quite right, the vowels skewed.

She said, "Hadn't you better scrub up, Gordon? Lunch will be served any minute."

That night Sam devised punishments for her rudeness, her pale hair twisted through his fingers, forcing her head into place.

On the weekend he stayed in his hotel room, the table that served him for a desk littered with carbon copies of statements and reports. He studied the photographs. Hamilton's face: pear-shaped, clean-shaven, ruched about the eyes. He was thirty-seven and looked ten years older.

A photograph of the jungle path where the body had been found pulled Sam's gaze. He returned to it again and again. He scrutinized it with the aid of a magnifying glass. At last he understood what it meant.

On Monday, before leaving for court, he penned a note to Nagel. *Ask the apu what Taylor bagged that afternoon. And search the bungalow.* He added a postscript: *I'm certain it was all her idea. But you'll never get either of them to admit it.*

The season began. Racing, flower shows, a fashion parade at the Grand Hotel. There were dances three nights a week at the Downhill: paper lanterns along the verandah, a five-piece Colombo band called The Sensations. The saxophonist went under the name of Freddie Fonseka, but his flat nose and woolly hair branded him a Kaffir. The Dutch had brought them over from Africa to deploy against the island's kings. The regiment's ferocity was legendary: those they didn't kill in battle they treated to castration, disembowelment, a *catalogue déraisonné* of protracted deaths. Fonseka was rumored to be leaving for Paris; he ended every night drunk on a foul cocktail of his own invention, three parts toddy to one of white rum and guava juice. Sam was of the opinion that such people were untameable.

Midweek the crowd was younger, Fonseka's saxophone more sweetly lunatic. These evenings soon acquired a reputation, so that stricter parents kept their daughters at home and men far outnumbered women. Yet couples always crowded the dance floor, or whispered where shadows pooled inkiest in the garden. Eurasian girls were known to be fast. Sam kept his eye on one of them: slender, long-waisted, a girl with a tilted smile and a wing of black hair. Grace Sinclair: father an English planter who hit the bottle, mother a village woman. Grace worked at Cargills, behind the millinery counter, and was clever with her fingers, sewing all her own clothes. One dress, a sheath of jacaranda-blue satin cut on the bias, inspired some of Sam's gaudier ruminations as he sat in court, hearing a witness recite the fluent lies they had rehearsed together, seeing Grace's muscles move under the clinging cloth.

He ran around with her for a week or two, then dropped her. Girls like that expected no better.

Besides, Claudia and Jaya were up for the season. At his brother-in-law's insistence Sam moved into their house, a mock-Tudor cottage with sloping green lawns and seven bedrooms. He loved the prickly, dark-green smell of the pine tree outside his window. At midday in April its shade still struck cold; or so it seemed to him, standing beneath its arms with his eyes shut, breathing scented air.

He had thought England would smell like that: deep and crisp and even.

The house was full of guests and visitors dropped in at all hours. Fonseka showed up one midnight, rolling drunk in a sharkskin jacket, and vomited into a satinwood umbrella stand. The sickly scent of ganja perfumed the night. At three in the morning Jaya was cha-chaing with the wife of a minor Venetian aristocrat. Later he perched on the piano stool and sang, "They're changing sex at Buckingham Palace, His Highness will now be addressed as Alice . . ."

Once, Sam would have dismissed his brother-in-law's gaping need for novelty and clamor as nothing more than quintessential foolishness. Now he was disturbed by nuances he sensed rather than understood. In that mood, even the presence of the saxophonist could seem sinister. Would his father—or Jaya's—have tolerated that creature under his roof?

At the height of the season, Jaya turned up to the Governor's Ball wearing a dinner jacket and a sarong. An aide showed him the door. The incident did the rounds as a witticism: "Heard Jaya's latest?" But Sam knew from Claudia that his brother-in-law had exchanged letters with Gandhi. In that house, with its fox-hunting prints on the stairs and its bound volumes of *Chums* in the breakfast room, he was vouchsafed a vision of what lay ahead. Politics. Change. He sweated through a nightmare in which he was trying to find his way home, to a house that lay behind a high stone wall, and that he glimpsed, from time to time, at the end of a lane or through trees; but the path he followed left him floundering on the side of a hill, where there were only low, dark leaves for cover, and riders approaching.

Instinct catapulted him toward the source of all his craving. Maud was staying with friends, in a house overlooking the lake. He called on her late one Saturday morning and found her taking breakfast with Marcus Fernando in a summerhouse webbed with creamy jasmine. Marcus had the remains of an egg hopper in front of him and a dot of yolk on his chin. He greeted Sam extravagantly and avoided meeting his eye. Maud offered her cheek, still gnawing at a wing: he smelled garlic and Elizabeth Arden.

Nine out of ten women would have chosen not to face the merciless silver light reflected up by the lake. Sam accepted a cup of tea and drank it while cataloging her chipped nail varnish, a black hair coiled on the rim of her plate, a smear of lipstick on her glass. Long ago he had realized that disgust was the only reliable weapon against his need.

She told him—and Marcus, of course; it would be all over the hill station by dinner—that the Jayasinghes had begun to remark on Claudia's failure to have a child. Ayurvedic treatment had been mooted, consultations with leading gynecologists in Colombo and London having failed to produce a result.

"Could be a charm," said Marcus. "Happened to our gardener's daughter. Her husband called in a soothsayer, who found human hair and nail clippings buried near the entrance to their compound. Within a year she had a baby. Only a girl, mind you."

Claudia had not uttered a word about any of this, although Sam had concocted occasions to be alone with her. He made a point of quizzing her about her relations with Jaya; and whenever a discreet opportunity arose, examined what he could of her flesh to ensure that she was no longer mutilating herself. Her manner had often struck him as evasive, but evasion was her natural mode. Now it occurred to him that she might be contriving to deny her husband his conjugal rights. His knees came together in a little spasm of delight.

"I don't know what's wrong with that child," Maud was saying. "It's always problems and whatnot." She arched her back and stretched her arms, languid movements that invited inspection. "In my day we never needed doctors to make babies." She was wearing a mint-green chiffon housecoat over bottle-green pajamas. And a necklace Sam had never seen before, square-cut topazes linked with gold.

When he stood up to leave, she said, "Cheerio, Sam," and brought the palms of her hands together in the traditional way. It was done lightly, her yellow gaze mocking. But he had noticed that Jaya used the gesture systematically these days in lieu of shaking hands.

One morning he woke up and found he was famous.

Success exposes a man's true nature while adversity encourages dissimulation. Nevertheless Sam was unprepared for the generosity with which Nagel played down his own part in bringing the Hamilton case to a conclusion. The superintendent made it plain—to his superiors in the force, to the reporters who besieged him—that the crucial tip-off had come from Sam Obeysekere. He himself could claim no credit for solving the mystery, said Nagel, in a much-quoted interview. He was no more than *the instrument of another man's brilliance*.

Taylor's arrest for the murder of Angus Hamilton made the front page of every newspaper in the island; there was even a paragraph in the London *Times*. Details of the case could not be discussed, pending the trial; and Sam took care to remind the reporters who arrived from Colombo and Calcutta and even Singapore of the presumption of innocence. They parroted his platitudes, and filled up their columns with trivia, gross flattery (*the dashing Mr. Sam Obeysekere* . . .) and lurid speculations about Taylor's character and motives.

A photograph of Sam appeared above the caption *Our Sherlock Holmes*. He cut it out of the newspaper with his nail scissors and kept it until the end of his days between the pages of *The Pilgrim's Progress*, bound in royal-blue boards, the first prize he had won, for General Proficiency, at Neddy's.

He received offers from twenty-seven marriage brokers.

In Shivanathan's dry congratulations, he heard the grinding crank of envy. He remembered that Shiva, too, had been privy to Nagel's story, but had failed to see its significance. The entire affair was an illustration of the difference between flair and a mechanical ability.

The coolies from Rowanside were charged with the theft of Hamilton's watch and the obstruction of justice. Shiva's defense took the line that as both men were illiterate, they had seen only a decorative hieroglyph in the planter's initials and had no idea of the significance of their find. It was a typically lawyerly contortion. But the case was heard by a magistrate who had been in the colony just over six weeks: not quite long enough to erode his intention of keeping an open mind. He sentenced the pair to eight lashes apiece, a sentimentality from which his career would never recover.

One day, the two men were waiting for Sam as he emerged from court. They prostrated themselves before him and kissed his shoes. A shriveled crone in a dull red cotton sari crept forward and handed him a twist of picture cord from which was suspended a cylindrical copper amulet, bound with scarlet thread and greasy to the touch. Her Tamil was whispered and in any case unintelligible to him, but he gathered he was to wear it around his neck.

At the Downhill that evening, standing at the bar with his instep on the brass rail, he put his hand into his pocket and encountered the thing. As soon as he could do so unobserved, he dropped it into the nearest wastepaper basket.

The court ruled that the Fernando brothers' patrimony was to be divided equally between them: exactly as their father's will had provided. Marcus and his brothers embraced tearfully, assuring each other that their feud had been a misunderstanding fostered by the bally lawyers. That night they threw a riotous party to which none of their counsel was invited. The next day Ronnie brought charges against Marcus and Clifford for invading his dressing room while intoxicated and defecating in his slippers.

Taylor's trial came up before the Colombo Assizes, some weeks after Sam had returned home. Seats in the public gallery were awarded by lottery. Whenever he had a spare half-hour, he pushed his way through the crowds awaiting news of the latest developments in the Hamilton case, nodded at the officers on the door and found himself a place at the back of the courtroom. Despite the discretion of his entrance, heads always turned.

Fellows he had never set eyes on before—Tamils, by the look of them—accosted him in the Hulftsdorf corridors or in the street, and seized his hand. Baskets of Jaffna mangoes arrived daily at his chambers. But on the third morning of the trial there was a polecat, its throat cut, left at his door.

Nagel gave his evidence with commendable calm. A week before the trial opened he had been returned to the rank of chief inspector. The trick to carrying off any egregious move is to treat it as preordained, a matter of destiny not policy. The officer who replaced Nagel had twelve years' seniority over him; ergo, he was better fitted for the post. It was obvious to everyone who met him that the new superintendent, plucked from the malarial lethargy of the east coast where he had spent his days lying in a hammock strung between two jamfruit trees, was a lumbering blockhead. But he was the senior man. That he happened to be English was irrelevant.

Once, in the previous century, a private from Bradford had faced a court-martial over the knifing of his quartermaster in a Pettah brawl. But Taylor was the first Englishman in the colony to be tried for murder. Like all novel situations it elicited predictable sentiments. A famous London silk, William Earnshaw, was retained for the defense. His fee, reputed to be outrageous, was to be met out of a fighting fund set up by Taylor's countrymen.

An anonymous pamphlet appeared, hinting in three languages at a British conspiracy to pervert the course of justice. Sam, pressed for his opinion, would say only that he had every confidence in trial by jury.

All this time, he was conscious that he had received no reply to the letter he had sent Sir George indicating his willingness to enter the judiciary. An Additional District Judgeship had recently fallen vacant. Soft prickles of expectation ran over Sam's scalp at the news. Now that the acuteness of his mind had been so dazzlingly demonstrated, a judgeship was no more than he might look forward to. He allowed himself to hint as much to Billy Mohideen, his rather pushy junior, over a drink in chambers.

Mohideen eyed him oddly. "Well, but . . ." He broke off.

"Go on."

"No, nothing." But then Mohideen could not help himself; he resembled one of those lead-weighted toys that cannot lie down. "You see, you are putting a noose around an English neck, isn't it."

"I brought a murderer to justice." He remembered that he had never really liked Mohideen. It was the double whiskey, downed too fast, that had led him to confide in the oily little squirt. "I think you'll find that's the crux of it."

"Oh, but can you be sure, Obey?"

"I flatter myself that I know what counts with Sir George rather better than you do, old chap."

"No, no—I am referring to what you said two ticks ago about Taylor being a murderer." Mohideen bounced on his chair and beamed. "You are forgetting the presumption of innocence, isn't it. What is your situation if they find him Not Guilty?"

Sam was at his usual post at the back of the room when the court was shown an enlargement of the photograph that had provided his vital clue. James—"Jumbo"—Minton, who was leading the case for the Crown, drew the jury's attention to the single footprint clearly visible in a patch of mud to one side of the jungle path. Experts had established beyond doubt that the footprint was Hamilton's, said Minton. Would the murdered man have dismounted if accosted by strangers in the jungle? No. It was obvious—obvious, repeated Minton, fixing the jury with his famous fish-eyed stare—that Hamilton was on friendly terms with his assailant. The planter had so little reason to be suspicious of the man who came around the corner of that deserted track carrying a shotgun that he got off his horse and walked a few steps with him.

"Perhaps the murderer persuaded him to dismount by pretending to have seen something of interest in the jungle. That we shall never know. But what we do know," thundered Minton, aiming both his chins at the dock, "what we know beyond a shadow of a doubt, by his own admission, is that the accused was out with a gun that afternoon. For the purpose of shooting pigeon, according to his statement. And yet, gentlemen of the jury, he returned home empty-handed that evening."

Minton's oratory was bruising. It left Sam untouched. His brain toiled on the mill where Billy Mohideen's insinuations had set it. Now the silence from the KA's office appeared wholly sinister. Yet he refused to believe that the color of Taylor's skin could outweigh his guilt; and he was certain that the man slumped like a sack in the dock was guilty.

The next day he called on Sir George. The KA was affable and vague. He spoke in labyrinthine periphrases of shifting circumstances and offered his visitor a bull's-eye from a brown paper bag.

Finally, there was only the sound of sucking.

A trapdoor swung open inside him.

Sir George skipped ahead on his tiny feet to open the door. With his shapely red fingers on the handle, he said, "Word to the wise. The judiciary . . . Personal discretion, don't you know. Limelight not entirely . . ." He shifted the sweet across to his other cheek and turned the brass doorknob.

Twenty-four hours later, it was official: Shivanathan had an Additional District Judgeship. The appointment was not without genius. Putting a Ceylonese on the Bench quelled the hullabaloo over the Hamilton case, while the choice of a Tamil engendered rancor and division in nationalist quarters.

For the rest of Sam's life he would associate the scent of peppermint with betrayal.

Earnshaw set about unraveling the prosecution's case with the apologetic air of a maiden aunt called on to point out the dropped stitches in someone else's knitting. He was a trim little man with a large head that photographed handsomely. Where Minton bullied, Earnshaw flattered. Juries loved him for it. In cross-examination he took witnesses by the hand, walked them with infinite sympathy into quagmires.

Nagel found himself admitting that Taylor's failure to bag any game was proof of nothing more than a bad afternoon's shooting. As for the canvas holdall with Taylor's fingerprints on it that had been found, half charred, on the rubbish heap behind the bungalow, anyone could have placed it there. Were there not several other people, asked Earnshaw kindly, the White Falls coolies, for instance, and Hamilton's servants, who knew about and had access to the rubbish heap on the side of the hill? Nagel had to concede that there were. His client's fingerprints proved only that he had handled the bag, went on Earnshaw—as, indeed, Taylor had readily admitted. Since he had often helped Hamilton divide up the estate's wages, there was nothing surprising or sinister in that.

When Sam took off his jacket at night he would find that the courtroom wall had left a streak of powdery white distemper across the shoulders. But he was leaning there as usual, wedged in beside a potted palm, when Earnshaw made his only mistake.

The defense called Yvette Taylor.

She was wearing a lavender maternity dress, with a matching coatee. Her voice, with its distinctive vowels, trembled a little on the oath. The judge, old Matthew Coote, peering at her with his head tilted, called for a chair. A carafe of water and a tumbler were placed within her reach.

The sight of her affected Sam as directly as a blow. Her smallness. The straight fair hair held off her face with a flowered clip. Yet he could see very well that by any conventional measure she was not pretty. This hurt him. One of the instincts she aroused was protective.

Earnshaw, solicitous as a father, was leading her through her questions. These were innocuous at first: how long had she been married, where had she met Taylor, and so on. She answered softly but with precision. Having set his witness at ease, Counsel moved on to the events of the day on which Hamilton had died. Mrs. Taylor corroborated the evidence already given by the apu, gazing at Earnshaw with her small colorless eyes.

The jury—British to a man, shop keepers, shipping agents, an engineer, the manager of a plumbago mine—watched Mrs. Taylor, shifting their thighs. Her clothes, the pale pink color she had applied to her mouth, even the high mound of her stomach, each element of her appearance colluded in the impression of a child impersonating an adult. Sam found himself wondering if her condition was genuine, or a ploy suggested by Earnshaw to win sympathy. He allowed himself the brief fantasy of ripping her dress open, disclosing the cushion strapped to her taut white flesh.

And then Yvette Taylor faltered. She drank some water, grasping the tumbler with both hands. Justice Coote, leaning forward and adjusting his gold-rimmed spectacles, enquired if she was quite well. Tears pooled in her eyes but she nodded her head.

Earnshaw had been asking Mrs. Taylor about life at White Falls, a line of questioning designed to establish Hamilton's generosity toward the couple and the longstanding friendship between the two men.

Justice Coote now directed him to repeat the question he had just put to the witness.

It was possible, as Sam later swore, that a trace of unease stiffened the loose line of Counsel's bearing at that moment. Earnshaw's voice kept its habitual mildness, but he looked very intently at his witness, as if to remind her that the question served a purely rhetorical purpose: "Mrs. Taylor, can you conceive of any reason why your husband might have wished to harm Angus Hamilton, his oldest friend and a generous benefactor to you both?"

"Yes," whispered Yvette Taylor.

The monosyllable brought Sam upright at his post. Taylor, with a strangled noise, half rose in the dock. His wife turned her soft white face to him. "I'm so sorry. But I've promised before God . . ."

Earnshaw said hastily, "My Lord, the witness is clearly not fit to continue. I request . . ."

But Mrs. Taylor had risen to her feet. With her hands clasped in front of her, like a dutiful performer, she gazed up at Justice Coote and embarked on her story.

She spoke in jerky rushes but there was no mistaking the significance of what she said. For some time before his death, she had felt uncomfortable in Hamilton's company. He had a way, she whispered, of looking at her. Once, he had walked into her bathroom as she was preparing for her bath. He mumbled some excuse about looking for Taylor, flagrantly trumped up, since they both knew her husband was playing billiards at the club.

On the day before Hamilton died, he had returned to the bungalow halfway through the morning. This was unexpected. After breakfast, both men were usually away until lunch. Her husband was in the factory that day, where the sifter that separated the coarser tea leaves from the finer had broken down. She was in their bedroom, sorting linen for the dhobi, when Hamilton came in and shut the door behind him. He said that he was mad for her. He said . . . "All kinds of things," confided the faint voice, audible everywhere in the coffinlike hush of the court.

In her distress, Yvette Taylor had blurted that she was going to have a child, hoping that the news would bring the planter to his senses. Instead, "It seemed to excite him," said that terrible whisper. Hamilton took hold of her roughly, clamped his hand over her mouth.

At that moment, with the planter's weight forcing her backwards onto the bed, a horn sounded at the bottom of the hill. It was the usual signal that a car was on its way to the bungalow. Hamilton let her go, and she fell back onto the coverlet. She heard him leave by the side door. Minutes later, a cheerful voice was calling out at the front of the house. Yvette Taylor smoothed her hair, arranged her clothes and went out to greet a planter's wife who was dropping off jumble for a sale in aid of the mission school.

She kept to her room for the rest of the day, telling the apu, and her husband when he returned, that she had a headache. But as darkness fell and she heard Hamilton's heavy tread coming and going about the bungalow, she was seized by terror. She begged Taylor to take her away at once. He was baffled, of course, and dismissed her tears as the "nerves" that habitually overcome a woman in her condition. Finally, she told him what had happened that morning. And ever since, she whispered to Justice Coote, she had been afraid.

With every eye directed at it, the lavender dress swayed. Glass and carafe crashed to the floor.

In the second before the tumult, Sam saw Jumbo Minton's gap-toothed grin. In barely eleven minutes, Taylor had been delivered to the hangman.

At the cocktail party Sam attended that evening no one talked of anything but the sensational turn taken by the Hamilton case. He was the center of a knot of women with smooth, bare arms. Aloysius Drieberg, his head of chambers, took him aside and confided that his doctor had advised him to ease out of the harness while there was still time. He pressed Sam's hand to confirm what he was offering; they would talk on Monday, they agreed.

Later, with sheeted rain and drivers lining up to bring cars in under the porch, his hostess took advantage of thunder and umbrellas to murmur that she was always alone between two and three in the afternoon. She had a mole at the corner of her thin magenta mouth and pearls as plump as eyeballs in the folds of her neck. Everyone knew that her husband kept two mistresses and forty-three cats in a house by the Wellawatte Canal.

Insomnia, which would eventually transform his nights into ragged holes held together with threads of sleep, was already a moth blundering softly into Sam's dreams. At four he came awake to clammy darkness and the certainty that Yvette Taylor was lying. Yet everything she had said proved him right about Taylor.

Somewhere near at hand a leaky gutter or garden tap dripped onto stone at unpredictable intervals. Its maddening irregularity syncopated the conundrum that was still occupying him when the servant-boy came in with bed tea. What monstrous calculation lay behind the woman's decision to condemn her husband when Earnshaw had demolished the case against him?

Sam was the only churchgoer in the house. Iris no longer left her room, and Kumar used her illness as an excuse to spend Sunday mornings pottering around the back garden in his pajama bottoms. He had taken to keeping chickens in a wired enclosure just off the kitchen verandah, where he liked to supervise the mixing of their feed. The diets he devised were elaborate and erratic, fluctuating with whichever manual or expert he was swearing by at the time. Two servants had already given notice.

That Sunday, the grizzled houseboy relieved Sam of his hat and hymn book and informed him that Green Crescent *nonamahatheya* and Jayasinghe *mahatheya* were in the drawing room. He found Kumar on the settee, a bush shirt buttoned in crooked haste above his striped pajamas, his hand brushing Maud's knee. Jaya sat on her far side, with his head thrown back so that his furry throat was exposed. A bottle with a silver teaspoon protruding from its neck lay aslant in an ice bucket. Sam had walked in on a dispute about whose breasts champagne glasses were modeled after. Jaya was for Marie Antoinette, while Kumar was groping for a name he couldn't recall: "Famous tart. Married that short army bugger." Maud construed this, correctly, as denoting the Empress Josephine.

Afterward, Sam was unable to remember which of the trio informed him that Claudia was expecting a child. The intelligence ricocheted around his brain and lodged itself as a headache behind his left eyebrow. "Where is she?" he asked, conscious of his hands dangling by his thighs.

"Who?" asked Maud, genuinely puzzled. "Oh—Claudia? Don't be silly, Sam, she's at home, lying down."

Kumar, above whose ear a delicate white feather lay curled, was offering him a glass of champagne. The room was crammed, like all the rooms Sam had known, with dark furniture, brass jardinières, silver candlesticks, stuffed birds, tapestry cushions, tasseled lampshades, china shepherdesses, jasper jugs, painted boxes with sliding lids inlaid with mother-of-pearl. He had never coveted objects, but at that moment understood why men do. A collector runs his fingers over each round or angled surface and is comforted by the heft of the world; without which there is only space, curved as a belly, a humming darkness.

When dawn broke on Monday, Taylor was found dead in his cell. He had fashioned a rope in the classic manner, using a torn-up sheet; but had bungled the job and taken a long time to die.

The note he left, subsequently printed in every newspaper in the island, professed his innocence. He admitted that his wife had told him of the incident with Hamilton. *But God forgive me, I didn't believe her, knowing Angus as I did, and thinking that my wife's condition must have caused her to misunderstand or exaggerate some harmless, clumsy action on his part. I swear I never harmed him. I believe he was killed for the money, by the coolies. But I fear that it will go ill with me now, for even the one person whose love I prize above all the world's riches believes me guilty of murder. And so it is best, for the sake of the child, to end it all.*

No one believed a word of it. Why would an innocent man kill himself? It was agreed, however, that Taylor had been precipitate. He would almost certainly have got off. Earnshaw was swift to point out that Yvette Taylor's evidence was uncorroborated. And one of the jurors told a newspaper reporter that he had been tormented all weekend by the delicate problem of how a sentence of death might be carried out. That a native should hang an Englishman was unthinkable. But could one count on the government, always unreliable over essentials, to go to the expense of bringing in a hangman from Home? That uncertainty alone was enough, said the juror, to ensure that he, for one, would not have returned a Guilty verdict.

Yvette Taylor spent the rest of her confinement in an Anglican convent in the hills. A subscription was got up for her. Sam donated an anonymous five rupees.

Some months later a squat paragraph in a newspaper caught his eye. She had left the island with her baby, a girl. Hamilton's firm had paid her passage home. The reporter had allowed himself a final flourish: *Far from our shores, may no shadow of the Hamilton case ever mar the untainted brow, the soft dark gaze, of the infant whose sweet innocence stands as the coda to those tragic events.*

Half a rasher congealed on Sam's plate as he stared at the newsprint, picturing her in a sheltered corner of the deck, the child in her arms, her face a colorless blur turned this way and that, as a worm swivels its blind head. Around her, an ocean swelled and sank unnoticed.

The day after the trial collapsed, Nagel resigned from the force. It was understood and approved as a gesture of principle: he had been treated shamefully. Sam intended to write to him. It would be an affair of half a morning to pull a silken string or two on the poor devil's behalf. But the new arrangements at chambers claimed all his attention. Before he knew it, weeks had piled up like the gold-lettered cards on the hall table. He was elected president of the Old Edwardians' Association. His patronage was sought by the Kennel Club, and Christian Ladies Against Socialism.

At the Customs and Excise Ball, with the daughter of a copra millionaire on his arm, he learned that Nagel had emigrated. To Australia, said Sam's informant; but someone else chipped in, insisting it was Rhodesia. At any rate, a country waiting to be invented. It would suit Nagel well, Sam thought; he was a man cast in the heroic mold.

Yet he was unable to shake off the sensation that something had slipped from his grasp.

His longing for Claudia grew urgent. The thought of the creature engorging itself within her, distending the small waist he had been able to circle with his hands, was repellent. He pictured it as an eye: jellied, rotating in darkness. Fearing that its mass had pitched her off balance, he needed assurance that its effect was in fact steadying. But when he dropped in at Green Crescent, fingers crossed for luck, he was confronted by Jaya, and a priest tricked out in yellow like a bally pineapple. His brother-in-law was devoid of all spiritual feeling; of that he was certain. But the needle of Jaya's ambition had settled on the north of nationalist zeal, and Buddhism was intrinsic to the cause.

Jaya crushed Sam to his breast, then explained that Claudia was resting and had asked not to be disturbed. "But stay, stay," he urged, while the monk's shaven indigo head turned to study the visitor. "We're holding a *pirith* ceremony this afternoon."

Of *pirith* Sam knew only that it involved chanting. That was quite enough.

Everywhere he went, men flattered him to his face and maligned him behind his back. He recognized this for what it was, incontrovertible proof of success. But there were entire days when his life seemed a thing of cardboard and paint, and a gale raged offstage, mocking him with losses.

He knew it was time he married.

III

The jungle moved within the walls.

Leonard Woolf

The copra millionaire's daughter satisfied the criteria on which he would not compromise: she was plain, and the inventory of her dowry exceeded a dozen foolscap pages. What was more, she had been educated in a seminary for young ladies presided over by two sisters from Aberdeen. Her ambitions were contained by drawn-thread work and the novels of Sir Walter Scott, which she read every year, returning to *Waverley* as soon as she had closed *Castle Dangerous*. It was true that her parents left something to be desired, as in-laws usually do. They spoke Sinhalese at home and the mother wore nothing but saris. To offset these drawbacks, they were elderly, mild and rarely ventured into Colombo, preferring their rambling estate near the 27-mile post at Kaltura.

He would be marrying into a family that had been Christian for five generations. But the old people's primitivism expressed itself in their insistence on having his horoscope drawn up by their astrologer, who scrutinized it for information about his health, financial prospects, compatibility with his fiancée's chart, and so on. These particulars having been deemed satisfactory, further consultations were required to determine an auspicious date for the wedding. Why her parents chose to believe that the girl's well-being would be determined by the slant of planets rather than by the estates, investments and lakhs of rupees they had settled on her surpassed Sam's understanding. But he submitted to their requirements as an anthropologist conforms to the practices of the tribe he is studying: with the tolerance that accompanies the certainty of reward.

Her name was Leela. He called her Lily, if anything. They never met unchaperoned. But on visits to Colombo she stayed with a cousin, a jovial matron with enlightened views on courtship who found excuses to leave the young couple alone in her drawing room from time to time. On one such occasion, wishing to test the girl's modesty, he placed his hand on her knee. Her distress was acute and unfeigned. He desisted at once, apologizing. Her unremarkable proportions scarcely affected him; he was excited by smallness, with its aura of violation. Still, the articulation of power is its own aphrodisiac. He looked forward to his wedding night with clinical ardor.

Claudia's son was born at daybreak on the 14th of January. In the house next door, the Jayasinghes' Tamil neighbors smiled to hear him cry. They had risen early in honor of the Hindu harvest festival of Thai Pongal, when barefoot pilgrims crowd into temples to offer up rice and vegetables to the god of the sun. Thus joyfulness and ceremony attended the child's entry into the world.

His ayah slept at the foot of his cot on a mat woven from coconut fronds. When he was twenty hours old, a noise awoke her. Through the dissolving meshes of sleep, she saw a figure in a long white gown bent over the baby. As she struggled to her feet the apparition straightened. By the time the ayah began screaming, she was the only one alive in the room.

Servants stumbling along a corridor toward the commotion at the front of the house met their mistress gliding on bare feet in the opposite direction. They flattened themselves against the wall to let her pass; but as they said later, she appeared not to notice them. A few claimed to have seen that she was concealing something in the folds of her nightdress. They all agreed she was smiling.

It was Jaya who found her, in the damp weeds among the plantain trees by the back wall, the bottle of Lysol empty beside her. She was not smiling then; and no one who saw her doubted the agony of her end.

Sam was able to go on living after she chose not to by becoming more himself. This would be his lifelong tribute to her. It affirmed her wisdom in choosing oblivion over monstrosity, the last lucent expression of a mind giving way to darkness.

He began by seeking out someone to punish. There was the abomination she had married. At Claudia's funeral, a furtive ceremony boycotted by the Jayasinghe clan, her husband wept as men did not, in that time and place, weep for their wives. Sam watched, stone-eyed, from the opposite side of her grave. In that public grief he saw only the inadequate expiation of private remorse.

Afterward, when the handful of mourners had converged on Kumar and Iris's drawing room, Jaya drew him aside. "I found this in her almirah," he muttered, fumbling in a pocket.

A letter, Sam thought. She had left a letter. Not for him, but for Jaya. He felt like a man who has missed the last step on a stair.

Jaya held out a small sooty sphere hung with gold. He moved his hand and two blue eyes flipped open in his palm.

Sam put out a finger. The thing was smooth and cool to the touch.

Jaya shuddered. "It's horrible," he said. "Like a charm."

"It's a doll's head," countered Sam. The turmoil of his emotions did not prevent him noting how fluently his brother-in-law resorted to superstition. Really, the veneer of Jaya's civilization could be picked off with a thumbnail.

"But look how it's been colored black. It has to be a message."

Jaya's voice had risen. Any moment now it would attract attention, and there would be a scene: probing, exclamations. Sam plunged his hands into his pockets, short-circuiting the impulse to snatch the vile little object from Jaya and crush it underfoot.

"It doesn't mean anything," he said. "A broken doll. She kept things like that."

After a minute Jaya said, "She used to talk about you."

Small cold feet trod the length of Sam's spine.

"About when you were children." Jaya's voice had thickened. "How could you have . . ." But here he produced a handkerchief, flashily monogrammed, into which he made coarse, trumpeting noises.

Sam closed his eyes. Not because he gave a hoot for his sister's prattle, but because the slide from the second to the third person is always chilling. Whenever he thought of Claudia, he had pictured her face turned to his. Now he saw himself as a thing trundled across a stage, a little varnished manikin pushed hither and thither for private entertainment.

A few weeks later Jaya converted to Buddhism. Thirteen months after Claudia had been laid in her grave he announced his engagement to a moon-faced Kandyan virgin, descended from aristocrats who had led a failed rebellion against the British. Sam interpreted these signs, and every subsequent step in his brother-in-law's career, as proof that Claudia would always have been sacrificed to mythology and ambition.

But Jaya, spiraling into history's orbit, was beyond his reach.

Besides, Jaya had only married her. There was the parent who had delivered her up to him.

Sam was at the passenger terminal to meet her ship.

With her usual disregard for proper sentiment, Maud had decided to go abroad as her daughter's stomach swelled. "My last fine careless rapture and whatnot. Do you realize this wretched infant will make me an *aachi*?" So she had exclaimed, resplendent in green lace, scattering cigarette ash on her guests, at the party Jaya had thrown for her before she left.

Claudia had been allowed to attend the first hour. Afterward, Sam sat with her as she lay on her bed, her hand jumping in his, while downstairs the gramophone alternated with the piano in grinding out fun. Her hair lay loose on her pillow. He remembered smoothing it behind her small ears; making a feeble joke about the "affluence of incohol." It was the last time he saw her alive.

With her flawless instinct for the disreputable, Maud had hooked up with Jaya's Venetians. Italians! Treacly eyes, a religion that was eight parts nonsense and two parts sentiment. The countess had worn tails to Maud's party and kissed her full on the mouth on arrival. The couple had an Abyssinian in their retinue, a long-limbed man with a shaven head who neither spoke nor smiled. Rumor had it that he serviced both husband and wife with unflickering indifference.

Their group was trailing its permutations along the wintry Mediterranean coast when Claudia died. The telegram followed Maud from one gilded, chilly hotel to another for over a week, until it caught up with her beside the Bay of Naples on the afternoon of her fifty-first birthday.

Rain was falling when her ship docked in Colombo. The boom of waves crashing against the breakwater was in Sam's ears when an old woman draped in black put a hand scribbled with violet veins on his arm. He had looked straight past her, scanning the passengers disembarking under umbrellas. She saw that she had disconcerted him, and smiled her crooked smile. Sooner or later every son sees his mother as a quantity of female flesh. But for the first time in his life, on that bilge-smelling morning, he experienced her presence only as an absence of desire.

She took a cigarette from a silver case. Her porter hung about ostentatiously. "Give the man a whatnot," she said and began coughing.

He fumbled for a coin. She said, "How stingy you are, Sam." It was spoken with the disinterest of a naturalist remarking on the behavior of apes. Then she sank to her knees on the shining pavement.

Kumar summoned his doctor, who diagnosed bronchial pneumonia with pleurisy. There was already Iris, who required round-the-clock care; and the doctor, a straight-browed Tamil, waggled the neckless head set like a ball on his shoulders and warned that Maud's condition was acute. Within an hour she was in a nursing home. Until she was pronounced out of danger, Sam prayed every night and every morning that she would be spared. He wanted her to live a long time.

When she could receive visitors he went to see her. A leather dressing case lay on her coverlet. Her lips and nails had been colored their usual crimson, and she was wearing a bed jacket of tawny quilted satin. But a line had been crossed. She had left for Italy a handsome, middle-aged woman. Now, although her skin was close-grained as linen, her eyes magnificent, these things reminded him of the last yellow roses that had clung to the wall under his window in Oxford: not so much an echo of summer as evidence that the glory was gone.

He asked where she intended to live when she left the nursing home. "Don't imagine you can go back to Kumar," he said, forestalling her. "Iris is dying. He's told me he doesn't want you there."

That was not strictly true. But he had surmised it from the old boy's eloquent silence on the subject of Maud. Besides, the lawyer who had drawn up Iris's will was an Old Edwardian. Sam knew that after disposing of her jewelry and personal effects among an assortment of nieces, Iris had left the residue of her small estate to Kumar. She had added a line in her own hand, made clumsy with illness, under the clerk's copperplate: *I beg you to have nothing more to do with her*.

On Maud's bedside table, a vulgar gold basket held two dozen sprays of orchids, an extravagance of bruised kisses. She reached behind them and slid out a long buff envelope. "The deeds to Bentota. Jaya's given them back to me. I'll put the house up for sale and rent a little place in Colombo."

The ceiling fan creaked round and round. Sam was conscious of the blood being forced around his veins; of everything that repeated itself and was beyond his control.

At last, he said, "You don't really imagine the Bentota bungalow is worth anything, do you? Selling it will barely cover the bills you've run up here."

Maud said, "You could pay them yourself. Now that you're marrying money."

"I'm afraid Lily and I will have considerable expenses of our own." There was a small waxy stain on the gray coverlet. He picked at this scab. "A young couple just starting out, don't you know."

The silence wound itself tighter.

Being Maud, she rallied. A narrow hand wove a nonchalant arc through the air: "Something will come up."

He leaned across her, to her dressing case. Then, taking hold of her wrist, he folded her fingers around a tortoiseshell handle. "I don't think so," he said. "Not any longer."

She hurled the mirror at him as he was leaving. It caught the green-painted rail at the foot of her bed. "Seven years' bad luck," he said, and shut the door.

It was Kumar, in the end, who rescued her, taking the Bentota property off her hands at a price well above market value; a generosity that dropped like sourness into his relations with Sam, curdling them forever. The money enabled Maud to hang on in Colombo, where she parked herself on a series of acquaintances, moving on every few months when hints hardened into ultimatums.

Sam waited. His rivals at the Bar liked to say that he bored the defense into submission. When the jibe made its way back to him—as it was bound to do, since friends rarely deny themselves the pleasure of relaying abuse—he smiled. Only a fool distinguishes between outwitting an opponent and outlasting him.

A fortnight before he married, Sam fell in love.

In matters of the heart his instincts were neurotic but not self-destructive. Where he had loved, he had suffered. The lesson was not lost on him. It led him to discover an outlet for tenderness unshadowed by the menace of rejection.

The house stood by the sea, at the end of one of the lanes that protruded from Galle Road like the teeth of a dirt-caked comb. There were still fields there in those years, emerald parcels of *kurrakkan* and *keera*, and low, thatched huts set among thickets of plantain. Across the lane, the lichen-embossed wall and ironwork gates of Allenby House suggested an opposing army.

From the moment he first saw the place Sam wanted to possess it: the mild lions lounging on the gateposts, the cobalt rectangles of Bohemian glass in the window on the landing, the pedimented portico, the verandah floored in white marble squares with black diamonds at each corner. It had stood empty for close to a decade. Halfway through the previous century Allenby, the third son of a third son, had arrived in the colony with four shillings and a change of twill trousers. He got into coffee and amassed such a fortune that his deerhound fed from a golden dish. But the leaf blight came in 1869, and Allenby shot the dog and hanged himself. The house changed hands a dozen times. It had last been owned by a Danish bandmaster, who had modernized the plumbing. His wax-faced wife burned with increasing boldness for her Tamil tailor. One evening, with guests for dinner and the best silver, she left the room with a murmured excuse. Minutes later, they heard her scream. She was found clinging to the newel, with a tape measure twisted about her neck. In between there had been minor catastrophes, a stonemason crippled in a fall, a baby born with a flipper at its shoulder in lieu of an arm.

Sam put his hand on a brocade curtain in the dining room and came across a bat, bulging like a tumor in the tarnished folds. Mildew had papered an entire wall. In every room the sea could be heard, sighing in its bed. From an upstairs window he looked down at coconut trees slanted like pins and a row of clumsy black stitches. Beyond the railway line waves lowered their woolly heads and butted the shore.

A watchman dressed in a filthy *banian* and sarong trailed Sam through high-ceilinged rooms full of aqueous light, spelling out a catalog of deterrents. These were a judicious blend of the domestic and the gothic: blocked drains, a cloudy shape on the stairs, rotten floorboards, a room into which the mongrel bitch nursing its mastitis on the verandah would not venture. Children with matted hair and mucus-ringed nostrils crept out like cockroaches from their squalid quarters beyond the kitchen to gape at the visitor. The superstitions that had lowered the price of the house to the point where it cost little more than the value of the acres in which it stood left Sam unmoved. In a bathroom where a broad-leafed sapling was growing out of a skirting board he closed his eyes, summoning his sister's ghost. She had left him nothing: no sign, no token of their understanding. Remorse at his lack of vigilance crashed about his heart with the obduracy of breakers.

The exterior of the house, once faced with dark yellow stucco, had weathered to ochre and lemon. Claudia had owned a dress that color. He could recall its faint sheen in a dim corridor; a fabric-covered button grazed his ear. Among garden beds turned rank and wild, the watchman droned in his wake. Sam sprang up the steps two at a time and entered the house once more, half believing she would be waiting at the foot of the stairs. He would take her hand and lead her out into the gold day. Fish would leap and sing in the sea.

Wide-eyed and rigid on her bridal bed, his wife could not understand, then or ever, why he was the one who wept as he went about his onslaught. In all the years to come she would endure their encounters with the aid of the mantra that a merciful instinct devised for her on that first night. *Flora. Augusta. Rowena. Amy. Flora. Augusta. Rowena. Amy.* He laid his wet face against her shoulder and ripped her open again, and Sir Walter's heroines sustained her in the dark.

At his wedding reception Sam had stipulated that his mother's glass was not to be refilled between toasts. Maud countered this with the simple tactic of following a waiter out to the hotel kitchen and returning with a bottle in each hand. Then she went around the room informing everyone, from his gaping in-laws to the band leader, that he had married the girl for her money. "Look at her—face like the backside of a bus, poor child." She waltzed cheek-to-cheek with men Sam's age, while their wives displayed an overwhelming interest in the contents of their beaded handbags. He watched, flint-masked, from the bridal table.

At last, he took her in his arms and she swayed with him over the parquet. Her head lay twisted on his shoulder. They glided past a mirrored pilaster and he marveled that a tender word from this rouged carcass could once have been his most avid desire. Yet even as he steered her into the center of the floor, he was claimed by a vision in which she was restored to youth and radiance, and he climbed into her bed and was gathered to her breast. Leela, encased in baleen and satin cut on the bias, glimpsed his face at that moment and misread, as she was bound to, the rapture inscribed there.

Leaves mocked gravity, rising into the air. There they resolved themselves into a billow of jade butterflies. He had hired six men from the docks and turned them loose in the grounds of Allenby House. For two days they crept about with machetes and knives, impervious to the jeering of crows. When they had finished he possessed a lawn, plumbago hedges, brick-edged canna beds, clumps of scarlet and mustard croton, disciplined arabesques of stephanotis and thunbergia. He went out to inspect their work and was particularly pleased with the discovery of a *bulath* vine, woven around the trunk of a *lovi* tree. Its cordate leaves could be sold to the betel women who used them to wrap the small fragrant parcels of areca-nut parings and lime that constituted their trade. The double row of coconut trees against the seaside wall represented a far more lucrative source of revenue; but he had that instinct for the acquisition of wealth that is as appreciative of a coin on a pavement as of the deeds to a diamond mine.

As a married man with a household of his own, he was incurring expenses inconceivable in his bachelor days. When he inspected the monthly accounts he required Leela to keep, his fingernail left a trail of faintly shiny grooves where it had scored the column of figures in consternation. *One dozen coconut-shell spoons: Rs* 0.20. Why did they need a dozen? "Because otherwise they are two cents each," replied his wife.

He grunted, and moved on to the cost of kerosene. What Leela didn't say was that the cookwoman had asked her for more spoons in order to avoid the contamination of vegetable dishes by utensils that had come into contact with meat.

In the early months of their marriage, Sam would send his peon out to the Pettah now and then to check on the prices his wife had listed for a pound of sugar or a bar of Sunlight soap. He suffered a twinge of disappointment on uncovering her systematic honesty.

Now he called together the six men who had restored order to his garden and put this question to them: "What is gardening?"

The rich were like the sun, disease, the pull of currents: which is to say, arbitrary and potent. Each man feared, instantly, that this riddle would be the means that deprived him of his day's wages. They stared dull-eyed at the *hamuduruwo*'s shoes.

At last, one of the men took half a step forward. His legs were two black twigs, the circumference of each knee identical to that of the ankle.

Sam said again, raising his voice, "What is gardening?"

"*Hamudurawanai*, it is preventing things from growing."

This man, whose name was Tissa, remained in Sam's employment for thirty-four years. On Christmas morning when the *hamuduruwo* and *nonamahatheya* returned from church, the gardener would be waiting on the back verandah, accompanied by his wife and a row of children arranged like a stair, one new step every year. Each child received a coin, a soft drink, a paper cone of homemade toffees from the *nonamahatheya*'s hand.

But their father's inclinations lay in a direction quite other than his gradated progeny would imply. The extent of the grounds necessitated employing a gardener's boy, and Tissa was allowed to handpick his assistant from the families that overflowed like sewage in the tenements. It was in the hollow chests and uncallused flesh of these children that the gardener found pleasure. A new recruit soon learned to stay quite still for the minute or two the act required at the start of each day in the dank outhouse where rats crawled over gardening forks, and cockroaches cracked underfoot. Tissa was tender with these boys, spoiling them with *beedis* and other small gifts: a sesame sweet, a marble enclosing a twist of flame.

When a boy's voice broke, Tissa returned him to the streets. About this he was implacable, although at such partings he often wept and the boy with him.

He was a wonderful gardener. In a place where palings burst overnight into leaf and no talent was required to bring forth life from the earth, Tissa's genius lay in conjuring absence. He was the artist who reveals objects by painting the emptiness that surrounds them, the composer whose music shapes itself around silence.

Paradoxically, joy represented itself to the gardener as repletion: a seer fish curry of which he might eat his fill.

There was a room downstairs, opening off the verandah opposite the kitchen, about which the servants began to complain. It started with a stocky, swaybacked girl called Soma. She said that she could no longer clean the room, because while she dusted or swept something watched her. It was the kind of talk that is taken up like a bad habit. Within days there were reports that a light had been seen there late at night. The cookwoman related how she had been woken by a thunderous crash, as of heavy furniture toppling from a height. Other servants complained of a muffled banging; of an odor they identified variously as putrefaction and bitter oranges.

It was Leela who alerted him to what was going on. This was in the first months of their life together, when the silence swirling between them was still only ankle deep and she had no reason to fear it. She would sit back in her chair after their evening meal, her hands folded on her belly, and offer him segments of her day, fresh peeled. He was of the opinion that this talk of haunting was bally nonsense. But he agreed that something had to be done about it. The next day he called the servants together and informed them that he intended to spend the night in the haunted room.

It contained a four-poster bed carved with sailing ships, a cupboard, an assortment of straight-backed chairs with yawning rattan seats or broken legs. He had a mattress carried downstairs, the bed made up. While this was going on, a russet and turquoise hen stepped onto the verandah and over the threshold of the room, wobbling its head.

"You see," he said to the servants, attempting lightheartedness and mastery at a stroke. "Everyone knows animals shun a haunted room. So here is proof that there is nothing to fear."

That they would contradict the *hamuduruwo* was unthinkable. But he knew what they were not saying from the way they found absorbing interest in their work. *A hen is only a stupid bird. A snake, that would be something. Even a crow*. It made him want to shout, I'm not the one who has it all wrong! It was his misfortune to live among a literal people. An English education is a prerequisite for distinguishing irony from ignorance or untruth.

He read *The Woman in White* until midnight by the light of a kerosene lamp, that wing of the house not having been wired for electricity. A few hours later, he could not have said what woke him. The lamp had gone out. The smell was very bad and easily identifiable as drains; he had forgotten to shut the door to the bathroom. For a while he lay with his knees squeezed together, silently repeating her name. The room swam in moonlight and shadows. But he could not persuade himself that there was a yellow dress in the folds of the curtain. He was alone with the whine of mosquitoes, having overlooked the precaution of a net.

At last he went into the bathroom and replaced the plug in the washbasin. Then he managed to get the lamp going again and read until dawn. When he heard the servants moving about, he put on his dressing gown and went outside, calling for tea. The sky was moonstone feathered with gray.

At breakfast Leela looked at him with her small stupid eyes and said a prescient thing: "Perhaps ghosts show themselves only to people who need to see them." This annoyed him. He picked up his newspaper and ignored her for the rest of the week.

The episode had a curious postscript: his wristwatch had run down at two forty-three, although he was sure he had wound it as usual before placing it under his pillow. Neither he nor the experts he took it to were able to set it ticking again.

At weddings it was customary to set aside a portion of the cake to be eaten at the christening that was expected to take place within a year. Ten months after his marriage, Sam's wife presented him with a daughter. The baby weighed six pounds and two ounces. For the past eleven days she had lain motionless under her mother's ribs, a discreet guest choosing to slip away without commotion.

The midwife wrapped the small body in a towel and smuggled it out of the room, while Leela lay back on her pillows, sweaty and elated. She was waiting to hear the child cry. After an interval, she asked the woman who was sponging her face and neck why the baby was so quiet, and was told to shut her eyes and try to sleep. Then she was left alone. The walls in that room were washed a milky green, a color she would detest for the rest of her life.

Sam arrived a few hours later, after the tournament in which he had been placed fourth in the Men's Singles, and told her what had happened. When she grasped what he was saying and began to whimper, he left the room.

On the evening she came downstairs for the first time, they sat at opposite ends of a rosewood oval and ate mock turtle soup, mutton cutlets with lime pickle, and jaggery pudding. Halfway through the meal he remarked that he was looking forward to an early night. It was his usual signal to her. She understood then, with awful clarity, that the reason he displayed no grief was that he felt none.

Time was his great ally. The day came, as he had known it would, when Maud had sold or pawned everything of value that she owned. That in itself required little prescience. But this was where he displayed insight into the social mechanism: he understood that power always comes down to accountancy. Without wealth, a woman who is no longer young is no longer desirable. It is a principle scored across cultures, etched into the species. He knew it would not fail to search out his mother.

One evening the letter he had known would arrive was waiting in the brass tray on his desk. He noted the second-class stamp; and the envelope, which was the kind that could be bought singly from a *kadai* and caused ink to smudge. It lay on his upturned palm. He thought of all the letters that had surely preceded it, the appeals addressed to everyone she had ever known. They had failed her, of course, the cronies, the lovers, the sycophants, the protégés, all the people she had once preferred to her children, the great, glittering wheel of society rotating and returning her to him.

He had to pull over twice and ask for directions. When at last he found the house, in a laneway off Fife Road, there was no street lighting and he almost stepped into an open drain when he got out of the car. The servant who came to the gate scratching her scalp yawned in his face. On a verandah lit by a bare light bulb with a nimbus of insects, a youth wearing a sarong lolled on a chair with one knee cocked. He eyed Sam with frank curiosity and didn't have the decency to get to his feet.

Maud received her caller with aplomb, even though he had arrived without notice. She stood, one slim hand resting on the jamb, in a doorway that opened off the verandah. "Isn't this a convenient spot?" she screeched over the blare of her landlord's wireless. "I go for a walk every morning, right around the links. Ritzy and I always meant to take up golf. All those marvelously ugly socks and whatnot."

The reference to his father he interpreted as a brazen attempt at blackmail. He ignored it, and the bright falsity of her tone. Her cramped, airless room told him everything he needed to know. He pulled out one of the straight-backed chairs tucked in under a card table and sat down. Before him spread a drift of papers, bottles of nail varnish, a dirty teacup, a saucer that had served as an ashtray, hairpins, three mauve tissue-paper roses in a plaster vase, little pots of face cream, the usual sluttish disarray he associated with his mother. A bottle of Stephens Ink caught his eye. He pictured her clearing a space at the table before sitting down to compose the letter in which she asked him to *tide her over for a few months*. He wondered how many drafts it had taken to hit on the brittle nonchalance of that phrase; and felt his glance hooked by a wickerwork spiral from the wastepaper basket unraveling in a corner.

Maud drew a bottle and two cloudy tumblers from a varnished almirah. She arranged herself with her spine propped against the buttoned headboard of her bed and fanned her face with a pleated newspaper.

Sipping without enthusiasm at flat soda water, Sam noticed two black-strapped rubber slippers arrayed side by side under the bed. The soles, worn thin, showed the indent of his mother's heel and the ball of her foot, and he remembered that she walked with her weight rolled over to her instep, so that all her shoes were eventually pulled out of shape. The sight affected him queerly. He turned his head away.

"Heard from Jaya lately?" he enquired to give himself countenance.

A five-strong coterie had resigned from the Ceylon National

Congress the previous month. In a blaze of oratory and denunciation the quintet had announced the birth of the People's Party. Its platform was vague yet menacing. A return to village values, the restoration of land to its traditional owners, the dignity of labor. The British affected indifference; a nursery squabble, that was the line. The Communists sulked in public, but Billy Mohideen swore he had evidence of a midnight meeting at Green Crescent.

The president of the new party was a former dux of Queen's and a graduate of the LSE. But there was a toothiness to his jaw. In photographs he had the air of an aggrieved rodent. It was his handsome right-hand man the newspapers loved. Sam, confronted with grainy images of Jaya addressing a mass rally in a malarial outstation, had sensed the first stirring of something large and with a capacity for rage. At the same time, he couldn't help filtering the new party's provocative stance and popular following through the clichés of a schoolboy story: rebellious Fourth Formers taking on the prefects in Congress, egged on by rowdy juniors. In this way he failed to understand the power of the phenomenon he was witnessing.

He said, "What do you suppose is the position of a former mother-in-law in the village scheme of things? Perhaps you could apply to have a little hut of your own in the back garden at Green Crescent."

"It's not as if you can't afford to rent a place for me," said Maud. "How much did that girl pay you to marry her?"

But he knew he had the upper hand. "There is always a home for you," he said. "At Lokugama."

His chair must have been riddled with bed bugs. All night he tore at the backs of his thighs, exultant when he recalled her face.

There were two suitcases and a steamer trunk on the back seat of his car and a second trunk in the back. "Things," said Maud, vaguely and grandly, in answer to his irritated question. "Frocks and whatnot."

She was of a generation that believed in carriage. She sat upright, her gaze fixed straight ahead. As they were passing under the living arch thrown across the road by the bo tree at Kaltura, she lit another cigarette. "When I think of all those years you cadged off Kumar and Iris. One minute it was how you couldn't afford to tip the servants at Christmas, the next you were boasting how you'd fleeced some poor devil in court."

The sea came into view: translucent green close in, solid blue farther out, everywhere flecked with light. "How many rooms do you have in that hideous yellow house of yours?" asked Maud, not turning her head.

He had always been rather proud of the dash with which he drove. Now the car surged forward, nosing between a bullock cart and a colonnade of coconut trees. When he had completed the maneuver he said, "There's my wife to consider. And in time, our children. You're not an influence I would wish to expose them to." He had rehearsed these phrases and was pleased to have the occasion to deliver them.

The journey to Lokugama took three hours. Side by side, they sat in silence. His eyes kept returning to the trunk that filled up the rearview mirror. Frocks! It was plain she had failed to grasp what her life was to be like.

She spent thirteen years there. It sounded like a sentence. But he was punctilious in his solicitude, motoring down for a weekend every month. On these visits he settled the servants' wages, went over the market chits and folded three notes into a stiff blue envelope that he propped on the tallboy in his mother's bedroom.

To his wife, and everyone else who enquired, he said that Maud had decided it was time she lived quietly, away from Colombo. "You know how it is with old folk," he observed, over tea in the pavilion at the Queen's–St. Edward's cricket match. "They reach that time of life when they want to take stock." He brandished an asparagus roll. "*Cultiver son jardin* and whatnot." In those first months he was helpless before an urge to imitate his mother—a verbal tic, a characteristic gesture in which the fingers of one hand were flung outward. Wanting her gone, he found himself compelled to conjure her presence.

At a party to mark a silver wedding anniversary, he parried questions with a light laugh. "You know Mater." The telltale flip of his hand. "She's always been a *gamarala* at heart."

On the whole this picture of rural quietism was unconvincing. Catching the whiff of scandal, one or two of Maud's more persistent acquaintances motored down to Lokugama to dig out the true state of affairs. But the gates were kept padlocked and the bungalow keeper had orders to turn visitors away, saying that the *nonamahatheya* had been unwell and was resting. This gave rise to the story that Maud Obeysekere, notorious as a bad hat, had contracted something unmentionable and was being kept out of sight by her son.

For a while this rumor could be observed perching here and there like a crow. Then it flapped away. People stopped asking after his mother. She was an old woman, easily forgotten.

For the girl he had married, time was a stony plain stretching in every direction. Anniversaries were marked by the packages of matted blood that slid from between her legs at intervals. These objects were borne away from her in covered bedpans; occasionally she flushed one down the lavatory herself. She could not have said what they were exactly. But they were not children. They had no faces.

That first time the midwife, a kind woman who suffered from varicose veins, told her that the baby was a girl, her skull covered in soft black curls. In Leela's dreams this child was not dead, but beat uselessly with tiny bloody fists on the rocks and earth piled over her. Sometimes, even at yellow midday, she would hear a faint, terrible scrabbling that died away as soon as she lifted her head. Once, entering the dining room, she became convinced that something was trapped in the sideboard. She flung its doors wide. Damask tablecloths, silver trays, Delft platters: they taunted her with the mute indifference of things.

She came to hate the house. It was an arrangement of monumental boxes, each with its own lock and key. She had grown up in an ancient sprawling edifice designed without interior doors; a curtain hung over a doorway provided privacy while allowing the free circulation of air. In Allenby House each room was a cell, into which more prisons had been fitted: cupboards, chests, tallboys, cabinets, chiffoniers, trunks, rifle cases, document boxes, scent bottles, biscuit tins, cheese dishes, spice jars, tea caddies, decanters, a stool with a hinged lid, a glass bell encasing wax flowers, so many tombs where a soul might flail for all eternity. No sooner had she settled to her sewing or bent her gaze over a letter than a compulsion she was powerless to direct brought her to her feet. All day she went in and out of rooms, climbed and descended stairs. a servant looking up from the hall might see her standing there, the mass of her planted solid on the landing yet faintly nebulous along the line of a shoulder or hip in a way that occasioned unease in the onlooker.

In every room the sea mourned with her. Yet she shunned the upstairs windows on the seaward side of the house. Her mind unfolded that view into the flat blue planes of a schoolroom map, and she would recall the fear she had felt on first realizing that nothing but the treachery of water lay between the island on which she stood and a continent of ice. Now and then as she wandered through the house, small things stopped her in her tracks: a fan of red chilies drying in the sun, the gardenias Soma floated in cut-glass bowls. But the sea was like love: a vast, glittering instability.

In those terrible years even Sir Walter failed her. Narrative, an optimistic form, assumes that it is worth turning the page; it is predicated on development and progression. That life might *move on*, a sentiment echoed by well-meaning relatives, struck Leela as monstrous. Sequences of sentences she had had by heart for years now chilled her. She had all the books removed from her room and placed in a trunk, where those brown or faded crimson boards could no longer mock her with the relentless ambition of their contents.

Sam's affinity for the house intensified in tandem with his wife's aversion. The symmetry of its design, the harmony of its proportions laid a salve on his soul. He drew its air into his lungs, and his life grew light and sumptuous. Tender with gratitude, he ministered to its needs like a considerate lover anticipating his mistress's desire. Masons repaired its crumbling brickwork. Electricians rewired the upper floor, cursing their predecessors and the rats that had gnawed through their workmanship with admirable evenhandedness. The cookwoman's uncle, a doddery individual with a wispy gray topknot who appeared at the back door one day to cadge a cup of tea, revealed himself as a plumber of genius: within the space of a morning he had set water gurgling again in the downstairs cistern and unblocked the pantry tap. A carver from Galle who specialized in *mal lella* was hired to restore the damaged fretwork above doors and windows. The missing roof tiles were replaced. Shutters that had warped tight over a decade of monsoons were eased open, planed to fit once more into window frames. One morning Sam went out into the garden and found an ossuary on the lawn: the remains of birds and small mammals whose carcasses had clogged the guttering for years.

All but the most urgent work took place gradually, over weeks that lengthened into months. He would place his hand, palm open, against wood or plaster, and know where the house desired his attention: here in the chinked creaking of boards, there in the musky stench seeping from a cupboard.

His face became known in the salesrooms of auction houses. He picked up a massive ebony chiffonier for a song. An eight-inch vase glazed in damson pink and gold cost him as much as he pulled in in two months. He bought an astrolabe. He acquired three portraits, in oval frames, of men who had the air of dim aristocrats. He bought eighteenth-century soup ladles, a chest of drawers with beveled edges, two music stands, a bone stamp box, a hideous electric chandelier. Other things, a pair of biscuit-colored Meissen cups painted with flowers and fruit, a nest of straight-legged teak tables, he rejected with barely a glance. It was as if the house spoke through him, so that he turned away from the exquisite silver nutmeg grater the auctioneer had set aside for his inspection because the phrase *a set of ivory-handled fish knives* had floated into his mind. He crossed to a display cabinet, shifted a basket of tiles depicting the activities of cobalt Chinamen and located the knives in a box lined with maroon silk, the whole bordering on the commonplace but urgently necessary to him.

In this way, with time, he felt the loss of Claudia less keenly. It was not that the house replaced his sister but that it came to function like the puckered tissue that grows over a wound, the presence that betrays an original absence. He gave no sign of understanding that his life had been a series of substitutions. He might spend an afternoon gazing from an upstairs window, while the sky turned gray and swollen like a tick and nails of rain were driven into the sea.

A boyhood devilry with firecrackers had claimed the tip of the Lokugama bungalow keeper's little finger. Even at the time, in the swirl of shock and pain, Sirisena was not sorry. The missing phalanx conferred distinction.

His ancestors were fishermen. To Buddhists the work was abhorrent since it necessitated taking life. Then a fleet of sallow Portuguese priests arrived, their lines baited with salvation. The despised fisher caste rushed to nibble at this god who loved their kind. The boy saw Catholicism, too, as synonymous with difference. When paper lanterns glowed in the village for Vesak, the fisher huts were holes of briny darkness.

Sirisena's father drowned. His mother married a brute. The boy turned his back on beatings and the sea. Inland there was a Carmelite convent with a whitewashed chapel, the Counter-Reformation unscrolling beneath coconut plumes and the ravishing spread of flamboyante.

He clutched a chit from a priest. The nuns found him work: digging a well, relieving the night watchman. One morning he looked at a girl in the kitchens. Thereafter she always stirred a spoon of condensed milk into his tea. Marriage to a Tamil: it was yet another sign that he had been singled out for an uncommon destiny.

They had a child, a boy with a large lolling head. In their sister house in the hills the nuns had a special wing for unfortunates. It was sheer charity on their part to take the baby. Yet Padma could not reconcile herself to the loss. She turned sullen. Sirisena saw suddenly how coarse she was. She picked a louse from her scalp and squashed it between her thumbnails.

They were encouraged to make their future elsewhere. The sisters resolved it, like all difficulty, with an adamantine sweetness. A situation was found for the pair, the ease of their duties pointed out. They arrived at Lokugama on an evening when the moon was full and saw the house before them, pearl-pale in the jungle.

Even when daylight revealed rats' nests, and rafters patched with sky, Sirisena remained joyful. He paced verandahs, studied the dim outlines of the frescoes on the gateposts. He counted the coconut trees. His wife, uprooting yams that had seeded and run wild, paused in her labors. She understood that she had married a fool. Look at him now, delirious because he had the use of a heavy black bicycle. In her dreams a flat-eyed baby mewled. She lay on her mat with aching nipples.

There were no more children. At night the animal breath of the jungle licked their necks. As the years wore on it became difficult to see these things—barrenness, isolation—as marks of favor. There were days when the bungalow keeper knew he was cursed. His wife cooked with *gingelly* oil, in the Tamil fashion. In the thatched booth of a tea boutique at the junction with the trunk road, a tot of illegal toddy eased his nausea.

When the *hamuduruwo* announced that his mother would be living at Lokugama, purpose was restored to Sirisena. Overnight his former air of an energetic bird returned: an alertness to his step, a round bright eye cocked at his surrounds. On the coconut estates that had once belonged to the Obeysekeres, there were villagers who could remember the old days at the house. The bungalow keeper grew avid for their stories. A child employed solely to fold table napkins into lotuses. The head servant who disciplined underlings with tablespoonfuls of castor oil. A Chinese seamstress who filled the house with scarlet crepe paper dragons when the bullock cart bringing pots of poinsettia from up-country overturned on a hairpin bend one Christmas. Sirisena led former servants from room to room, his heart knocking with pleasure as they detailed vanished opulence. A clock as tall as a man that showed the phases of the moon. The fifteen curries served daily at lunch. There was a septuagenarian who evoked a gramophone with a turquoise-glazed horn and a chandelier strung with faceted rainbows as vividly as if these objects were painted on the cataracts that blinded him.

Then the *nonamahatheya* arrived, and was not as Sirisena had envisaged. Nevertheless he looked at her and thought of chrome, he thought of a curtain rising in silvery swags as the lights dimmed and of white ships gliding like queens into a harbor. The bright vague web of yearning within him lashed itself about her presence. He dropped a fistful of pink newborn mice into four inches of water. There were places where everything was new and clean, where no one struggled.

For Maud, each day discharged an identical freight of loneliness, monotony and long, voracious mosquitoes. Hardest to bear was the heat. When she lay in bed, the air was so heavy she felt its weight upon her. Her skin grew damp beneath its touch.

The house was dwarfed by its backdrop of trees, so that it appeared to crouch low on its haunches. In fact it had ceilings eighteen feet high, designed for coolness. Its walls were inset with lattice, its verandahs screened with rattan blinds that could be lowered against the sun and sprayed with water. These were stratagems that presupposed currents of air, since an island race is fated to take its bearings from the sea. But the breeze that ruffled the coast was strangled by leafy ropes as soon as it ventured into the hinterland. The air was not air at all, thought Maud, felled on the verandah at ten in the morning, but a woven yellow haze. Spiders and green-veined orchids lived suspended in its honeyed weft.

She began to unpack a trunk and reached a layer of photographs in pokerwork frames. Ritzy failing to look sinister with a cutlass between his teeth. Herself at the same costume party, a slave-girl whose gauzy attire displayed tantalizing traceries of flesh. Claudia unsmiling on her wedding day, Sam authoritative in a morning suit. Was it chance, wondered Maud, that preserved her children in images so much more formal than their parents? She picked up the photograph of Sam and studied his face. Why didn't she hate him? Wouldn't loathing be more natural than the massive indifference he triggered in her? He was her first born, the only child left to her, and a door within her slammed shut in his presence.

It had been the state of affairs between them for as long as she could remember. Once, coming away from a prize-giving at Neddy's, her husband had said, "I say, old thing, you should try harder with Sam." "Should I?" said Maud, as startled by the fact of the reproach as by the point it delivered. "Yes." After a minute, "Do you think he minds?" she had asked. "I should say so." Maud whistled—a vulgar habit she was cultivating. She had tried to concentrate on her son, to see him whole. It was useless. In her mind, she was always inspecting him from a height. The air between them was at once clear and impenetrable. Diamond-bright, diamond-hard: it characterized her manner with the boy. Among a set that valued astringency in human relations, her style passed as good form.

In those first months at Lokugama her dreams were of landscapes where the boundary between earth and water was blurred. She began each day charged with the promise of mutability. At night she walked beside waves or was carried on slow river currents to a boat that lifted and fell and leaned to meet her. How could she not long for deliverance?

Yet a terrible jauntiness informed the notes she soon began composing. These were directed to friends who lived abroad: the Venetians, an Argentine industrialist, a stockbroker from Surrey, a Basque poet, a cluster of faded English civil servants. Within weeks she was writing compulsively, five or six bright, cloying letters a day. Colorful detail was her forte. She described *a troop of monkeys with sorrowful faces, speeding through the treetops*. She called up *manes of saffron-hued lantana*. Pride dictated that loneliness and despair, the companions on whom she closed her eyes every night, could never be cited. Instead, a blocked and stinking lavatory became *our preposterous plumbing*.

By the end of the third month it was plain her allowance wouldn't run to the postage. She borrowed two rupees from the bungalow keeper and went on writing. *I wish you could see this marvelous old place. My father-in-law had latticed ducts set in the floor to blow air up the skirts of dancing ladies*. Or: *I have been gorging myself on rambutans. Such fruit! Spiked scarlet globes the size of a hen's egg, split open with a thumbnail to yield segments of delectable white flesh*.

All routine offers consolation. The truism extends also to cliché, to the comfort found in worn patterns of words. If Maud wrote of bougainvillea it was unfailingly *rampant*. The jungle *teemed with life*. The scent of temple flowers *flooded the evening air*. Language was a net, ready knotted, in which to capture the formless insistence of the world around her: to hold it still and render it legible.

Rain fell. When it stopped, thousands of wings filled the house. The insects flew into Maud's nostrils and beat in her ears. They drowned in a sauceboat. They seethed on her plate, shedding wings. They clotted every surface with their corpses. Half an hour later she seized a pen and wrote: *Never imagine that it is dull here. A continuous wave of squirrels, bats, hens, lizards, frogs, ants, wasps, beetles and crickets washes through this house. This morning brought the novel diversion of a swarm of winged termites*.

It was not her intention to deceive. There is an old instinct, at work in bordellos and the relations of East and West, to convert the unbearable into the picturesque. It enables a sordid existence to be endured, on one side, and witnessed, on the other, with something like equanimity. A visitor to Lokugama would have seen plaster that peeled like diseased skin, sagging rattan, the mildewy bloom of wood unpolished for decades. A horn at the gate would send Maud scuttling from the verandah, hissing for the bungalow keeper. That same evening she could sit at the dining table, its scratched varnish sticky along her bare arms, and evoke *the intoxicating scent of jasmine* or *the emerald flash of a parrot's wing*. The prose that thousands before her had applied like antiseptic to the island gushed from her nib. Rats thundered in the rafters. *Did you know*, she found herself writing, *that according to legend this was the Garden of Eden?*

In the weeks leading to the monsoon heat stacked up like yellow bricks. By afternoon all life was walled in. The sun was a ripe fruit, oozing toward collapse. Insects vanished, swallowed by the cracked earth. There were no birds.

Prickly heat, an affliction Maud thought she had discarded with the tedium of childhood, returned in angry lumps in the folds of her knees and elbows. Her nails left ribbons of skin in their wake. One morning dhobi itch had stamped its rosettes along the line of a collarbone. Sweat passing over the inflamed skin stung so painfully that she wept. This sweat was a further indignity: it poured down her flanks, broke out on her forehead, gathered in the intimate creases of her flesh. She would wake in the night to find a soaking sheet twisted about her hips.

From one day to the next her body became repellent to her. She became grateful for isolation, certain that she stank. Between breakfast and lunch she had doused a dozen handkerchiefs in eau de cologne and wiped herself down. She squandered a whole vial of orange water, upending it in her bath. The monsoon arrived and the weather cooled by three perceptible degrees, and still the clothes she put on when she rose were musky with sweat by eleven.

At last she sent Sirisena into town with a chit for the doctor. When he came, he heard out her symptoms and asked two questions. Then he fingered his tie, with his gaze averted, and named her condition. Maud was dumbfounded: it was so simple and so absolute. Accustomed to regard herself as singular, she was unprepared for this last proof of commonality with her sex.

The oak-framed cheval glass that had occupied a corner of her bedroom when she came to Lokugama as a bride had long since given way to an oblong of pocked mirror. Maud braced herself and let her housecoat fall. Then she took an inventory: twin purses of skin each with its warty stud, a little round loaf, a fistful of graying lichen. Below and above she had not the fortitude to venture.

For a week she craved gin, drunk neat. She had a need of clarity. Night after night, Claudia appeared in her dreams: gliding in and out of doorways in a long pale nightgown rocking a doll-like infant; or curled in her bed, a child herself, with a little silky cushion jammed between her knees.

Maud woke, stippled with sweat. She recognized the dream: its sequences had haunted her in the weeks after Claudia's death when she had lain in the nursing home with pneumonia. Later, when fever and the delirium it brought had cleared, and pain no longer scoured her lungs, the dream images, too, had faded.

Jaya had been her first visitor. The instant he loomed in the doorway, she asked a question consisting of a single word.

"I don't know." He advanced into the antiseptic space between them. "She was afraid there would be something wrong with the baby. But he was perfect. Perfect." His huge hands sketched a small shape. "One of those little crests of hair . . ." He sank onto a chair, and placed his palms over his face. In this way he avoided her eyes.

It was the only time they spoke of it. There was the disgrace of murder compounded with suicide, best smothered in silence; and then, Maud nurtured an explanation that she didn't care to voice. Her son-in-law was careless. She had warned him, in the first months of his marriage. "Ritzy and I had an understanding," she had said. "But don't imagine Claudia will put up with it. These girls today want the whole show." Then she handed him the battered little cardboard rectangle the dhobi had returned with the *mahatheya*'s shirts. The demure face of an old friend's wife smiled out from its scarring of creases.

Jaya had laughed the thing off. Nevertheless, she had jolted him into discretion. But Maud knew that old patterns have a way of asserting themselves. She pictured Claudia, nine months pregnant, opening a book and coming across a photograph. She saw the girl lifting the blotter on Jaya's desk and reading a letter she found there. There were pockets of pure anguish in her daughter. As a child, she had been shaken by bouts of baffling tears. An array of little fetishes, broken toys and household oddments, small unsightly items no one quite liked to touch, provided her with a queer kind of comfort at such moments. It was easy to imagine her overwhelmed by the discovery of her husband's faithlessness, swept along on a cold black current of despair. Watching Jaya weep beside a florist's arrangement of scentless blooms, Maud knew he was ravaged by the same suspicion. It was torment enough, she decided.

Now, thinking of the last terrible minutes of her daughter's life, she rose from her bed at Lokugama. She hunted out every carafe in the night-shadowed house and dashed them one by one against the tiles of the verandah. The act brought no release. At six in the morning Sirisena found her still sitting there, surrounded by broken glass. He was obliged to step gingerly when he returned with a broom. It was the kind of thing that did not occur to those who went about the world wearing shoes.

The postcard showed the Promenade des Anglais. *Bellissima, We are dying of envy. Here it is foul, the mistral all day and no one simpatico. Next week we sail for New York. Carlo kisses your ravishing hands, and so do I. Your loving Giulia*. Maud propped it against the Bakelite salt cellar while lunching on curried ash plantain. She had it by heart before she realized it carried no forwarding address.

Christmas brought a little loaf of envelopes, bland sentiments, cautious expressions of goodwill, a sheaf of impenetrable free verse from the poet. Sir Alban's card, robins and a wreath of holly, bore a handwritten addendum to its Compliments of the Season: *Took in a rather delightful Sapphic show yesterday. One of the girls long and brown, like you. Poor old Mulligatawny had to be put down in August. P.S. Charlotte died last spring*. The stockbroker sent two blunt lines asking her not to write. *It causes awkwardness at home*.

These communiqués barely registered with Maud. By then she was covering forty pages a day, epistles she rolled up and slipped into mildewing shoes or tucked behind a cushion and forgot. Her style grew daily wilder, more fabulous. Even a mildly attentive reader would have diagnosed a dislocation. In a country where night arrived with the haste of a curtain lowered on a flop, she insisted on *twilight*. While a monsoonal wind ripped a limb from the mango tree, she could write with no sense of incongruity of *spice-laden breezes*.

In the intervals between letters, she would rise from the dining table to drift in and out of rooms where no one had breathed for years. The absurd topography of the house had always eluded her. There was a step between two corridors that served no purpose except to make her stumble. She spent a morning in search of a room she remembered, a pleasant bay with a fern-filled alcove where Claudia had played the piano. Dust stirred and settled. Thwarted, Maud slammed the door on a mournful little cubicle at the end of a passage. Midstride she halted, retraced her steps. The Lindahl had stood there, under the window that memory had embellished with leaves and curved air.

Cockroaches, glossy as dates, fled from her slippers. She saw no one. Yet a presence walked with her. She stepped aside, to allow it space. It wished her no ill, but she felt the stir of its longing. What are ghosts but things we cannot bear to remember? Sometimes, on entering a room she was certain something had altered, a chair angled differently, a drawer pulled open. In the doorway of a shuttered room, one hand on the jamb, she knew that this scene had already occurred.

Meals occasioned small spears of anticipation that pierced the cottoned tedium of Leela's day. Her first dreamy thoughts, on not quite waking, were of improbable dishes, vanilla-scented poppadoms or trifle spiked with fennel. All day Soma went back and forth from the kitchen bearing fried breadfruit chips in a silver epergne or a rose-patterned plate piled with prawn crackers. There were mornings when the *nonamahatheya* devoured four pots of chocolate custard or a platter of fish patties. She ate jack *mallung* heaped on crackers. She kept a jar of pumpkin preserve at hand. In the concentration she brought to bear on flavors and textures, she discovered a kind of steadying. In those years her jaws worked nonstop.

On the morning of her twenty-sixth birthday she looked in her mirror and saw how flesh had accrued around her waist. She had thickened at the hips, like a candle. Layers of flesh blunted the line of her nose, the curve of her jaw. As she gazed at herself appalled, there was another face beside her own, a child's face with tumbled black curls. It vanished in an instant. When the knocking in her chest quieted she set a chair in front of her glass and remained there all day.

The incident marked a turning point. Independently of her volition, the grinding mechanism of survival intervened. One day she woke up and the armor welded around her chest had vanished. It no longer hurt to breathe.

Her days gravitated toward the angle of a side verandah, screened with waist-high trellis. On this ambiguous site neither inside nor outside the house, she created a bower. It contained a rattan-seat planter's chair piled with kapok cushions, a velvet footstool, her porcupine-quill workbox and a palm-leaf fan edged with tortoiseshell. Pots grouped by her chair held mother-in-law's tongue and philodendron. Maidenhair spilt from coir-lined hanging baskets. Sam, coming upon her there one morning as she sat with folded hands in watery green light, thought of a slug clamped moistly to its leaf, and shuddered, and went away without a word.

Months passed. Leela nibbled iced biscuits from a tin and watched a monsoon demonstrate its architecture of rain. Gray-green growths that crumbled to the touch appeared in the interstices of the trelliswork. Garments arrayed on a clotheshorse remained clammy for a week. Sliding into her shoe, her toes encountered a webbed dampness: spores that had burst into vegetable being in the interval of an hour.

She woke from a doze one afternoon and sensed the scrutiny of small bright eyes. She tracked them to a frieze of geckos with translucent veined stomachs on the side of a pillar. Her stillness attracted birds, chameleons, the little squirrels whose striped backs showed where they had been stroked by a god's fingers. A pale stucco mansion took shape on a cornice, the wasps ignoring her as they flew in and out of their nest. A tailor bird took hold of two leaves at the extremity of a slender twig and sewed them together at their edges, using a thread made of vegetable fiber and its bill for a needle. For days it flew back and forth from the shoeflower tree that grew by the verandah, tiny feathers and scraps of cottony down protruding from its beak. These the bird pushed between the two leaves it had stitched together, while its perch swayed under its feet. It had chosen the thinnest twig in order to protect its young from snakes and other predators. Leela watched the leaf nest quiver and spin with each breeze, and envied the bird inside, rocking in soft darkness, with small hearts beating beneath her wing.

In the early years of Maud's marriage the house at Lokugama had not been connected to the municipal water supply. She could remember an era when a servant staggered between the kitchen well and her bathroom, a bucket at either end of the pole slung across his shoulders. Later, in the grip of one of his ruinous schemes, Henry called in a Manchester firm to do the plumbing. In Maud's bathroom a dado of bottle-green tiles stretched around the walls beneath a band of stylized pink tulips. The thick copper piping, now dripping verdigris, still functioned to capacity, filling the massive bath in one hundred and twelve seconds.

Twice a day she would mount the shallow teak steps beside the tub and lower herself, inch by voluptuous inch, into the water. There was a whiff of mud, not unpleasant, about Lokugama water; sometimes it contained a leaf, once a tiny transparent snail. But in less than ten minutes it was a clammy chemise that adhered to her skin. The taps affixed to the tub were beautiful, brass and green-glazed majolica, each topped with a smiling dolphin. Maud fell into the habit of addressing them, cursing the tepid bathwater and her own greed, for she had smoked the last Players in her morning ration of twelve well before that hour.

Soon she was talking to everything, the earthenware goblet with a beaded lace cover in which boiled water was stored, a brown asparagus fern crisped in a blue luster bowl. There came an evening when she began one of her screeds, conjured *a silvery downpour* halfway down the sixth page and in midsentence abandoned the enterprise forever.

Her voice flowed out to occupy the space that the letters had filled. It went on and on. She sang "Lead, kindly Light" and rugby choruses of elaborate obscenity. She conducted baroque conversations with herself, scrolls and whorls of defense and recrimination. When she fell silent her ears filled with an awful clamor, a muttering that crescendoed to screeches and fell away as keening. Maud identified it as the racket of a million microscopic jaws, the scraping of antennae, the whirr of wings, the striving of worms, the march of long, golden millipedes, all the life she had called silence and disregarded. There were nights when jackals howled as they swept past on their hunt, their screams ceasing abruptly at the highest pitch of ferocity. Their noise was terrible, their silence worse. Yet the other was more ghastly still. She lay under her mosquito net chanting "The Charge of the Light Brigade" to drown out its claims.

At the far end of the house, Padma, with her husband deep inside her, heard the pitch and fall of that recital. The servants' room was pungent with coconut oil. On a tea chest draped with a length of eau-de-Nil satin that had once been a pajama leg, a lamp glowed before an eight-inch plaster statue of the Virgin: a wedding gift from the nuns. At some point on their tossing voyage from Liverpool six hundred shoddily stowed madonnas had suffered fractured halos and chipped hands. When the crate was levered open in Colombo a shrewd bishop converted pecuniary disappointment into the conviction that deserving orphans the island over would see only the gorgeousness of gold paint, the horizon-blue sweep of that mantle.

The pair laboring in the room knew they were envied. They ate rice twice a day, they had a tiled roof over their heads, the work of caring for an old woman and a dilapidated house could not be described as arduous. Yet long after the shadows rearing on the wall beside her had quieted, Padma lay sleepless. This was the compass of it, rotting in the jungle with those cracked tones invading her skull. She knew the place was *moospainthu*. It blighted her cooking. Curries emerged from that kitchen as bland as milk, or so fiery they drew tears. Sauces refused to thicken. A jungle fowl simmered for two hours ended as bone wound with glutinous string. Liquids evaporated or boiled over as soon as she glanced away. Even dishes that seemed faultless when eaten returned to the back of the throat as a putrid tang.

Her husband scoffed at her talk of enchantment. He passed freely through the house, untroubled by its humors. There were seasons when Padma saw milky molecules coalesce on a verandah or gather in a doorway. The contrast between light and shade was more violently marked at these times. Forms sharpened, a table or pillar taking on an etched distinctiveness, the world waxing resolute in the face of an encroachment. Sirisena noticed nothing. Padma kept to the kitchen, where a stew ruined inexplicably. She crossed herself. In the enclosure where chickens pecked she scraped charred flesh from the pot, her nostrils flaring against the crusty stench.

There was a snake coiled on Maud's pillow. She shouted and sprang away, but when Sirisena came running in it was only her housecoat, a careless twist of chiffon. The lid of a tureen became a mirror that reflected everything except her face. She reached for a cake of gardenia soap and found it fringed with fish hooks. There was also a bird, feathered brown and dusty purple, perched on a brass curtain rod or stepping along the back of a chair; or, horribly, gazing up at her, a prickle of claws along her instep.

At the far end of an empty verandah, a child slid into view. His arms were folded over an object he clutched to his chest but his face was in shadow. She took half a step forward and he wasn't there. But what set her heart knocking was the certainty, sudden as a blow, that something essential had eluded her.

The place itself eroded the distinction between perception and hallucination. It hung a devil mask in a flamboyante tree, a bold gray langur monkey whose mocking face presided over the drive. It impaled a turquoise rag on a twig and then, when Maud reached for it, bewitched by that brilliance, slipped a rotting wing into her fingers. Nothing was as it seemed. Nothing stayed the same. Flowers staged brief, violent dramas, blazing and dropping within the day. A cloud burst and sticks exploded into tender green leaves. A scratch on the bungalow keeper's heel blossomed overnight, unfolding petals of yellow pus. Maud turned her head away from a bloated pi dog that lay stinking by the roadside, held fast in a trembling mesh of red ants; an hour later it had been picked clean of all corruption.

The alchemy of change, hostile to all patterning, worked with dizzying swiftness. The carter who carried away the nightsoil from the servants' lavatory was always accompanied by his daughter, a capering four-year-old in a filthy pink skirt. One morning the little girl was not there. Her father wept by the kitchen door, relating how the child, usually as robust as a coconut, had complained of a stiff neck the previous afternoon and was dead by nightfall. For the first time in Maud's life there was nothing to distract her from these mutations. They induced nausea, like lines of print held too close to the eye. It was a matter of perspective. Trying to adjust itself, her mind swung a little loose on its hinges.

Looking back on those months, she would picture them marbled with lunacy. She continued to observe the rituals that keep a life from fraying, but observed them oddly, a bath lit with candles at midnight, a table set under the mango tree at four in the afternoon. Ordinary things, some ugly, entranced her. She might turn a spoon in her hands for hours, as if to discover its function or marvel at its perfection. She studied the small jeweled flies that settled on the slice of papaw before her and made no motion to disturb their feeding. For two or three days at a stretch her mind would be inhabited by a detailed eroticism, bright lewd images succeeding each other swiftly like postcards thumbed to excite desire: the bungalow keeper naked and priapic before her, her cousin Iris stroking a faceless girl who knelt between her thighs.

It was an interval of heightened, almost painful sensations. Objects she had handled unthinkingly—a towel, a nail file—turned velvety and repulsive to the touch. Colors flared more forcefully, and translated themselves into flavors, the blue-black of a crow experienced as a thick plummy sweetness, the scarlet of canna rising in her nose like mustard. The place would not be reduced to background. It cast nets of leaves about her. It caressed her arms with its warm yellow tongue.

Madness seemed as inviting as cool sheets. She spent an afternoon crouching in her almirah, among the discarded skins of her evening gowns. After a while the conviction came to her that this finery should not be left to rot in the dark. The next morning she trod the length of the verandah in bare feet and midnight-blue lace. Sam found her glittery-eyed in a carapace of bronze beading, her greasy playing cards fanned out before her. He caught a whiff of spice. She turned her head and he saw that she had inserted a clove in each earlobe in lieu of a jewel.

He had opened his mouth to inform her that she had stepped over a boundary, when she rose from her chair. Even barefoot she was taller by half a head. He tightened his lips, carried his bouquet of chits to his room, slipped the car into gear while the sky was still dim the next morning.

When the doctor confirmed what Leela already knew, she registered only the dull anticipation that her condition now aroused in her. But this time she began each day vomiting into a blue-rimmed enamel basin. It went on for hour after hour. There was a respite in the afternoon, when she trembled with exhaustion on her bed, a hummock of feeble flesh with a handkerchief soaked in eau de cologne across her temples. Shark cooked in a white curry that contains fenugreek seeds encourages the flow of a woman's milk, so she forced herself to swallow a few spoonfuls with rice each day. *Nivithi sambol* too was prepared daily, as spinach develops a baby's brain. Then Soma was holding the *nonamahatheya*'s head over the basin again. Four months later when the vomiting ended, the child had still not dislodged itself.

There was a prickling sensation, like pins and needles, running along Leela's arms. She realized it was hope, exercising itself with the caution of a limb grown numb from disuse.

The first time, she had sewn and embroidered dozens of baby shirts in graded sizes. Also bibs and satin-stitched pillow slips, and bath sheets with yellow ducks appliquéd along the borders. One day she opened a chest that had remained padlocked for years and folded back layers of tissue paper. Soma, padding in with her broom, found the *nonama-*

hatheya surrounded by scraps of lace and lawn and cotton. Leela held up an exquisite little shirt, white shantung with blue smocking at the yoke and wrists, for the girl to admire. But Soma recoiled. Here was the source of the evil, she declared, in her slow, flat voice, these ghost babies hungry for life and sucking it out of her mistress. Their presence in the house was *moospainthu*.

The next day Tissa sent his boy to the kitchen door to say there were two Rodi women at the gate. Buddhists shunned contact with the Rodiya, considering them unclean; yet they made their living by begging and were rarely turned away from a house. They were believed to possess second sight and the evil eye, and it was judged unwise to cross them.

Usually it fell to Tissa's boy to deposit food and coins in their trowel-shaped bowls, which he was careful not to touch. That afternoon the *nonamahatheya* herself came out of the house, carrying boiled rice, curried bitter gourd, salt fish and a rustling parcel done up in brown paper. The Rodi women under the jacaranda watched in silence as the bulky figure crossed the lawn, an ungainly woman rendered clumsier by pregnancy. Approaching those emaciated effigies, with sweat pooling under her breasts, Leela was aware of how much space she occupied in the world.

In a mud-colored sling across her chest one of the beggars carried a baby with yellow crusts along its eyes. It was to this woman that Leela presented her parcel. At that, the other Rodiya seized her hand, turned it over, ran the ball of her thumb hard across Leela's palm. "The child will be a boy," she said. "Healthy, strong. There is nothing to fear."

She was turning away from them when the woman with the baby spoke. "The first one will come for you before your son's milk teeth have fallen."

One evening the lights dipped and flickered. Then they went out. That in itself was not unusual; the supply of electricity to Lokugama was at best unreliable. But then a woman screamed from the rear of the house: a drawn-out wail followed by three strangulated notes. Frozen on the verandah, Maud thought, Sirisena has murdered his wife. Now he will come after me.

After an eternity dull footsteps approached. The bungalow keeper carried a candle stuck to a saucer. Maud looked at his hands, club-thumbed and blunt-edged, and hoped it would be over quickly.

He said, "*Nonamahatheya*, dinner is served."

Afterward, when he was clearing the table, she asked, "Who was that woman screaming at the back?"

"That was the devil-bird."

At once her mind was brushed with purple and brown feathers, a curved beak waiting for the moment her attention faltered. But Sirisena went on talking. "In our village they say there was a woman whose husband killed her because he suspected the child she was carrying was not his. He buried her body with the child still alive inside her. Now she roams the jungle at night, and from time to time she cries out to warn another woman of violent death."

She asked what this bird looked like.

He shook his head. "No one has ever seen it. But it cries, *Magai lamaya ko? Magai lamaya ko?*"

"Where is my child."

He said, "These are only stories."

A week later he returned from market bringing news of a girl who had been discovered in a jungle grave with her throat cut. The police sergeant had put his boot on the corpse of a chameleon that lay nearby. "That's the mark of the devil-bird. It always leaves a dead lizard to show that it passed."

At times Maud was convinced that the walls pressed about her, a ceiling lower than she recalled, a corridor narrowing at her step. Yet the house was emptier than it had ever been. As a girl, she had passed through its overstuffed rooms and understood at once what she was witnessing: the delusion that, given an adequate weight of chesterfields and candelabra, sufficient swathes of linen and plum-red velvet, domesticity would prevail in that setting. In certain moods she had been apt to see the illogic of Sir Stanley's architecture as expressing a fundamental dissonance between the bones of order that held the household rigidly upright and the decay at work everywhere under that roof.

It was a sentiment that had overwhelmed her one evening, in the third year of her marriage, halfway through one of her famous cold buffet suppers: such a waste of endeavor, this pitting of talk and jellied venison against the soft snarl of the jungle. She set down her glass. Twenty yards from the gate, lamplight and braided music and embroidered satin shoes might never have existed.

Now, as she trailed her own footprints in and out of rooms, Maud thought how greatly the house had improved since Sam had stripped it. A tension had seeped from its shell, dissipating through yawning boards and cracked panes. She lingered in an echoing chamber that bats had colonized one year; although it had been scraped clean of excrement, the smell was still bad. Yet the sullen resentment that used to sour the breath of the place was gone.

She flipped a little nipple and shadows rolled into corners. But electricity in that house cast a weak, grayish light. It suggested something haggard waiting just beyond its reach.

The bird with the dragging, purple wings no longer tormented her. Instead, footsteps sounded along the verandah, a dry pattering as of grains spilling from a sack. Maud thought of the child she had glimpsed with his arms folded to his chest. She told herself he was a creature concocted by her brain, a thing of addled chemistry. Nevertheless she lay awake at night, listening. Something was sobbing on the other side of the wall. Years before, when she herself was still a girl, one of her children had died in that room. Her lips framed a soundless question: *Magai lamaya ko? Magai lamaya ko?*

In the weeks following Leo's death Maud had willed herself not to think of him. It was not, after all, so difficult. He had spent only two hundred days in the world. She slept fourteen hours a night, having swallowed the powders prescribed for her. Later, when she allowed herself to remember him—on the anniversary of his birth, or death—she found that the baby was no longer himself but a cluster of sensations associated with him: sadness, a vague odor of cloves, the crimson and ivory upholstery of the Panhard his father had bought soon after he was born. Now, precise images of Leo's flesh flowed through her mind: a kinked toe on his left foot, the downy sphere of his skull. His clean pink yawn. "Little lion," she said, and blew onto his scalp. "Little beast." He batted the air above his chest.

Maud was not a woman who thrilled to babies. She handed her newborns over to an ayah, and took off for a week's shooting as soon as she could. But Leo had exercised power over her. She found excuses to keep him in Colombo: he was mildly jaundiced at birth, there was the to-do of his christening, then Claudia went down with measles and to install the baby at Lokugama with the other children was to risk infection. It was not that her days orbited around the infant. The Kaiser's second cousin visited the island a month after Leo was born, and Ritzy gave him a magnificent hunt in the hills near Hatton. It was the event of the year. Leo was left in Colombo for the nine days of its duration. No one thought anything of it: it was an era when children were in plentiful supply, and therefore accorded neither influence nor status. On the last evening in camp Maud hacked off an aide's curls with her hunting knife, after which he was ducked in a jungle pool for a breach of form. People would talk about it for years. She was dazzling that night and she never once thought of Leo. Even after she had returned to Colombo, whole days might pass when she saw the baby for five minutes or not at all. Nevertheless an invisible cord ran between them. Now and then each tweaked it, testing.

She could remember her surprise when Ritzy suggested spending a few days at Lokugama. Her husband loved the place, yet usually shunned it. "Because you can't lose money fast enough there," Maud would say, the charge teasing at first but growing vinegary over time. He admitted it straight away: one of the infuriating things about Ritzy was that their rows were wholly one-sided.

He was a charming, jug- eared man. He adored Maud. She had been married to him for six weeks before it dawned on her that he adored everyone: his lardy cousin Sybil who sang hymns at birthday parties, the one-eyed gram seller who squatted by a culvert in Sea Street behind her basins of deviled pulses. The impartiality of his affection was maddening. Maud flaunted conquests, dangling her desirability before his eyes. It was useless; he knew nothing of jealousy. He kept a florist in a flat in Bambalapitiya, a liaison that pre-dated his marriage. Well-wishers hastened to apprise his nineteen-year-old bride of the arrangement. Maud opened the Obeysekere Bible to the family chronicle recorded at the back and dragged a heavy black line through the details of her marriage. *A hideous mistake*, she wrote above it.

"But what can I do, old thing?" said Ritzy. "Jilt poor Nesta?" He swore it had been years since the florist and he did anything but play cards with her wheelchair-bound mother. "Rummy with Mummy. What's the harm?"

In the end Maud believed him. The only lies he told involved horseflesh. "Ritzy doesn't keep his flowery little friend for plucking and whatnot," she declared to confidantes. "She's just another way he can waste money." The setup in Bambalapitiya persisted until the day an Afghan moneylender's ultimatum obliged Ritzy to choose between Nesta Buultjens and a quarter share in an Irish colt, after which nothing more was ever heard of her.

That was something else Maud understood in time: her husband's pliancy was threaded with steel. He endowed a lying-in hospital for women who gave birth on the Lokugama estates, and paid a benefit to the families of workers who fell ill; yet one of the laborers, a man of low caste, found himself sacked on the spot for not removing his shirt on entering his employer's compound. Ritzy's voice quavered as he recounted the tale, but that he might have acted otherwise never occurred to him.

Lokugama drew and focused his inflexibility. He could not imagine, for instance, that his children might live with their parents in Colombo. "Lokugama is where we come from. Sam and Claudia belong there." It suited Maud well enough. There was a relentlessness to small children. Their needs glided with frightening rapidity into demands; she experienced their wants like so many sticky little hands dragging at her skirts. All the same, the implacability of her husband's ruling exasperated her. It was years before she realized the significance Lokugama held for him, and then it was a thing intuited. The British had entered the country's bloodstream like a malady which proves so resistant that the host organism adapts itself to accommodate it. Ritzy, who openly declared that he found nationalists a bore, felt no dissatisfaction with colonial rule. But in a part of the island where Europeans had held power for over three hundred years, Lokugama was still a symbol of his people's enduring worth; it represented a different order, thought Maud, an older, organic world.

Like all mythic sites it was of course best not frequented.

Nevertheless, when Leo was six months old, it was Ritzy who proposed a visit to Lokugama. It was time the children got to know their brother, he said. But Leo's ayah, informed of the excursion, played the merry devil at the idea of getting into a car, imploring the *hamuduruwo* and *nonamahatheya* on her knees. So she was packed off on the early train, with the baby.

Afterward Maud would remember how they had dawdled that day. They rose late. Then Sybil arrived and settled herself on a leather ottoman with her ankles crossed. Over the next hour she told them about a journey she had made to China, where she had been crucified for her faith. "But I didn't mind. They ravished me first, you see. *Most* interesting." Ritzy sat beside her, refreshing her ginger beer and ignoring his wife's frowns. Then the Panhard refused to start. When they finally did get away, they were held up at a level crossing where the barrier was down because a bullock had been knifed in a brawl between two carters twenty yards down the track. At the Lokugama turnoff they decided to detour into the town for cocktails at the Oriental. The sun had set when they finally turned into the driveway, half a bottle of champagne wedged between Maud's shoes. They were met by the blaze of too many lamps and the silhouette of a buggy crouching before the verandah.

Old Dr. van Dort was waiting at the top of the steps. He came forward and folded her hand in his cold fingers. "Now you must be a brave girl." The baby had been found dead in his cot, he said. Maud wondered briefly why a man of his age had taken it into his head to play the fool. He was clinging to her hand with such force that her rings bit into her flesh. Then Leo's ayah ran out onto the verandah with her hair streaming and threw herself at the *hamuduruwo*'s feet.

A lifetime later Maud prowled the corridors of Lokugama repeating the doctor's words: "You must try not to distress yourself, the poor little chap just fell asleep and didn't wake up." She tried singing it. She essayed different keys, experimented with ragtime and blues. She reeled past the courtyard in a flurry of tulle, pushed open the door of the room next to hers. "Don't distress yourself now, girl," she bawled. "Poor lil' man just done fell fast a-sleeeep."

Before Dr. van Dort left he had dosed her on brandy mixed with something that tasted funny. Leo's round head lay on the sleeve of her new yellow traveling costume. She counted five silk-covered buttons running up from her wrist, while the moon dangled over the trees like a broken fingernail. A rasping noise went on and on. She heard it plainly. It was the sound of her breath when they pried him away from her; but that was one of the things she failed to understand.

Very early each morning, before the sun sprang over the horizon spoiling for a fight, it became Maud's habit to walk the four miles that led from the house to the junction with the trunk road. On one side of the Lokugama road, the jungle reached deep into the hinterland. Along the other lay the old Obeysekere estates, now divided between three absentee landlords. The coconut plantations spread almost to the crossroads, where a few thatched huts and a tea boutique squatted beside a paddy field. She bought her cigarettes at the boutique and lit the first one from the smoldering rope that dangled beside the entrance. Sitting on a culvert with her knees apart, she exhaled blue smoke roses. Five exquisite minutes passed.

The *kadai* owner rested his elbows on the plank that served him as a counter. Maud was wearing a dress that reached to her ankles, grass-green georgette bedraggled around the hem, and her rubber slippers. The spectacle of her degradation gave focus to a delirium he improvised upon a cross-eyed Malay girl on the last Thursday of each month. When the old woman walked away he spat very accurately, a scarlet betel jet that arced to earth an inch short of that green skirt.

One morning, on her way back to the house, Maud halted beside a track that cut through an apron of scrub and vanished into the jungle. The sun had only just burst above the trees but ferocity was already shimmering along the rutted dirt ahead. She looked away, toward the shade. It was one of those merciful intervals when the jungle cacophony had muted to a seashell murmur. She crossed the scrub and walked a little way into the trees, hearing the thwap of her slippers. Her narrow eyes turned this way and that. The jungle hummed with small flies that settled at once on her arms. Vines put out green claws to rake her hair. But the monumental canopy was not as dense as it appeared from the road. Leaf shadows lay along her path, and in between them, leaves of light.

Her father, a bony, vivid man with a taste for women and morphine, had drowned in the rip off Trincomalee on Maud's sixteenth birthday. Dr. Rajaratne's wife had imagined that she was avenging herself on him by succumbing to puerperal fever three days after their child was born. Her death was in fact a relief to her husband, who was as ill suited to discretion as to the infliction of pain. He had wanted a son but was accustomed to disappointment. He taught Maud to bowl and shoot, how to dock a pointer's tail, the correct way to skin a leopard.

She was twelve when she claimed her first trophy, a gray wanderoo. As soon as she swung the slim Maynard rifle skyward the silence exploded with guttural shrieks, *wah-wah-wah*, and the troop, some ten or twelve monkeys, was off through the treetops. But she was lucky. A large male convulsed, clutched at the surrounding branches, then fell ninety feet through space with outstretched limbs. It thudded to earth almost at the girl's feet. She had thought every bone in the big body would be broken but on examining the corpse detected only a snapped femur. Her bullet had ripped through the flesh of its left shoulder. It was quite dead.

Hunting expeditions, in Maud's experience, were tremendous affairs, orchestrated with the obsessive precision of campaigns. Cooks, porters, trackers, trappers, game bearers and dog handlers set out days in advance. When the hunting party arrived in camp, a makeshift compound awaited them: sleeping and cooking huts, a storehouse, latrines, shelters for the dogs and the servants.

After she married it had fallen to Maud to compile the foolscap lists of provisions required for a shoot, checking the stores on the morning the advance party was due to leave, a satisfying line drawn through each item with a red crayon. Now, wandering through the jungle at Lokugama, she chanted those lists aloud from memory. Three bags of flour, twelve pounds of sugar, two pounds of tea and three of coffee, tins of jam, butter, ham, sardines, mackerel, meat paste and crackers, table salt, chilies, curry stuffs, coconuts, limes, fifteen gunnysacks of rice, two sacks of orange lentils, ten pounds of potatoes, two tins of dripping, three jars of Crosse & Blackwell pickles, a dozen slabs of chocolate, a dozen tins of Ideal milk, a flask of brandy, eighteen bottles of whiskey, two dozen of arrack (for the servants), sundry bundles of tobacco (ditto). The trackers and bearers had to provide their own food, bought with money advanced for the purpose; about this it was necessary to be firm. "Lanterns, matches, candles, kerosene oil, a soiled-linen bag, a coconut scraper," sang Maud. "Saucepans, frying pans, ladles, knives, a knife board, cutlery, plates, mugs, camp stools, ropes, nails, an axe, soap, towels, bedding, butter, muslin netting, citronella oil, quinine, potassium permanganate, aspirin, Burnol, bandages, a tin cutter, Ritzy's blasted ukulele." Four pounds of coarse salt and four of alum for preserving skins. A spare toothbrush. Half a dozen bottles of brown rum for a never-neglected, last-night ritual under the stars. The fine calibration of these provisions was a matter of pride with her. She had been known to breakfast on curried sardines and woodapple jam on the morning they struck camp, determined that no surplus would mar the elegance of her calculations.

It occurred to Maud, weeks after she first ventured into the trees, that the jungle where she now walked every day was the first she had entered alone and unarmed. The realization brought her to a halt. She pondered it with the aid of a cigarette taken from the grubby sequined evening bag that swung from her wrist. After a while she decided that to have been granted a different perspective, at her age, was no small thing.

She plucked a frond from a fern growing by the track. It was a game children played. You placed the leaf on the inside of your arm, on the silky skin below the elbow, then pressed down hard. When you took the frond away, a silvery tattoo remained stamped on your flesh.

It served as the seal on a vow Maud made to the gods of the place: to live with, instead of against, whatever they demanded of her. She put her head back and cursed her clumsy shoes and attempted a waltz. One hundred and twenty feet overhead, the winking leaves spun with her.

The dhobi returned her batiste nightdress folded like a moth, the pin-tucks on the yoke exquisitely smoothed. Two nights later when she lifted it from a drawer, Maud discovered the brown hoofprint of an iron scorched into the back of the garment.

No one guards against trivial losses, which is why they lodge directly in the heart. Maud sat on her bed, the ruined nightdress across her knees, and looked about her. What she saw was an angled space that had sheltered her as a child, a secret place formed by the junction of two walls and a rattan-backed settee draped with a leopard skin. One morning she peered through the rattan and saw her father's mustache graze a lady's hand. The kiss was not unusual but the lady was. Ada Thornton, scrubbed, dish-faced, as incongruous in Dr. Rajaratne's catalog of conquests as a toad in a bed of carnations. At the brush of his lips she flushed a fierce, painful scarlet. Seconds later the air had turned foul. Within days Maud would realize that the stirring of Thornton's emotions could always be counted on to trigger her flatulence.

Everything about the new governess was soft, her voice, her round blue eyes, her touch on the piano, most of all her heart. She melted and spread, a toffee left in the sun. When a terrier suspected of rabies had to be shot, Thornton dug the grave herself and folded her good crepe blouse about the body. Four sets of girls had outgrown her like gingham. She gave love, because she could not do otherwise, but suffered no illusion of being loved in return. She knew she was ridiculous. Her hair was the color of a mirror and still she thrilled to the world, its brutality and extravagance.

From Thornton, who had been in the colony for only thirty months, Maud learned to rub the dogs with *kohamba* oil as a specific against fleas. The wood of the tree was much prized for bookcases, said Thornton, as silverfish were repelled by its aroma. She picked the yellow flowers of the *ranawara* bush, dried them in the sun and brewed them into a tea that she drank twice a day. "*Cassia auriculata*. Excellent for purifying the blood."

Dr. Rajaratne, Edinburgh trained, was skeptical. When a villager was carried into his surgery, he sent for Thornton. Six weeks earlier, the man's arm had been clawed by a bear, the flesh ripped away between shoulder and elbow. A fool had packed the wound with dung. "Miss Thornton, this is what advanced gangrene looks like," said Dr. Rajaratne. He was a kind man. He had seen Europeans come unstuck. There was the German surveyor who had taken up abode in a cave in the jungle in order to eat berries and practice chanting; he wore a saffron robe and died of malnutrition. Dr. Rajaratne wanted the governess to see ancient wisdom for what it was: superstition and a terrifying ignorance of hygiene.

But he was mistaken about her. Where knowledge was at stake, it was not romanticism that propelled Thornton but a steely curiosity. She asked questions: what was *chunam*? how many yards of cloth went into a sarong? what measures was the government taking to combat rinderpest? That she conducted her enquiries among villagers as well as educated people was disconcerting. It led Dr. Rajaratne to misdiagnose as sentimentality what was in fact an instinct for impartiality. In the purest sense she was the better scientist of the two.

Thornton insisted on a sisal hat and white cotton gloves, and when Maud was thus attired grasped her hand and led her half a mile to the paddy fields on the edge of their outstation town. They watched women winnowing rice, tossing it into the air from flat baskets. A buffalo with corrugated flanks waited with terrible patience to be led to the threshing floor where beasts trod the grains from the straw.

Padda boats with thatched roofs slipped along the river. To Maud, the gentle reek that enveloped this part of the town was an unremarkable fact, like the cast in the servant-boy's eye or the warty skin of a custard apple. It was Thornton, craning over a parapet, who pointed out that the stench rose from the coconut branches and husks rotting in the water until they had decayed sufficiently to be beaten for fiber.

Among the things Maud knew were her times tables and the 23rd Psalm. She knew Arthur's knights and Alfred's cakes. Education, in her experience, involved books. That the world around her merited her attention was a novel idea. Conservative as only a seven-year-old can be, she regarded it with mistrust.

Throughout the years they spent together Thornton would unleash contradictory sentiments in Maud. One evening she saw the governess, believing herself unobserved, retrieve one of the doctor's shirts from the dirty clothes basket, and sniff at it with her eyes closed. This was at once thrilling and ludicrous. Dr. Rajaratne, cognizant of the poor creature's suffering, exploited it with aplomb. He suggested, for instance, that she take charge of the surgery accounts. "Dear Miss Thornton, you have such exquisite penmanship," he sighed, bending so close over the ledger that their shoulders brushed, with the result that the air turned noxious and Thornton sat up long after the household had retired, trying to reconcile columns of unreconcilable figures.

When the servants went home to their villages for Sinhalese New Year, Thornton cooked and scrubbed and swept the leaves from the drive with an *ekel* broom. She herself was entitled to half a day off a week and one full day each month, but the notion was theoretical. Every now and then Dr. Rajaratne overlooked the matter of her wages. Yet he always addressed her with kindness and courtesy, and was mindful to ensure that she was out of earshot when he whistled "The Lass with the Delicate Air," winking at Maud as the child writhed in her chair with laughter.

Here is a curious anomaly. Humility, unselfishness, devotion are qualities that scarcely affect us. Are they not our due? But a mole studding a cheek, a hat pinned at an unfortunate slant, a weakness for china kittens or prints of dying cottagers, these things grate our nerves raw. A trick Thornton had of peering at objects with her chin just slightly lifted had the ability to enrage Maud. At the bottom of the garden she mimicked the Englishwoman's stance, and stumped flat-footed in circles glaring at ripening guavas. As an exorcism it was a fiasco. There continued to be moments when the mere sight of Thornton acted on her as the shriek of fingernails on a blackboard.

It was above all the governess's infatuation with Dr. Rajaratne that his daughter could not bear. As Maud grew out of childhood, Thornton's unassuming slavery of the heart worked on her acutely. Like the governess's flatulence it could be broached only in comic terms, and then never to her face. Compassion struggled in Maud; uselessly, like a puppy in a sack. The changes in her body made her ruthless in all that concerned an eroticism she was ruled by but could not articulate.

Around this time a Mrs. de Zilva was a frequent caller at the surgery. Scented, parasoled, gorgeously female, she invited Maud to spend the day at her house. The girl returned with a Kandyan silver bangle, an enameled powder compact, a new way to arrange her hair. Some months previously she had come across a book in a case her father had forgotten to lock and learned much from its illustrations. The nature of his relations with her new friend was more or less plain to her. Dr. Rajaratne being the pole of her own fixations, Maud might well have resented Mrs. de Zilva. Instead, she was mesmerized. Charmaine this, Charmaine that. The name was always on her tongue. Simultaneously, her irritation with Thornton grew as unbearable as lace that pricks under the arms. It was a reaction not unmixed with self-protection. Thornton was the crow with stiff wings nailed to a tree. The girl cawed and wheeled away.

Snooping through the governess's room, Maud grew furious at the discovery of a broken cuff link with her father's monogram secreted in a handkerchief case. She hurled the glittering little object through the bars of the window and saw it swallowed by leaves. At lunch she stared at Thornton and complimented her father on his new onyx links. The governess turned scarlet. Wind seeped noiselessly from her. Maud shot meaningful smiles at her father until Thornton intercepted one of them. The tormented thing lowered her head. Her fork clattered on her plate. Maud hated herself. She dug her nails into the back of her wrist and spoke loudly, brightly: "Daddy! Can you please tell Piyadasa not to bring durians home from the market? They stink like anything." In her room she threw herself face down on her coverlet and wept. How could she have said such a thing? She was vile.

When she rose, she twisted up her hair and fastened it in place with a tortoiseshell comb. She admired her ears, set so sweetly on her head. Her reflection was dazzling. The swell of her breasts delectable. She was giddy with power. Already men's eyes slid sideways at her. Thornton was a fool. It was her own fault that people laughed at her. She invited humiliation. I shall never be like that, vowed Maud, stroking the mulberry length of her nipples. If I love a man, he will never know it. He will be my slave. Pictures of what she might command this slave to do flickered across her mind.

A week after Maud's thirteenth birthday, a letter came for Thornton. The aunt who had raised her had tripped over her cat and broken a hip. Duty rose plain as a cliff before Ada Thornton. It was essential to climb, and not think about the drop.

On the day before she sailed she called Maud to her room. The girl found her surrounded by piles of blued, shapeless undergarments. A trunk stood open against one wall. It contained old birthday greetings made by Maud, skeleton leaves glued crookedly to scraps of card; also seven china kittens. It was plain that Thornton did not possess the kind of mind that can pack.

The parcel she handed Maud rustled like dry wings. Within the folds of brittle, yellowing paper lay a snowy nightdress: old-fashioned, yet exquisite even to the girl's judgmental eye, each of its three dozen stitched button loops a tiny work of art. Maud stood before Thornton's looking glass, the nightdress flattened against her body. Her tongue slithered out to caress her upper lip. She was thinking that it would take a long time to undo those buttons; and how a man might be driven wild by the delay.

"I made it when I was not much older than you are," said Thornton's soft burr behind her. "But I never had an occasion to wear it."

That evening they drank Thornton's health in madeira wine. Maud presented the traveler with a coral brooch that had belonged to her mother. All week she had been gently attentive to Thornton, ensuring that the governess's favorite curries and *sambols* succeeded each other at mealtimes. For herself, she contemplated the parting with equanimity. Thornton belonged to her childhood. That her adult years would be lived in the new century was thrilling. On a visit to the capital she had witnessed the phenomenon of electricity. It was like being vouchsafed a vision of her future.

Dr. Rajaratne had retired to his room that night when there was a knock at the door. He gazed dreamy-eyed on Thornton. Her hair hung over her shoulders and she was clad in a dressing gown made of some eminently sensible material. When she released her grip on its folds, it opened on bare flesh. Dr. Rajaratne felt no alarm; the scene was consistent with the chemistry of the opiate in his veins.

"A vision," he said, recounting the incident to his apothecary, while Maud leaned against the wall by the open window. "Pukka flashing eyes and floating hair, like the chappie says."

The apothecary asked a question, lewd and to the point.

"My God, no," Maud heard her father say. There was a faint chink of glass. "But I think I touched something. Flabby. Like a pudding gone cold."

The eavesdropper strolled away, stretching her arms to the sun.

Half a century later, she was the single thread left of their knot. Thornton, her father, the apothecary, all gone. Even the nightdress, which might have outlasted the lot of them. I must have been mad to entrust it to the dhobi, thought Maud. But it was only the most recent mistake. She rose, and began to pace about the room; as if it might yet be possible to return to that place where everything first went wrong, and set out again, differently.

The child was named Henry, after his paternal grandfather. Leela had known all along that this would be the case but had secretly yearned for Quentin or Nigel, and had spent the last dreamy months of her confinement weaving epic adventures in which the boy fought injustice under a crimson banner and was hailed as a hero in banqueting halls. Then he arrived, furious and urgent, and she forgot everything except that she adored him. An indigo stain spread over the small of his back. That was the way with all newborns, they assured her, adding that the birthmark would vanish after a week. She wept at this intelligence, and pressed her lips to the puckered blue skin. He was perfect. She wanted to eat him.

She knew six years of happiness. Harry had a tortoise, two puppies, a pony, a tank of rainbow fish. The house was a tree, putting out fresh leaves, charged with birds; if it had motives of its own they were entirely benign. Children caroled from the swing on the lawn, or took flight along corridors like a shower of arrows. Her son swerved past her on the stairs. For a whole week he ran everywhere, arms outstretched, making a humming noise that threatened to drive the household mad.

The women who brought their children to play with Harry fell into conversation with his mother. To the usual noises of the house was added the ching of bangles sliding along arms. An only child in a household ruled by the gods of duty and abstinence, Leela had been a serious, self-conscious girl. Now, for a brief, delicious interval, she yielded to frivolity. There were shopping expeditions to the Fort. A morning was spent reviewing the merits of L'Heure Bleue and Chanel No 5. Samples of poplin or crepe de chine, fanning out with pinked edges from their cardboard backing, made their way from hand to hand. A length of rose moiré silk was draped about a torso, while Leela stood with her head angled, then stepped forward to pull the soft folds into a more artful arrangement. Her flair for design earned her a mild envy. The patterns she cut from newspaper brought compliments and outbursts of squabbling.

She was unused to admiration. It fizzed in her through afternoons tinted the pale gold of champagne. Meanwhile her husband continued to live his life as if she played no part in it. This had been the state of affairs between them for so long that she had ceased to expect anything else. But now a little tendril of vanity uncurled within her. She submitted to the exquisite torture of eyebrow plucking. A tortoiseshell shoehorn crammed her feet, which were broad and somewhat splayed, into crocodile-skin shoes strapped roguishly across the instep. She exchanged her lifeless garments for shaped bodices with lace inserts, and skirts that molded themselves around her hips. Toweling herself dry after her bath, she escaped into a timid dream in which a petal-soft mouth fluttered the length of her thigh.

Sam, who had long been blind to her, was transfixed one evening by the pigeon-toed apparition descending the stairs on a cloud of French musk, a visor of powder clamped over its face. "My God!" he said. "Have you seen yourself lately?" His wife froze, clung to the newel with a rose-tipped brown paw.

Later she crept upstairs to the mirror in her bedroom. What she saw caused her to weep: flesh that merited no more than the loathing he regularly expressed on it.

Between the furred paper covers of an exercise book, Maud began to keep a diary. It was a custom Thornton had encouraged, reading aloud entries from her own journal: a list of birds observed on an outing, the medicinal properties of nux vomica, scraps of verse copied from a magazine, the progress of an experiment in which cochineal-stained water inched up the stem of a snowy balsam. There was something ridiculous and tiresome about the enterprise; as with so much that emanated from Thornton. Even as a girl Maud sensed that it was absurd to go about the world pen in hand, as if its variety and chaos and appalling detail could be corseted within royal-blue copperplate. It was very English: that mania for description and constraint. At the same time, and this too was typical of Thornton, the project was not without heroism. All dissection requires curiosity and a sturdiness of nerve; even if wholeness is sacrificed in the process.

Now, at the opposite pole of womanhood, as her body embarked on its clumsy accommodation of age, Maud found herself taking up the ritual as lightly as she had once abandoned it. Her diary was, in a way, a tribute to Thornton, a form of atonement. Dashed off, sporadic, it was nevertheless an agent of analysis and order; an intuitive counter to the swirling hyperbole that had infected her letters.

This morning I followed the monkeys. The undergrowth here is relatively sparse. Rough tracks have been hacked out between the trees, and once accustomed to the gloom my eye easily picks out the telltale blazes on trunks and stumps. The flying column of monkeys called a halt every few hundred yards to rest and peer down at my progress. As soon as I drew near, they were off again. Wood pigeon went flying up, also shama, kondayas, blackbirds, a shock of blossom-headed parakeets. Flock is what I meant, but my pen insisted otherwise.

I've remembered something from that day, all those years ago, when I shot my first monkey. Not long afterward, Daddy brought down another. It crashed some way off and Carom bounded after it. We followed the tip of his white tail and found the monkey staring skyward. The shaggy fur on its chest lifted, although there was no breeze. Daddy bent down, then motioned me closer to look at what he had found: a huge-eyed baby clinging to its dead mother. It was probably no more than a week old. Carom's muzzle approached and I saw the tiny thing trembling with renewed force. Daddy pried it free, very gently. It fitted into the palm of his hand. He took his knife from his bag, thrust the point of its blade into the monkey's occiput and gave it a slight turn.

For years I had quite forgotten that little monkey. Today I can think of nothing else.

A thread of light between the ropy arms of banyans led Maud to a stream, no more than a few feet wide. Where the opposite bank sloped to the water, the earth had been churned and pocked by animals coming down to drink. A faint stirring of the air could be felt there, out of the shelter of the trees. Maud licked a finger and held it up. Then she walked a little way downwind to a patch of bushy scrub, where she settled beneath overhanging leaves, and waited.

Although she was on the alert, eyes straining to pick up density or movement, she didn't see the mouse deer until it had stepped out of the bushes on the far bank and straightened its back. It was no bigger than a hare, with pencil-thin legs and frail ebony hooves. Among trees, light and shadow would play over its mottled coat in perfect camouflage. She pictured it slipping through the jungle, weightless as leaves.

Thereafter she made her way to the stream every morning, remaining there until the sun rose too high for animals to come down to the water. The mouse deer and its mate rarely failed to appear. For the space of a season they were accompanied by a fawn, an elfin creature. It lowered its head and butted its mother's flanks. It lay down on the bank, occupying an area no larger than Maud's hand. Then a babbler flew up in a jitter of leaves and all three deer vanished as if bewitched, not a shiver of grass to betray the direction of their flight.

Sambhur drank at that sluggish stream, high-antlered deer bulky as elks. There were black-naped hares, also squirrels, pretty little *rilawa* monkeys and the ubiquitous wanderoos. Teal circled low, whistling plaintively. Three of the birds waddled down to the water while their sentinel stood motionless, with craned neck, on the spot where it had alighted. A pair of stilts paused in their feeding to preen an ebony wing, or drowsed, poised on one long leg in the mud.

An anteater nosed its way down the bank one morning, back arched high, an apparition from prehistory. Maud chilled at the sight. As a girl she had seen one of these creatures thrust the gelatinous blade of its tongue deep into the passages of an anthill and withdraw it encased in a quivering black scabbard. There is also something repellent about the way an anteater walks, the curved claws of its forefeet pointing backwards, like pavement beggars with broken bones set forever at sickening angles. Yet watching this one now, as it rose on its hind legs, swiveling its head as it sniffed for food, Maud acknowledged the perfection in its clanking design; in the shield-shaped plates of clear gray horn that defended it from jackals and leopards and the cobra's fangs, row after regular row laid close against the skin, an archetype of imbrication.

Sam could not fail to notice the change in her. She was still grotesque, knees apart as she inhaled smoke, a worm of ash trembling on her ridiculous dress. He considered her with the impartiality of a summing up from the Bench: a bony face above a corded throat, arms shrouded in loose flesh. The familiar, arrogant tilt of her head merely ludicrous now, a shred of defiant scarlet still clinging to the flagpole while crows strip the carcasses below.

Yet in some subtle way she had altered. There was a lightness in her. He could not rid himself of the peculiar idea that she would appear at Allenby House. Her breath settled on the bones at the base of his skull as he made his way down the stairs. He went into his office room and found himself peering over his shoulder, certain he would find her lounging by the door.

At last curiosity triumphed over his distaste for servants' gossip, and he asked Sirisena how the *nonamahatheya* spent her time. The bungalow keeper replied that she went for walks. Sam looked out, incredulous, at the vegetation pawing at the walls. Going for a walk: it was an activity he associated with buds fattening in an English hedgerow. Where could one walk here? "In the jungle," said the bungalow keeper, which only compounded the riddle.

In the old days Maud had dressed for shoots in sensible twill, and narrow boots hand-turned on a lathe in Burlington Arcade. Later she had switched to trousers, reasoning that they were disreputable, practical and flattered her figure to the point of obscenity. Now her progress through tunnels of restless leaves was marked by scraps of taffeta or organdy spiked on twigs, a scattering of diamanté like starfall. Skirts that had belled over parquet snagged on thorns and were tugged free with little hisses of protest. Hems came undone and trailed behind her, gathering earth and leaves.

Maud went home and hacked away the sticky burrs of love grass with pinking shears. She used a double strand of cotton to sew up the lips of jagged tears. The dhobi clucked his tongue over these crooked white scars, then beat her dresses limp against a rock to rid them of stains.

For Padma, that ruined incarnation passing through the house and compound was yet another sign that the place was cursed. Yet for her and her husband these years, on the whole, brought an interval of grace. Any long marriage is subject to variations of tempo. The eroticism that had first drawn those two together returned in force at this time. There were mornings when they could scarcely credit the bliss they had harbored. It instructed them in the savoring of other, small pleasures. A mynah, fallen from its nest and hand reared, that returned to peck rice from their palms. Ambrosial half-moons cut from a round red cheese, a gift from the *hamuduruwo* that the *nonamahatheya* failed to eat at Christmas.

There remained one facet of her marriage that never failed to elicit Leela's gratitude: every day she witnessed the love that Harry drew from his father. She saw Sam steal up behind the child, scoop him into his arms, whirl him into the air. He helped Harry mount his pony and walked him in circles around the garden or up and down the lane, showing the boy how to hold himself in the saddle, adjusting his grip on the reins. He held his son on his knee and taught Harry his letters out of a book salvaged from his own childhood: *A is for Army, That dies for the Queen, It's the very best Army, That ever was seen.*

There was this symptom, most telling of all: he lavished money on his son. When Harry lay in bed with measles a box arrived, larger than the child, covered with foreign stamps and sealed with emerald wax. It contained one hundred and eighty-five hollowcast soldiers, including two rare British Camel Corps as deployed in the relief of Khartoum. Harry arranged battle formations on his coverlet, murmuring with delight.

Yet it was also apparent to Leela, watching with her old uncontroversial skirts swathed about her on the lawn, that love manifested itself in her husband as a craving for perfection. As Sam crouched beside the child to demonstrate once again the turn of a wrist on releasing a ball, she saw that patience might be only a by-product of implacability. At that, a brief spasm of fear clutched her heart.

And the boy always chose his mother, making his preference clear with the casual cruelty of those who have not yet learned to dissimulate. One morning he came crying into the house, having cut open both knees in a fall. His father exclaimed and half rose from his chair; but the child trotted straight past, to his mother. Over the small heaving body, Leela saw her husband's face.

Maud's eyes snapped open to the night noises of Lokugama, frogs, creaking blinds, bandicoots in the rafters, the sawing of her own breath. Then a child cried out in the room next door. "Polecats, *nonamahatheya*," said the bungalow keeper the next morning. It was true that there had been heavy rain the previous week, enough to have driven polecats indoors to nest in the roof. But she knew it was not a polecat she had heard.

There were three halved coconut shells, each cradling a paste of boiled rice, condensed milk and strychnine. Sirisena climbed into the roof through a trapdoor on the back verandah while his wife held the ladder steady. Padma was wrapped, as usual, in a blue cotton sari, her eyes fastened on the ground. She said something to her husband, her Tamil seething like bubbles. Maud leaned against a verandah post, smoking. The bungalow keeper clambered down, the muscles of his buttocks moving beneath his sarong. His feet were soled with gray skin half an inch thick. Long bare toes like fingers felt for each rung as he descended.

As soon as Sirisena looked at the *nonamahatheya*, he knew her thoughts had alighted elsewhere. She was a disappointment to him: her attention was fluid and could not be diverted to flow solely in his direction. The legend of the devil-bird had pricked her into reaction, so he had ventured another tale, this one involving a farmer and his unfaithful wife. *Gama katha*: stories people told in villages, gathered around a cooking fire at night. He had pictured himself producing them one by one, coins drawn glinting from a purse. But as soon as he began to speak she had gazed at him blankly. A little later he heard her blundering about the house, crooning to herself. Now, while he was still slapping his palms together to rid them of dust, she swerved away. She came to a halt in the doorway of the room next to hers, one hand on the jamb. So she might remain for an hour.

The child cried again the following night.

Maud knew there was nothing in that room, only a small filthy pillow in which mice had once nested and the spoor of her slippers on the dusty floorboards.

Toward dawn, a tap gushed in the courtyard. But there was no tap there.

The morning was cloud-flanneled, and a section of guttering swung loose from a corner of the verandah. Perhaps that was what she had heard, rain cascading from the broken gutter. That was the genius of the place at work again, concocting undecidability.

A few weeks later, she returned to the room where Leo had died and found that the pillow had vanished. She knew she had seen it lying near the skirting board under the window. If she closed her eyes she could summon a corner of striped ticking, smell the musty dampness of kapok.

She asked the bungalow keeper if he had thrown the thing away. He denied all knowledge of it, swore he hadn't entered the room in years. It proved nothing. A servant would never admit to having removed a household object, however dilapidated, without permission. It could be construed as theft.

The thatched *kadai* at the Lokugama turnoff where Maud bought her cigarettes had metamorphosed into a concrete shop, with a hinged door painted the green of sugar almonds and a poster distributed by the Dig for Victory campaign. The boutique keeper now spent his days slouched in a carved armchair, surrounded by lesser men. His shop hummed with the expectant murmur of rendezvous and transaction. Villagers stood entranced before pyramids of tinned luncheon meat and crackers. Enameled basins overflowed with graded rosy or brown growths, since rice was rationed and everyone was condemned to a diet of yams.

Every hour the khaki blur of jeeps appeared and faded on the trunk road. The boutique keeper wore his striped sarong low on his waist to accommodate his soft round belly. It was one of the marks of his new ease, like the walnut-cased wireless on its shelf behind the counter and the mirror etched with swans that doubled his mistress's humiliations. None of these things afforded him the twist of joy that came with the sight of white men, stripped to the waist, laboring like coolies at clearing a path through the jungle.

In the first year of the war, ignoring ridicule, he had acquired a truck with a hundredweight of rust under its hood. Then he unloosed his twelve-year-old nephew on the carcass. The obstinacy and range of this child were remarkable. He crossed his arms over his chest and haggled with thugs. At a workshop on the edge of the town he watched, and wheedled assistance. He flashed a knife at shanty-dwellers scrambling through refuse for the same coveted section of rubber tubing or metal flange, and hoarded screws with half- or three-quarter-inch threads in an oily cocoa tin. His hands were callused and always filthy, his conversation fluent in pistons and connecting rods. At the end of eleven months he summoned his uncle to a ceremony. With his teeth clamped on his lower lip, he jiggled a length of copper wire. They heard an engine turn over.

There came a January when an incantation was in every mouth: Kampar, Batu Pahat, Slim River. The *kadai* keeper probed a troublesome molar with a matchstick and concluded an alliance with an up-country market gardener. He found himself a driver. The rivulet of soldiers pouring into the country swelled to a white cataract, and he called on their quartermaster. His truck coasted down from the hills with the bland vegetables dear to the English, cauliflowers, lettuces, cabbages large as heads. The first baby with russet hair was born in a drainpipe, twin gray lamps startling in its wizened brown face.

Sam sent Leela and the boy up-country when Singapore fell. Colombo emptied in days, the population interpreting editorials about the brave little island chosen to staunch the flow of tyranny as a coded admission of the nightmare to follow.

Alone at Allenby House, he found that Claudia's presence had grown vivid. This happened, from time to time: a brief brightening of memory. An arrangement of cushions on a settee molded itself to her form. By the door of the music room, he heard soundless melodies flow from her fingers. In those weeks glazed with public dread, he was aware as never before of time as matter: habitually opaque and dense, a medium through which he advanced only by means of a tremendous exertion, it would give way, without warning, to a fold of drapery, easily disturbed. Through a window in a courtroom he glimpsed his sister in a treed alley in Hyde Park. He sat like a rock in his armchair at the club because she knelt before him in a frilled pinafore, laying out a feast of pyramidal mud cakes and magenta petals on a lawn. Fixed things—cause and effect, the physical laws—seemed fluent. His sense of smell sharpened. A light green scent detached itself from the routine reek of damp and rot, the bass note of the tropics. For a brief interval, a world he had systematically disregarded acquired power over him. He saw the new moon through glass and crossed his fingers to avert misfortune. The sight of two magpies on a telephone wire filled him with unreasonable joy.

Then it ended. A chap with a commission in the Ceylon Light Infantry tipped him the word that Allenby House was on a list of private residences to be requisitioned for British officers. That night Sam rose from his bed and passed through silent rooms, while the sea complained endlessly about the ice at its feet. Now and then his fingertips found their blind way to glass or carved wood. The idea of strangers going casually about the house, opening its doors and yawning in its corridors, filled him with disgust. He lay face down on Harry's bed, persuading himself it still held the child's smell. The dalmatian tied up for the night on the back verandah lifted its muzzle and studied him. He entered a downstairs lavatory and tugged vengefully on the porcelain handle of the chain.

The warning screams had scarcely begun when the beggars deploying their sores by the Colombo breakwater on Easter Sunday saw the ship-crowded harbor erupt with blossoms that pulsed rose at the edges. A fish market was hit in the same raid; also a wing of the lunatic asylum. A madman escaped into a universe where giant metal insects flew up from the trees to dance and blaze in the sky.

Kumar's name was among those that figured on the register of the dead. Ten days earlier he had drunk a glass of sherbert and contracted typhoid. A buffoon's death, thought Sam. Nevertheless there was now the possibility that the old boy had done the decent thing and returned the Bentota bungalow to him. For twenty-four hours he found himself susceptible to certain objects—a fluted vase, a paperweight, a string of beads around a shopgirl's throat—and was at a loss to explain why he noticed these things. Then, as he paused in the act of pulling on a sock, he thought *glass*, and *greenness*, and the memory rolled and sparkled before him: a green glass ball caught in a net of foam, beside a woman's boot, pearl-gray kid splashed with seawater. He reached for the green marvel and heard his mother say, "How clever you are, darling." It was the sole residue of a day spent at Bentota in the third year of his life.

All through his childhood the cool green buoy had remained on a shelf in his room, but he could not recall having seen it after he went to Neddy's. It had sunk irretrievably under the flow of time along with everything else that had been damaged or lost or discarded. His chest tightened with longing for the old house at Bentota, for a clean wide selvage that bore no resemblance to the paltry beaches of the capital. He pictured a blue ocean tottering about his son, and yellow grains tracked onto a red-polished floor.

But it transpired that Kumar had left everything to a Miss Hope Galhena. She was twenty years old and a student at the Muttukrishna Polytechnic. Learning to type had been Kumar's last whim. Four machines of different make were discovered in his office room, along with a sheaf of misspelled observations about a quick brown fox and Miss Galhena's charms. In encouraging a cousin with expectations to contest the will, Sam found a measure of consolation.

It was an era that had the force of a bad dream and collapsed as swiftly. In the Bay of Bengal a hundred ships were sunk in a week, but enemy air reconnaissance, working without radar, failed to detect the Eastern Fleet as it lurked among the Maldivian atolls. Like the Easter dogfights, this might have been viewed objectively as no more than a minor impediment to Japanese hallucinations. But war, like dreaming, abounds in disproportion. Generals who had held it a small matter to overrun a continent now faltered at the conquest of an island.

Regiments from the Middle East and Africa were diverted to the colony to train for jungle combat, the Japanese having administered lessons in strategy with a vividness unavailable to Sandhurst. The muscled necks of British servicemen displayed their sunburn like so many defiant little flags; they signaled stiffened resistance and a return to order. With Malaya and the Dutch colonies lost, fortunes were made in rubber, the trees slaughter-tapped to maximize yield. It was a situation conducive to trade and theft, speculation and profit; on these activities the root of Empire had always fattened.

By the end of the year the Japanese ships and their carrier-based bombers had swiveled to meet the Americans in the Pacific, and the civilians who had fled to the hills were drifting back to Colombo. Sergeants lavished promises and NAAFI chocolates on girls from decent families. To filch a Wren's beret from her head became every schoolboy's dearest ambition. Airstrips parted the island's leafy hair.

No envelope bearing the government crest arrived at Allenby House. Recalling his informant's eyes, slitted with malice as he warned of balls bowled down a marble pitch and Eurasian nurses smuggled into bedrooms, Sam could not understand how he had ever credited the report. It exemplified the era. Everyone claimed to have the inside information, rumors vied with each other in outlandishness: yellow ladies ringing for chrysanthemum tea at Raffles, white wraiths fitting railway sleepers in the Burmese jungle.

Mountbatten set up his headquarters in the botanical gardens outside Kandy. The Allied counterthrust into the archipelagos and jungles to the east was formulated in the shade of a Javan willow. Wireless bulletins that had once threatened invasion turned into a recital of names Sam associated with adultery, having in his youth been agreeably scandalized by the stories of Somerset Maugham.

On an afternoon in 1943, as he strolled among the weekend crowds on Galle Face Green flanked by his wife and son, Sam saw a man nibbling a pink cloud. Thirty seconds later in the slope of those shoulders he recognized John Shivanathan.

Leela ducked her head as usual when Sam said, "This is my wife," but she could not help smiling. The sight of a grown man in a tie with sticky lips delighted her. Meanwhile the stranger had her son's fingers in his own and was leading him across sun-tormented grass to a knot of food vendors. Since Kumar's death, the menace of contagion had united Harry's parents in a spasm of precautions. Every vegetable in Allenby House that could not be peeled was washed in three changes of potassium permanganate solution. The reek of ammonia seeped through walls. All-out assaults were conducted on the cockroaches that milder campaigns had failed to eradicate. Leela scoured the child's hands with coal tar soap on the hour, and twice before meals. Yet here he was, advancing upon his parents with a repository of disease in each fist.

Shivanathan thrust a rosy puff into Sam's hand, lifted his hat to Leela and was gone.

For a moment Sam was lost. It is difficult to expostulate while grasping a stick of candy floss. Then the past came flying into his mind like a stone. "*He's no oil lamp*. That was how Claudia described him. Blighter used to hang around and bore the poor girl for hours."

Harry said unexpectedly, "No oil painting." He was at the age when he noticed patterns of words and parroted them.

"Quite right! No oil painting either!" Before he had realized what he was doing, Sam's mouth was full of sugar. "It's a miracle how Shiva's got on. District Judge of Panadura. Advisor to the State Council. Billy Mohideen told me the latest—he's been inviting fellows to dinner and reading them a lot of bilge he's written about the ancient rhythms of village life."

"He seemed kind," ventured Leela.

"He was there that night at the Downhill. Heard everything Nagel said. But all he could think about was his precious coolies. Couldn't make the leap to Taylor." Sam's teeth met in sweet pink air. "A plodder," he announced.

Seedlings thrust upward between stones, there were furry outbreaks of green on rock and leafy tendrils fused to rusting iron. Once, Maud had thought of that opulence as immoderate, a blind vegetable excess that overran every weak thing it encountered. Now she found it pleasing that life renewed itself cell by cell, that it was assertive and tenacious.

In March the flamboyante tree was hung with scarlet panicles. *Poinciana. Poinciana* something. It was the year of Maud's lists. At the bottom of one of her trunks she had found a volume swaddled in a paisley shawl: *The Ceylon Gardener's Handbook*, the morocco on its spine worn loose and her father's name on the flyleaf, Cyril Rajaratne, 1878. *Cassia fistula*, Indian laburnum, known in Sinhalese as *ehela*. *Tamarindus indica*, tamarind, *siyambala*. She quizzed Padma for the Tamil names of roots and herbs that lay about the kitchen and noted down her replies. Ginger translated as *inji*, garlic as *vella-vengam*. The fiery tongues of the *niyangala* creeper ran through the compound, licking trees. Bright pink amaryllis wove rugs for the earth. The beauty of the place waxed insistent. Maud's lists proliferated and flowered.

An entry in her diary might consist of a single notation—*dung beetle*, for instance, the bald syllables entirely inadequate to convey the concentrated purpose that emanated from the insect as it molded a ball of dung twice its own size from a half-dried cow pat, the slow hour spent watching as it inched this treasure backwards to its lair. Grasses, snails, the withering of a shrub, white birds like torn clouds over ripening paddy: once Maud had begun to notice these things, they were always there, waiting for her attention. She came and went from the house with sprays of leaves and samples of berries in a jet-fringed bag; she read of the medicinal properties of plants that flourished casually in the vast green dispensary of the jungle, and learned how to name them in four languages. Knowledge was a discipline in which she found pleasure, even if it was helpless against a power that asserted itself now and then over the years.

When that happened, things slipped out of their elements. A human face might peer at her from the chipped brickwork of a wall. Mosses grew eyes and moved. Tiny fish, vivid as gems, glowed briefly among ferns. Four headless mandarins in funereal kimonos paraded before her, on a log where a row of cormorants had stood with wings stretched wide as they pecked lice from their pinions. Once, in the unambiguous glare of noon, a figure walked less than six feet ahead of her on the road. It was neither male nor female, and its skin was a luminous coppery blue.

These phenomena no longer disturbed Maud. They were integral to the place in a way her presence was not. If whatever sent them had a message for her, it would be revealed in time. She accepted them, and they left her alone.

Between the jungle and the dhobi, her finery gradually fell to pieces. Fragments of georgette rotted into the earth. Birds braided strips of chiffon into their nests. Once she saw a weaverbird with a scrap she recognized in its bill, and recalled the legend that says the weaverbird studs its nest with fireflies to light it up at night. She would have liked to witness this, the gleam of phosphorescence illuminating a twist of muddied lace, the last glory of sea-green foam that had spun to Viennese waltzes.

Every few months a *bolanool* man called at the house, a Moor with a withered hand and a tin trunk carried on his head. He traveled at an unhurried pace, content to squat for hours over a cup of thrice-sugared tea. Maud's purchases seldom ran to more than a packet of needles or a ball of Glasgow thread, but the Moor always insisted on unpacking his entire box for her. Like all peddlars he understood magic. Its performance required him to conjure a world stocked with marvels, the residue of every child's dreams. A flotilla of shallow trays would materialize on the verandah, each packed tight with ribbons and combs and tiny cakes of sandalwood soap. The Moor might slide a thimble painted with poppies into Maud's hand or a little japanned cylinder crammed with glass-headed pins. Small bright things have their own potency; she would find herself buying a card of round green buttons or a skein of scarlet embroidery silk, objects she had no use for but coveted with a child's uncomplicated greed.

When the Moor next appeared she asked to see the flat bales of cotton and muslin he kept in the bottom of his dented trunk. Within minutes he had draped the verandah in florid swags, the bales slapping out under his good hand. Maud chose two lengths of flowered chintz, one coral, the other yellow, each stamped along the selvage with its identifying brand, a tiger's striped head. Out of them she fashioned a trousseau of waistless sacks, supplemented with glittering oddments: a stole worked in silver flowers, a belt with a jeweled buckle.

In the Moor's opinion, the old lady in the big house was mad. It was not a contemptuous assessment. He was a man in whom religious feeling expressed itself as a wide tolerance; madness, in his view, was not altogether divorced from saintliness. It seemed evident to him that the woman whose crazy weaving through the jungle was remarked on in villages for miles around had been brushed by the same finger as the ash-smeared holy men who wandered the Hindu pilgrim routes wild-eyed with god and self-mortification.

He was a tall man with sharp cheekbones and a quick tongue. In his presence the verandah bloomed into a small civilized stage hung with trumpery. He would haggle ruthlessly over a card bound with rickrack braid or a length of Pettah lace; then offer, at no cost, that rarest commodity, good conversation.

Sam spent the evening at a house set well back from the road in an acre of flowering trees and softly luxuriant ferns. It was an establishment that guaranteed hygiene and discretion. The girl he chose was new. Her breasts were scarcely larger than their violet-brown aureoles, the faintest swelling above her ribs. Flint-jawed, this elf dealt with him unmercifully. At such times he found himself transported. Mrs. Timms imposed her regal features on the face blooming above him and he clawed at the sheet in ecstasy.

Petrol was rationed but there was a rickshaw stand at the junction. His nerve-endings tingled as he walked up a street where branches met overhead. The moon was a silver sprat held in a mesh of leaves. When he lowered his gaze, he saw a patch of white moving ahead of him. He recognized the uniform above the sturdy calves and remembered that a group of Wrens was billeted in a compound at the head of the road. It lay barely two hundred yards away. But at Christmas there had been a minor scandal about a gang of youths who surrounded an English nurse when she was walking back from the cinema one evening. They had asked her to kiss one of them, a prospect she described as *too frightful for words*.

The thock-thock of the girl's heels masked his quickened steps. "Please excuse me!" he began, reaching for his hat.

She gave a tiny shriek and spun around. "Don't touch me," she screamed. "You beastly little nigger."

He settled his hat back on his head. "My dear young lady," he said, "please forgive me. I took you for a strumpet but I see now that you are much too ugly." The terror on her waxy features hardened to fury as he strode past her.

A week later, while he was knotting his tie, he heard the first sentence on the early bulletin and switched off the wireless. He walked down the stairs with care. It seemed a long way.

The breakfast service, rimmed with blue and gold fleur-de-lis, was one of the few tolerable items his wife had inherited from her mother. He ignored the newspaper folded beside his plate, although the headline was plainly visible: *Labor Landslide!* Nevertheless, knowledge persisted like a headache.

Thanks to the war, it had been years since he had tasted decent marmalade. His son knew nothing but the pineapple jam in the middle of the table, runny and oversweet in its faceted glass dish. The English had gone mad. Now it would be only a matter of time before they extricated themselves from the island as if they had never been there. A century and a half swilled down the drain like a discharge not referred to in polite company. And there he would be, high and dry and thousands of fellows like him, craving the amber subtleties of marmalade and obliged to make do with pineapple bally jam.

At the other end of the gleaming rosewood his wife was smearing onion *sambol* on buttered toast. It was a habit he had not been able to break her of. The whiff of Maldive fish depressed him every morning. His son sat between them, head tucked over his plate, eating spoonfuls of neutral boiled egg.

Sam's gaze alighted on the dalmatian stretched panting in the doorway, where the servant was obliged to step over it as he came and went with dishes. "Poor old Winston," he said, attempting lightheartedness, for the child's sake. "I suppose we should take him out and put a bullet between his eyes."

He intercepted the glance Harry shot at his mother, to which she replied with a slight shake of her head. The next moment, to Sam's horror, he found that his eyes had filled with tears. He was so very tired of being misunderstood.

From the talk that rolled around the circle of drinkers at the *kadai*, Sirisena learned that he belonged to an Aryan race. Tamils were Dravidians, therefore inferior. There was a man, a *mahatheya*, said the boutique keeper, who had spoken of these things at a meeting in the town. Although he was a gentleman, he had worn a sarong and addressed the crowd as equals. He had promised land for everyone, and bellies full of rice. The Sinhalese were the rightful rulers of their country: the day was coming when they would reclaim its sacred space for themselves and rid the island of all usurpers.

As Sirisena's wheels ploughed homeward, a cloud settled over the moon. He thought of a hen fluffing out her breast over an egg. At such moments old dreams revived, a pearly gleam at the edge of his vision.

He woke to pain that jolted between the base of his skull and his temples. Toddy was cheaper than arrack but produced a more sickening aftermath. He held his head under the tepid flow from the kitchen tap. Padma scraped the flesh from coconuts and ignored him. He stepped into the bright hateful morning and trod on a small bundle of nut-brown feathers lying in the dirt.

When he had finished cleaning the *nonamahatheya*'s bathroom, the floor was hazardous with slopped water. He smoothed the coverlet over her bed but left the sheets rumpled. At mealtimes he slapped dishes down in front of her, curries coated in a glistening scum of oil. She noticed nothing. This maddened him. In the pantry he poured coffee into a luminous, dinted pot, then spat into it. He wanted to hit the old woman until her hair turned dark and matted, and she whimpered in the dust at his feet. He wanted to clasp her knees and beg: *Help me to escape from my life.*

Maud had her own preoccupations. These, increasingly, had to do with the treachery of her body. There were days when stilettos of pain pierced her chest. Sometimes the floor dipped when she rose from her chair. One afternoon she found herself standing under the flamboyante with flies crawling along her arms and no memory of how she came to be there.

Deer would always bend their heads to a leafy cress that grew by the stream. Maud had witnessed the sight a thousand times before she connected it with Thornton's voice: "A general tonic and purifier of the blood." Thereafter Padma had instructions to prepare *gotukola* leaves mixed with shredded coconut every day. Maud persuaded herself that the *sambol* heightened her energy, yet knew she had reached that age when she would never again be free of the demands of a failing mechanism. At best, on a good day, it would let her off with a throbbing toe or a tenderness about her gums. Her lungs scratched. A knee locked itself into immobility. "Such mediocrity of design," she fumed. "Any cabinet carpentered in a village is sturdier."

She spoke this aloud, unintentionally. Sirisena, feverish for a sign, materialized at once in the doorway. She studied his small unmanageable face. His yearning communicated itself to her, but thinned and diffuse: a distant commotion. The ready self-pity of the old opened its arms to her. It admitted no neediness but its own.

The electricity failed three evenings in succession and they ran out of candles. It was the kind of minor domestic crisis that restored the bungalow keeper's sense of self-worth. Conscious of quiet mastery, he filled leaf-shaped lamps with coconut oil and arrayed them on the flat-topped verandah wall. Maud sat entranced before a row of clay lamps no bigger than a child's palm, each cupping a rag wick and a beating golden heart.

No soldier returns from war without a plunder of stories. Men who had been stationed near Lokugama carried home the tale of a woman with eyes like cold yellow gems who wandered the jungles of Ceylon dressed for a ball. In the torn light under the trees she had the aspect of a young girl, barely marriageable; then she turned her head to reveal a grinning crone.

Variants of this narrative surfaced in Solihull and Nairobi. It was embellished on an expedition to the Amazon, footnoted in an ashram in Poona, disputed on a farm near Dubbo. There was a version in which the woman had been reared by leopards and craved human flesh, the gown in which she prowled the jungle having been ripped from her first victim. Alternatively, she was the sad, mad product of an incestuous coupling, hidden away by her family and governed by the delusion that she was a sought-after débutante. Sometimes the figure in the trees was a ghost, the daughter of a Dutch governor, who had fallen in love with a foot soldier. Her father had the man taken deep into the jungle, where he was chained to a tree and left to the wild animals. The girl learned of his fate as she dressed for the garrison ball. Bejeweled, arrayed in laces and silks, she slipped from the fort that night and vanished without trace.

There were those who claimed that the woman in the jungle appeared only to soldiers who would die in combat. Others, that the vision guaranteed safe passage through the war. She glided on six inches of air, she crept on all fours, she walked abroad on moonless nights, or at that hour when the last star still glimmers palely above the horizon. There were always these constants, however: a violence from which everything sprang, the fabulous incongruity of her clothes.

When the pain first manifested itself Leela thought it was temporary, brought on by the green mango *achacharu* she loved and ate by the dishful. She dosed herself with Kruschen salts and waited for it to pass.

Later she knew it would not. She said nothing. She wanted her son to remember an afternoon of light and water they had spent together by a lake up-country. She had held him on her lap and pointed out the colors of a kingfisher: the back a deep lilac, rich blue wings edged with ultramarine, a snow-white belly, red feet and a carmine bill. If she complained now, what would he retain of her? A handful of brutally accurate photographs; the memory of hushed voices, a woman lying like a grub inside the milky-green cocoon of a sickroom.

There came a day when she stopped eating, unnoticed by all except Soma, who noticed everything; still she kept finding her way downstairs to her chair on the verandah. There were hours when her needle was a weight she could barely lift, as in a dream. But a border of gros point lotuses flowered beneath her fingers. It surrounded a parade of caparisoned elephants, drummers, dancers and a crimson-petaled sun. She made, in those last weeks, a set of six chair backs, thousands of stitches. But she left the sixth unfinished because a shadow fell across her knees and she looked up to see her daughter step forward to claim her.

With his canteen of filtered water thudding against his white shirt, Harry ran all the way down the lane to show his mother what the morning had brought: a tooth threaded with blood, the hole in his smile.

Filing away the papers that concerned his wife's death, Sam came across the certificate of their marriage. It was the date that made him pause. Fifteen years; and already she was blurring like fine print, he couldn't recall with certainty how tall she was, or the particular gracelessness with which she held her body.

One memory, however, remained with him to the end of his days. It was a Friday afternoon before the war. He had allowed a junior advocate to stand him lunch at the Jersey Hotel in the Fort and told him a good one over the deviled prawns: *Old Mother Hubbard she went to the cupboard to get the postman a letter. When she got there the cupboard was bare—so they did it without. Which was better*. One of the eccentricities of the Jersey in those years was that instead of measuring out a peg, the bottle was brought to the table. At the end of the meal the waiter used his thumb to gauge how much had been drunk, and that was what went on the chit.

When Sam emerged into the street that afternoon, leaving his companion to settle the bill, a tramcar was rattling past. The *suriya* trees had dropped yellow blossoms on the pavements. In the violet shade of a line of rickshaws a child sat on his heels, puffing on a *beedi*.

Sam turned into Chatham Street and saw a shapeless female standing in front of Hidaramani's window. He looked again and recognized his wife, peering through the glass at a bolt of flame-colored cloth. Bright colors attracted her. He had put the kibosh on that sort of thing from the start; he didn't want to have to turn up to public functions with a bally parrot on his arm. Even now she was obediently clad in a dull blue garment drained of all light, as dreary as a wet morning. For a moment he considered taking her into the shop and inviting her to choose herself an extravagant length of cerise or scarlet. Not to have made up into a frock but to keep locked in her almirah, a furtive pleasure gleaming in that musky dimness. From time to time she would open the door and run her finger along its lustrous folds. But as he was about to greet her she turned and saw him, and the impulse faded. It had been such a long time since they had surprised each other.

He had three names, Henry Stanley Edward, and a fourth, Harry, but his mother always said *putha*, naming the relationship that bound him to her. In the park a few days after she vanished, he heard, "*Putha!* Where are you hiding, *putha*?" He let go of his ayah's hand and ran toward the voice. On the far side of a bed of flaming crotons he cannoned into an imposter in a pink sari. The lesson had to be administered three or four times before he understood that an act of his, committed in ignorance, had driven his mother away forever.

The compass of his grief led him unerringly to the only other person in the house who mourned with him. Soma had been a servant since she was ten years old, had weeded the headman's paddy fields since she was seven. On a scale of worth, she would have placed herself considerably below a buffalo. Yet this girl with her village ways possessed the ability, uncommon in any walk of life, to identify goodness at a glance. The other servants had mocked the *nonamahatheya*'s failure to question the rate at which rice sank in the wooden chest in the kitchen, had sniggered at the ease with which she was deceived over a discrepancy in the change brought back from market. In that perceived stupidity Soma had recognized the compliment of trust, and loved the dead woman for it.

Now she looked at the child and saw her own sorrow replicated in the set of that narrow body. He was a silent presence, swinging his legs on a pantry chair, while she scoured the dinginess from brass with a mixture of brick dust and lime juice. When she applied fresh pipeclay to the *hamuduruwo*'s tennis shoes, a shadow sidled around the corner of the house to squat beside her on the back verandah. She noticed that all neglected things hurt him. A discarded sweet wrapper, blown in from the lane, was a torment until he smoothed out its creases and placed it in a tin he kept in his toy cupboard. A shoe lying at a careless slant to its fellow required straightening so that it would not feel slighted. Soma set herself the task of exorcising the neediness from his face.

She began by talking to the child of whatever came into her mind. It was an ancient, banal remedy. It had emerged, uncorrupted, from the verdigris of privation that had stained her own childhood, when she drew comfort, night after night, from the voices of her parents, murmuring to each other in the dark. She spoke to Harry of the weather, and the sowing of paddy, and how to predict the sex of an unborn child. Her flat voice with its countrified locutions set out the taboos to be observed when cultivating a *bulath* garden, and the feminine appearance, neither too dark nor too pale, too thick nor too thin, of the perfect betel leaf. She told him the story of the age-old enmity between the cobra and the *polonga*, and of a rock pool, deep in the jungle, where on certain nights a drowned golden chariot gleamed. The place was guarded by giant eels. Of those who dared to challenge them, no more was heard. She described a rich man who was so stingy that he sold all his rice and ate only boiled jack. She spoke of her mother, who had died of a fire in her stomach, when she herself was a child. Afterward, her father took her on a journey. They walked for four days through the jungle. At night they slept on verandahs in strange villages, and she was frightened of devils and leopards. Then they came to a sprinkling of huts near the coast, and her mother's people. She was given a fried egg, the first she had eaten. The following morning her father gave her a silver ten-cent coin, and she understood that he was going away. It was the last time she saw him.

Once, she referred in passing to the *nonamahatheya*. At once Harry began to speak of something else, raising his voice over hers. Still, he had grown noisy again. That terrible watchful silence no longer accompanied him into a room. But the clear-water openness of his face had gone too, never to return.

With yellow soap and a scrap of coconut husk, Soma scrubbed grease from the clay *chatties* in which the lunchtime curries had cooked. The boy fetched a book and stood on a chair beside the veined porcelain sink, turning pages. One day she would hold her own children in thrall with stories of a land where cows flew through the sky, and a devil disguised himself as a dish painted with roses and pranced down the street on legs as skinny as a chicken's.

Those two heads close together were an affront. In the first instance there were the other servants. The powerless are necessarily alert to the whims of the powerful. The *nonamahatheya*'s fondness for Soma had attracted jibes that the girl was mostly too stupid to understand. Now here was the child singling her out all over again. Resentment simmered like broth. The boy's ayah was the jug from which it eventually poured, an overflowing of spite.

This woman, a crone with a pinched mouth, went to Sam and laid her tale before him. He heard her out in silence. She was Lokugama raised. He had sent for her when Harry was born, to Leela's dismay. She would have preferred to employ a young girl. But Agnes had been Sam's own ayah, and later Claudia's. He would admit no argument against her.

She told him that Soma was encouraging the child to make a garden for his mother beside the verandah where she used to sit. He had planted a flower bed with slips of coleus, because the dead woman had loved their bright leaves, and fashioned an edging from the spiky, coral-flushed shells she had helped him gather on a beach one morning. A stone dove with a broken wing served as a centerpiece. Around its neck Harry had placed the glass bangles, amethyst and sapphire and ruby, gorgeously rimmed with gold, that he had given his mother at Christmas.

When the woman had ended her recital, Sam said, "I will see to it."

It was the signal that she was to leave. But she lingered, unwilling to relinquish the pleasure of doing evil. "It is certain to be a charm," she repeated. And then, the formula with which she always prefaced a lie: "I have seen with my own eyes . . ."

"Go now," he thundered, outraged that she should presume to gossip with him.

Agnes crept back to the kitchen, her heart hammering with joy.

Her rigmarole about sorcery and charms Sam dismissed as the ignorance of her kind. But the substance of her insinuations remained, burrowing its way into his brain. He had been half conscious of the complicity between his son and that lumpish girl, but with the reluctance of a man who suspects his wife of adultery, thrusting away the evidence that will prove him a cuckold. Now the ayah's tale-bearing dragged the thing out from the trees and placed it like an ambush across his path. He went upstairs, unlaced his shoes, lay on his bed. Tissa's boy was dragging his *ekel* broom along the drive, raising a mindless shriek. The sea mimicked it like an idiot.

When Leela died, Sam had pictured his son at his knee, seeking his guidance. He understood that the child would miss his mother; that was only natural. At the same time it was no bad thing for the boy to step from the shelter of those petticoats. He had been babied by his mother, so that he was given to a dreamy foolishness. At night a light was left on in his room, wasting money, because he was afraid of *gonibillas*, the bogeymen with whom his ayah had once threatened him. When giants with rouged lips came stalking down the lane in glittering skirts, he was found trembling in an upstairs bathroom where he babbled about "the scissor man"; no amount of rational explanation about stilts could lure him out to watch the *bora kakul* men dance.

Very early on the morning after the funeral the child had gone into the garden with his watercolors and daubed paint on all the flowers he could reach, blotches and wavering stripes of unnatural color, rainbow streaks on creamy gardenias, emerald and purple smears on a bed of marigolds. Pressed for the rationale of this small but irritating offense, all he would say, eventually, was that he *wanted it to be different*.

Sam arranged tennis lessons. There was also swimming, three times a week before school, and cricket on Saturday morning. He had looked into his son's small remote face and longed to fashion a bridge between them. It occurred to him that while Latin was not taught at Neddy's until Standard 4, there was no harm in getting a head start on the other chaps. He drilled Harry at breakfast: *hanc civitatem, haec civitas. Infinitus est numerus stultorum*.

Crucially, he treated the six-year-old as an equal. In this way the child would understand that it was time to put away childishness. On Sundays they lunched in a restaurant. Harry studied menus longer than his arms, learned to calculate a five percent tip. Sam laid educational facts before him: for instance, that trial by ordeal was still quietly practiced at the turn of the century, when a witness had reported two villagers suspected of a crime required to thrust their hands into boiling oil under the supervision of their headman.

Billy Mohideen rolled to a stop by their table one day. The years had doubled Mohideen's tonnage; a youth in a beautiful sky-blue shirt treading daintily in his wake created the impression of a child bowling a giant hoop. Mohideen introduced this apparition as *an upcoming star in our mercantile firmament*. One of his catamites more likely, thought Sam, eyeing the blighter's cushiony indigo lips. Really, Mohideen was shameless. He waggled a fleshy pink palm in Sam's direction, exclaiming, "The famous Obey!" In his mouth it sounded like a warning; a veiled reference to infection, perhaps.

Sam said, "I was just discussing the Hamilton case with Harry, here." He paused to let this sink in. "Destined for the Bar, this one. Or perhaps the Bench. We haven't decided."

"Hamilton case," said Mohideen meditatively. "Oh yes, *Hamilton* case. My God, all those years vanished like two ticks." He dropped his voice. "Pukka shame about that show, Obey. Jolly high time the English packed up, isn't it."

His creature yawned, fluttering the tips of his fingers against his mouth. His nails were trimmed but had a suspicious sheen.

"Mind you," said Mohideen, still in that conspiratorial murmur, "even then there were fellows saying it served you right for saving coolies." A contented squeak escaped him. "So when our chaps take over, your *persona* could still be *non grata*, isn't it."

Sam said, "Don't let me detain you, old boy. At our age, it's so difficult to stay erect after a feed."

It flew past Mohideen of course, but he saw the other blink.

Now, studying the molded acanthus leaves on his bedroom ceiling, Sam was swept with sadness. Everything he reached for eluded him. Harry received his overtures with the polite reserve that had always characterized their relations, while choosing to moon about behind a servant. Yvette Taylor's face rose before his eyes. A man had loved her insanely. Her bloodless lips and greenish pallor had received a corpse as their due. Sometimes it seemed that the whole world was privy to a secret withheld from him. He recognized this for self-pity but remained imprisoned in its logic. It required punishment.

He sent for Soma the next morning, after Harry had left for school. It was only the eleventh day of the month; but she would be paid in full, in lieu of notice. He informed her of these facts, all she needed to know. Then he took up his newspaper.

She was the kind of person who breathes noisily. He put down his paper in irritation. "I shall be leaving for court in half an hour," he said. "Have your box ready for inspection." In Sinhalese he always used the lowest form of address, suitable for animals, because anyone who deserved respect spoke English.

With her eyes directed at the gleaming parquet, for it would have been offensive to look at the *hamuduruwo*'s face, Soma asked, "Is my work unsatisfactory?"

He got to his feet. "Twenty-nine minutes," he said, and left the room.

She was waiting for him on the front verandah. Her box was a length of striped material, spread on a table to display its contents. Using a ruler, he sifted through her possessions. She owned two spare jackets and a flowered cloth. A towel. A small blue tin of talcum, a veined sliver of soap, a box of tooth powder, a comb, a needle skewered through a spool of white cotton.

A purse woven from coconut leaves contained a rupee note as soft as a rag, a few coins, two hairpins and a tiny wooden elephant, brightly painted, its flanks superbly curved. He picked up the exquisite little object, no larger than a date but satisfyingly solid on his palm, and sensed the girl's fear. He recognized the elephant, of course: one of a pair from the Noah's Ark, hand-carved on a Swiss mountain, that he had presented to Harry on the child's third birthday.

"What is this doing here?"

"Harry baby gave it to me, *hamudurawanai*."

At once he grasped the potent symbolism of the gift, one half of two. He slipped the toy into his pocket. "This isn't yours to keep," he said.

It could have been much worse. He could have had her charged with theft. Still, her hand was unsteady when she made a cross beside her name in his wages book to show that she had received all the money due to her.

All that remained was to supply her with a chit. He went into his office room, took a sheet of notepaper and wrote: *The bearer, Somawathi, has been in my employment as a servant woman for sixteen years. Her work is satisfactory but her character is marred by a certain slyness.*

He was halfway down the steps to the car waiting under the portico when she said, "*Hamudurawanai*."

When he turned, she said, "Harry baby." Then she stopped.

"What?"

But she only stood there, moving her head a little.

From a recess of his trunk, the *bolanool* man produced a greasy fold of leather with a lump in it. A water-worn yellow pebble rolled on Maud's palm. "A snake stone," said the Moor. "A charm against snake bite."

It was no larger than a chickpea, faintly luminous in shadow. "A cobra carries it in his mouth. At night, he places it on the ground and watches over it. He will defend it with his life."

She set it by her plate at lunch, and saw Sirisena eye it. When she held it out to him, he turned it in the tips of his fingers.

"You climb a tree in which a cobra lives and wait until nightfall," said Maud. "When the snake comes out from his hollow in the trunk, he places his stone on the ground beside him. Its shining attracts fire-flies, which cobras love to eat. Then you part the leaves very carefully and empty a bag of ashes over the stone. The cobra circles the tree all night, searching for his lost treasure. In the morning you climb down and take the stone. The snake will never return to that place."

In the kitchen, where his wife was grinding chilies, the bungalow keeper reported the conversation.

"That thing will draw snakes into the house," said Padma at once. "You must get rid of it."

"How am I to do that? Do you imagine she won't miss it?"

Padma sighed. She had never set eyes on the sea but conceived of it as akin to the stupidity of men: immeasurable, eternal.

The trunk road was intersected by a flow of greenish-brown water. Sirisena left his bicycle by the bridge and clambered down to the stream. There he remained for over an hour, his sarong tucked up around his thighs, rummaging in wet sand. To the dhobi children who came swarming around him, he replied that he was looking for a gold chain. The clasp must have been weak, he told them. He had been leaning over the parapet of the bridge when the chain and its tiny gold cross slithered from his neck and into the water below. The children helped him search for it, wading out through clots of foam.

When he had found what he was looking for, he rose to go. "The chain!" cried the children. "What about your chain?"

"Keep it," he said, with royal munificence. "If you find it, you may keep it."

The next day, while the old woman was taking her bath, he effected the switch. Then he dropped the snake stone down the disused kitchen well. Not a moment too soon. His wife, catching a movement from the corner of her eye as she split open a coconut, turned to see a ribbon gliding in from the back verandah. Her blade sliced through the air with admirable precision, almost severing the flat head from its body. On examination it turned out to be a rat snake, harmless to men. But that one, as Padma remarked, was only the first.

For months the dhobi children found themselves unable to pass the spot below the bridge without pausing to scan the stream. Reason said the chain had long been washed away on the current. Still they looked, and stirred the sand with agile toes.

Then the monsoon arrived and the stream was a braided amber torrent. On the trunk of the massive banyan that grew near the dhobi colony measurements were marked off in white paint. Every day another six inches of bark had been swallowed by the water. A small jackwood cabinet flashed past, a china face with blue eyes pressed sideways against the glass. Mottled green river lizards, thicker than a man's arm, appeared in the crowns of trees. It was the season of delirium and miracles.

"The chain! There!" screamed the smallest child, dancing through mud, oiled plaits whipping around her head. But there was nothing, only light and linked water.

That his son might ever come to harm filled Sam with terror and rage. He wanted to keep him safe. He wanted him to shine. Icy cords wound about his ribs as the eight-year-old served ball after ball into the net.

There was worse: the boy was placed thirteenth in a class of nineteen. It was arranged that twice a week after school and every Saturday afternoon Harry would see the new deputy head of the junior school for an hour and a half of coaching. Barlow had been a housemaster at St. Paul's. A weak chest had kept him out of the army, he said apologetically, and now it had driven him to seek warmer climes. He was a short, fair man who smelled pleasantly of pipe tobacco. His wife had been killed in one of the first raids over London. Once again his tone was apologetic, although it was difficult to see in what way he was to blame.

Over time, Sam realized that Barlow's manner was a tic. The schoolmaster could not help sounding contrite: about the shocking-pink gorgeousness of the anthuriums that flared on his verandah in a humus of his own devising, about the tail-end collapse of the Queen's First XI. It was faintly irritating. Yet the man's gaze was so level and so desolate. Sam decided that he had never recovered from the ignominy of missing the war. The death of his wife would have compounded the poor devil's torment. *Dulce et decorum:* it would not have been an empty tag to a man like Barlow. The diagnosis of another's infirmity is always gratifying. Sam's manner toward the Englishman grew expansive, paternal.

One Sunday, Harry asked if he might stop having coaching. They were in the middle of a slap-up feed of noodles and crab claws at the Mandarin Inn. His father had been talking about his own school days: pranks, a poem that had won a prize. The request had framed itself on Harry's tongue.

His father said, not angrily, "Why?"

Harry considered the clouded water in his fingerbowl, studied the crimson paper globe suspended overhead. He could see it was a reasonable question. Yet he was unable to answer it. Yet his father expected an answer. The instant before paralysis seized him, the smooth amber plane of a waiter's jaw provided rescue. "I don't like Mr. Barlow's mustache," he announced.

The schoolmaster's upper lip, nutmeg flecked with ash, neat as a German park, passed before Sam's eyes. After a moment, he smiled. "Doesn't like his mustache! That's a good one!" There were times when his son appeared intensely alien: no flesh of his flesh but a fierce compression of motives operating from dense opacity. This was deeply unnerving. When it happened, amusement was one of two modes available to him.

Harry was aware of having stepped to the limit of solid ground. He could not understand how, a minute earlier, his father's anger had seemed preferable to Mr. Barlow's mustache. The mistake frightened him. He must not make it again. When Mr. Barlow pressed his mouth against his own, the roughness of his mustache was after all far from unbearable. And those sixty seconds of prickling discomfort were accompanied by a sensation that was at once troubling and agreeable, that returned to stir the core of him as he swung his legs under the tablecloth and sucked sweet white flesh from a scarlet claw.

For five terms he would continue to visit the Englishman for coaching. Barlow was a gifted teacher, methodical yet intuitive. Harry's marks did, in fact, improve.

In the two new nations to the north, Muslims and Hindus were celebrating independence by slaughtering each other. Sam contemplated a row of zinnias beside a path, their rayed petals and flat, gaudy colors. There was nothing sinister about the sight. Yet his breathing tightened. As soon as he opened his eyes every morning it was waiting, an unspecified dread that built through the day like cumulus massing on the horizon. At last he sent his peon to the P&O office in the Fort with instructions to reserve a first-class berth to Southampton and set about scheduling work to accommodate his absence. He had to go while there was still time, before everything changed.

An obstacle presented itself at this juncture. Harry was recuperating from chicken pox, still scabby about the shins. The virulence had manifested itself in his body with particular intensity. Well after it had peaked, he still tired easily. Now the doctor prescribed rest, a prolonged break from school. There was no question of him entering the boarding house at Neddy's for three months, as Sam had envisaged. But at the thought of canceling or postponing a journey that had assumed talismanic status in his mind, he was gripped by apprehension.

He decided to take the child and his ayah to Lokugama. It was a solution that had the added attraction of being certain to irritate his mother. But the isolation of the place scratched at his nerves. What if

Harry should suffer a relapse and require a doctor one night? The telephone was still a rarity in outstations, but he arranged, by dint of barefaced bribery and covert menace, to have a line installed by the time he was to sail. It seemed to him that the very presence of a telephone would keep his son from misfortune, as a man carries an umbrella to insure against rain. He could recognize the argument as one that swam in the sightless depths of unreason. But in everything to do with his son he dwelt in the maze of irrationality and obsession that was the pattern of his love.

He cranked down his window and surveyed them, an old woman wreathed in fierce blue smoke, a pigeon-toed child in dazzling socks. They had the same eyes: runnels of light set deep under the brow. His heart shivered. He drove away.

My grandson is a gnome of a boy. A cap of rough black hair, and he is at that unflattering stage when a child's head is too large for his body. The Obeysekere ears. Sometimes, when Ritzy was being exasperating, I would picture grasping him by those handles and tipping the foolishness out of him.

The child swings his legs and stares at me. I stare back. What shall we find to say to each other?

Harry's finger sank into the waxy yellow brain that sat on the pantry table in a wrapping of leaves. For a week they breakfasted on buffalo curds and that pale-gold sweetness, fresh from the comb. "The test of good honey," said his grandmother, licking her spoon, "is that it pricks in the throat on the way down."

It went to swell the little mound of information Harry was garnering at Lokugama. The powerless can never be certain when the powerful will move against them, nor how they will be required to defend themselves, so children, like servants, put together an ant hoard of guesses and shreds of knowledge; an archive of oddments whose detail a general might envy.

The boy learned the weekly roll call of beggars, starting with the leprous mother and daughter who presented themselves at the door every Monday and ending with the man with no legs whose wheeled plank labored up the drive on Saturday at noon. He examined a bandicoot caught in a trap, a rat the length and weight of a cat, whose flesh, his grandmother assured him, tasted like suckling pork when curried. He found the branch of the mango tree where red ants had slung their nest. He watched a monkey with a fringed face and a baby draped around her neck sip from the soup plate that caught drips from the tap outside the kitchen. He knew that a rusting bath planted with marigolds marked the place where Sirisena kept eight rupee notes buried in a Huntley & Palmer biscuit tin. He was privy to the slow vegetable drama of a bo tree asphyxiating in the corded embrace of a ficus. He crawled down a mongoose path beneath a matting of lantana, ignoring everything that had been drilled into him about snakes, and encountered a large dead boy whose green-speckled hands curved around a flute.

Like all solitary lives, Maud's had worn itself a smooth groove of routine. Harry's effect on it was jarring. It was a matter of small things. He sat in a chair she considered hers. She picked up a goblet to pour herself a glass of water and found he had emptied it. Lights left on in empty rooms blazed his passage through the house. A leather pouffe was moved out onto the verandah, a side table shifted. She ate little and rapidly, while he had inherited his mother's keen appreciation of food, chewing his way through three solid courses long after Maud had put down her spoon.

Vanity played its part in her agitation. She held herself rigidly in his presence, afraid that her body would humiliate her with the leakings and mutterings of old age. Her stomach thundered and her fingers clenched on the arms of her chair. He was not a beautiful child but he had the gloss of all young creatures. She was sixty-eight years old. Her feet were ropy with veins. She folded her hands into fists to hide ridged fingernails, and grew conscious of the faded shapelessness of her clothes.

Over the years she had spent at Lokugama, Maud had fallen into the habit of talking to herself. Passing an open door, Harry saw that she was alone. Yet she was addressing someone. It was one of the things about her that frightened him.

They played Chinese checkers before dinner and cribbage after. Night in that place brought an absolute blackness such as the boy had never encountered. It seemed to him that the jungle stepped closer to the house after dark, when jackals screamed and murdered among the trees. Wheels of insects spun about the weak verandah lights. A tiny gecko fell from a rafter to lie among the counters on the checkerboard. Harry's mother had shown him how to feed these lizards, with grains of boiled rice impaled on the point of an *ekel*. He picked up the small beating body and hurled it into the dark.

Maud insisted that they play for cash. Then she fleeced Harry of all his pocket money. She had spied on his possessions and knew of the clay till, painted to resemble a tomato and weighty with coins, that he kept in a drawer. To count money after lamplight was to attract robbers. He pointed this out. She was waiting for him the next morning, with a rust-red rock. The till had only a single slot. In order to retrieve its contents it was necessary to smash it, an everyday parable about the kinship of loss and gain. Harry placed the tomato on a table and stood back. At the hard torrent of copper and silver, a wire strung tight in him gave.

The coins in front of Maud mounted, while his own heap diminished. He glanced away, then snapped around. She was whisking a counter into a more advantageous position.

"Of course I'm cheating," said Maud. "The question is, why aren't you?"

"Pater says you're shameless."

"There, for once, he is quite right."

"Jesus Christ!" said Harry, a trifle self-consciously.

It marked the beginning of their alliance.

A little parade stepped from the undergrowth. Chinked light brushed the silky feathers of a jungle fowl's neck and his arched green tail. Maud halted to watch six brown hens trail him across the path and heard leaves crack behind her. When the last bird had vanished, she raised her voice: "Hurry up—I'm waiting." The child arrived at her side with a skipping rush of relief.

There were blue eyes underfoot. Harry ground one into the dirt, taking courage as the petals blackened beneath his heel. The gloomy silence under the trees unnerved him, but not as much as the patter that would break out without warning. "Only leaves," said Maud, but he was certain that the noise was animate and malevolent.

Sometimes the same huge whispering enveloped the house after dark. Then he was afraid to lift his gaze from the cards in his hand. His grandmother won easily, narrowed her eyes and mocked him.

Maud drew the child's attention to the purple trumpets of *ruta attana* and its poisonous, prickly green fruit. She showed him a *talakiriya*, a small tree with milky juice that blisters the skin. He learned to pick out the drooping branches of the *goraka* tree, whose leaves and lobed fruit act as an aperient, and the gray-barked *domba* that is used for cart poles. In bed at night the names of trees burst in his mind like stars: *hingul, tammana, keena, sapu.* He knew satinwood as a ball-and-claw sideboard, ebony as a set of admiralty-backed chairs. With his grandmother he stood beneath breathing trees, tilting his face to the heavy green vault above, and had to place his palm against a trunk to steady himself against giddiness.

One of the spry barbets that flew about the garden developed an interest in Harry. It would follow him around the compound, alighting on a branch or a wall to regard him with fondness. He led his men in a daredevil charge on the golden battlements of an abandoned anthill, and the bird fluttered its wings to cheer their victory. He thought it tracked him on his walks with Maud but could not be sure. The jungle was full of those small green parrots and the *kukra-kukra-kukra* of their insistent call.

When the temperature was less than ninety-six degrees, shadows showed violet. In the middle of the day they turned blue. If he stood on the verandah in the afternoon and sniffed, he could smell the heat. "Always going in the sun without a hat," scolded his ayah. "You will become black like a dirty Tamil person."

He stepped along packed red earth beside Maud. In his mind he skirted his grandmother with caution, as if she were a piece of furniture against which he might scrape his shin. The old woman stood fresh-peeled cinnamon quills in jars, drenching the air with scent. She went about the house in bare feet, like a servant. She picked up a drumstick from her plate and sucked flesh from bone with wet noises. Her arms and legs were meshed in silvery scales of drying skin. She said *stomach* instead of *tummy*. She cut cigarettes in half to make them last longer. Her nails were unpolished and the color of horn.

These were confusing signs. He had absorbed, at a very early age, the distinction between a *woman* and a *lady*. In his grandmother's presence these terms slid toward that disturbing category of words he could not at once fasten to a thing: *teapot* and *kettle* caused the same queasiness to stir in him, or *orange* and *yellow*, ideas that slipped in his mind like a soapy plate gliding through Soma's fingers on its way to disaster. He had not intended to, but found himself gripping his grandmother's knotted hand.

The child's presence in the house released an unquietness. It was not altogether hostile. A row of mud cakes decorated with crimson petals pulled from a Barberton daisy was set out on a step for Harry one morning. A white pebble winked between each crumbling cake.

At that hour of the evening when the sky turns inky blue and children are driven in from their games, he heard a soft voice call from the crotons, "Ready!"

The monsoon rolled in the distance, like thunder. Sweat glued Harry's shirt to his skin. He was walking along the back verandah, past the room next to his grandmother's, when he found himself breathing icy air. His ayah had told him that a baby had died within those walls. His head grew hot with fright.

A boy at school by the name of Rex Ebert had an uncle who had served in Burma. Wounded in action, he had a leg that unscrewed and an artificial eye. Harry had seen him, straight-spined and stiff-gaited, at a cricket match, where he had given off no more than the usual adult charge of menace. Yet Rex swore that at night his uncle took himself apart entirely, so that nothing was left in his room. It was information Harry would have given a great deal to unknow.

If he found himself alone he ran, from the dining table to his bedroom, between verandah and pantry. As he fled he kept his head lowered and would not glance to left or right. He sniffed all morning rather than fetch the handkerchief that waited at the far end of shadow-filled corridors. The lavatory was an ordeal in a class of its own, a dank chamber where he crouched on a mahogany seat with his chin tucked on his chest. To look up was to risk facing whatever might be standing in the doorway. He learned to move his bowels every third day, forging a lifelong link between anxiety and constipation.

Clouds of white butterflies with pale green underwings streamed into the compound one morning, signaling that the monsoon was on its way. The day was as still as a pond but tiny fingers of air stroked Harry's scalp and set it tingling.

A clinging odor was remarked on by everyone in the house. The smell came and went at unpredictable intervals and was predominantly sweet, as if a bottle of scent had been left unstoppered in a room. Yet in a moment it could turn foul. The stretching of nerves, characteristic of the season, was thus exacerbated. A dish of fried sprats sprang from the bungalow keeper's hand. Harry's ayah sliced open her heel on a shard of bottle glass.

A formal arrangement of squares was found chalked on the verandah one morning. Hopscotch was a girl's game. Harry would have scorned it at home. Here he scoured garden beds for a smooth, flat stone. His *butta* landed in the first, second and third squares. The boy aimed at the fourth until his arm ached. "Jesus Christ!" he muttered, whenever he remembered. At each attempt the stone fell on a line, or outside the chalked squares.

He lay in his room, working up to the test of courage he had devised. There was no breeze but he heard the jungle creaking. He thought of a story he liked about pirates and flying fish. For a moment he was the boy on the bowsprit, with white birds following.

His ayah snored on her mat across the doorway. Damp and the urine of polecats had drawn a brown map of Africa on the ceiling. He gouged a lump of dry, gray matter from a nostril. Then he rose and stepped over his ayah, dropping the snot into her open mouth. She shifted and muttered and didn't wake.

During his illness and convalescence all spices had been omitted from his diet. In the pantry he scooped lime pickle from a dish and licked his fingers. He filled a tumbler from the ceramic water filter. It tasted faintly of dust.

Thus fortified, he returned to the room where the baby had died and went in. It contained only a faint, sweet reek and the corpses of flies. Somewhat disappointed, he wandered out again.

A sofa with elaborately scrolled ends leaned against one wall of the verandah that ran around the courtyard, its broken leg propped up on half a brick. He lay on its sagging rattan, with his feet resting on one of the scrolls. The second toe on his right foot overshot his big toe by half an inch. This was *moospainthu*. The courtyard was a cauldron of light with a blue enamel lid. He fell asleep and woke screaming.

A rat's tail lay across his ayah's shriveled chest. She coiled the plait into a gray knot and speared it with hairpins. All the while she scolded him: her practiced eye had spotted the smear on his chin. "*Aiyo*," she whined to Maud, who was lowering herself onto the sofa. "You see how disobedient he is? He steals food that gives him bad dreams. If he falls ill, the *hamuduruwo* will say it is my fault. But what am I to do?"

Rattan had stamped itself into the boy's cheek and arm, a trellis of cinnamon flesh. He turned his head and looked at Maud. "I dreamed I was in that room," he said. "And there was a cushion on the floor. And a thing in a net."

"What kind of thing?" she asked.

He answered without hesitation. "A hand like mine."

On Harry's last day at Lokugama, the household was woken at dawn by a bulletlike downpour that exhausted itself almost at once. Over a fortnight there had been a series of these eccentric starts to the monsoon. Even now the sky was as gray as a bucket but the air remained heavy and close, with no sign of the singing winds that would sweep in when the rain arrived to stay.

But an hour later the trees around the house were bowing until they groaned. The first drops of rain fell like fat fish. Harry's ayah scuttled between rooms, hiding scissors and knives in cupboards, draping towels over mirrors as lightning splintered the enormous sky.

Soon rain poured straight down as if a tap had been left open overhead. While Sam was still explaining that flooding had rendered the roads impassable, the line went dead.

Maud remained in the hall, clutching the receiver. Why had Leo's room contained a cushion, rather than a pillow, in Harry's dream? What did the substitution signify?

She thought of Claudia, and her special cushion—no different from any other—that the little girl insisted on jamming between her knees when she slept. Maud could remember the child's fierce attachment to the thing, how she had trailed that silky blue package everywhere, dragging it through grass and over earth so that its sheen dulled and its piping frayed. At last it began to disintegrate, and was wrested from her grasp while she stiffened her body, and thrown away while she screamed.

Rain crashed on the roof. Maud's spine prickled. She turned to see a child approaching fast, his shirt a pale smear in the rain-darkened hall. Harry ran past and out onto the verandah.

There he swung himself up onto the wall and extended first one stick leg and then the other into the downpour. Far from the regimenting forces of pavements and lampposts, wind and water were larger, more elemental things; he needed to express his solidarity with them. Children always side with monsoons, thrilling to the assault on stability. It was an instinct the boy would never quite outgrow.

The coconut trees against the wall swayed and ducked behind each other, and clouds blew through their feathered heads like smoke. Water foamed in the compound and raced down the drive, where puddles boiled with caramel bubbles. Curtains of rain turned the day so dark that lights were required in the house. But switches clicked uselessly; electricity put up only a feeble struggle against the monsoon. To Harry's delight, the bungalow keeper produced bunches of candles from the pantry. He was allowed to stick them onto saucers. With candles, there was always the hope that someone would get hot wax on his fingers.

By the time lunch was cleared away, tiles had been wrenched from the roof and the household had run out of buckets. The distinction between inside and outside blurred as rooms filled up with falling rain. Basins, saucepans and an enameled chamberpot were placed wherever someone was bound to trip over them. Furniture hauled into unfamiliar positions out of the way of leaks provided a further hazard. There were groans, and hands clamped to bruised shins.

Leaves turned black and rain fell in ropes. When it stopped, late in the afternoon, steam rose from the drive. In half an hour it would pour again. Meanwhile the sun shone as if clouds were a fanciful notion that would never amount to anything.

All night, sky and leaves dripped. Harry flailed in his bed. His lids snapped open. He had said cushion. But he meant pillow. He realized that now. *Pillow. Cushion.* But then he wasn't sure. One or the other lay beneath his cheek. *Cushion. Pillow.* They melted and merged. They wavered and became sleep.

In the morning, Maud called Harry to her and gave him her snake stone. She told him the legend associated with it, shouting over the din of the rain. A squall of wind carried a pestilential stench into the room. The stone rolled on the child's palm: a dull little nugget, ochre-tinged.

At lunchtime it was discovered that an act of municipal heroism had restored the supply of electricity. Harry raced in and out of rooms, puffing his cheeks and blowing out candles with great gusty breaths. A horn tooted at the gate. Maud thought, How am I to live, not seeing his face?

❖

She was lying on her coverlet, sleepless in the dark, when her bed began to shake. The door crashed on its hinges, drawers opened and slammed shut. One by one, her fingers were forced back from a bedpost. There was a weight on her chest, so that she fought for air. Coverlet and sheets were ripped from beneath her. Very clearly, above the rage, a thin sobbing went on and on. None of this was as frightening as the sense of a frustrated, furious presence. Its warm breath was in her ear.

When it ended, a minute later, she rose from the disordered bed. "I am a stupid old woman," said Maud to whatever was listening. Her fingers groped for the switch on the standard lamp, but everything was already clear.

God knows what that old fool of a doctor gave me to knock me out. It settled like fog on my brain, obscuring everything that happened that night.

Hours after I had fallen into bed, I found myself on the back verandah. Every step I took was weighty and effortful, like striding through water. Dr. van Dort had taken Leo away with him, but I had either forgotten or didn't care. Instinct propelled me toward the room where he had last drawn breath. The door was open. And on the threshold I walked into a child.

That was the vision that sank into my mind and lay buried there all these years. It governed me from that moment, I realize that now. But I had understood everything the wrong way round.

It seemed essential to write it all down, to pull knowledge, at least, from the wreckage of love. Maud saw a garden laid waste by thirst, soft blooms crisped on the stem. Her pen sped as if charmed.

I should have seen what Harry's dream meant straight away. A cushion that replaced a pillow: that was the crucial detail. It held the key to what happened to Leo.

Rain fell, the noise clamorous on the roof. When she tried to rise from the table, the walls swayed about her. She steadied herself, gripping the back of her chair.

Her diary was in her hand when she passed onto the verandah. She could not have said what she was doing; only that she was intent on reparation. Wind feathered her nightdress and someone called her name. Light flashing from the sky obliterated the courtyard. Trees filled the void, green fists bursting as far as she could see, rimmed with restless blue at the horizon. Her father lifted his hat and waved to her from that shore. The girl beside him held out her hands, strung with a ruby-red necklace. A dog with a snow-tipped tail wove in and out of view, and Iris, in strapless satin, was tangoing with a man in striped pajamas.

Other figures drew near, her dead gathering to greet her. A pigeon-toed woman, deep in conversation with Thornton. A jug-eared pirate who blew kisses. He lifted a fold of leopard skin and Maud saw the round-headed baby in his arms.

Rain drummed joyfully on the tiles, and was answered by the pounding at Maud's temples. The door of Leo's room gave at her touch. What she saw within, the scene glowing softly as if painted on glass, was a child with his arms folded over his chest. Then he let the pillow fall and ran forward to meet her.

Maud felt full of life, its force streaming through her limbs. A tremendous sense of well-being wrapped itself about her. She stumbled into its embrace and slept like a baby.

The bungalow keeper was a man who yawned often and tremendously, cracking his jaw. He was still retying his sarong and blinking sleep from his eyes when he saw the bundle lying on the verandah.

At the other end of the day, long after the burble of conjecture had subsided, and the doctor had finished issuing contradictory orders and driven away, Sirisena remembered the exercise book. It still lay like a broken bird near the door where he had found her. By the dim verandah light, his thumb rifled pages. That he could neither read nor write was one of the sources of his rage. Its lightning crazed through him now. The book cost five cents at any *kadai*; and represented everything that would always elude him.

The moon eased itself out from under a weight of clouds. When the bungalow keeper turned away from the decaying breath of the rubbish heap he saw the house before him, coated in silver light. For an instant it appeared utterly unfamiliar: a place he had visited only in a dream. Then the vision righted itself and he was returned to the world.

The last time Sam saw his mother was on a February morning in 1948. The English were leaving, with the haste instinctive to thieves. As he drove out of Colombo he kept the heel of his hand on the horn. The crowd thickened wherever a festive *pandal* arched over the road, its bamboo struts and crosspiece festooned with flowers and strings of colored bulbs.

The sea hissed on his right. The waves were up, whisked into sloppy peaks. Spray blew onto the hood of his car where the road embraced a headland of dark rock. Everything was changing: the sea crept forward and back, maps were altered grain by grain. Even when he turned off the coast road, he was conscious of that twisting vastness at his back. It propelled him forward, inland, toward certainty.

Maud lay propped against pillows. Her eyes were turned to a corner of the ceiling. She had been lying there, silent, the left side of her jaw dragged loose, for eight weeks. The doctor insisted that it was only a minor stroke. Yet life ebbed from her, a steady leaking.

The room was dim, dust-furred. The nurse slumped by the door took advantage, like all her kind. Sam saw, with irritation, that a sticky spoon with a tarnished handle lay on the drawn-thread tray cloth on the bedside table. His wife had stitched that mat, and the matching runner on the chest of drawers. Now both were creased, stained, the tray cloth was rust spotted. The table itself was cluttered with smeared tumblers, and bottles labeled in an apothecary's italics. But the doctor, who drove out to see Maud every few days, said that she was making no progress. "Lost interest. It happens all the time."

This doctor, whose name was Dickie Meerwald, had a birthmark on his left cheek, curving around his socket, where the raised skin was mulberry hued. He held his head awkwardly, angling the bad side down toward his shoulder. If not for the stain he would have been an imposing man: sharp-featured, flat-stomached. Sam remembered him from Neddy's, a new boy in too-long navy-blue shorts standing at an angle to the boundary wall. The jolt when he turned his head: a flipped coin coming down on the side of calamity.

Saucers of water had been placed under the legs of the dining table. At dinner the bungalow keeper said that the ants were bad that year. Sam hadn't troubled to telephone ahead, so ate unpolished country rice, fried snake beans and coconut *sambol*, like the servants. But the cook-woman had opened a tin and curried some mackerel for him. The fire-works began while the dishes were being carried in. He chewed slowly, to the sound of distant explosions.

The following morning he went in to see Maud and found himself calculating how many years had passed since they had last touched each other. He sat beside the bed with his hands on his knees. There was a sickroom smell of musty sheets and Brand's Essence of Chicken. His eyes alighted on his mother's slippers, the indent of her heel and the ball of her foot plainly visible in the worn rubber. He wrenched his gaze away.

His chair creaked when he brought his knees together. Maud's lids flew open. Her eyes had remained beautiful: leaf-shaped, the unclouded amber of old. For one long radiant moment, he thought she had seen him clearly: not as he appeared, but as he was. "How clever you are," she would say. She would say, "My marvelous boy."

He picked up the case he had set on her bedside table. Made of ma-hogany and lined with royal-blue silk, it held eight cut-glass bottles with silver-gilded stoppers and mounts, a silver-backed clothes brush and a shaving pot. He had acquired it in a lot, along with a pair of vine-clustered grape scissors and a papier-mâché card tray, at an auction house on Bullers Road, obeying the usual imperative that directed his purchases. It was only after the auctioneer had knocked everything down to him that he spotted the initials twined on the lid of the case.

The past was retrievable; at that moment he was certain of it. Time dissolved, slipped sideways in that room. The girl who was his mother stopped him in his flight. She would not let him pass, but steadied him in her arms. He angled the case and traced its gold lettering with a finger that trembled: *H. W. P. O.* "Look," he said. "It belonged to Pater."

Maud gave no sign of having understood or even heard. But when he was at the door she said, her voice clear, "Only eight bottles, Ritzy?" Then her crooked, irresistible smile. "I suppose I smashed the other two."

That night, in Colombo, the noise jangled him awake. He had dozed off in his office room, feet up on a low table. A Christmas fly, seduced by the lamp at his elbow, was disintegrating in half an inch of brandy. Still cobwebby with sleep he swung his feet down, and pins and needles tattooed prickles along the muscles of his calves. The telephone squatting on his desk like a sooty imp shrieked again, bloated with self-importance.

He knew at once what this midnight summons signified. The operator went off the line and he heard the bungalow keeper's voice, buzzing with static and the thrill of bad news. It drowned out the sound of the sea. But he knew it was there, a rolling darkness to which he would come.

❖

Eight years later, in 1956, what was now called the Sinhalese People's Party won government in a landslide victory at the polls. Sam gave it as his opinion that the elections had been rigged; he knew fellows who knew other fellows who had witnessed the bribery and voter intimidation at first hand. The chaps—decent chaps with *backgrounds*—who had taken over the burden of government from the British woke up to find themselves in opposition, scrambling for scapegoats and explanations.

The new Minister of Culture—Jungle Jaya, as an inspired columnist dubbed him—appeared in every newspaper, massive, genial, wreathed in marigolds and temple flowers. At the club Sam ran into a fellow from Neddy's who swore that Jaya had slept with the wives of every one of his fellow ministers. This despite the gargantuan paunch, dragging at him like guilt, that rendered the act almost impossible. It was common knowledge in government circles, said Sam's informant, that the Minister accomplished sexual intercourse only with the aid of a ramp designed to facilitate the copulation of elephants.

At the Queen's–St. Edward's match Jaya showed up in a sarong, his silver and blue rosette pinned to a Nehru collar. When he presented the cup to the winning team—Queen's, with four wickets in hand, as it happened—he remarked that it was only when watching a game of cricket that he could understand why so many intelligent men had believed in the honorable intentions of the British. He seemed not to notice the flushed presence on the same stage of Warden Radford and half a dozen English masters. The boys cheered, as boys do. Jaya clambered into the back of an open truck with the rowdiest of them and drove around Colombo, serenading schoolgirls with caddish songs. It was bally bad form from start to finish.

At Neddy's Harry had one of those nondescript careers. For a few months at the age of fourteen he displayed an enthusiasm for hockey, which evaporated as soon as his house selected him as a reserve. Once, he was placed third in Geography; the maps he drew were exquisite. His reports typically characterized him as *a pleasant boy.* The lack of interest he inspired in his teachers was manifest.

Sam sometimes thought that this ordinariness was itself a kind of talent, and not unenviable: it freed his son from the knotted anxiety that had attended his own successes at school. Is there any torment in adult life keener than that suffered by a clever child hanging around the noticeboard where the results will be posted? Yet the next moment he would be speared by anger: why couldn't the boy make an effort, when was contentment with mediocrity not symptomatic of a mediocre mind?

The years lengthened, breathing slowly.

Harry had his tonsils out.

He was left-handed.

He rode his bicycle everywhere.

He went to the pictures, or swimming at Mount Lavinia, with friends from school. They shared a brief craze for cramming themselves into telephone booths, a fad that swept the city and attracted the disfavor of newspaper editors.

He asked for and received a camera one Christmas.

He was allergic to penicillin.

He had a pen pal in Oslo.

He had inherited his mother's weakness for clear, bright colors. His bedroom was scattered with a confetti of cheap objects that had caught his eye on Pettah pavements: two china eggcups manufactured in Japan, one scarlet, the other leaf green; a turquoise tin mug with a crimson rim; a plastic orange.

He loved eggs scrambled with green chilies, and an American improbably named Elvis.

He wrote to the manufacturers of Ponds Vanishing Cream to avail himself of their free offer: an autographed photograph of their model, the film star Miss Kamala Devi, *Loveliness Personified.*

He had the same shoe size as his father. And like him, he couldn't hold a tune.

These were the things Sam knew about his son when the boy left for Oxford in his twentieth year. After eighteen months of cramming, Harry had been offered a place at his father's college; the question of what he was to read had proved almost as problematic. He had dropped Latin after scraping through his O Levels, and even Sam was obliged to acknowledge that he had no aptitude for the law. Probed about the future, Harry was typically malleable and vague: he could see himself in the Civil Service, he wouldn't mind tea, he hadn't altogether ruled out teaching. It was plain that he could not be left to steer his own course. Sam wrote to his old tutor. Fisher, now the Senior Fellow, suggested that the boy read history. *It does a young man no lasting harm.* Thus it was settled.

On the evening before Harry sailed, Sam stood him dinner at a hotel by the sea. It was a grand old place: atrocious architecture and beautiful décor. The boy chose a table on the pillared verandah. At the far end of the dining room a quartet was playing "Under the Bridges of Paris." The music reached them in dashes, interrupted by the breakers from India hurling themselves at the sea wall.

This was before the ban on all imported goods. Champagne arrived while they were waiting for their baked crab. Harry lit a Gold Flake, fumbling it a little. He was still new to smoking, having taken it up while cramming for his exams. Noting his awkwardness, Sam thought of all the rites the boy had yet to negotiate and with what negligence the world could crush him. He gripped his knife. This circumvented the impulse that would have him clasp his son's wrist and cry, Don't leave me.

He said, "Your grandmother was a great smoker," the words a blurted link between two needs. But it sounded harsh: accusatory and flat. Harry swiveled his head away.

A trolley of dishes with silver lids glided past. The scent of cardamom arrived to muddle the sea tang of salt and sewage.

Harry said, "Did you know that curry comes from a Tamil word? *Kari*, meaning a sauce."

"I say!" He eyed his son. "What an extraordinary thing to know. Where did you pick that up?"

Harry shrugged. Sam saw that it was, inexplicably, the wrong question. He resented the unreasonableness of this.

As always, silence was the solder they applied to the cracks between them.

The quartet played "Blue Skirt Waltz," followed by "As Time Goes By."

Sam said, "Great thing to be a young fellow with Oxford waiting like a book."

He said, "A May Ball, you know."

He said, "Nosing down the river in a punt. The willows. And those birds, let me think what they're called. Sedge warblers?"

Harry looked into his empty glass. He drank like a young man, thirstily. He looked up and said, "Granny told me you were refused a tryout for the tennis teams. And that the stories you wrote for the college magazine were always returned. They didn't even open the envelope."

Sam could see Harry's lips moving, but knew that these little razor-tipped shafts had been loosed in hell. He wanted to put his arms up before his face. The realization that the boy had carried that information within him all these years, like an illness, was unbearable. Sam had never spoken of these slights. He had forgotten them himself. It was like that game he had played as a child, where a fellow came up noiselessly behind you and drove his knees into the backs of yours and what you felt above all, as you went down, was that you had been a fool.

There was a weight in his breast pocket, the gold lighter he had had engraved with his son's initials. He put his hand to his chest.

Harry said, "Why do you never talk about what they did to you? Why is it always water meadows and the deer at Magdalen?"

On a planet where men are moved by a superior mechanism it might have been apparent to Sam that belligerence was the coating with which the boy was trying to swallow his nerves. As it was, he managed only to say, "She must have got it all from Jaya. He had cronies at Oxford. Threads of third-hand gossip, spun out of all proportion." It clattered between them, sounding tinny and worthless, like one of the new coins the government had minted.

The boy's face remained ungiving. This time the silence had a different quality, as of a blind alley.

Harry sailed at midday on the *Orion*. His father's old overcoat, freshly brushed, lay across his bunk. It pinched under the arms, but Sam had insisted. "Just to tide you over," he said again, now. He stooped, caressed one of the hairy sleeves. "Get yourself measured up as soon as you can. Jermyn Street. You have the address?"

Harry nodded.

His father picked up the heavy coat. He patted it, scraped at a loose thread that wasn't there, laid the coat down again with great tenderness. "Mustn't get stuck with this old fellow."

He shook Harry's hand when the bell sounded. A motor launch was waiting to carry visitors to shore. He stood at the stern, heedless of spray, his gaze on the rail that was receding like hope. That evening, he realized that he had forgotten to wave his handkerchief. His footsteps followed him in and out of echoing rooms, and he could not forgive himself the omission.

Weeks later his coat arrived in layered brown paper, along with a black-and-white postcard of the Sheldonian. *Meadows stony*, said the inscription in Harry's backward sloping hand. The parcel had been opened and inexpertly done up again. It was a wonder the coat hadn't been pinched. Sam wouldn't put anything past the light-fingered blighters at the post office. Whenever he sifted through the envelopes waiting for him on his desk and found nothing with an Oxford postmark, he pictured a clerk with oiled hair slitting open an envelope with foreign stamps in case it contained banknotes. With time, the attributes of this individual became very clear to him: the nylon shirt yellowing in the armpits, the stacked aluminum lunch carrier with its film of greasy curry. He had a word to the postmaster general, who promised to look into the matter. Nothing changed, of course. The PMG was not actually a fellow one knew. This was happening more and more, chaps arriving out of nowhere like cracks in a wall.

History, for all its shortcomings, is supremely impersonal. Sam could see its effect on lives other than his own, patterns he had thought eternal wrenched into new configurations. A fellow's shoes growing shabbier as inflation corroded his pension. Silver-haired girls one had danced with wilting in line for a bus under the fierce blue eye of noon. Nevertheless he was unable to shake off the suspicion that a unique malice had singled him out. It was not that misfortune came his way. Rather that his star dimmed; or perhaps it was simply that others brightened. One morning no different from all the others, between the upward and the downward scratch of his pen, he understood that the zenith toward which he labored already lay behind him.

There was nothing to suggest this in the dark paneling of his chambers, or the twenty-six crimson spines of *Principles of Roman–Dutch Law* in the French-polished case behind his desk. He had taken silk just before the war. His reputation was secure. His practice flourished; years ago it had reached the stage where it could scarcely do otherwise. Lesser men still fawned on him and courted his patronage. But one post-independence cabinet succeeded the other, and the Bench was never mooted. Yet he was sure he had the finest legal mind in the island.

All government appointments were political, of course; merit didn't enter into it. His views on the state of the country were widely known and he wasn't about to sing a different bally tune. Jaya's old jibe, *Obey by name, Obey by nature*, crawled once more over the convolutions of his brain. He was never going to give them the satisfaction of seeing him mash stringhoppers between his fingers while coconut gravy dripped down his arm. The fear of appearing foolish if he changes his mind may bind a man to a course of action more securely than any oath. He began giving small formal dinners every year on May 24. Sam Obeysekere's Empire Day do: word got around. He felt it was a plucky, rather fine gesture: the Collector in the doomed residency running up the standard. At the same time he resented the role. It had been imposed on him. They had thrust him into anachronism.

One day he switched on the wireless halfway through a jingle: *Hentley, Hentley, Shirts the dhobi cannot tear* . . . He was scarcely aware of listening. But later he discovered the word *sanforized* embedded in his memory. *Sanforized. Sanforized.* He batted it away and it returned to the attack. What did it mean? He suspected that everyone else knew. *Sanforized. Sanforized.* How could he find out, without revealing ignorance? Where was the dictionary to which he could refer?

On an April morning limp with heat, he stood in his dressing room and found himself shouting. "I'm the detective," he bellowed at a rack of listless ties. "I'm the coming man."

On Harry's twenty-first birthday, he came into money from his mother's family. He had been at Oxford for four terms. He wrote to Sam, thanking him for his telegram of congratulations, and the bank draft. A brief paragraph added, as if it were an afterthought, that he had left the university and was living *with friends* in Yorkshire. There was a view of moors, he wrote. He intended to find work as a gardener, *or perhaps in forestry*. To set a seed in the earth and see it grow was all he wanted to do.

Sam took a Quickshaws taxi to the airport. There he crossed the tarmac and boarded his first airplane. A scented china doll with yellow hair piled on her head leaned across him to adjust a buckle. Her cone-shaped breasts were an inch away from his lips. He squeezed his knees together. Over Switzerland the plane ran into turbulence and he moaned as she lurched across the aisle and into his arms. Together they dipped toward the lights of Europe, an orange sodium code that for a long ravishing moment he believed he could crack with her assistance.

For five days he heard nothing but the ringing in his ears. Against this metallic score, England unfolded as a soundless hallucination. Double-deckers exhibited their scarlet rumps in choked streets. Girls' bleached faces swayed above their collars like flowers that refuse to open. At Paddington an ancient female with pink-rimmed eyes and a fox stole barred his way, mouthing furious instructions; at last he gathered that he had been taken for a porter. He was outraged and humiliated—among the crowds pushing past there had been more than one smile—yet you could see how it had happened. He had never seen so many brown and black faces in London. Whenever he ventured into the street he encountered women shivering in saris or gaudy robes, a bright plumage of embroidered cloth escaping from the camouflage of dirt-colored raincoats and stretched cardigans. Once, if you had met a creature like that in London you would have known she was a princess. Now there was every chance she would turn out to be a tea plucker. The February sky was an iron cap clamped down as tight as a headache. The exchange rate was a practical joke.

He was afraid that Harry would not come. But he did, seventeen minutes late. He was wearing a coat with a hood and wooden toggles, quite plainly not from Jermyn Street. His face had filled out. His hair was too long. Father and son shook hands, directed smiles at each other's shoulders.

Sam had decided to stand the boy lunch at the Savoy, to demonstrate his goodwill. It was an error. They were shown to a table half obscured by a potted palm, with a view of a wall. The prices were dizzying. Harry said something to their waiter. After a long interval, he was brought a plate of pale leaves and slices of whitish-yellow tomato.

"What? What?" The din in Sam's skull had sunk to a drone, but all external noise still reached him thickened with silence. Harry's lips moved. "Vegetarian?" His son nodded. "Why?" Harry gazed at the cruet, spoke briefly. Sam caught the word *life*. "Not a Buddhist as well?" Harry shook his head. "Well, that's a relief," he shrieked, and saw the boy flinch.

Sam had promised himself that he would not speak of Oxford over lunch. Words trembled on his lips but he held heroically to his course. They shouted platitudes at each other at intervals. The effort this required was exhausting. Harry enquired about friends from Neddy's. Sam had no idea what they were up to. He made his way through another gluey forkful of veal *à la normande*, all the while conscious that every facet of the scene—the atrocious food, the bored waiters, the mingled scents of hothouse gardenias and roasting flesh—was conspiring against him. There stole upon him the same helpless rage he felt when a jury, ignoring legal argument, common sense and directions from the Bench, returned a verdict of Not Guilty.

At last it was over. Outside, the rain had let up and an east wind was rubbing the day raw. Harry produced a frightful checked muffler that he wound about his throat. He hadn't shaved. Sam had a sudden, terrifying premonition that he was about to walk away and leave everything unsaid between them forever. "A stroll!" he bellowed and grasped his son's elbow.

They walked in the park with bent heads past sodden earth and drowned green lawns. There was no one about. Boughs dripped noiselessly. Dark birds blew about the sky like debris.

At a place where hooves had churned the footpath into milky tea, Sam halted. "No real damage done. Saw Fisher yesterday. They'll have you back."

Harry began to say something.

"Have to speak up!"

"I've made up my mind."

"Finish your degree. Then we'll see."

Harry shook his head.

"The money won't last forever. How will you get by then?"

Again, the boy shook his head. He said, "Don't worry about me. I'll be all right."

"What?"

"I'll be all right! Don't worry!" Then, unexpectedly, Harry smiled. His face, released from watchfulness, was vivid with charm. "Here we are," he roared, "at the heart of the Empire, shouting at each other across two feet of mud."

Sam slapped him, open-palmed.

Harry took half a step backwards. He placed his hand against his cheek. He said, every word distinct, "I've always hated you." Then he walked away.

Life is bearable only if it can be understood as a set of narrative strategies. In the endless struggle to explain our destinies we search for cause and effect, for recurrent patterns of climax and dénouement; we need beginnings, villains, we seek the hidden correlation between a rainy afternoon remembered from childhood and a letter that doesn't arrive forty years later.

It was routine among Sam's acquaintances, as they stiffened into age, to date the decline of the island from the departure of the British. After that everything followed with the inevitability of history: new stamps, hula hoops, ration books, flocked nylon, rising prices, a falling currency, Coca-Cola, cabinet ministers in sarongs, ladies in trouser suits, failed coups, successful assassinations, race riots and a national anthem no one knew the words to. A generation was left marooned on verandahs, eking out its grievances like whiskey and sodas. Land reforms! The Twist!

After Sam retired he became a familiar figure in Colpetty, stepping straight-backed through the streets every morning with a malacca cane. He wore a straw boater and a sand-colored suit, and noted evidence that standards had deteriorated. A brass tap on a stand pipe at the junction of two streets that hadn't worked for months. Drains painted with velvet slime. The insolence of rickshaw coolies. Three dead rats arrayed on a potholed pavement. Yellow phlegm gobbed in a doorway. A constable on point duty who wiped his nose on the back of a smeared cotton glove. Dust-streaked double-deckers, pensioned from London, fixed in the traffic and coughing up exhaust like old men with terminal illnesses. The tide of filth that mounted the pavements, crept over walls, plastered the façade of every public building. He would return to breakfast well satisfied: it was no more than the fools deserved.

Tissa had gone, claimed by a cancer that gnawed through his pancreas in four weeks. He was succeeded by a series of anonymous laborers, hired for two or three days a week. Such men knew nothing about gardening. They treated their days at Allenby House as a respite from the spine-cracking labor that waited for them on building sites or the docks, and were usually to be found scratching at the vegetable beds near the kitchen, hoping for a cup of tea. Patches of mange appeared on the lawn. No longer renewed every six months, the earth in the flowerpots along the verandah turned gray, and the plants they held withered. An arbor collapsed under the weight of clumping jasmine. Seeds grew skyward where they fell. Shrubs rose and put out woody arms and choked each other. Wild blue pools of morning glory advanced by stealth. Throughout the garden there were fresh new leaves and silky shoots, the ancient, anonymous green life that thrived on neglect.

Whenever its disorder impinged too far on his consciousness Sam would sack the man he had hired, then replace him with another of the same kind. It was a ritual, satisfying and meaningless. It appeased his sense that something had to be done, but saved him the expense of a full-time gardener. The government was up to its systematic rookery. The price of a *chundi* of rice! The cost of butter! Devising ingenious household economies was one of the pleasures of Sam's retirement. Visitors were served drinks in thimble-sized glasses. He had the bulbs removed from half the lamps in the house and tolerated nothing brighter than forty watts in the rest. His servants were allowed meat or fish no more than twice a week. Then he gave notice to the lot of them and employed a cook servant-boy, a round-chinned youth named Ranil from a village near Lokugama.

Ranil had unexpected talents. He replaced the worn rattan in all the chairs, holding down the long new canes with his toes as he wove them together. Using a mixture of sugar and powdered borax he rid the house of cockroaches, and was capable, when he put his mind to it, of turning out a halfway decent Irish stew. But in the matter of social instinct he was a blank slate. On his first day at Allenby House he presented the Visitors' Book to the fellow who came to the door with a cobra in a basket. Sam, inspecting the entry that night, saw an unintelligible squiggle, followed by careful block letters: ONE SNAKCHARMER.

One morning a dog with a large head was lying on the verandah. It was collarless and of uncertain pedigree, but its toffee-colored fur was sleek. At the sight of Sam, it rolled over and presented him with its unguarded belly. Then it righted itself, inched forward and licked his left shoe. It did not appear rabid. Nevertheless it was an unattractive brute. He sent Ranil to make enquiries among the neighbors but they denied all knowledge of the animal.

The dog arrived the year after the fields across the lane from Allenby House had been torn up by machinery. Bird-bodied men in cages of bamboo scaffolding buried the clawed earth under three pastel cubes of surpassing ugliness. They had been designed by an upstart in dark glasses who passed himself off as an architect and was rumored to have been paid a lakh for his vandalism. A *lakh!* The houses were owned by three brothers. One made films about a secret agent called Jamis Banda, another worked in advertising, the third ran an agency that transported tourists to coral reefs and wildlife sanctuaries. These occupations struck Sam as flimsy and dubious. A man might be a carpenter or a shopkeeper or a cinnamon peeler, he might be a general or a shipping clerk, there was a lineage and weight to such work, it anchored a man in the world. Modernity found expression not in revolutions or acts of parliament but in a series of small terrible jolts. One airless afternoon you noticed that respectable women were wearing lime green or that the basin from which a crone was hawking velvet tamarinds to passing schoolboys was molded from plastic, and you realized that the world had changed utterly, in ways that far exceeded the sweep of your comprehension.

Sam suspected one or all of his new neighbors of spying on him through the slits of their sly louver windows. They possessed transistor radios. Their wives wore frosted lipstick and drove Mini-Minors, their unspeakable sons swaggered up the lane with little fingers linked and combs protruding from their hip pockets. The air around them was hard edged, yet nonchalant and bright. In a chain of days hung with small shameful failures of memory, so that Sam would begin a sentence with rock underfoot and find himself, three words later, dropping through rushing air, a line of a poem he had learned as a schoolboy hammered at his brain: *They are all gone into the world of light.* "The world of light," he repeated aloud. "The world of light." It suggested cellophane, and angular chairs fashioned from blond wood. He stepped out each day from dim rooms of solid brick and mortar into a world as insubstantial and alluring as images projected on a screen.

His neighbors were implicated in the matter of the stray dog, of that he was certain. He slipped a looped cord around the animal's neck and told Ranil to take it to the Pettah and turn it loose. This was done. But the next day the dog was there again, flattening itself on the verandah. Its tail thumped when Sam appeared. What was he to do? He laid his hand on the springy fur and found a bloated gray tick on its neck. He pried it free and was about to hurl it into a flower bed, when the dog took it very gently from his fingers and ate it. It was not an unintelligent beast, but it loved him abjectly. It lay across the lavatory door and squirmed with joy when he emerged.

There was a day when, in the very act of stepping over its belly, he became aware that he found its devotion pleasing. The realization was succeeded by a hot humiliation: to be tickled by the good opinion of an animal! He made one or two further attempts to be rid of the dog, even driving it himself to Nugegoda junction and turning it out of the car. A week later it padded up the drive, ears laid back, hip bones more sculpted. Sam looked up the number for the dog catcher in the telephone book but could not bring himself to make the call. The dog pressed its body against his legs. Eventually he named it Watson: for its good nature, and stubborn loyalty. He ignored it, mostly. It ignored everyone else.

At a party for a retiring assize judge, he was accosted by a sucked chicken bone with a face like a fist: Mrs. Malini Mendis, the country's only lady advocate. Her grandfather had been a letter writer sitting cross-legged on a pavement in the Pettah; Mrs. Mendis was a graduate of Girton. Sam disliked her, of course. Quite apart from anything else, she was wearing an electric-blue sari. He would have grimaced and passed on, but she thrust a stuffed chili under his nose and said, "Now just the other day, your name came up."

Her voice was the sort described as fluting, which meant it could stun an elephant at twenty paces. "Denis de Saram's birthday party. We were talking about famous trials, that kind of thing. One of Denis's ancient aunties had a long rigmarole about a murdered planter. Harrison? Hamilton? The case Don Jayasinghe solved. Denis's auntie said you prosecuted but lost, because the English hushed it all up. I said, Are you telling me Sam Obeysekere used to be anti-British? Because as long as I've known him, his veins have run with Bovril."

It took her a little while to recover from her own wit. He passed the time in contemplation of her altogether remarkable sideburns.

Then he said, "You know, I ran into Nanette Raymond last week. I never see that girl without remembering how fondly poor old Bunny used to speak of her."

An embolism had killed Bunny Mendis while he toiled above the ravishing Nanette on a heat-clogged afternoon the previous year. Sooner or later, few could resist reminding his widow of these facts. But the Mendis woman's stretched white smile didn't falter. Sam was almost moved.

The idea, iridescent as an archangel's wing, came to him the next day. Now that he was alone at Allenby House, he had made his bedroom on the ground floor. The dust-sheeted rooms upstairs had the melancholy air of all things that have outlasted their purpose. Still, he climbed the veined stairs from time to time and stood at a window that looked seaward. At daybreak water and sky were a thin, opalescent mist. Once, he saw a fleet of etched black boats dissolve in it. But he preferred the night hours, when the sea detached itself from the land as a different darkness and the windows of the mail train pouring itself along the coast were a border of golden rectangles stamped on sooty velvet.

That evening the racket of the train's passing reminded him that Mrs. Mendis's mother had killed herself by stepping in front of an up-country express. At the time the event had defined her daughter; but now, just a few short years later, he had not thought of it at all in the course of their encounter. Knowledge became smudged with terrifying swiftness, forms faded and merged. At that moment he realized that he had to write about the Hamilton case. Once so widely known and discussed, it was slipping from public memory, glimpsed now and then only in grotesque distortion. He discovered that he was trembling a little from the force of the revelation. Yet the thing appeared to him whole and clear, so that he knew he was not mistaken. A book inviting to hand and eye, calf-bound, printed on linen paper. No desiccated lawyer's chronicle, but a tale that winged to the heart of things, life skimmed quivering onto the page. He gripped the sill and saw that he would write about himself, that this would give his story its human ballast.

He looked at the star-crowded sky and thought, There will be no mistaking the facts.

The moon was thin-edged, irregular as a pearl.

He thought, and a small wave lifted under his heart, he thought, Harry will understand.

After breakfast Sam would give Ranil his instructions for the day. Then he attended to correspondence, read the legal journals he still subscribed to, listed his personal expenditure from the previous day in a notebook. After that there were callers to receive. These were invariably obscure young men in search of endorsement of one kind or another. They sat on the edge of their verandah chairs in heroically snowy shirts, their knees jiggling in that common way, clutching a letter of introduction from men who were themselves of no importance, one of Sam's old clerks perhaps, or a minor official he had come across outstation and could no longer remember. The young men sought employment at the Transport Board or the Ministry of Agriculture, posts that carried a monthly salary of seventy or eighty chips and were contested by hundreds of their kind. They had identical stories, of ailing mothers to support and younger brothers to put through school. To these narratives Sam no longer listened. But he always scribbled a few lines on the young man's behalf and watched the sheet of headed notepaper stored away with painful care in a used brown envelope or between the pages of a blue-ruled exercise book. He was flattered by these requests, of course. At the same time he knew that it was useless, that if the fellow had any prospects he would not have been on Sam's verandah in the first place but importuning a cabinet minister or a senior civil servant or indeed one or other of the pastel trio across the lane.

At his feet Watson growled softly in his throat. He was jealous of all visitors, and would rise and place his body sideways between Sam and whoever came into the room. Sometimes all that was required was Sam's signature, as a justice of the peace, on a statutory declaration. Sometimes it was an old peon who had fallen on hard times. Once it was a loafer with a shifty, rolling gaze, who claimed to be Tissa's eldest son and tried to touch Sam for a loan. He stank of toddy and was wearing trousers. Bally cheek from beginning to end. But mostly it was the young men. These he was incapable of turning away. Each was a version of Harry, who might even at that moment be standing in front of an ineffectual codger in shirt sleeves who represented everything he understood as success.

Between a quarter- and half-past ten he would leave the house, ignoring the young men, who rose to their feet when he emerged from his office room. He walked down the drive, accompanied by Watson. At the gate the dog always raised his hind leg against the left-hand post. Then he would scratch lustily at the earth, scraping up grass and sending small stones flying. Sam would stand at the gate, looking up the lane, hands clasped on his stick. The face of the lion on the seaward side had blurred. Watson, an indolent beast, panted in the striped shade of the jacaranda.

During the monsoon the dog stood under dripping leaves, his gaze doleful. If the schools had awarded a rain holiday, two brats in plastic raincoats would emerge from a pastel house and hurry to the head of the lane, where they launched a flotilla of newspaper boats in the ditch. They had to run to keep pace with the downward rush, righting boats that capsized, poking sticks at those that floundered to urge them on. Their toes curled in the red mud. Sam looked on from the shelter of curved ebony petals. His own newspapers were bundled, tied with string and sold for wrapping at the rate of one cent a pound to the man who came to the kitchen door four times a year with a pair of scales and iron weights. The children's paper boats fetched up sodden against gratings, or were swept irretrievably under culverts. There was a certain frisson to be derived from the spectacle of this waste.

The post brought brick-high stacks for the houses across the lane. Sam himself was an assiduous letter writer, keeping up with colleagues who had retired to outstations, pursuing cronies who had emigrated to New South Wales. He had always had a prodigious memory for dates. He remembered the birthdays of third cousins and anniversaries overlooked by those whose acts they commemorated. Despite the cost of postage, he was particularly attentive to correspondents who lived abroad. The blue edge of an aerogram protruding from the postman's fist signaled a small explosion of hope. Sam would find his mouth full of saliva. The years passed, and his haul thinned. Yet even when there were six or seven letters it took only a moment to ascertain that there was nothing from Harry.

He would make his way back up the drive, sucking in his cheeks, then releasing them. The house waited for him, stuffed with useless objects: toast racks, clocks, chests of folded linen, plump putti nestled in the gilded molding of a frame.

At Christmas and in the week leading up to his birthday anticipation flickered constantly in him, as a frayed wire exposes the jumping current within. He was beset by tiny acute pains that shifted their source as soon as he had tracked them to eyeball or wrist. When he thought of his son he saw a window streaked with rain that he could not wipe clean. Once—a bad December—he sat for over an hour behind his desk. He still had the address in Yorkshire. Christmas flies, drawn to the lamp, left a litter of taffeta wings on his blotter. But when he placed his hands on the arms of his chair and levered himself upright, ligaments creaking defiance, the sheet of ivory paper in front of him remained unblemished. He was owed an apology. It was up to the boy to make the first move. A son stands to his father in the same relation as beasts to man. This was one of the granite foundations on which he had built his life. It was not a question of refusing to go forward; rather that he had arrived at a limit. He took his handkerchief from his pocket and blew his nose. He thought, People used to wave a hanky to say goodbye. But he couldn't remember the last time he had seen it.

After dinner, and long into the night, he sat at his desk, working on the memoir that would set out the events of the Hamilton case. At first, as he polished his style and buffed his epigrams, he knew only intense pleasure. It was inherent to the task: where is the man who does not enjoy talking about himself? And then, every writer knows the elation of beginnings. Greater than these delights, however, was the satisfaction of puncturing the sanctimonious bubble with which Jaya had contrived to surround himself during his life, and which a hundred bleating eulogies and fawning Sunday features enshrined as truth after his death. Sam would call history to testify against mythology. A just verdict! His pen raced toward the sweet prospect. Now and then, in its haste, his nib caught in the paper. His pages were punctured with tiny holes, a scattering of gunshot.

Later he would think that this had been his mistake, to allow himself to be seduced on his journey to the heart of the Hamilton case. He had dawdled. He had followed the temptation of meandering tracks and found himself doubting the way forward. Impossible now to recover the *élan* of his start. Two nights and a day might pass and he would have written only a single sentence. He retraced his steps; cast this or that phrase differently. He made a fair copy of the manuscript. The Hamilton case beckoned. He was there, at the edge of the thicket. And still he hesitated, and looked over his shoulder and was pursued by a bewilderment that advanced on him like time.

He might be proposing a toast at a Bar Association dinner, or negotiating a flight of stairs while pain streamed to his knees from his spine, his mind fixed on the task at hand, when he would be nudged by an unease he found difficult to classify. Then the ill-defined impression that he had missed something—*a vital clue* was the formulation that came unbidden to him—would keep him company for days, a smudge at the edge of his vision. If he jerked his head around quickly enough he might spot it.

This tic, very pronounced at times, was remarked upon by everyone who knew him. In the market, Ranil sat on a sack of lentils and gave it as his opinion that the *hamuduruwo* was beset by ghosts. The remark was a testimony to his insight.

On a rain-shrouded night in 1963, Jaya's car had skidded on a bend near Kadugannawa Pass. He died with a steering wheel embedded in his chest. Sam recalled the black border around his newspaper; the photograph of the crumpled hood. At the time, he had exulted at the supreme justice of it: Jaya crashing into a rocky embankment, like the country he had guided into disaster with such reckless disregard for the rules. The telephone was ringing before he had reached the end of the first column: a chap he knew from Neddy's, inviting him to a discreet celebration in Cinnamon Gardens that evening. By the time he returned to the table, his toast had grown cold. He rattled the handbell. Ranil came in, after a delay. Sam was about to tick the blighter off; then he saw that the boy was crying.

Now, during the sleepless hours he spent hunched in a chair, cross-examining the past like an unreliable witness, he was haunted by the possibility that he had chosen unwisely. By daylight he knew this to be absurd. But at night the sound of the sea reached him more distinctly. Its repetitions, which were never wholly identical, hinted at infinite subtleties of interpretation. He was unable to articulate why he should find this disturbing. There was only the unbearable thought that everything might have been different.

Beneath the baleful murmur of ceiling fans, the British Council library offered the *Times*, the *Spectator, Punch*. In this way entire afternoons were rendered tolerable. Each day was a campaign conducted in hostile territory where meticulous discipline was required to keep moving forward, outflanking tedium. He still played tennis every Wednesday and Saturday; and turned up, vervain scented, at AGMs, where he could be counted on to dispute obscure points of order. Other men, his contemporaries, succeeded in overcoming boredom only to be assaulted by despair. Then there were only two courses open to them, death or emigration. He outmaneuvered loneliness by failing to recognize it, a devastating strategy.

One day, as he was leaving the library, his attention snagged on the rosewood stand of Recent Acquisitions. The book was called *Serendipity*; but it was the name below that had drawn his eye. His first thought: When was inadequacy ever a bar to ambition? Nevertheless, as he picked up the volume there was a needle of jealousy in his heart—Shivanathan, the author of a collection of stories!

At the Loans desk, he tapped the crudely tinted illustration on the cover. "I know this fellow."

The librarian, rifling through his box of index cards, nodded without raising his eyes.

"Oh yes—we were at Neddy's together. One of those plodders. Worked his way up, worked his way up. But they passed him over for the Supreme Court."

Even the silly asses at the Ministry got it right from time to time. Like everyone in the legal fraternity, Sam knew that Shivanathan had come under an official cloud. Details were sketchy, but Billy Mohideen had insisted the blighter was suspected of taking bribes. Nothing could be proved, said Mohideen, but the Supreme Court was out of the question. It so happened, however, that the vacancy arose shortly after the riots in '58, when everything was reflected in the distorting mirror of race. The cry went up that Shiva had been overlooked because he was a Tamil.

While the controversy billowed about him, Shivanathan had accepted a post abroad; somewhere that didn't count, like Canada. At this recollection, Sam's resentment began to ease. He flipped through the book, a cheap local edition, noticing the coarse paper, misspellings and smudged, uneven type. A biographical note informed him that the author was *Emeritus Professor of Low* at a university in Vancouver. The little rush of glee carried Sam along Galle Road, so that he bore the exhausted afternoon with equanimity. The sloganed, filthy walls, the blue petrol stink and glaring windshields, the house-high advertisements for Bata Shoes: he smiled with gentle forbearance on them all.

At sunset bats rose from the tree at the top of the lane to stencil the sky. Sam opened Shivanathan's book, savored the pretentious subtitle—*Island Epiphanies*—and prepared to be entertained. "There will be breasts that resemble mangoes," he announced to the decanter at his elbow. "Hair lustrous with coconut oil will alternately ripple and cascade. And I very much fear there'll be a barefoot old woman in spotless white who eats curries with her fingers and performs simple devotions to her gods."

Two hours of contented skimming proved him right in every particular. He put down the book, awarded himself a third whiskey and went in to dinner.

For years now he had taken his meals at a gate-legged table in his office room. At eight Ranil came in with a fish cutlet, boiled French beans, tinned beetroot, white bread and butter. Afterward there was orange jelly. Everything was indifferently cooked, the beans falling apart, the jelly resilient as rubber; but to care overmuch about food is a sign of weak character. Between courses he opened Shiva's book at random and read, with deep pleasure, a sentence involving *a maiden* and *delicately cupped hands*.

Over the jelly, his amusement turned rancid. Shiva had taken the cuneiform in which the world manifested itself and reduced it to a script suitable for the nursery: *H is for Hut. L is for Lotus.* His version of reality resembled the simple drawings in flat, bright colors that adorn kindergarten walls: a typical lotus, a typical hut. And those terrible little pictures, drained of all complexity, were hailed by his publishers as *authentic glimpses of an island paradise*. Here I am, thought Sam, with my orange jelly and my *Collected Works of Shakespeare*, I'm part of it all too, like it or not, I'm as authentic as any bally mango.

The last story in the book was by far the longest. He saved it until he had swallowed the last spoonful, intending to relish it like a sweet.

He read quickly at first, then slowly, and a pale moth drugged on light drowned in the coffee grown cold in his cup.

When he was halfway down the last page, the night mail dragged past at the bottom of the lane. Minutes later it reached the bend in the track and cried out, a beast that could endure no longer.

He flipped pages until he found the beginning of the story, and read it through once more.

"Death of a Planter" was set in an outstation in the 1930s. It centered on a bored Englishwoman named Cynthia Wilmot, who was married to the superintendent of a rubber plantation. Mrs. Wilmot had been amusing herself with a man called Cameron, her husband's oldest friend, who managed the adjoining estate. The story opened at the point where she had thrown him over for Vernon Danby, the local magistrate. Consumed by jealous hatred, Cameron threatened to lay the tale of her infidelities before her husband; whereupon the lovers colluded to murder him.

Cameron's body was found beside an isolated estate road very early one morning. The police looked for the killer among his workers, as Cameron was a notoriously harsh employer. A coolie was arrested and interrogated. But nothing could be proved against the man, despite the best efforts of the police, and eventually he was released. (Here, the flow of the story was interrupted by a page of predictable sentiments about the plight of the estate worker, plucked from his native India to labor on the plantations of the profiteering British. The sole merit of the passage was to stamp Shiva's blatant pastiche of Maugham with a clumsiness that was wholly original.)

It was then, a few weeks after the crime, that the murderers revealed their genius and the true viciousness of their scheme. Danby befriended an English reporter who was visiting the district and contrived to direct suspicion at Mrs. Wilmot's husband. The reporter, *a Londoner with the high opinion of himself that brands a fool*, leapt at the opportunity to play sleuth. Within days, following the trail of insinuation and false evidence artfully laid by Danby, he had "discovered" the identity of the murderer. True to the principles of detective fiction, his investigations "proved" that the crime had been committed by the least likely suspect: Wilmot, the dead man's best friend.

Wilmot protested his innocence, but was arrested and tried for murder. He stood to gain financially from Cameron's death, having come into a sizable legacy from his friend. Yet at trial the case for the prosecution was shown to be flimsy, with little direct evidence linking the accused to the crime.

At this crucial juncture Cynthia Wilmot took the witness stand. There, playing her role with consummate artistry, she "broke down" under cross-examination and confessed to her affair with Cameron. She told the court of her fears that Wilmot had discovered what was going on. She also retracted the alibi she had originally provided, now admitting that she had slept so soundly throughout the night of the murder that she could not swear to her husband's presence at her side. Everyone understood what she did not actually say: that this unnaturally deep sleep had been brought on by the cup of Horlicks served to her at bedtime by the accused and doctored with a draught for his own murderous ends.

The jury returned a Guilty verdict, which was upheld on appeal, and Wilmot went to his death in a prison yard one morning.

His widow, tearful and upright to the last, sailed for New Zealand, where Danby joined her after a judicious interval.

The reporter, whose genius was feted on three continents, turned his account of the murder into a bestselling book, accepted an outrageously high fee from a London broadsheet to write the occasional column celebrating his own brilliance, and lived a long, contented and useless life.

Much later, while a corner of his brain noted with puzzlement that the decanter was almost empty, Sam thought of Shivanathan cultivating his spite over the years until it erupted at last into this grotesque flower. It demonstrated what he had always known: that no one is too untalented to excel at envy.

Yvette Taylor had been capable of anything. Hadn't he always suspected her of setting that weak fool Taylor on his murderous course? Beyond that, Shiva's theory was preposterous. To imply that Nagel was guilty of cold-blooded collusion in the deaths of two men was fanciful enough. But to suggest that Sam himself had been instrumental in fulfilling the murderers' design proved only that a diseased mind is a great maker of fictions.

The high opinion of himself that brands a fool. There would be smiles in Hulftsdorf when that one did the rounds.

From the row of royal-blue bindings, he selected the volume he wanted straight away. The bookcase had a glass door locked with a key, protecting its contents from the monsoon's rot; but silverfish have in common with thoughts the capacity to ravage as they please. He shook the book gently, dislodging a papery shower of wings from the binding on the spine, noticing that the silver crest and motto on the cover were still bright: *Semper Vincit.* Inside, entire sections displayed the insects' tattoos, but the cutting he had placed there forty years earlier remained intact. He carried it over to the lamp and examined the photograph with the tender amazement we reserve for our younger selves. *Our Sherlock Holmes:* as an embrocation, it was extraordinarily soothing.

With supreme disregard for the British Council's injunctions he went through Shivanathan's book with his pen in his hand, circling literals, underlining errors of fact, annotating legal points, calling attention to the grosser stylistic blunders with an exclamation mark in the margin. All the while an old trouble flickered just below the surface of his mind. Something he had noticed but not heeded at the time. It came again, a faint tug traveling up the taut stretch of years. Any moment he would wind it in. But then it darted away, vanishing into opacity where he couldn't follow.

When he looked up he saw what he had long ceased hoping for, a fold of yellow skirt in the mess of shadows beyond the bookcase. At once he was released, the core of him unclenching. There would be time yet to set everything right. He rose from his chair in a single painless movement, supple as a boy. She was gone on the instant. But when he opened his eyes the memory of happiness remained, a streak of brightness like the first thread of day unspooling along the horizon.

It was a Saturday. There were no young men waiting on the verandah. Half-past ten found him at his usual post, by the gate. A dull discomfort was coursing the length of the arm that had been cramped under his body when he woke. He stretched and flexed the limb but was unable to dislodge the ache. There was a scuttling among the white-haired mango stones and blackened plantain skins in the ditch; a rat perhaps, or a chameleon. Watson cocked his head, but declined to investigate.

The stand on the postman's bicycle was broken. He propped it against a telephone pole and fed envelope after envelope into the slits in the gateposts of the pastel houses across the way. Then he looked across at Sam and shook his head. He could just as well have signaled this information as he freewheeled down the lane, but had chosen to keep his victim in suspense. This despite relieving him of five chips at Christmas.

Fury knocked at Sam's breastbone. But he remained planted where he was, gazing up the lane as if absorbed in the red tilt of the earth, the vacant blue sky. He was very well aware that this charade lacked conviction, but was unable to prevent himself from acting it out.

At last the postman reached the crest of the lane, standing on his pedals, and turned into the main road; no doubt to snicker in a tea boutique at the old codger to whom no one had written in a month.

Sam had forgotten his stick. Hands paddling the air beside his thighs he made his way up the drive, measuring out the distance three paces at a time. His head jerked sideways. *Sanforized. Sanforized.* It beat in his mind like heavy-plumed wings. They could replace sonnets with *sandesha* poems in every classroom if they liked; both were irrelevant. The generations to come would take their bearings from *A Hentley shirt is smart and neat, And keeps you cool in tropic heat* . . .

As he neared the house, he halted. Its paint, unrenewed in five years, had faded once more to a lemony ochre. It was a color he couldn't see without thinking of Claudia. Yet that morning it seemed to him that something was amiss. He continued to stare at the house, his neck thrust forward in the collar that had grown too loose. But the sun edged past the roofline and struck him. He lowered his head and shuffled forward into the portico, and Watson's cold nose came to fit itself into his palm.

At that moment there rose in his mind a picture of the Taylors' dog, its hindquarters writhing in ecstasy as it greeted Nagel like an old friend. The scene presented itself to him with sparkling clarity: a withered geranium leaf on the snowy gravel, the silvery feathering on the spaniel's paws. The past shuddered, then reconfigured itself differently. A life might turn on such a reversal.

He dismissed it at once. The slobbering kisses of a dog: what did they prove? Not that he could understand now why he had ever granted the Hamilton case any significance. Why had he set out to disentangle its chain of cause and effect? He had allowed a sideshow to distract him from the drama of his own history. Nagel, the Taylors, Hamilton glass-eyed on the jungle floor: they swirled about him and crumbled to dust. He barely noticed. He caressed his chest, where the ache had intensified.

Something lurched in him, a small vital cog or pivot, and he no longer had the strength to ram it into place.

With painful care he brought his left foot up to join the right one on the lowest step. The effort had to be repeated five times. An age later he arrived on the verandah. There he stood stone-still to recover, and thought, But it was Mater, not Claudia, who wore that shade of yellow.

Words he might have spoken, soft declarations of need, shifted in his thoughts like a breeze lifting papers in a room. He pictured a child rising from his bed, he traced his trajectory along the night corridors of Lokugama: a whiff of spiced air, the ghost with his face waiting at the mirrored end of a passage, rust-colored hexagons cool under his feet. He would climb into his mother's arms and lay his confession before her. His life would change key.

Alternatives glimmered, a different kind of existence opening now and then like a view. A morning when the arrow flight of his son shot him straight to Leela, who gathered the weeping child to her and held him close on her knee. Sam had thought, It is as simple as that! He looked at his wife, her broad, plain face infused with love, and saw how glorious she was. He was visited by a yearning for absolution so physical that his flesh slicked with sweat. Then it passed. He fell back in his chair. The course of his life was as fixed as a mathematical rule.

Now at last he understood that character—compulsion, will, impulse, propensity, aversion—might accrete and solidify around a central mistake. When Claudia had woken him in the sleeping house that afternoon, the first thing he saw when he followed her into the baby's room was her little satin-stitched pillow. She disliked being parted from it. But there it lay in Leo's cot, the embroidery loosened and grubby where her finger worked it as she slept.

The two children stood side by side, looking down on the small body. There was a blister of white paint on the wood near Sam's thumb. He picked at it. "Baby gone?" whispered Claudia. He watched the smile slip off and on her face.

He was eight years old. He made a slow circuit of the cot. He even had the wit to smooth the snarled netting into place. Then the baby's ayah muttered in her sleep and shifted on her mat. An eternity passed. When the woman's bubbling breath began to rise and fall again, he led his sister to her bed, and for sixty seconds gazed at her and marveled.

The afternoon and evening passed in a wheezing rush. All through the tumult of discovery, he seemed to be holding his breath. He had only to speak. But his brother was dead. Nothing he might say could set that life chirping again. While across the table there was Claudia. She sat upright on her chair crayoning a doll's face black. The circle of their family had gaped briefly to admit Leo. Now it had sprung closed again. He walked around the table and stood beside his sister, and pincered her wrist between finger and thumb. He chafed her soft skin back and forth. She neither pulled away nor screamed. In this way he set his mark on her. She looked at him, and her face was vivid with understanding.

His tutor possessed the English genius for sidestepping unpleasantness. Summoning a rotten tooth, he spent the evening barricaded within his room. No one paid any heed to the children left alive. They dined on water biscuits and the ruins of a blancmange. Their father appeared at the door, gazed at them and padded away again in his blue velvet slippers. Hearing those dull steps, Sam remembered the overseer's son prostrated on the verandah. His father had not sought to punish the boy, just as he himself had not sought the elimination of Leo. Yet it had fallen to them both to restore equilibrium in the disruptive wake of a crime. Exaltation was rolling through him, when a splinter of fear punctured his mood: Claudia's pillow still lay in their brother's cot.

Squeezing his knees together, he prayed for time. He rang for a servant, had a bed carried into his room and made up for his sister. But she would not settle, plucking at the overlong *banian* that served her as a nightdress. At last Sam went out onto the back verandah, to a sofa scattered with cushions. He returned with one of them. She rubbed its silky piping along the side of her finger, stroking it into her dreams.

It was well past midnight when the reek of oil of cloves retreated from the corridor and an amber line no longer showed at the bottom of the Englishman's door. The boy ran through the house on silent feet. He eased the pillow from the empty cot, a lump of embroidered matter in his arms. Slipping from the room, he collided with his mother.

Hours after he had watched, limp-muscled with longing, as she rocked his brother's inert flesh, Maud was still wearing the yellow traveling costume in which she had arrived at Lokugama. Her hair had worked loose and was bunched around her face. She stood in the doorway, one raised arm on the jamb, and the lamp on the verandah rimmed her sleeve with gold. She looked from his face to the pillow in his arms. He saw revulsion seep into her eyes and fled, a button at her elbow grazing his ear as he passed.

He lay in his bed with a sheet over his face, and shivered in monsoonal heat. His first thought: it was a hideous mistake. His mother had seen everything from the wrong angle. He had been judged guilty of a crime he had not committed. Each blow of his heart protested the unfairness of it. He dreaded and longed for explanation, for her step in the corridor.

Instead, old evils arrived to torment him. He crouched beside Claudia, urging her to tweak a fold in the usurper's dimpled thigh. He constructed mythologies in which their brother had been stolen and replaced with a devil's nestling. What she had done, she had done to please him. She had carried out his desire as surely as if he had guided her hand.

By the time dawn came with its diseased light, he had grown reconciled to the distortion of events. He rose and went out into the compound, and hurled the pillow over the wall to rot in the jungle. That his mother thought him hateful was no more than he deserved. For the rest of his days his understanding of justice would be molded to that skewed design. Now, at the bleak end of the arc of his life, frozen on the verandah of Allenby House, he saw with the extraordinary lucidity that was pouring through him like pain that the boy trembling under a sheet was only the first for whom he had found no forgiveness.

Watson was whining in the depths of the hall. When Sam raised his eyes he saw a woman at the foot of the stairs, her hand on the newel. He heard a commotion that he took for the sea; but then he realized that the floor of the verandah had lifted. In thickening light he was pitched forward on a flow of white marble tiles with black diamonds at each corner. Her arms flew wide and love burst against his ribs, and he went joyfully into the dark.

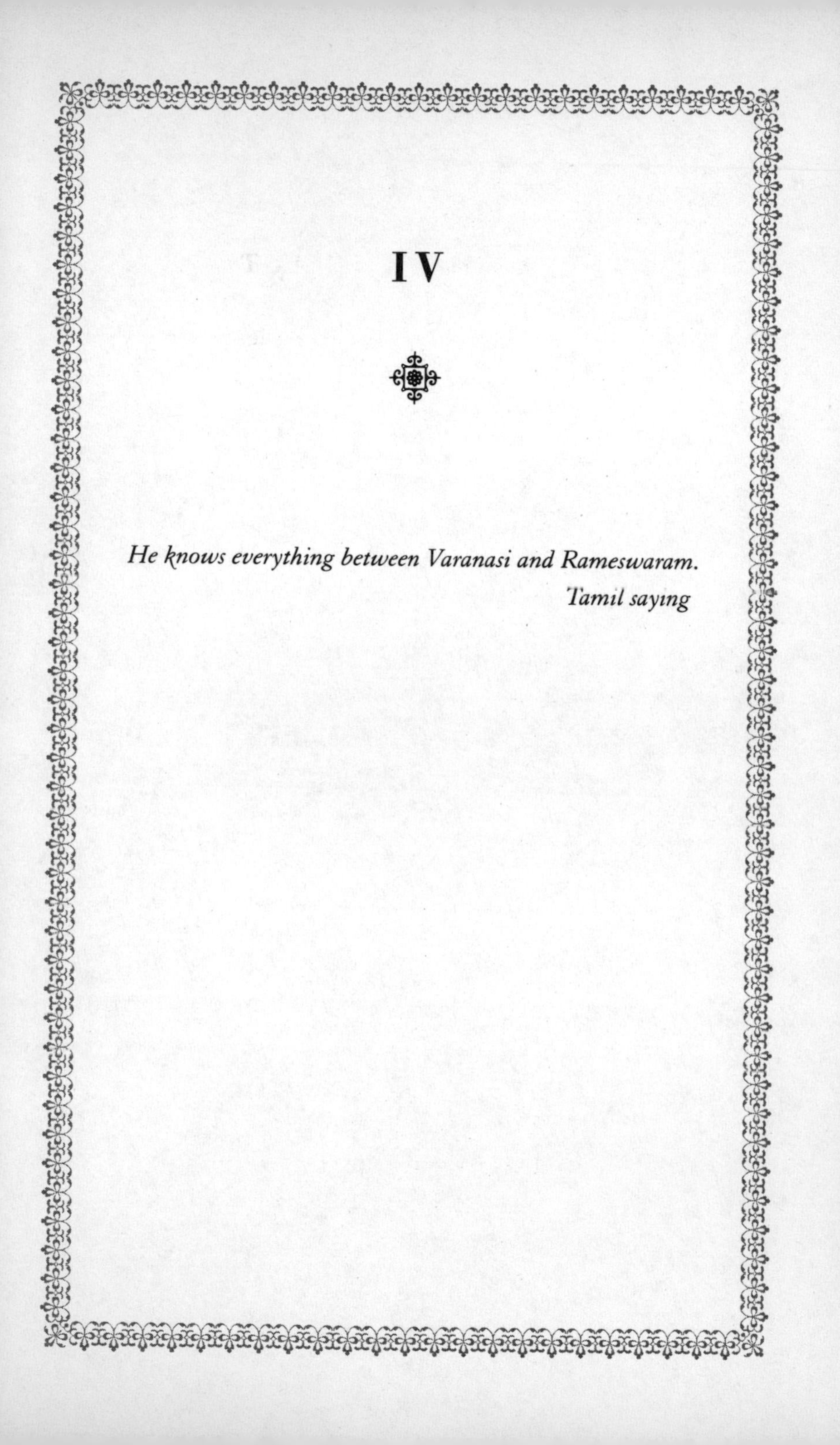

IV

He knows everything between Varanasi and Rameswaram.

Tamil saying

Harry Obeysekere, Esq.
Allenby House
Allenby Lane
Colombo 3
Ceylon

28 February 1971

Dear Harry,

I remember it well. You must have been how old—three? four? Your eyes stretched wide when I handed you that stick of pink sugar. But you wouldn't let yourself taste it until you had trotted back to your mother with her share. She had a gentle face.

You ask about your father. There's not a lot I can tell you. We were friends briefly, a lifetime ago. It grieves me to hear that he sat up with one of my books on the night before he died. He would surely have disliked what he read.

One Saturday when we were cycling back to school after a swim at Mount Lavinia, he called over his shoulder, "Look at that, will you. That's magnificent." I slowed and turned my head. The wall was faded and embroidered with mildew, but had once been painted kingfisher blue. By the doorstep someone had set three kerosene tins, rust laced, planted with golden cannas. We were both boarders at Neddy's that year.

The manuscript you enclosed is remarkable. Here and there it terrifies. *In cahoots with some ne'er-do-wells. A cold collation in my set.* He had the gift of perfect mimicry, you see. It won him every prize on the classics side. If you would put your hand on the key to him, study that ventriloquism. I find it unbearably sad.

Jaya argued that it kept us captive, locked in the structures of an alien way of thought. But what else did we have? Jaya's solution was the vernacular. As theory, it was sound. Nevertheless, we went on reaching for English. How could it have been otherwise? We had ingested the language. It streamed through our lungs, fired our synapses. It turned to waste in our bowels. It fed muscle and bone. In this context the word *alien* is not unproblematic.

You see, we were a generation that spoke always in quotation. Even Jaya's oratory derived from the civilization it denounced. Because at some point quotation had become our native mode. There was no original. No beneath, before, beyond. It was a question of rote thinking. Of the stock response and the preordained concept. I catch myself at it still, rolling out ready-made phrases like any well-drilled schoolboy. *Not unproblematic*. Did you hear it, there? It works insidiously. In the placement of an adverb. The choice of a cadence. Only in my case the pastiche is gross. I never had your father's ear.

He was one of those sincere, aggrieved people. He would go up to a fellow and harangue him in detail about the flaws in his game; and then bound over to him the next day, beaming, racquet in hand. Nine times out of ten he was turned down, and not always politely; and each time the rebuff caught him unprepared. You could see it pained him. A thinning of the mouth. It was a devastating lesson in how a man might see every detail with perfect clarity and yet misread the shape of the whole.

The first thing one noticed about your father was that plume of hair. It was a trial to him. In a burst of disclosure he told me he thought it conveyed an impression of coarseness. He spent five minutes each morning plastering it flat with a comb dipped in water.

He was avuncular with me, well disposed but essentially remote. We were not close. There was the difference in age, all-important in the stratified society of school. Besides, there was something in him that precluded intimacy. I diagnosed it as ambition, recognizing the symptoms in myself. The virus was endemic at Neddy's. Now I think that fear went to compound the hard little nugget at his core. What other people thought of him mattered acutely. He feared judgment. Like all imposters, he feared exposure. You are familiar perhaps with the pathology of psychosis? The tragedy of the psychotic is that he lives in terror of a breakdown which has in fact already occurred. So it was with your father. He strove to perfect a performance that had never deceived his audience.

There was an evening when he looked up from his book and asked how one pronounces Marylebone. I suggested he enquire of one of the masters. A bleak despair crept over his features. "Then they would know," he said.

"Know what?"

"That I'm not one of them," he blurted.

I came down with pneumonia after two terms and was a day boy when I returned. Thereafter I knew him only in flashes. He nods at me on a landing, sea and sky two bands of different blue beyond his shoulder. He gives me five hundred lines for having my hands in my pockets. As a prefect he was, of course, a disciplinarian. It was wholly in character. The dread of being judged articulated as a need to punish.

Of his relations with his family I can tell you very little. He never spoke of home. Well, none of us did. It was not exactly encouraged. Neddy's constituted our world, sufficient unto itself. But I knew, vaguely, that his people were grand. And rather fast. There was a whiff of scandal. Bills that went unpaid. He was among those regularly summoned to the bursar's office, which always meant trouble over fees. From those interviews he would return stone-eyed.

I remember a sports meet when a lady in a jade-colored hat turned every head. She was your grandmother. I didn't know which I coveted more, the silver flask she produced when tea was served or the diamanté-collared Great Dane at her side. It strolled up to Warden Metcalfe's prize begonias and urinated on them in front of the entire school. My mother bristled beside me. "All show and humbug," she hissed.

My sister and your aunt were in the same year at school. Both outcasts, I think, Anne conscious of her stick and dragging leg, Claudia, who had been educated at home, suffering from her ignorance of the rituals that govern school life. She spent the day at our house now and then. A girl with long eyes. Her upward glance produces a streak of topaz brilliance, snuffed out straight away. Anne used to tease me about her. It was true that in her presence I became more awkward and tongue-tied than usual. Her shyness drew me; it was not a quality I associated with beautiful young girls.

I tried to pump Anne. "What is she like? What do you talk about?"

"Everything but you," said my sister. She had a sardonic vein.

"Well, but what exactly?"

But she wouldn't say. And Claudia left school after a year, when she turned sixteen. My sister kept in touch for a while, but her attention was increasingly on her studies. Claudia dropped out of our orbit, as people do.

I saw her one more time, when I was a proctor practicing upcountry. It was the year of the Hamilton case. She was married by then, mistress of a house washed through night and day with a flux of people. In those years Jaya was still sniffing out the form that his convictions would assume and had yet to discover the tonic effect of anti-Tamil rhetoric on a political career. He had helped me with a submission to the Crown about conditions on the tea estates, and I was grateful for his advice. But when I took up his invitation to drop in one evening, I confess I was moved chiefly by the desire to see his wife.

Yet when she entered the room I failed to notice her. Then, beyond a wedge of dark jackets, I saw your father turn his head. I traced his gaze to a Japanese screen in a corner; and found her there, half obscured, in the dimmest recess of the room. I had forgotten how small she was. Her cocktail gown and cigarette holder looked outlandish, frippery filched for a game.

When she looked up to find me three paces away, no glimmer of recollection disturbed that topaz stare. Her glazed smile remained in place. A swirl of platitudes, light as flies, passed between us. I looked away, the bubbles of pleasant anticipation that had effervesced in my veins all day gone flat on the instant, and met your father's eyes. They were faintly amused.

In my next letter to Anne I recounted this little episode. Her reply is beside me. After some wholly gratuitous observations about masculine vanity, she continues: *I never told you about the time I saw a wreath of blisters on Claudia's shin. When I pressed her for an explanation, she admitted she had applied a lighted cheroot to her flesh. It was nothing, she said. An "experiment." Her face, usually so sweet, flickered with cunning as she produced the word, fished up to please me with its scientific ring. Even an ignoramus like you might know that self-inflicted wounds signal low self-esteem? Her idea of her own worth functioned in inverse ratio to the power she accorded others. Her brother, above all. Sam this, Sam that: so she chirped endlessly. I would say she was terrified of him.*

I suggest you do not place any store on that last remark. Anne, whose opinion of me was set at affectionate scorn, was a stranger to the more tender fraternal sentiments. And her medical studies having newly led her to the mire of psychoanalysis, it was a time when she was predisposed to find unwholesome depths beneath the most innocent surfaces. I report her comments only as corroboration of the undertow that ran between Claudia and your father. It rubbed me a little raw, that private strand of emotion. It felt exclusive. Contemptuous. I brooded on it for three days, then shook myself like a dog. Absurd to entertain jealousy in that quarter. He was only her brother, after all.

One incident I recall dates from '40 or '41. At any rate, the early part of the war. I was District Judge of Galle, and when I heard that Jaya would be addressing a rally some twenty miles away, I offered to put him up for the night. We were allies still, exchanging letters and ideas, gorging ourselves on fried rice and deviled crabs at the Mandarin Inn whenever I was in Colombo. I applauded his break with the brown sahibs in Congress. He encouraged my tentative steps into fiction, arranging a meeting with a friend who edited the little magazine where my first story was published.

I plucked him from the usual throng of sycophants and petitioners, and drove fast along back roads where the jungle streamed past and monkeys fled into the trees. I couldn't wait to quiz him about the speech his leader had made the previous evening. Its references to the purity of the Sinhalese race had kicked up an almighty stink.

"Did you hear what Congress called him? Our Führer in waiting."

Jaya, overflowing on the narrow seat, hooted with laughter. "I knew it would put the wind up those buggers."

"Yes, but . . ." I glanced sideways. He had his elbow propped on the window and his face showed only the most serene good cheer. "Did he run it past you?" I asked.

He laughed again. "I wrote every word of it."

"But it's preposterous," I blurted. "It's so . . . so third rate."

"Not the cadences," he replied. "They're first rate." A flattened coin of light rolled along the dash, skimming from the gold-rimmed dial on his wrist. He began to sing: "On the road to Mandalay, Where the flying fishes play, And the dawn comes up like *thun-der* . . ." He broke off. "Isn't it *rousing*." He sang the last line again. "Third-rate sentiments. First-rate cadences. You see?"

By then we had turned onto the trunk road. I was about to argue when my attention was caught by a shard of brightness under the trees that crowded close to the road in those days. As I said, we were traveling fast. I had barely registered the apparition when we had left it well behind.

"My God!" said Jaya, twisting to peer in the direction we had come. "Did you see . . . ?"

"Yes."

He slumped back in his seat. "That was Maud Obeysekere," he announced.

"My God!" A jade-hatted vision shimmered through my mind. I tried to fit it to the ruin I had glimpsed. "Are you sure?"

"The Obeysekeres have a place near here."

"But did you see . . . ?"

"Yes."

She had been wearing a dress that rippled and shone, a cascade of light. Sequins, perhaps, or silver beading. There was something unsettling about the sight. A sense of dislocation. Even today, the discrepancy between that gown and its setting troubles me. It suggested the perversion of some fundamental law. You will forgive me for saying it suggested insanity.

"She was a grand old girl." Jaya's voice was flat.

"Should we go back?"

He was silent for a minute. "Better not," he said at last.

Jaya never spoke of his first marriage. It was assumed that the Obeysekere connection was an embarrassment. His second wife, whose family tree was an impeccable record of Buddhist piety and opposition to colonial rule, was so much more congruent with the public man. And then, of course, there was the shame of your aunt Claudia's death. The story given out by the Jayasinghes was that her child had lived only a few hours, whereupon grief had driven his mother to take her own life. But there were rumors, as there always are in such cases. Unofficial narratives of a complicit doctor and bribes paid to an ayah to hush up a greater scandal. No wonder Jaya kept off the subject. But I always thought his silence was also a form of self-rebuke. He had failed with Claudia, you see, and he was not a man accustomed to failure.

We drove without speaking for some miles. The vine-shrouded banyans thinned, and coconut trees took their place. A curve in the road brought us out onto the coast. The sea was blue and infinitely creased, a sheet of silk pulled over the life that rolled and muttered below.

Jaya said, "Did you ever go there? To Obey's family place?"

I shook my head. "They were living in Colombo when I knew them."

If I had probed then, he would have spoken freely about Claudia. I am sure of it. He was expecting my questions; hoping for them, even. But I was in no mood to be beguiled by private romances. The rhetoric reported in my newspaper that morning had enraged me; but anger is a lively emotion. Now I felt only a dull despair. Nationalism, for me, was a sentiment as large as light. I was just beginning to understand that it could be reduced to something as petty and merciless as the glint of ambition.

Beside me, Jaya stirred. I sensed him calculating whether or not to go on.

"There was another brother," he said at last. "Died when he was a baby. It was Claudia who found him." From the corner of my eye, I saw him studying me. "Can you imagine it? She was three years old. She got up from an afternoon nap and went to look at the baby. He was just lying there in his cot. She told me she'd never heard the word *dead*. But she knew it described him."

The VOC shield carved above the massive entrance to the fort had come into sight when he next spoke. "I could never rid her of the idea that she was somehow to blame. It was Obey who had put that notion into her head, of course."

Ever since I read your letter I have been pondering how to answer you about the Hamilton case. You are quite correct in surmising that "Death of a Planter" is a transposition of its elements. But when you ask if it is true that your father's investigation brought about the death of an innocent man, all I can tell you is that I used to think so. It was a hypothesis that drew on the flimsiest data. The way two people didn't look at each other. And this detail: the newspaper report of Mrs. Taylor's departure from the island mentions her infant's *soft dark gaze*. I read that clipping thirty times over as many years before I realized why it had hooked my attention. Both Taylor and his wife had eyes of the palest blue. You will remember Mendel's law on that point: two light-eyed people cannot have a dark-eyed child.

Does that constitute proof? No court would accept an arabesque issuing from a reporter's overwrought pen as evidence. Even if the remark could be verified as fact, it would scarcely pin Nagel to the murder. The father of Yvette Taylor's child might have been someone else entirely—why not? Hamilton himself leaps at once to mind. Perhaps the only lie Mrs. Taylor told in the witness box was that he did not succeed in raping her. Perhaps she was to be pitied. Such a bloodless little thing. You would swear she was transparent. But the depths were smoky. She was like a crystal. A man might hold her in his hand. He might turn her this way and that, and read what he wished in her.

When I wrote "Death of a Planter" I suppressed those doubts. The case against Nagel and Mrs. Taylor was not implausible, and the novel delight of prosecution revealed itself to me like a whore disrobing. I relished the finesse, the complex pleasure of the thing. By the time I laid down my pen I had quite persuaded myself that the pair in the dock were guilty. Then last month you wrote to me. Since then all my old uncertainties have revived; only strengthened now, more vigorous.

You see, I share your father's fascination with detective fiction. I was perusing his defense of it with no little enjoyment, when a name made me pause. The next moment recognition brought me upright in my chair. Twenty-five years have passed since I read *Hercule Poirot's Christmas*. I have never owned a copy of the book. Yet I saw that I had—quite unconsciously—plucked out the crucial elements of Mrs. Christie's plot and grafted them onto the Hamilton case. A policeman who commits murder. A dark-eyed child with light-eyed parents. I had believed, preening myself, that my theory about Nagel and Mrs. Taylor sprang from shrewd observation and deductive logic. Now I saw that I had fallen for an old enchantment. I had mistaken the world for a book.

Your father would have understood. He knew the force of narrative patterning. It threw him Taylor: a weak man, Hamilton's best friend, the least likely suspect. His guilt had been elaborated in the pages of a hundred detective novels. Perhaps he did murder Hamilton. Who knows? What is beyond all reasonable doubt is that he fitted the plot.

And then there was his wife. Has it ever struck you that detective fiction teaches suspicious reading? *Take no one at his word. Nothing is as it seems.* Those are its iron principles, the legacy it bequeaths its addicts. You will notice the resemblance to psychoanalysis; I annoy my sister by claiming that it was Poe, not Freud, who founded her discipline.

Your father was a sophisticated reader, fluent in the conventions. That Yvette Taylor constructed herself as a victim was in itself cause for suspicion. He looked for the latent confession beneath the occluding surface. That business of the lavender coatee. The small hand resting like a badge of virtue on her swollen belly. She had overdone the symbolism, like any Sunday scribbler. In the signs of innocence he recognized guilt. As I said, he was a sophisticated reader.

All Hulftsdorf knew your father's opinion of Mrs. Taylor. I, for one, shared it. Keep in mind her costume, and the way she went to pieces in the witness box. It suggested greasepaint. It looked stage-managed. So when I came to write about the Hamilton case, it was with an untroubled conscience that I winched her viciousness a notch tighter. You could call it the curse of belatedness. Murder, like love, offers only a handful of variants. The story has always already been told; it feeds on ever more ingenious twists. To accuse Mrs. Taylor of doing no more than orchestrating the murder of Hamilton now reeked of old hat. So I described an adultress who had arranged the deaths of two men and made a fool of a third. Understand that I was certain I had discovered the truth. It never crossed my mind that the Yvette Taylor I had conjured might have been determined from start to finish by narrative necessity.

Naturally none of this precludes the possibility of her guilt.

Sometimes the endless shifting of figure and ground drives me to despair. I long, like you, for the consolation of certainty. But murder, like all art, generates interpretation and resists explanation. Why do you suppose that your father, having set out to establish the facts of the Hamilton case, found himself unable to do so? Have you never noticed how testimony falters under interrogation?

But I am only postponing the moment of confession. There is another turn of the screw.

On an evening in 1957 I saw Jaya for the last time. The murderous events of the following May were still months away. But violence already hung in the air. A charred van helpless on its back, bottle glass frosting a pavement. All over the island there were these premonitory spurts of temper.

I had spent three months in the western province, hearing the assizes. Rigidity sets in quicker in the outstations, preference embalmed as prejudice in the beat of a pulse. Episodes that might have remained unrelated in the capital were stringing themselves together on a common thread of hatred. I returned to Colombo in the grip of a headache, certain that the small acts of savagery breaking out around me were emissaries from the future.

That night I lay in the clammy shroud of a fever and memories of Jaya swelled to fill my skull. I repeated his name aloud. We had broken years before. In the aftermath of his speech calling for the compulsory repatriation to India of all plantation Tamils, we flung extravagant insults at each other. The icy memorandum in which I queried the legality of his Sinhala Only bill went unanswered. But now, with a migraine pounding at my temples, it was clear to me that Jaya alone could reverse our island's drift to brutality. I grew delirious. I walked on the ceiling of my bedroom. I flew over an amethyst sea on which Jaya and I strolled, devising the principles of a radiant new grammar.

He agreed to see me. His secretary returned my telephone call within the hour. Three evenings later I presented myself at the house in Green Crescent. A stir of breeze along the road carried the scent of night-flowering jasmine, scrambled with the ripeness of excrement. At the gate a sentry consulted a list, then slapped his rifle to his shoulder. I no longer trod the light-seared heights of my dreams as I made my way up the drive. Nevertheless I went to the encounter buoyant with hope.

I had rehearsed with care. *Proceed calmly*, I advised myself. *At the same time, be unequivocal. Flatter him but let him understand that you have his measure.* At the top of four stairs I walked into his embrace. Before we had crossed the verandah, his arm like a log across my shoulders, I was confessing fears, babbling entreaties, doling out rebukes, proposing methodologies, contradicting myself and starting over again. "You have the PM's ear," I cried, and bit my tongue. The pain brought me to something like my senses.

In his office room Jaya sat me in a chair carved by a Dutchman. He unlocked an oak cabinet and drew out a decanter. He put a glass of cognac in my hand and produced the pipe he no longer smoked in public. Then he said, "What I have always loved in you, Shiva, is that you are never judicious. An admirable quality in any man, and a great one in a judge." I knew then that he would not move a finger to save us. Jaya's compliments were always a symptom of disengagement.

No need to dwell on what followed. I reasoned like a sensible man, then like a lunatic. He smiled and drew on his pipe. What none of his chroniclers will tell you is that politics mattered to Jaya *up to a point.* Words flowed from him and men wept or committed murder. But he entertained no causal relation between these phenomena. He saw no reason why his Tamil friends could not overlook his oratory; or why his Sinhalese supporters could not overlook his friends. Rivals in his party cried hypocrisy. It was a crude assessment. He polished his speeches until they flashed like instruments. But their action in the world was a matter of indifference to him. He sought only that cool, perfect shine.

I think of it now as a profoundly modern sensibility. That Jaya—"Jungle Jaya"—possessed a near-mystical affinity with our island, a concentrated instinct for its core, has long been an article of faith. Useless to take issue with mythology, perhaps. But only consider the place. What do you see? For myself, an explosion of leaves. Wind that cracks trees. Iron-skinned jackfruit, heavy as lambs. A country governed by hyperbole, where love and hate are operatically scored. The dial stuck on fortissimo. The needle shaking past the last calibration. Jaya met its opulence with a cool grid of irony and dialectic. It was counterintuitive, a new way of looking at the world. Technical, abstracting. Very twentieth century.

But my sister will tell you that what we seek to repress returns distorted. Emotion is not so easily excluded from history, you see. Jaya lived to see his theorems of national pride codified into a geometry of racial hatred. The exquisite rigor of the grid turned schematic, its glitter vicious. I think it brought him to a private despair. I have never believed it was misfortune that sent his tires spinning on the road to Kandy. For years he had barricaded himself in that monstrous house of flesh. I think he fled from it, in the end, into truth.

When I rose to leave that evening, I mumbled something sour about his disdain "not only for men but for justice." We both knew it was the deadliest charge in my repertoire. Once, that fact would have amused him. But now my contempt grated. He set his pipe down and studied me. "Why, Shiva—you of all chaps know that justice is a slippery beast."

I gazed at him dully. We no longer seemed to have anything worth saying to each other.

"You remember the Hamilton case."

It was not a question. I made no answer.

He said, "I know about Velu."

The connection took a moment. Then the spark: Velu was the man who had found Hamilton's watch. The illumination accompanied by a little shock of astonishment that Jaya should have retained the name.

He misread my surprise. "You're wondering how I found out. Have you forgotten that we went about those coolie lines together, you and I, enquiring into conditions on the estates? Those men knew my face. They counted me as an ally. It didn't matter to them that I was a Sinhalese. Do you find that galling, Shiva?"

A carriage clock roosting on a pile of document boxes was clucking like a demented fowl. I raised my voice: "You're talking in riddles."

He reached for the decanter and angled it over my glass. I hesitated. But curiosity and cognac is a potent mixture. I sank back into my chair and waited.

"Nadesan." Jaya's gaze was mild, even friendly. "Marimuttu Nadesan. Mean anything to you?"

A short, whippy man with a milky white shutter pulled down over his left eyeball. I said slowly, "He worked in the factory on Rowanside. Like Velu. There was trouble about trying to organize a union."

"Earned himself a boot up the backside and a discharge ticket." Jaya had his pipe going again. He was wearing a loose batik shirt, loudly patterned, over a snowy sarong. That kind of getup suited his bulk, a suggestion of regality in the drapes. I had worshiped him at Neddy's. I had believed him finer than the rest of us, a denizen of the hills come down to the plains, a boy following the clean curve of a ball through the wide future. Of course when people fail to live up to our illusions, we find it impossible to forgive them. So I studied Jaya as he lounged there under that lamp, a large soft man with a syrupy drink at his elbow, and wanted to inform him that he had come to resemble a statue of himself.

He was telling me that Nadesan had called on him one evening. There, in that very room. "We talked of this and that," said Jaya, and I allowed myself a vinegary smile. I knew the deft empathy with which Jaya could unravel a man's defenses. It was a gift, I suppose. Like his prodigious memory. This detail, for instance, preserved from a decades-old conversation: that in forty-eight hours Nadesan had eaten only a slice of bread and sugar. "He was in a bad way, poor bugger. But he thought that in Colombo there would be a chance of picking up work on the docks. No *kangany* would hire him up-country."

At first Jaya assumed his visitor was trying to cadge a meal and a few rupees. "I was reaching for my pocket. But Nadesan was after help of a different kind."

He paused. His gaze rolled over me; that deadly mildness. I had trained myself to counter it with composure. Only now, as his glance flicked away, I caught the satisfaction in it; and saw, too late, that poise might be as revealing as agitation.

When he spoke, he might have been remarking on the weather. "Nadesan knew who had murdered Hamilton."

I helped myself to more cognac.

He said that Velu and Nadesan had been drinking together. Taylor had just hanged himself. On the estates, in the bungalows and the lines alike, it was the only topic of conversation. But Velu went further. He put his mouth close to Nadesan's ear and breathed what he had done. He was very cock-a-hoop at the latest turn of events: the sweetness of it, an Englishman dying in place of a coolie.

"He told Nadesan he had planned the murder for months, tracking Hamilton each time he returned with the wages along the shortcut through the jungle. When the evening he had settled on arrived, he waited until he heard Hamilton's horse. Then he flung himself face down beside the path and lay still, his gun concealed beside him.

"Hamilton reined in his horse. Several slow seconds later, Velu heard him dismounting. A chink of brass. The dull tread of a boot. Hamilton had taken three steps when Velu sprang to his feet and shot him. At the last minute he snatched up the dead man's watch; but panicked as he ran and dropped it behind a bush."

My years on the Bench had tuned my ear to perfect pitch: the recital rang false from start to finish. Which was of a piece with Velu; as I recalled, the man was born to swagger.

I began with the most obvious flaw his story. "Velu tried to pawn Hamilton's watch. Why would a murderer draw attention to himself?"

Jaya gestured with his pipe: Who knows? "It was a calculated risk. He chose a Tamil pawnbroker, remember. The fellow might not have gone to the police. And Velu took good care that his father was present when he pretended to stumble on the watch. The old man had worked on Rowanside for forty years. The *periya dorai* himself went down to the police station to put in a good word for him. A gold watch . . . Even Nagel could understand the temptation. But everyone who knew the old man swore he would never have had anything to do with murder.

"And then Velu had a glorious stroke of luck. Obey showed up. Obey!" Jaya grimaced like a schoolboy. "Conferring in hushed tones with that arrogant dolt Nagel. Examining clues with his magnifying glass. A coolie was far too crude a suspect for him. No psychology, you see. In his view people like Velu murdered brutishly from tedious motives. So the great detective dreamed up his crackpot theory about Taylor and persuaded Nagel to arrest him."

I tried to interrupt, but Jaya was in full flight. "The utterly incredible thing is that both Obey and the DSP believed they were giving their careers a boost. It still amazes me. Did you know that Billy Mohideen tried to warn Obey? Waste of time, of course." He thrust out his chest. "*I know the English, old boy. Fair play and all that.*" He gave a little snort. "God, what a stiff-necked fool."

"But none of it hangs together." I rose from my chair and began to pace about the room. "Why would Nadesan do the dirty on Velu? Hamilton stood for everything he hated. Why would he denounce a fellow worker for killing him?"

"Because it was Velu's father who went to see the *dorai* and told him that Nadesan was a Red trying to stir things up on Rowanside. The old man was desperate to crawl back on side. And Nadesan discovered that socialism is a very poor insulation against the craving for revenge."

"So why not go straight to the police?"

"You think they would have believed him? A Bolshie agitator? It would have sounded like a cock-and-bull yarn cooked up to discredit Velu and his father."

I was shaking my head. "It's all wrong. What happened to the money? And where would Velu have got hold of a gun?"

Again that dismissive wave of his pipe. "A fellow like that always knows how to get his hands on a gun."

"What about the money?" I repeated. "One of the bags was found half burned behind Hamilton's bungalow. How do you square that with Velu being the murderer?"

Jaya was looking down, fiddling with the amber mouthpiece of his pipe. "Brilliant, unformulated cunning," he replied after a moment. "I don't suppose he planned it. But the night was rainy, moonless. Easy to creep down a hill and toss a couple of canvas holdalls onto the White Falls rubbish heap. If they were found, suspicion would fall on Hamilton's own household. Which is exactly what happened."

"But the money itself," I insisted. "Surely you don't believe Velu left it to burn? The man made forty cents a day. Think of the temptation. It would have begun with tots of arrack for his cronies. A bottle of whiskey for himself. Gold nose studs for his mother. And Nagel would have had him behind bars before the undertakers had finished measuring Hamilton for his coffin."

Jaya had his pipe going again. In the blue smoke rolling between us, I thought I glimpsed the edge of his smile. But all he said, peaceably enough, was, "I haven't got to the end of what Nadesan had to say."

He paused. "Well?" I said, impatient with these histrionics but obliging him nevertheless with his cue. "What happened?"

"Velu died," answered Jaya. "The night after Nadesan was sent packing. He picked a fight during a game of cards and someone slashed his throat open with a broken bottle. Gambling was banned on Rowanside. No one would admit to being at the game. All the men provided each other with alibis. The police didn't press too hard—you couldn't expect them to exert themselves over a dead coolie—and that was that."

"It's the one plausible thing you've said," I snapped. "Your ending at least is in character with a toddy-fueled loudmouth. But that drivel about murdering Hamilton! It's obvious Velu invented the whole story to impress Nadesan. A socialist will believe anything as long as it's sufficiently incredible."

When he laughed I turned away.

I was standing by a long window that gave onto the night-filled garden. As I peered up at the sky with its worn sliver of moon, it occurred to me that darkness was what was always there, the ground on which the world was painted. Each day the canvas grew further abraded, and a little more darkness showed through.

Behind me, Jaya went on talking. Nadesan had begged him to go to the police, he said. Vouch for his character, act as an intermediary. Get him reinstated on one of the estates. "He was afraid the Red dawn wouldn't rise over the hills without him. One of those fellows with a mission, Nadesan."

I took off my spectacles, rubbed my eyes. "What did you do?" I asked.

"I told him not to be a damn fool. An Englishman had hanged himself. No one wanted to dig up a stink around that corpse. I slipped him ten chips and advised him to get himself a one-way passage on the next boat to Madras."

It was irresistible. "Of course. The blueprint of your grand plan for all Tamils."

Thirty seconds of ticking silence went by. Then he said, in that same mild, implacable tone, "You know, you were a shade too insistent about the money."

I turned on my heel.

This time there was no missing his smile. "Oh, Nadesan knew everything. He knew that Velu confessed to you, and that you ordered him to keep his mouth shut. You said that at worst Hamilton's watch would cost him a few months with hard labor, and that there was no need to put up his hand for the gallows. You were a man of the law a long way after you were a Tamil, my friend."

I tried to say something. He put down his pipe and began to applaud: a slow, ironic clapping. "A first-rate brain. I always envied you that, Shiva. The way you turned their prejudices against them. A coolie: by definition, a brute. If a creature like that had murdered Hamilton, the motive had to be robbery. Base gain. Inconceivable that such a man might murder impersonally, from principle. Inconceivable that Hamilton might simply have been the unlucky representative of a race Velu had every reason to detest. You grasped that straight away, didn't you? The nonappearance of the money was the psychological weak point in the case against Velu. It unsettled Nagel. Made him receptive to Obey's romance about Taylor."

He tilted his glass, and for a moment the orange liquid lent its carnival tint to his face. "You were right to muzzle Velu," he said. "A dead Englishman—what did it matter? They shouldn't have been here in the first place. That was the real crime, the one that counted. Your submission about the plantations was on a desk in London. The revelation that Hamilton had been murdered by a coolie would have damaged your cause beyond repair."

At the first syllables he cut across my protest. "You and I have always been realists, although we rave like dreamers. Velu got off. You got your judgeship. There were reforms on the estates. Keep those things in mind, when you come here with your po-faced prattle about justice."

He swallowed the last of the aerated water and set his tumbler down with a click. "Now bugger off," he said, pleasantly.

I swear it was a lie. A foul lie concocted by that drunken fool Velu. No need to labor its contradictions. Its idiocies. The gaps that stand out as stark as nooses. Do you think I could have watched Taylor tried for a crime I knew he hadn't committed? That my hatred of imperialism skewed reason to the point where I was indifferent to the murder of Englishmen?

Yet I sense your hesitation. By placing Jaya's accusation at the end of my account, I've lent it credence. We believe the explanation we hear last. It's one of the ways in which narrative influences our perception of truth. We crave finality, an end to interpretation, not seeing that this too, the tying up of all loose ends in the last chapter, is only a storyteller's ruse. The device runs contrary to experience, wouldn't you say? Time never simplifies—it unravels and complicates. Guilty parties show up everywhere. The plot does nothing but thicken.

But you will have to make up your own mind about my part in the Hamilton case. It's true that if Velu had been arrested for the murder, the official line on up-country Tamils would have hardened. So you could take me for an unreliable narrator, objecting to flaws in Jaya's story in order to obscure my guilt. Perhaps you have heard a rumor linking my name with something fishy and unspecified? It was not long after my conversation with Jaya that I first encountered it. The taint of corruption. In time it cost me my appointment to the Supreme Court. Its breath has pursued me across half the globe. I detect its odor in air-freshened common rooms where silence falls as soon as I appear. So believe, if you like, that I wrote "Death of a Planter" with the intention of clouding the truth. That I threw suspicion on Nagel and Mrs. Taylor in order to divert it, once and for all, from myself.

There remains the possibility that Jaya whipped up the whole rigmarole from air, Nadesan's visit and all, to slather over my protest at his government's treatment of my people. No way of telling if that's true, of course. But I can give you my word that his accusation was false. Bearing witness to lies: it's the closest we can come to truth in an age of suspicion.

You ask who murdered Hamilton? Understand that when you drag out the past you find yourself standing over a corpse. You circle it and it lies there unbreathing. The slant of the light eludes you. A dog barks in the night and you fail to hear it. The stench of pipeclay or ghee chokes every molecule of air but stops short of your nostrils. Because the things that changed everything always resist interrogation. So you list the evidence before your eyes, and miss the stain trickling down the stairs. History, like any other verdict, is not a matter of fact but a point of view. To be honest, I am tired of history. It has been going on for a long time.

You asked about your father and I have told you a great deal about myself. Forgive an old man's egotism. I hope the detour has not been entirely irrelevant.

We had just called for the other half that evening at the Downhill when he said, without preamble, "Remember the canna house?"

At first, nothing. Then a hinge swung back. I saw two boys wheeling down a sand-rutted lane, salt-streaked blue and a glorious burst of gold.

He said, "There's a certain kind of English room. Lamplight, those heavy-headed dahlias, dented Georgian sugar tongs, two wing armchairs, Regency frames on striped wallpaper, a square teapot on a bamboo table. Talk as reassuring as the swish of curtains meeting against November gloom." He leaned forward, gripping the arms of his chair. "If you picture everything together," he said, "cannas, dahlias, kerosene tins, that bally teapot, it looks a shambles, of course. But why suppose that the opposite of incongruity is coherence? There's also sterility. This mania for one thing or the other."

Then Nagel walked into the club and our lives changed course.

These days I have an inkling of what your father was trying to say. I think he glimpsed, obscurely, that we were being written by the grand narratives of our age. Nationalism, empire, socialism, capitalism. It was necessary to choose between them. You picked a story and stuck with it, saw out the plot to its predictable outcome. He was no exception. As the product of an idea, he was superb. Only it walled him off from so much he might have loved.

For myself, I tried to write about that love. You have seen the result. Pretty little tales, tricked out with guavas and temple bells. It seemed a way forward. I persuaded myself that a girl with oiled hair threading her way barefoot through a paddy field was more authentic than a man downing a cocktail, one glossy shoe resting on a polished rail. After all, the girl stood for a way of life uncorrupted by the West. That fixation on purity! It branded me a creature of my age. In its service I perfected a rhetorical sleight of hand as slick as any magician's patter. *Coconut oil. Paddy field.* Hey presto.

An ash-smeared sadhu. The fragrance of cumin. I pulled them from my hat in earnest good faith when I first ventured into fiction. And my stories proved very popular with readers in the West. They wrote to tell me so. *Your work is so exotic. So marvelously authentic.* When the flatulent rumbles of self-satisfaction subsided, I saw that what I had taken for the markers of truth functioned as the signs of exoticism. The colonizer returns as a tourist, you see. And he is mad for difference. That is the luxury commodity we now supply, as we once kept him in cinnamon and sapphires. The prose may be as insipid as rice cooked without salt. No matter: call up a monsoon or the rustle of a sari, and watch him salivate.

Literature as souvenir: I confess I traded in it. Tales as sweetly banal as the incense peddled in every mall here in Vancouver; each trite sentence a small act of cynicism. I had stumbled on my métier, I told myself, as my books went into fourth and fifth printings, and students wrote requesting interviews for their theses on New Literatures in English.

But Jaya was wrong about me. I am only intermittently a cynic. If you knew what visions I used to tend, when I was young and drank coffee in brass tumblers until all hours designing the paradise to come. Well, history is a great unmaker of dreams. But the ruins of my romanticism persist: the belief, stubborn as a weed, that art aspires to truth, not success; an itch to begin again, differently. So that night after night I sit here shuffling oddments, laying out the past in imaginary spreads. Two children, side by side, peering at a corpse. A woman dressed for a ball walking down an arcade of leaves. Brocade curtains patterned with rot. *Sambol* spooned onto a Limoges plate. Each hygienic Canadian dawn finds me a little further advanced in invention and imitation, drawn on by a tale as shot through with impurities as history itself.

I envy you, in your house by the sea. Lately I've kept an old map to hand. A cockeyed Portuguese projection, continents rolled up and jammed into corners, Europa at the center dragging the world out of true. Yet I find it straight away, every time: Ceylon, *Ceilao,* syllables I repeat secretly, willing myself there, where the world ends in plunging blue and the flip of a monster's tail.

I loved the dash of it, as a boy: a small island riding an ocean and nothing to break the fall.

Shivanathan

ACKNOWLEDGMENTS

The Hamilton Case draws on the following books: Douglas G. Browne and E. V. Tullet, *Bernard Spilsbury: His Life and Cases;* Rodney Ferdinands, *Proud & Prejudiced: The Story of the Burghers of Sri Lanka;* Yasmine Gooneratne, *Relative Merits;* James Manor, *The Expedient Utopian: Bandaranaike and Ceylon;* Douglas Raffel, *In Ruhunu Jungles;* John D. Rogers, *Crime, Justice and Society in Colonial Sri Lanka;* Gamini Salgado, *The True Paradise;* R. L. Spittel, *Far-Off Things* and *Wild Ceylon;* Leonard Woolf, *Growing: An Autobiography of the Years 1904–1911.* Readers will have already noticed my debt to Agatha Christie's *Hercule Poirot's Christmas* and Somerset Maugham's "Footprints in the Jungle."

My research was facilitated by the Victor Melder Sri Lanka Library in Melbourne. I am grateful to Victor for giving me the run of this remarkable archive.

My thanks go also to my editors, Pat Strachan, Jane Palfreyman and Alison Samuel, for their encouragement and perceptive criticism; to Chandani Lokugé, who patiently answered questions about Sinhalese culture; and to Chris Andrews, Sara White and Mark Williams, who kindly read drafts of the novel and improved it with their good advice. Special thanks are due to Dr. Walter Perera of the University of Peradeniya, a stranger who gave generously of his time and erudition. Also to Sarah Lutyens, whose flawless sense of direction kept me from losing my way.

In 1942 the Caxton Press published a book called *The Pope Murder Case*, a true crime account of the murder of an English tea planter in Ceylon and the trial of his killers. The author, O. L. de Kretser, was my father. His book has no direct bearing on the events imagined here. But it is one of the ghosts that haunt these pages.

THE HAMILTON CASE

A novel by

Michelle de Kretser

A Reading Group Guide

A CONVERSATION WITH MICHELLE DE KRETSER

The Hamilton Case is set in Ceylon (now Sri Lanka), where you grew up. Do the experiences that you and your family had while in Ceylon figure in the novel?*

Only obliquely. What seeps into the novel from my childhood is what you might call its atmosphere: that sense of a gorgeous, seductive, yet rather menacing landscape, for instance, that I retain from the gardens I played in—green and pleasant places, yet so rampant, so lush, that they threatened to overrun any weak thing they encountered. My memories of once-grand old houses, full of shadows and hauntings, also made their way into the book.

On a wider level, my family, and thousands of others like us, the English-speaking descendants of Dutch and British colonizers, left post-independence Ceylon as the island's politics changed. So I was aware from an early age of the way small private lives are shaped by large historical events, like the breakup of the British Empire. The idea that the private and public spheres are inextricably linked is integral to *The Hamilton Case*.

How would you explain the ways in which The Hamilton Case *differs from a traditional detective story?*

In a classic 1930s-style detective novel, the detective gathers everyone together at the end of the book and explains how the murder was done and whodunit. I decided that in the final section of my book, a character would reconsider crimes that had previously seemed resolved. I liked the idea of having several equally plausible solutions to mysteries; it seemed a neat metaphor for the modern belief that there is more than one way of seeing the world, more than one valid way to understand reality.

I guess also that traditional detective fiction places far greater emphasis on situation than character, whereas *The Hamilton Case* is above all the portrait of its "detective," Sam.

Given that you left your homeland when you were fourteen years old, did The Hamilton Case *require extensive research and travel to Sri Lanka?*

I was superstitiously determined *not* to return to Sri Lanka to research the novel. In the first place, I felt that what I remembered of the island was more than enough to recreate its landscapes and so on for readers. And, then, Sri Lanka today is a very different place from the Ceylon in which I grew up, let alone the colonial Ceylon of my parents' generation. I was writing about a country that no longer exists—a ghost country, which, like all ghosts, depends on memory and narrative to conjure its existence. It seemed important, therefore, not to muddle that remembered, imagined world with the reality of contemporary Sri Lanka. Of course I had to research aspects of the novel—elephant hunting, for instance, which I'm glad to say isn't part of my experience!—but I did so solely in libraries.

Your main character, Sam Obeysekere, says, "What I remember most about my parents is that they weren't there." How do his withholding parents affect Sam's fate?

Sam has a very inadequate idea of how to express love because he has little direct experience of these things. In the upper-class, British-influenced set to which his parents belong, it is "bad form" to show emotion. Consequently, the personal relationships Sam forms are predicated on the exercise of power rather than trust or tenderness.

Your first novel, The Rose Grower, *was set against the backdrop of the French Revolution, and* The Hamilton Case *takes place during social upheaval in Ceylon. Do you think characters can be revealed more fully in troubled times?*

Yes, indeed. Social change is interesting because it obliges people to make choices—and is therefore very revealing of character.

QUESTIONS AND TOPICS FOR DISCUSSION

1. Michelle de Kretser once said in an interview that "people who are not well loved do not know how to love well in turn." How does Sam exemplify this statement?

2. How does Sam's schooling at St. Edward's ("Neddy's") and Oxford influence his social and political opinions?

3. Sam's sister, Claudia, ends her life tragically. What aspects of her past and present did she find unbearable?

4. Sam and Jaya come from similar privileged Sinhalese backgrounds. What is at the root of their animosity? How do their hopes for Ceylon's future differ?

5. Sam reveres all things English. How does this reverence affect his attitude toward his mother, Maud, and his choice of Leela as his wife?

6. How is "the fabulous flotsam of Empire" reflected in the decorative objects in Sam's childhood and marital houses?

7. The Ceylonese jungle is a powerful physical presence in this novel, especially as it slowly takes over the estate to which Maud is exiled at Lokugama. What kind of metaphorical presence does it have? How does it complement Maud's decline?

8. Would you say that Sam — as a widower whose grown son is estranged from him — is most dismayed by the loss of his family, his fall from professional grace, or the cessation of English rule in Ceylon in 1948?

9. How does the use of different points of view in each of the four parts of *The Hamilton Case* enlarge our understanding of the characters and their country?

10. At the end of *The Hamilton Case,* Shivanathan writes that "history, like any other verdict, is not a matter of fact but a point of view." Do you agree? Discuss.

ABOUT THE AUTHOR

Michelle de Kretser is a Sri Lankan who has lived in Australia since 1972. Her first novel, *The Rose Grower,* was published in 1999. She has taught literature at Melbourne University and worked as an editor and reviewer. *The Hamilton Case* received the Commonwealth Writers Best Book Prize, SE Asia and South Pacific region, and the Encore Award for best second novel of the year.